PENGUIN

THE ILIAD

The Greeks believed that the *Iliad* and the *Odyssey* were compiled
by HOMER, and seven Greek cities claim to be the place of his
birth. Nothing is known of his life or date, nor can it be proved
that the same person compiled both works at the same time, but
the quality and unity of the structure in each book indicates one
author, who may for convenience be called Homer. Modern
scholarship now places him somewhere in Ionia in about 700 B.C.

•

E. V. RIEU, editor of the Penguin Classics from 1944 to 1964,
was born in 1887 and was a scholar of St Paul's school and of
Balliol College, Oxford. He was appointed Manager of the
Oxford University Press in Bombay in 1912, and served in the
Mahratta Light Infantry during the First World War. He worked
as Educational Manager and Managing Director for Methuen &
Co. until 1936, when he became their Academic and Literary
Adviser. He was President of the Virgil Society in 1951, and Vice-
President of the Royal Society of Literature in 1958. Among his
publications are *The Flattered Flying Fish and other poems*, and
translations of the *Odyssey*, the *Iliad*, Virgil's *Pastoral Poems*, the
Voyage of Argo and *The Four Gospels*, in Penguin Classics. In 1968
he was awarded the Benson Medal. He died in 1972.

HOMER

THE ILIAD

TRANSLATED BY
E. V. RIEU

PENGUIN BOOKS

PENGUIN BOOKS

Published by the Penguin Group
27 Wrights Lane, London W8 5TZ, England
Viking Penguin Inc., 40 West 23rd Street, New York, New York 10010, USA
Penguin Books Australia Ltd, Ringwood, Victoria, Australia
Penguin Books Canada Ltd, 2801 John Street, Markham, Ontario, Canada L3R 1B4
Penguin Books (NZ) Ltd, 182–190 Wairau Road, Auckland 10, New Zealand

Penguin Books Ltd, Registered Offices: Harmondsworth, Middlesex, England

This translation first published 1950
43 45 47 49 50 48 46 44

Made and printed in Great Britain by
Richard Clay Ltd, Bungay, Suffolk
Filmset in Monophoto Bembo

CONTENTS

INTRODUCTION

THE Greeks looked on the *Iliad* as Homer's major work. It was the Story of Achilles, and not the Wanderings of Odysseus as might have been expected, that Alexander the Great took with him as a bedside book on his adventurous campaigns. I myself used not to accept this verdict, and I felt that many modern readers would agree with me. It was therefore with some trepidation that I bade farewell to the *Odyssey* and braced myself for the task of translating the *Iliad*, which I had not read through as a whole for twelve years. I soon began to have very different feelings, and now that I have finished the work I am completely reassured. The Greeks were right.

It is a question, not of any difference in skill, but of artistic levels. The *Odyssey*, with its happy ending, presents the romantic view of life: the *Iliad* is a tragedy.* To paint the Odyssean picture, convincing, just, and beautiful as it is, Homer took his easel to the lower slopes of Mount Olympus, which are pleasant, green, and wooded. It was a good spot, for the Muses certainly come down and play there. But to compose the *Iliad*, he moved higher up the mountain-side, nearer to the eternal snows and to the very homes of the Muses and the other gods. From there he had a different and a clearer view of the same landscape. Some of the mists had dissolved, the sun beat pitilessly on the snow, and a number of new things, many of them very terrible and lovely, came into sight. Homer himself became, if possible, even more human. He had climbed high; he had faced and solved some of the ultimate enigmas; and he could afford to smile both at the ant-like activities of men and the more awe-inspiring pageant of the gods. I am therefore very confident when I assure those who already know the *Odyssey* that they will be brought closer to tears by

* I am not implying in what follows that we really know which of them Homer wrote first.

the death of a single horse in the *Iliad* than by the killing of the whole gang of Suitors; closer too to laughter; and closer, if they follow Homer to the Olympian eminence from which he looks out on the world, to the heights where tears and laughter cease to count.

The plot of the *Iliad* is simple. King Agamemnon the imperial overlord of Greece (or Achaea, as Homer calls it) has, with his brother Menelaus of Sparta, induced the princes who owe him allegiance to join forces with him against King Priam of Troy, because Paris, one of Priam's sons, has run away with Menelaus' wife, the beautiful Helen of Argos. The Achaean forces have for nine years been encamped beside their ships on the shore near Troy, but without bringing the matter to a conclusion, though they have captured and looted a number of towns in Trojan territory, under the dashing leadership of Achilles son of Peleus, Prince of the Myrmidons, the most redoubtable and the most unruly of Agamemnon's royal supporters. The success of these raiding parties leads to a feud between Achilles and his Commander-in-Chief. Agamemnon has been allotted the girl Chryseis as his prize, and he refuses to give her up to her father, a local priest of Apollo, when he comes to the camp with ransom for her release. The priest prays to his god; a plague ensues; and Agamemnon is forced by the strength of public feeling to give up the girl and so propitiate the angry god. But he recoups himself by confiscating one of Achilles' own prizes, a girl named Briseis. Achilles in high dudgeon refuses to fight any more and withdraws the Myrmidon force from the battlefield. After an abortive truce, intended to allow Menelaus and Paris to settle their quarrel by single combat, the two armies meet, and as a result of Achilles' absence from the field the Achaeans, who have hitherto kept the Trojan forces penned up in Troy or close to their own city walls, are slowly but surely put on the defensive. They are even forced to make a trench and a wall round their ships and huts. But these defences are eventually stormed by Hector the Trojan Commander-in-Chief, who succeeds in setting fire to one of the Achaean ships. At this point Achilles, who has remained obdurate to all entreaties, yields to the extent of permitting his squire and closest friend Patroclus to lead the Myrmidon force to the rescue of the hard-pressed Achaeans. Patroclus brilliantly succeeds in this mission, but he goes too far and is killed under the walls of Troy by Hector. This disaster brings Achilles to life. In an access of rage with Hector and grief for his comrade he reconciles himself with Agamemnon, takes the field once more, hurls the panic-stricken Trojans back into their town, and finally kills Hector. Not content with this revenge, he savagely maltreats the body of his fallen enemy. Hector's father, King Priam, in his grief and horror, is inspired by the gods to visit Achilles in his camp by night, in order to recover his son's body.* Achilles relents; and the *Iliad* ends with an uneasy truce for the funeral of Hector.

Such is the framework of the story. Unlike those who describe the plot of a thriller on its dust-cover, I have disclosed the end. And I have done this, with no fear of spoiling the tale, in order to bring out the fact that the *Iliad* is a fine example of the Greek method of constructing a story or a play. In most cases, since the matter was traditional, the end was already known to the audience when they sat down to the beginning, and the author had to secure his effects by other methods than that of surprise. He could of course show a greater or lesser degree of originality in the details of his composition. In the *Odyssey*, for instance, it was a stroke of dramatic genius to break the narrative by causing Odysseus to recite his own adventures to the Phaeacian nobles in the shadowy hall of King Alcinous. And in the case of the *Iliad*, Homer's first audiences must have been delighted by the daring humour with which he presented the comedy of Olympus; for I believe this to have been one of his major contributions to the old story of the Trojan War. But apart from such innovations, Homer employs two devices, both of

* The Achaeans attached even more importance than we do to the proper disposal of their dead. See the ghost of Patroclus on the subject (XXIII, p. 414).

which are typical of Greek art. First, like the Attic dramatists, far from feeling that his hearers' foreknowledge is a handicap, he makes capital out of it by giving them confidential asides. The ominous remark that follows Hector's promise to Dolon of the horses of Achilles is a case in point. Again, the effect of the magnificent speech in which Achilles repudiates Agamemnon's overtures is heightened by the fact that Achilles really thinks that Destiny leaves him free to go home unscathed, whereas we know that he will be dragged back into the war by the killing of his dearest friend and in the end (or rather beyond it) will himself be killed. Which brings me to a further point. The action of the *Iliad* covers only fifty days in a ten years' war. But by a skilful extension of the device I am discussing, Homer causes two shadows to add their sombre significance to every page, that of the past and that of what is yet to come.

Secondly, Homer employs the device of delayed action. His hearers know what is coming, but not how or when. The sinister figure of Achilles is introduced at the beginning of the poem, but only to be withdrawn into the background till we reach Book IX. We are almost lulled into security – but not quite. There are too many references to the absentee for us to forget him. However, when Achilles does come into the foreground again, he removes himself once more with such a show of indomitable pride that we are left wondering how Homer is going to break this adamantine spirit. And we are not surprised to discover that it takes him nine tremendous Books to do so. The same artifice of suspense is used in the *Odyssey*. There too the chief figure is introduced in the beginning only to vanish and be talked about by other characters till he appears in person in Book V. Moreover, the parallel in technique extends to the conclusion of both works. In both, Book XXII brings the action to a climax (Hector is killed: the Suitors are disposed of); in Book XXIII we have a peaceful interlude (the Funeral Games: Odysseus is recognized by Penelope), and Book XXIV provides the resolution of the drama (Achilles obeys the gods and relents: Odysseus is reinstated by divine intervention). This similarity in their composition is one of the many things which incline me to the opinion that one man is the author of both works.

It will astonish people who know nothing of the 'Homeric question' to learn that these splendidly constructed poems, and especially the *Iliad*, have in the past been picked to pieces by the men who studied them most carefully and should presumably have admired them most. They alleged certain incongruities in the narrative and argued that the *Iliad* is the composite product of a number of poets of varying merit, who had not even the doubtful advantage of sitting in committee, but lived at different times and each patched up his predecessor's work, dropping many stitches in the course of this sartorial process. Now I think it is generally admitted that Homer did not invent the Story of Troy; also that it was the practice of ancient poets to build up their own edifice with the help of bricks taken from existing structures. In fact we should *expect* the *Iliad* to contain quite clear indications that it is the last of a long line of poems. Like Hermes as described by Priam, it bears every sign of good breeding and noble parentage. I have already referred to the evidence of advanced technique which is provided by certain elements in its construction. And I could add other points which in these latter days of literature we are too sophisticated to note with surprise or even to note at all, for instance that in Homer it is already an established convention that the author has been put by his Muse in a position to tell us everything his characters have said or thought, even their last soliloquies. If Homer invented all this technique it would be more than niggardly to deny him originality; but even if we take the likelier view that he inherited a great deal of it from previous poets, we have by no means shown that the *Iliad* was not his own.

We are left, in the end, with one kind of evidence, and that is psychological. To me, the proof of unity afforded by Homer's consistency in character-drawing is the most convincing of many. Note first that he does not describe his characters at length; he makes them disclose themselves by what they say and do in the scenes where they appear. Thetis, for instance, the mother of Achilles, is a sorrowful lady, who always has a grievance: her one obsession is her love for her illustrious but ill-starred son, on whose behalf she is ready to pester anyone from Zeus to Hephaestus. From the moment of her first introduction in Book I, through all the episodes in which she reappears, up to the last Book, Homer presents her with complete consistency – and that in scenes which have all been denied a right to their place in the *Iliad*. I argue that such a high degree of consistency would have proved impossible for more than a single author, particularly without the assistance, in one place or another, of a full-length portrait from the original creator's pen. The same is true if one follows the major figures – Athene, Odysseus, Nestor, or Helen herself – from the *Iliad* into the *Odyssey*. They are always themselves. I feel sure, on general literary grounds, that a fresh author taking them over could not have helped revealing his hand. In fact, any newcomer in the field of Epic poetry who was original enough to have 'contributed' to the *Iliad* or *Odyssey*, could not have failed, indeed would almost certainly have wished, to leave the imprint of his own mind on his characters. The Attic dramatists, who drew so largely on Homer, certainly showed this very human proclivity. It is difficult to recognize the characters of Homer in *their* portraits of Helen, Odysseus, Aias, and the rest.

However, it is inconsistencies in the narrative that were the chief weapons of those who tried to pick the *Iliad* to pieces. I cordially invite new readers to try to find some for themselves, though, unlike Achilles at the sports, I offer no 'splendid prizes' for this event. No marks will be given for the discovery of passages where Homer, after killing a man in battle, brings him back to life – this might happen to any author. One mark (out of ten) is allotted for the detection of minor incongruities in timing. For instance, Odysseus in the course of twenty-four hours, besides eating three dinners, does more things than the most energetic hero of a modern adventure story could have done in three days. But the taking of these little liberties with time is part of a dramatist's privilege, and Homer, particularly in the *Iliad*, is above all things dramatic. Half the poem consists of speeches and all the rest is put before us as though upon a stage – in fact, Homer invented drama before the theatre was invented to receive it. I might allot as much as two marks to the enquiring spirit who asks how it comes about in Book III that Priam, who has had the Achaean chieftains knocking at his gates for nine years, has to ask Helen who is who. But full marks will be given only for the detection of a real flaw which cannot be explained away – as can be done, in my opinion, with all the alleged literary crimes for which Homer was dismembered and served up piecemeal to Victorian schoolboys, myself included.

If we have now re-integrated Homer as one person, or at most two (for I believe I am in the minority in attributing the *Iliad* and *Odyssey* to a single author), the next thing that the reader will ask is where the story of the *Iliad* came from. I wish I could tell him. A great deal of scholarly research has been done on the question. It has become fairly certain that there was an earlier *Achilleis* or Story of Achilles, indeed several stories in which the angry young hero who refused to fight till the eleventh hour bore other names than that of Achilles. In fact, Homer himself gives us one of these, in which Meleager figures in the leading rôle, much as in the *Odyssey* he gives us the 'Wandering Prince' once with Odysseus as hero and once with Menelaus. Stories of the siege and sack of towns are by no means missing from the mythology of other races. And it is my surmise that the stories we read in Homer issued, with an esoteric or at least ritual content, from the mouths of wise men who lived long before him; that in the course of centuries they spread across the world, undergoing many changes of nomenclature and language, and sinking to the folklore level, where, even if they were not fully understood, they were at least enabled to survive by their intrinsic interest and excellence; and that in the age of Homer they were raised to what we recognize as the literary level. That is my impression. It would need a good deal to confirm it; and at this point I will only add my own belief that Homer himself did not realize the esoteric content of his tales, if any. He had his own approach to truth, but that was through art.

Is Homer's narrative in any sense historical? The answer is both yes and no. I do not think that, in telling the story of the Trojan War, he is giving us history, even in its most diluted form. There *was* a place called Troy (or Ilium) and we know that it was more than once destroyed. But even so, this ten years' war, as described by him and thrown back a few generations into the past, did not take place (even without the participation of the gods) either at Troy or, in my opinion, anywhere else. It was a fiction of a very special kind, which had existed long before Homer's time – a fiction that he adorned with the names of people whom his audience believed to be the ancestors of their own ruling princes, and some of whom we ourselves may well accept as having lived. If this view is correct, it enormously enhances the merit of Homer's achievement in building up the tale and the characters who make it. I would rather have the *Iliad* than a whole shelf of Bronze-Age war-reports, however accurate.

Besides, Homer does give us history – the history of his own world. That statement needs but little qualification. We know from the archaeological evidence that Homer attempts to archaeologize, even to take us into the Mycenaean Age. Nestor's cup is a case in point – a comparable vessel, with a couple of doves on top of it, was discovered at Mycenae. Yet in Homer's day there was no science of archaeology, no written history, to assist the historical novelist. Where then did he get these details from the past? I think there is only one answer. He took them from the work of previous poets, in much the same way as he took over from them much of their vocabulary, and even a number of their lines and ways of dealing with recurring situations. Yet in spite of this indebtedness, Homer leaves on our minds the impress of complete originality. It is his own observation of life that he depends on. I am not denying that he invokes the glamour of the mythical past when he

confronts Odysseus with the Sirens, or Meleager with the
Calydonian Boar. But I feel strongly that in all that matters
most, in describing the general structure of society, the rela-
tions of men and women to one another, and even the
physical circumstances of their existence, he is drawing from
contemporary models. I will go even further and say that he
could not have done otherwise and at the same time succeeded
in holding his audience, who, it must be remembered, did
not read him in a printed book with the assistance of learned
footnotes, but heard him recite his hexameters to the accom-
paniment of a lyre, as an after-dinner entertainment, while the
wine went round. I maintain that in such circumstances any
attempt to describe an alien world must have failed.

Homer, then, appealed to his hearers' minds through what
they knew. For instance, every member of his audience would
at once recognize the force of the homely simile in which the
Myrmidons are likened to a horde of wasps. By the same
token they must have known the lion; and for this reason I
mistrust the archaeologists who argue that in the period and
place in which they wish to locate Homer lions were extinct.
Would any narrator to-day, in his efforts to bring his story to
life, present his listeners every few minutes with a dodo in
action? If archaeology cannot fit Homer into a period which
contains lions and the rest of the things that he refers to in
familiar terms, I feel that archaeology must think again.
And to be quite frank it does so – every ten or twenty years.
At the moment it is fashionable to place Homer as late as
750 B.C. I myself would put him in the tenth century before
Christ. But the question of his date is extremely difficult,
and my only contention here is that Homer gives us a unified
picture of the world that he saw with his own eyes, whatever
its exact date may have been. In that sense Homer gives us
history – and history of a period about which, but for a few
broken relics, we should otherwise have known next to
nothing.

There is no need for me to describe Homer's world as
revealed in the *Iliad*. He does it a great deal better than I

could; he looks at it through the eyes of a poet. Hitherto I have discussed him mainly as a constructor of stories; and the problems involved were simple in comparison with the difficulty of assessing him as an imaginative poet. I can make only slanting approaches to this task, and must fall back on some of the new impressions that have crowded in upon me during the many years I have spent in the study of his mind.

I have been struck first by the realism, subtlety and modernity of Homer's character-drawing. When I say 'modernity' I do not mean that we shall meet such characters as Dolon, Paris, Diomedes or Briseis in Piccadilly, but that to Homer they were contemporary and true. He did not summon them from the legendary past: he created them out of his own experience of life. The deep impression of reality which they made upon me entirely banished from my mind (and I hope from my translation) the idea I had received in my schooldays that Homer was harking back to the so-called 'heroic age', when 'heroes' were apparently as common as blackberries. My illusions were shattered by a single reading of the sordid quarrel between Agamemnon and Achilles in Book I. I soon became convinced that human nature has not materially altered in the three thousand years since Homer wrote; that his people were a great deal more interesting than 'heroes'; that his poetic achievement in raising them to the tragic level was all the more sublime; and, incidentally, that his whole effect is obscured if one heroizes his men and gods by describing them and making them talk in a pompous and old-fashioned style. In other words, I found that Homer is depicting *us* in somewhat different circumstances. And I am not at all shaken in this conclusion when he makes his warriors hurl at each other lumps of rock 'even to lift which was a feat beyond the strength of any two men bred to-day.' That is merely a conventional tribute to the ancient belief that regression rather than progress is the rule in human affairs.

Another misapprehension that I rapidly corrected was concerned with the humour of Homer. 'Homeric laughter' is an unfortunate phrase. When the banqueters on Olympus are doubled up with laughter at the sight of the lame god Hephaestus bustling about in the hall, it is not Homer that is laughing, but the gods he has created. Nor is it pertinent to talk, as Dr Leaf did, of the 'savage humour' of his warriors. If you have just saved your own life in mortal combat by killing your enemy, it is ten to one that any joke that may spring to your lips will be completely lacking in urbanity. Homer is more of a realist than his critics, most of whom, I dare say, had never seen a battle. They do not even allow him to relieve a melancholy passage by a lighter interlude. When a hitch occurs in the cremation of Patroclus, and Iris hastens to help Achilles by bringing the Winds to bear on the situation, we are told by Dr Leaf (who does not fail to detect 'a touch of humour' here) that the whole scene 'falls below the dignity of its surroundings'; indeed, 'an interpolator' is blamed for the impropriety.

However, the point I wished to make is that Homer's own sense of humour is a very different thing from that of his creatures. It is a subtle, all-pervading essence, like the perfume of Here's imperishable olive-oil, which 'had only to be stirred for the scent to spread through Heaven and earth.' In his treatment of Heaven it is felt from the moment when Zeus comments with sad resignation on the domestic trouble that Thetis has let him in for, and it penetrates every Olympian scene till the last intervention of the gods, when the disguised Hermes compliments Priam on realizing that he comes of not ignoble parentage. What is so remarkable is the fact that Homer leaves us with the feeling not only that he believes in his gods but that they were indeed very worshipful and formidable powers. Moreover, the Greeks accepted him as their first theologian and the creator of the Olympian religion. I know that there have been other faiths whose devotees were not discouraged from laughing at their gods. But I still think that Homer's achievement in this respect is unique for a man of letters. And I cannot explain it.

But there is one fact to which I can point. The comic element is introduced almost solely on occasions when gods are *shown together*, in sympathetic or in hostile action. When dealing with mankind, each in his own capacity, they are far from amusing. Apollo and his Sister Artemis put up a ludicrous show when at war with their Uncle and their Father's Consort, but Apollo acting on his own in the first pages of the *Iliad* is a very serious and unpleasant person; and so is Artemis when King Oeneus has miscounted and she sends him the Calydonian Boar. Even Aphrodite, who cuts such a pathetic figure in a pitched battle, is a power whom Helen herself cannot trifle with when she, the goddess of love, is attending to her own business. This, I think, is how Homer saves the face of his gods – with one exception. He gives the War-god many terrible and bloody attributes, but he takes no pains to make us feel that he is much more than a bully. It is possible that the reason why he persistently degrades and ridicules Ares in a poem which is much concerned with battle, is that the *Iliad* was written not to glorify war (though it admits its fascination) but to emphasize its tragic futility.

Homer then reveres his gods, but rightly feels that it would be untrue to life to make these formidable creatures take one another as seriously as *he* takes each of them. They are members of a family and, as such, are all on much the same level, like the members of a human family, the father of which may be a terror to his office-boy but fulminates with less effect at home. Thus, for a realist like Homer, high comedy in Heaven was artistically inevitable.* And of course it was useful in a tragedy by way of relief or of contrast with the melancholy scene below. But Homer's humour is not confined to Olympus: it pervades the human drama too. Sometimes it comes into this by way of relief, as when Idomeneus and Meriones catch each other taking a rest in the middle of a very terrible battle, or in the brilliant description of the games that follow

---

* But the gods do not retaliate by laughing at mankind. On the contrary, except for some light-hearted backchat with their favourites (e.g. Athene and Diomedes, V, p. 114; or Athene and Odysseus, *Od.* XIII), they take men seriously and regard them as miserable though fascinating creatures. See Apollo on the subject, XXI, p. 392, or Zeus, XX, p. 366, and XVII, p. 328.

Patroclus' funeral. But this is not always so. The delightful account of Agamemnon's inspection of his troops, when the tactless Commander-in-Chief succeeds in ruffling the feelings of nearly all his senior officers, is not preceded by a passage where the tension is high. In the end, one is forced to the conclusion that Homer could not help seeing humour both on earth and in Heaven. He found it in the very texture of reality. And I hope that he was right.

Homer's diction is superb and it matches his observation. It is easy to rejoice in these and be content. But some of us are not so quickly satisfied: we wish to know how he achieves nobility. I myself have come to feel that his is the poetry not so much of words but of ideas – if it is possible to separate the two. I approach an understanding through the examination of the epithets which he uses in such abundance. Every manu-factured object that he mentions is well and truly made. A ship is always fast, well-benched and seaworthy; a spear is stout, long and sharp, and (we are charmed to note) it is its custom to throw a long shadow on the ground and also to be 'wind-fed' even when resting in a warrior's hand; that is to say, it looks back to the time when its shaft was part of an ash-tree on the windswept mountain-side, or else forward to the moment when it is going to hurtle through the air. Natural phenomena such as the rose-fingered dawn and the ambrosial and mysterious night are all given adjectives which search out the quintessence of their quality or beauty. Homer's men are all noble, peerless, brave, wise, or characterized by some other excellence; and his women are all lovely, or at least well-dressed and with hair beautifully done. What is the significance of this wholesale use of honorific epithets – epithets which often sound insincere or at least fall in most inappropriate places?* Scholars are inclined to explain them away as the decorative trappings of the Epic style, and as being for the most part a legacy to Homer from his pre-decessors' work. This does not satisfy me. If Homer did take

* Like our parliamentary expressions, e.g. 'the noble lord', or 'the honourable and gallant member for X'.

them over as trappings, his genius put them to a new use, which is a mirror to his own mind. When he calls a warrior brave or great-hearted just at the moment when he is behaving like an arrant coward, I do not think that he is being careless or conventional – he is seeing that warrior as he was, or will be, or indeed as he, in essence, is. When he talks of a beautiful and well-built chariot, he is not labouring under the delusion that all the workmanship of his day (excellent as it no doubt was) attained perfection. He has no use for a shoddy article, and what he sees in his mind's eye is the perfect thing. He does the same with people. Everything I have written earlier in this essay, if it is true, shows what a realist he is. But the reality that he sees has for his eye a certain transparence, through which he sees and records the ideal or higher reality. He puts me in mind of his own picture of Zeus when, sitting on Mount Ida, he wearies of watching the unending battle and turns 'his shining eyes into the distance', where, among other more satisfying things, he can survey 'the Abii, the most law-abiding folk on earth'.

I do not mean by this simile that Homer, when he calls a villain 'great-hearted', is indulging himself in illusion or wishful thinking, but that he is seeing reality at two levels. To which I might add that he sees good as more *real* than evil. It is as though he had anticipated Plato's Theory of Forms, according to which all earthly things are the imperfect and transitory copies of ideal Forms that have a permanent existence in Heaven. I like to fancy that Homer, more privileged than Plato, actually saw these Forms, and even, on one occasion, brought them down to earth. For it is this that he did when he gave immortal horses to Achilles. His attitude to animals in general repays the closest study *; but in these horses of Achilles, if the reader will follow them through their

---

* Unlike us, he has no superiority complex in relation to animals. He recognizes not only their essential qualities but their right to display them; he even shows sympathy with the wasp (XVI, p. 299) and he is the only writer I know who admires the intrepidity of the fly that keeps settling on one's nose (XVII, p. 331).

triumphs and their tears, I think he will admit that Homer has given us something unique. And he may also note an interesting point. When the Ideal is manifested in the work-a-day world, it does not put to shame the creatures of a day – it brings them nearer to itself. Thus, when Homer causes Pedasus, a mortal thoroughbred, to be put in as an outrigger with the divine horses of Achilles, he is careful to tell us that Pedasus, though he 'was only an ordinary horse', kept up with the immortal pair, and his subsequent death is one of the most poignant things we have to put up with in all the nightmare battles of the 'lamentable war'.

My theory that Homer's poetry gives us reality and superreality at the same time does, if it is correct, throw a little light on the central problem of the *Iliad*, the character of Achilles. We have seen in what a sordid light he is presented in the first Book. But this is only the beginning: we are to follow him through every stage of degradation to which the exasperating conditions of a long-drawn-out war can lead a character whose very strength is its weakness. Even his best friend and admirer Patroclus sees him as 'warping a noble nature to ignoble ends'. His pride becomes a monomania, and even his grief at the death of Patroclus, based as it is on injured self-esteem, produces no softening, but leads instead to an outburst of insensate cruelty and rage. Yet all along the gods are honouring Achilles and, with them, Homer somehow makes us feel that, behind all this, true greatness lies concealed. And in the end, in the memorable scene in which Achilles gives up Hector's corpse to his old father, we are allowed one glimpse of what the real Achilles is. I say 'is', not 'might have been', for I take it that the function of tragedy is not merely to mourn the wastage of virtue and to cry over spilt milk, but to hint at some ultimate solution, to suggest that if we could only look at things with the Olympian eye of Zeus we should see that, after all, the milk we were crying about is not really spilt.

At the end, I have added a Glossary giving a few facts about the more important characters in the tale. In compiling this I decided to say about these people only what Homer, our chief and earliest authority, permits, while adding in square brackets a little information that we glean from other writers. In the course of the work I hit on some interesting points, for example, the seniority of Paris to Hector, and the normality of Helen's parentage. I was also able to strengthen some of the impressions I had received from the text itself. Homer's main interest lies in the study of human beings and human gods. He is disposed to reject or tone down the grotesque and the supernormal. The beautiful Helen did not emerge from an egg, and, apart from one perfunctory reference to the Judgement of Paris, it was her human frailty and that of her seducer that led to the Trojan War. His handling of the gods and their many interventions and rescues in battle is much on a par with this. When Achilles is fighting the River-god Xanthus, we are left wondering all the time whether a demonic power is at work, or whether Achilles has not merely let himself in for the risk of being drowned by a river in spate. In a word, Homer is inclined to hover on the near side of the line that separates the natural and the supernatural – not that I, for one, object to crossing it now and then with such a guide.

E. V. R.

Highgate,
  September 1949.

Note to the 8th Printing

Since the above Introduction was written, Michael Ventris' decipherment of Linear B has opened a new era in Homeric studies, and Professor T. B. L. Webster, in *From Mycenae to Homer*, London (Methuen) 1958 and New York (Praeger), has taken full advantage of the opportunities now afforded of achieving greater exactitude in dating Homer's poems and tracing them to their sources. His brilliant work has convinced me that I was mistaken (on p. xv) in tentatively placing Homer as early as the tenth century B.C.; also that some of the earlier poetry to which I suggested (p. xiv) that Homer is indebted was that of the Mycenaeans themselves, whose literary work we still hope to discover.

June, 1959.   E. V. R.

I

THE QUARREL

The Wrath of Achilles is my theme, that fatal wrath which, in fulfilment of the will of Zeus, brought the Achaeans so much suffering and sent the gallant souls of many noblemen to Hades, leaving their bodies as carrion for the dogs and passing birds. Let us begin, goddess of song, with the angry parting that took place between Agamemnon King of Men and the great Achilles son of Peleus. Which of the gods was it that made them quarrel?

It was Apollo, Son of Zeus and Leto, who started the feud, when he punished the King for his discourtesy to Chryses, his priest, by inflicting a deadly plague on his army and destroying his men. Chryses had come to the Achaean ships to recover his captured daughter. He brought with him a generous ransom and carried the chaplet of the Archer-god Apollo on a golden staff in his hand. He appealed to the whole Achaean army, and most of all to its two commanders, the sons of Atreus.

'My lords, and you Achaean men-at-arms; you hope to sack King Priam's city and get home in safety. May the gods that live on Olympus grant your wish – on this condition, that you show your reverence for the Archer-god Apollo Son of Zeus by accepting this ransom and releasing my daughter.'

The troops applauded. They wished to see the priest respected and the tempting ransom taken. But this was not at all to King Agamemnon's liking. He cautioned the man severely and rudely dismissed him.

'Old man,' he said, 'do not let me catch you loitering by the hollow ships to-day, nor coming back again, or you may find the god's staff and chaplet a very poor defence. Far from agreeing to set your daughter free, I intend her to grow old in

Argos, in my house, a long way from her own country, work-ing at the loom and sharing my bed. Off with you now, and do not provoke me if you want to save your skin.'

The old man trembled and obeyed him. He went off with-out a word along the shore of the sounding sea. But when he found himself alone he prayed fervently to King Apollo, Son of Leto of the Lovely Locks. 'Hear me, god of the Silver Bow, Protector of Chryse and holy Cilla, and Lord Supreme of Tenedos. Smintheus, if ever I built you a shrine that de-lighted you, if ever I burnt you the fat thighs of a bull or a goat, grant me this wish. Let the Danaans pay with your arrows for my tears.'

Phoebus Apollo heard his prayer and came down in fury from the heights of Olympus with his bow and covered quiver on his back. As he set out, the arrows clanged on the shoulder of the angry god; and his descent was like nightfall. He sat down opposite the ships and shot an arrow, with a dreadful twang from his silver bow. He attacked the mules first and the nimble dogs; then he aimed his sharp arrows at the men, and struck again and again. Day and night innumer-able fires consumed the dead.

For nine days the god's arrows rained on the camp. On the tenth the troops were called to Assembly by order of Achilles – a measure that the white-armed goddess Here prompted him to take, in her concern for the Danaans whose destruction she was witnessing. When all had assembled and the gathering was complete, the great runner Achilles rose to address them:

"Agamemnon my lord, what with the fighting and the plague, I fear that our strength will soon be so reduced that any of us who are not dead by then will be forced to give up the struggle and sail for home But could we not consult a prophet or priest, or even some interpreter of dreams – for dreams too are sent by Zeus – and find out from him why Phoebus Apollo is so angry with us? He may be offended at some broken vow or some failure in our rites. If so, he might accept a savoury offering of sheep or of full-grown goats and save us from the plague.'

Achilles sat down, and Calchas son of Thestor rose to his feet. As an augur, Calchas had no rival in the camp. Past, present and future held no secrets from him; and it was his second sight, a gift he owed to Apollo, that had guided the Achaean fleet to Ilium. He was a loyal Argive, and it was in this spirit that he took the floor.

'Achilles,' he said, 'my royal lord, you have asked me to account for the Archer-King Apollo's wrath; and I will do so. But listen to me first. Will you swear to come forward and use all your eloquence and strength to protect me? I ask this of you, being well aware that I shall make an enemy of one whose authority is absolute among us and whose word is law to all Achaeans. A commoner is no match for a king whom he offends. Even if the king swallows his anger for the moment, he will nurse his grievance till the day when he can settle the account. Consider, then, whether you can guarantee my safety.'

'Dismiss your fears,' said the swift Achilles, 'and tell us anything you may have learnt from Heaven. For by Apollo Son of Zeus, the very god, Calchas, in whose name you reveal your oracles, I swear that as long as I am alive and in possession of my senses not a Danaan of them all, here by the hollow ships, shall hurt you, not even if the man you mean is Agamemnon, who bears the title of our overlord.'

At last the worthy seer plucked up his courage and spoke out. 'There is no question,' he said, 'of a broken vow or any shortcoming in our rites. The god is angry because Agamemnon insulted his priest, refusing to take the ransom and free his daughter. That is the reason for our present sufferings and for those to come. The Archer-King will not release us from this loathsome scourge till we give the bright-eyed lady back to her father, without recompense or ransom, and send holy offerings to Chryse. When that is done we might induce him to relent.'

Calchas sat down, and the noble son of Atreus, imperial Agamemnon, leapt up in anger. His heart was seething with black passion and his eyes were like points of flame. He rounded first on Calchas, full of menace.

'Prophet of evil,' he cried, 'never yet have you said a word
to my advantage. It is always trouble that you revel in fore-
telling. Not once have you fulfilled a prophecy of something
good – you have never even made one! And now you hold
forth as the army's seer, telling the men that the Archer-god is
persecuting them because I refused the ransom for the girl
Chryseis, princely though it was. And why did I refuse?
Because I chose to keep the girl and take her home. Indeed, I
like her better than my consort, Clytaemnestra. She is quite
as beautiful, and no less clever or skilful with her hands. Still,
I am willing to give her up, if that appears the wiser course. It
is my desire to see my people safe and sound, not perishing
like this. But you must let me have another prize at once, or
I shall be the only one of us with empty hands, a most im-
proper thing. You can see for yourselves that the prize I was
given is on its way elsewhere.'

The swift and excellent Achilles leapt to his feet. 'And
where,' he asked, 'does your majesty propose that our gallant
troops should find a fresh prize to satisfy your unexampled
greed? I have yet to hear of any public fund we have laid by.
The plunder we took from captured towns has been dis-
tributed, and it is more than we can ask of the men to re-
assemble that. No; give the girl back now, as the god de-
mands, and we will make you triple, fourfold, compensation,
if Zeus ever allows us to bring down the battlements of Troy.'

King Agamemnon took him up at once. 'You are a great
man, Prince Achilles, but do not imagine you can trick me
into that. I am not going to be outwitted or cajoled by you.
"Give up the girl," you say, hoping, I presume, to keep your
own prize safe. Do you expect me tamely to sit by while I
am robbed? No; if the army is prepared to give me a fresh
prize, chosen to suit my taste and to make up for my loss, I
have no more to say. If not, I shall come and help myself to
your prize, or that of Aias; or I shall walk off with Odysseus's.
And what an angry man I shall leave behind me! However,
we can deal with all that later on. For the moment, let us run
a black ship down into the friendly sea, give her a special

crew, embark the animals for sacrifice, and put the girl herself, Chryseis of the lovely cheeks, on board. And let some Councillor of ours go as captain – Aias, Idomeneus, the excellent Odysseus, or yourself, my lord, the most redoubtable man we could choose – to offer the sacrifice and win us back Apollo's favour.'

Achilles the great runner gave him a black look. 'You shameless schemer,' he cried, 'always aiming at a profitable deal! How can you expect any of the men to give you loyal service when you send them on a raid or into battle? It was no quarrel with the Trojan spearmen that brought *me* here to fight. They have never done *me* any harm. They have never lifted cow or horse of mine, nor ravaged any crop that the deep soil of Phthia grows to feed her men; for the roaring seas and many a dark range of mountains lie between us. The truth is that we joined the expedition to please you; yes, you unconscionable cur, to get satisfaction from the Trojans for Menelaus and yourself – a fact which you utterly ignore. And now comes this threat from you of all people to rob me of my prize, my hard-earned prize, which was a tribute from the ranks. It is not as though I am ever given as much as you when the Achaeans sack some thriving city of the Trojans. The heat and burden of the fighting fall on me, but when it comes to dealing out the loot, it is you that take the lion's share, leaving me to return exhausted from the field with something of my own, however small. So now I shall go back to Phthia. That is the best thing I can do – to sail home in my beaked ships. I see no point in staying here to be insulted while I pile up wealth and luxuries for you.'

'Take to your heels, by all means,' Agamemnon King of Men retorted, 'if you feel the urge to go. I am not begging you to stay on my account. There are others with me who will treat me with respect, and the Counsellor Zeus is first among them. Moreover, of all the princes here, you are the most disloyal to myself. To you, sedition, violence and fighting are the breath of life. What if you *are* a great soldier – who made you so but God? Go home now with your ships and

your men-at-arms and rule the Myrmidons. I have no use for
you: your anger leaves me cold. But mark my words. In
the same way as Phoebus Apollo is robbing me of Chryseis,
whom I propose to send off in my ship with my own crew,
I am going to pay a visit to your hut and take away the
beautiful Briseis, your prize, Achilles, to let you know that I
am more powerful than you, and to teach others not to bandy
words with me and openly defy their King.'

This cut Achilles to the quick. In his shaggy breast his heart
was torn between two courses, whether to draw his sharp
sword from his side, thrust his way through the crowd, and
kill King Agamemnon, or to control himself and check the
angry impulse. He was deep in this inward conflict, with his
long sword half unsheathed, when Athene came down to
him from heaven at the instance of the white-armed goddess
Here, who loved the two lords equally and was fretting for
them both. Athene stood behind him and seized him by his
golden locks. No one but Achilles was aware of her; the rest
saw nothing. He swung round in amazement, recognized
Pallas Athene at once – so terrible was the brilliance of her
eyes – and spoke out to her boldly: 'And why have you come
here, Daughter of aegis-bearing Zeus? Is it to witness the
arrogance of my lord Agamemnon? I tell you bluntly – and
I make no idle threats – that he stands to pay for this outrage
with his life.'

'I came from heaven,' replied Athene of the Flashing Eyes,
'in the hope of bringing you to your senses. It was Here,
goddess of the White Arms, that sent me down, loving the
two of you as she does and fretting for you both. Come now,
give up this strife and take your hand from your sword.
Sting him with words instead, and tell him what you mean to
do. Here is a prophecy for you – the day shall come when
gifts three times as valuable as what you now have lost will be
laid at your feet in payment for this outrage. Hold your hand,
then, and be advised by us.'

'Lady,' replied Achilles the great runner, 'when you two
goddesses command, a man must obey, however angry he

may be. Better for him if he does. The man who listens to the gods is listened to by them.'

With that he checked his great hand on the silver hilt and drove the long sword back into its scabbard, in obedience to Athene, who then set out for Olympus and the palace of aegis-bearing Zeus, where she rejoined the other gods.

Not that Achilles was appeased. He rounded on Atreides once again with bitter taunts. 'You drunken sot,' he cried, 'with the eyes of a dog and the courage of a doe! You never have the pluck to arm yourself and go into battle with the men or to join the other captains in an ambush – you would sooner die. It pays you better to stay in camp, filching the prizes of anyone that contradicts you, and flourishing at your people's cost because they are too feeble to resist – feeble indeed; or else, my lord, this act of brigandage would prove your last.

'But mark my words, for I am going to take a solemn oath. Look at this staff. Once cut from its stem in the hills, it can never put out leaves or twigs again. The billhook stripped it of its bark and foliage; it will sprout no more. Yet the men who in the name of Zeus safeguard our laws, the Judges of our nation, hold it in their hands. By this I swear (and I could not choose a better token) that the day is coming when the Achaeans one and all will miss me sorely, and you in your despair will be powerless to help them as they fall in their hundreds to Hector killer of men. Then, you will tear your heart out in remorse for having treated the best man in the expedition with contempt.'

The son of Peleus finished, flung down the staff with its golden studs, and resumed his seat, leaving Atreides to thunder at him from the other side. But Nestor now leapt up, Nestor, that master of the courteous word, the clear-voiced orator from Pylos, whose speech ran sweeter than honey off his tongue. He had already seen two generations come to life, grow up, and die in sacred Pylos, and now he ruled the third. Filled with benevolent concern, he took the floor. 'This is indeed enough to make Achaea weep!' he said. 'How happy

Priam and Priam's sons would be, how all the Trojans would
rejoice, if they could hear of this rift between you two who
are the leaders of the Danaans in policy and war. Listen to me.
You are both my juniors. And what is more, I have mixed in
the past with even better men than you and never failed to
carry weight with them, the finest men I have ever seen or
shall see, men like Peirithous and Dryas, Shepherd of the
People, Caeneus, Exadius, the godlike Polyphemus and
Aegeus' son, Theseus of heroic fame. They were the strongest
men that Earth has bred, the strongest men pitted against the
strongest enemies, a savage, mountain-dwelling tribe whom
they utterly destroyed. Those were the men whom I left my
home in Pylos to join. I travelled far to meet them, at their
own request. I played my independent part in their campaign.
And they were men whom not a soul on earth to-day could
face in battle. Still, they listened to what I said and followed
my advice. You two must do the same; you will not lose by
it. Agamemnon, forget the privilege of your rank, and do not
rob him of the girl. The army gave her to him: let him keep
his prize. And you, my lord Achilles, drop your contentious
bearing to the King. Through the authority he derives from
Zeus, a sceptred king has more than ordinary claims on our
respect. You, with a goddess for Mother, may be the stronger
of the two; yet Agamemnon is the better man, since he rules
more people. My lord Atreides, be appeased. I, Nestor, beg
you to relent towards Achilles, our mighty bulwark in the
stress of battle.'

'My venerable lord, no one could cavil at what you say,'
replied King Agamemnon. 'But this man wants to get the
whip-hand here; he wants to lord it over all of us, to play the
king, and to give us each our orders, though I know one who
is not going to stand for that. What if the everlasting gods did
make a spearman of him? Does that entitle him to use insult-
ing language?'

Here the noble Achilles broke in on the King: 'A pretty
nincompoop and craven I shall be called if I yield to you at
every point, no matter what you say. Command the rest, not

me. I have done with obedience to you. And here is another thing for you to ponder. I am not going to fight you or anybody else with my hands for this girl's sake. You gave her to me, and now you take her back. But of all else I have beside my good black ship, you shall not rob me of a single thing. Come now and try, so that the rest may see what happens. Your blood will soon be flowing in a dark stream down my spear.'

The two stood up, when the war of words was over, and dismissed the Assembly by the Achaean fleet. Achilles, with Patroclus and his men, made off to his trim ships and huts; while Atreides launched a fast vessel on the sea, chose twenty oarsmen to man her, and after embarking the cattle to be offered to the god, fetched Chryseis of the lovely cheeks and put her on board. The resourceful Odysseus went as captain, and when everyone was in, they set out along the highways of the sea.

Meanwhile Agamemnon made his people purify themselves by bathing. When they had washed the filth from their bodies in the salt water, they offered a rich sacrifice of bulls and goats to Apollo on the shore of the unharvested sea; and savoury odours, mixed with the curling smoke, went up into the sky.

While his men were engaged on these duties in the camp, Agamemnon did not forget his quarrel with Achilles and the threat he had made to him at the meeting. He called Talthybius and Eurybates, his two heralds and obedient squires, and said to them: 'Go to the hut of Achilles son of Peleus, take the lady Briseis into your custody, and bring her here. If he refuses to let her go, I shall come in force to fetch her, which will be all the worse for him.'

He sent them off, and with his stern injunction in their ears, the two men made their unwilling way along the shore of the barren sea, till they reached the encampment and ships of the Myrmidons, where they found the prince himself sitting by his own black ship and hut. It gave Achilles no pleasure to see them. They came to a halt, too timid and abashed before the prince to address him and tell him what they wanted. But he knew without being told, and broke the silence. 'Heralds,' he said, 'ambassadors of Zeus and men, I welcome you. Come forward. My quarrel is not with you but with Agamemnon, who sent you here to fetch the girl Briseis. My lord Patroclus, will you bring the lady out and hand her over to these men? I shall count on them to be my witnesses before the happy gods, before mankind, before the brutal king himself, if the Achaeans ever need me again to save them from disaster. The man is raving mad. If he had ever learnt to look ahead, he would be wondering now how he is going to save his army when they are fighting by the ships.' Patroclus did as his friend had told him, brought out Briseis of the lovely cheeks from the hut, and gave her up to the two men, who made their way back along the line of ships with the unhappy girl.

Withdrawing from his men, Achilles wept. He sat down by himself on the shore of the grey sea, and looked across the watery wilderness. Then, stretching out his arms, he poured out prayers to his Mother. 'Mother, since you, a goddess, gave me life, if only for a little while, surely Olympian Zeus the Thunderer owes me some measure of regard. But he pays me none. He has let me be flouted by imperial Agamemnon son of Atreus, who has robbed me of my prize and has her with him now.'

Achilles prayed and wept, and his Lady Mother heard him where she sat in the depths of the sea with her old Father. She rose swiftly from the grey water like a mist, came and sat by her weeping son, stroked him with her hand and spoke to him. 'My child,' she asked him, 'why these tears? What is it that has grieved you? Do not keep your sorrow to yourself, but tell me so that we may share it.'

Achilles of the swift feet sighed heavily. 'You know,' he said; 'and since you know, why should I tell you the whole story? We went to Thebe, Eëtion's sacred city; we sacked the place and brought back all our plunder, which the army shared out in the proper way, choosing Chryseis of the lovely cheeks as a special gift for Atreides. Presently Chryses, priest of the Archer-god Apollo, came to the ships of the bronze-clad Achaeans to set free his daughter, bringing a generous ransom and carrying the chaplet of the Archer Apollo on a golden staff in his hand. He importuned the whole Achaean army, but chiefly its two leaders, the Atreidae. The troops showed by their applause that they wished to see the priest respected and the tempting ransom taken. But this was not at all to Agamemnon's liking. He sent him packing, with a stern warning in his ears. So the old man went home in anger; but Apollo listened to his prayers, because he loved him dearly, and let his wicked arrows fly against the Argive army. The men fell thick and fast, for the god's shafts rained down on every part of our scattered camp. At last a seer who understood the Archer's will explained the matter to us. I rose at once and advised them to propitiate the god. This made Agamemnon furious. He leapt to his feet and threatened me. And now he has carried out his threats: the bright-eyed Achaeans are taking the girl to Chryse in a ship with offerings for the god, while the King's messengers have just gone from my hut with the other girl Briseis, whom the army gave to me.

'So now, if you have any power, protect your son. Go to Olympus, and if anything you have ever done or said has warmed the heart of Zeus, remind him of it as you pray to him. For instance, in my father's house I have often heard you proudly tell us how you alone among the gods saved Zeus the Darkener of the Skies from an inglorious fate, when some of the other Olympians – Here, Poseidon and Pallas Athene – had plotted to throw him into chains. You, goddess, went and saved him from that indignity. You quickly summoned to high Olympus the monster of the hundred arms whom the gods call Briareus, but mankind Aegaeon, a giant more powerful even than his father. He squatted by the Son of Cronos with such a show of force that the blessed gods slunk off in terror, leaving Zeus free.

'Sit by him now, clasp his knees, and remind him of that. Persuade him, if you can, to help the Trojans, to fling the Achaeans back on their ships, to pen them in against the sea and slaughter them. That would teach them to appreciate

their King. That would make imperial Agamemnon son of
Atreus realize what a fool he was to insult the noblest of them
all.'

'My son, my son!' said Thetis, bursting into tears. 'Was it
for this I nursed my ill-starred child? At least they might have
left you carefree and at ease beside the ships, since Fate has
given you so short a life, so little time. But it seems that you
are not only doomed to an early death but to a miserable life.
It was indeed an unlucky day when I brought you into the
world. However, I will go to snow-capped Olympus to tell
Zeus the Thunderer all this myself, and see whether I can
move him. Meanwhile, stay by your gallant ships, keep up
your feud with the Achaeans, and take no part in the fighting.
Yesterday, I must tell you, Zeus left for Ocean Stream to join
the worthy Ethiopians at a banquet, and all the gods went with
him. But in twelve days' time he will be back on Olympus,
and then you may rest assured that I shall go to his Bronze
Palace, where I will throw myself at his feet. I am convinced
that he will hear me.'

Thetis withdrew, leaving Achilles to his grief for the gentle
lady whom they had forced him to give up. Meanwhile
Odysseus and his men reached Chryse with the sacred offer-
ings. When they had brought their craft into the deep waters
of the port, they furled the sail and stowed it in the black ship's
hold, dropped the mast neatly into its crutch by letting down
the forestays, rowed her into her berth, cast anchor, made the
hawsers fast, and jumped out on the beach. The cattle for the
Archer-god were disembarked, and Chryseis stepped ashore
from the seagoing ship. Odysseus of the nimble wits led the
girl to the altar and gave her back to her father. 'Chryses,' he
said, 'Agamemnon King of Men has ordered me to bring you
your daughter and to make ceremonial offerings to Phoebus
on the Danaans' behalf, in the hope of pacifying the Archer-
King, who has struck their army a grievous blow.' Then he
handed the lady over to her father, who welcomed his
daughter with joy.

The offerings destined to do honour to the god were quickly

set in place round the well-built altar. The men rinsed their
hands and took up the sacrificial grains. Then Chryses lifted
up his arms and prayed aloud for them: 'Hear me, God of the
Silver Bow, Protector of Chryse and of holy Cilla, and Lord
Supreme of Tenedos! My last petition found you kind indeed:
you showed your regard for me and struck a mighty blow at
the Achaean army. Now grant me a second wish and save the
Danaans from their dreadful scourge.' Thus the old man
prayed; and Phoebus Apollo heard him.

When they had made their petitions and scattered the grain,
they first drew back the animals' heads, slit their throats and
flayed them. Then they cut out slices from the thighs, wrapped
them in folds of fat and laid raw meat above them. These
pieces the old priest burnt on the faggots, while he sprinkled
red wine over the flames and the young men gathered round
him with five-pronged forks in their hands. When the thighs
were burnt up and they had tasted the inner parts, they carved
the rest into small pieces, pierced them with skewers, roasted
them thoroughly, and drew them all off.

Their work done and the meal prepared, they fell to with a
good will on the feast, in which all had equal shares. When
their thirst and hunger were satisfied, the stewards filled the
mixing-bowls to the brim with wine, and after first pouring
out a few drops in each man's cup, served the whole com-
pany. And for the rest of the day these young Achaean
warriors made music to appease the god, praising the Great
Archer in a lovely song, to which Apollo listened with de-
light.

When the sun set and darkness fell, they lay down for sleep
by the hawsers of their ship. But as soon as Dawn had lit the
East with rosy hands, they set sail for the great Achaean camp,
taking advantage of a breeze the Archer-god had sent them.
They put up their mast and spread the white sail. The sail
swelled out, struck full by the wind, and a dark wave hissed
loudly round her stem as the vessel gathered way and sped
through the choppy seas, forging ahead on her course. Thus
they returned to the great Achaean camp, where they dragged

their black ship high up on the mainland sands and under-
pinned her with long props. This done, they scattered to their
several huts and ships.

Now all this time Achilles the great runner, the royal son
of Peleus, had been sitting by his fast ships, nursing his anger.
He not only kept away from the fighting but attended no
meetings of the Assembly, where a man can win renown. He
stayed where he was, eating his heart out and longing for the
sound and fury of battle.

Eleven days went by, and at dawn on the twelfth the ever-
lasting gods returned in full strength to Olympus, with Zeus
at their head. Thetis, remembering her son's instructions,
emerged in the morning from the depths of the sea, rose into
the broad sky and reached Olympus. She found all-seeing
Zeus sitting away from the rest on the topmost of Olympus'
many peaks. She sank to the ground beside him, put her left
arm round his knees, raised her right hand to touch his chin,
and so made her petition to the Royal Son of Cronos. 'Father
Zeus, if ever I have served you well among the gods, by word
or deed, grant me a wish and show your favour to my son. He
is already singled out for early death, and now Agamemnon
King of Men has affronted him. He has stolen his prize and
kept her for himself. Avenge my son, Olympian Judge, and
let the Trojans have the upper hand till the Achaeans pay him
due respect and make him full amends.'

The Marshaller of the Clouds made no reply to this. He sat
in silence for a long time, with Thetis clinging to his knees as
she had done throughout. At last she appealed to him once
more: 'Promise me faithfully and bow your head, or
else, since you have nothing to lose by doing so, refuse;
and I shall know that there is no god who counts for less
than I.'

Zeus the Cloud-gatherer was much perturbed. 'This is a
sorry business!' he exclaimed. 'You will make me fall foul
of Here, when she rails at me about it, as she will. Even as
things are, she scolds me constantly before the other gods and
accuses me of helping the Trojans in this war. However, leave

me now, or she may notice us; and I will see the matter through. But first, to reassure you, I will bow my head – and the immortals recognize no surer pledge from me than that. When I promise with a nod, there can be no deceit, no turning back, no missing of the mark.'

Zeus, as he finished, bowed his sable brows. The ambrosial locks rolled forward from the immortal head of the King, and high Olympus shook.

The affair was settled, and the two now parted. Thetis swung down from glittering Olympus into the salt sea depths, while Zeus went to his own palace. There the whole company of gods rose from their chairs in deference to their Father. There was not one that dared to keep his seat as he approached; they all stood up to greet him. Zeus sat down on his throne; and Here, looking at him, knew at once that he and Thetis of the Silver Feet, the Daughter of the Old Man of the Sea, had hatched a plot between them. She rounded instantly on Zeus. 'What goddess,' she asked, 'has been scheming with you now, you arch-deceiver? How like you it is, when my back is turned, to settle things in your own furtive way. You never of your own accord confide in me.'

'Here,' the Father of men and gods replied, 'do not expect to learn all my decisions. You would find the knowledge hard to bear, although you are my Consort. What it is right for you to hear, no god or man shall know before you. But when I choose to take a step without referring to the gods, you are not to cross-examine me about it.'

'Dread Son of Cronos,' said the ox-eyed Queen, 'what are you suggesting now? Surely it never was my way to pester you with questions. I have always let you make your own decisions in perfect peace. But now I have a shrewd idea that you have been talked round by Thetis of the Silver Feet, the Daughter of the Old Man of the Sea. She sat with you this morning and clasped your knees. This makes me think that you have pledged your word to her to support Achilles and let the Achaeans be slaughtered at the ships.'

'Madam,' replied the Cloud-compeller, 'you think too

much, and I can keep no secrets from you. But there is nothing you can *do*, except to turn my heart even more against you, which will be all the worse for yourself. If things are as you say, you may take it that my will is being done. Sit there in silence and be ruled by me, or all the gods in Olympus will not be strong enough to keep me off and save you from my unconquerable hands.'

This made the ox-eyed Queen of Heaven tremble, and curbing herself with an effort she sat still. Zeus had daunted all the other Heavenly Ones as well, and there was silence in his palace, till at last Hephaestus the great Artificer spoke up, in his anxiety to be of service to his Mother, white-armed Here. 'This is unbearable!' he exclaimed. 'A pretty pass we are coming to, with you two spoiling for a fight about mankind and setting the gods at loggerheads. How can a good dinner be enjoyed with so much trouble in the air? I do advise my Mother, who knows well enough what is best, to make her peace with my dear Father, Zeus, or she may draw another reprimand from him and our dinner be entirely spoilt. What if the Olympian, the Lord of the Lightning Flash, the strongest god in Heaven, should feel disposed to blast us from our seats? No, Mother, you must humbly ask his pardon, and the Olympian will be gracious to us again.'

As he said this, Hephaestus hurried forward with a two-handled cup and put it in his Mother's hand. 'Mother,' he said, 'be patient and swallow your resentment, or I that love you may see you beaten, here in front of me. A sorry sight for me – but what could I do to help you? The Olympian is a hard god to pit oneself against. Why, once before when I was trying hard to save you, he seized me by the foot and hurled me from the threshold of Heaven. I flew all day, and as the sun sank I fell half-dead in Lemnos, where I was picked up and looked after by the Sintians.'

The white-armed goddess Here smiled at this, and took the beaker from her Son, still smiling. Hephaestus then went on to serve the rest in turn, beginning from the left, with sweet nectar which he drew from the mixing-bowl; and a fit of helpless laughter seized the happy gods as they watched him bustling up and down the hall.

So the feast went on, all day till sundown. Each of them had his equal share and they all ate with zest. There was music too, from a beautiful harp played by Apollo, and from the Muses, who sang in turn delightfully. But when the bright lamp of the Sun had set, they all went home to bed in the separate houses that the great lame god Hephaestus had built for them with skilful hands. Olympian Zeus, Lord of the Lightning, also retired to the upper room where he usually slept, and settled down for the night, with Here of the Golden Throne beside him.

II

THE FORCES ARE DISPLAYED

THE other gods and all the fighting men slept through the night, but there was no easeful sleep for Zeus. He was wondering how he could vindicate Achilles and have the Achaeans slaughtered at the ships. He decided that the best way would be to send King Agamemnon a False Dream. So he summoned one and instructed it: 'Off with you, Evil Dream, to the Achaean ships. Go to Agamemnon son of Atreus in his hut and repeat to him exactly what I say. Tell him to prepare his long-haired Achaeans for battle at once. His chance of capturing the spacious city of Troy has come; for we immortals that live on Olympus are no longer divided on that issue. Here's pleading has brought all of us round, and the Trojans' fate is sealed.'

The Dream listened, set forth on its errand, and was soon at the Achaean ships, where it sought out King Agamemnon and found him lying fast asleep in his hut. Assuming the appearance of Nestor son of Neleus, the King's most valued Councillor, the Dream from Heaven leant over his bed and called him by his royal titles. 'Asleep?' it said. 'It is not right for a ruler who has the nation in his charge, a man with so much on his mind, to sleep all night. Listen to me carefully, and understand that I come to you from Zeus, who, far off as he is, is much concerned on your behalf and pities you. He wishes you to prepare your long-haired Achaeans for battle instantly. Your chance of capturing the spacious city of Troy has come; for the immortals that live on Olympus are no longer divided on that issue. Here's pleading has converted them all, and the Trojans' doom is sealed by Zeus. Bear this in mind, and do not let the memory escape you when you wake from your slumbers.'

With that the Dream went off, leaving the King with a false picture of the future in his mind. He imagined he would capture Priam's city on that very day, fool that he was. He little knew what Zeus intended, nor all the sufferings and groans he had in store for both sides in the bitter fighting still to come. When he woke from his sleep, the divine voice was ringing in his ears. He sat up on the bed and put on his soft tunic, a lovely new-made garment, and over that a flowing mantle. He bound a stout pair of sandals on his comely feet, slung a silver-studded sword from his shoulder, picked up the everlasting staff that was the sceptre of his line, and with this in his hand walked down to the ships where his bronze-clad army lay.

When Heavenly Dawn reached high Olympus, announcing day to Zeus and the other gods, Agamemnon ordered his clear-voiced heralds to summon the long-haired Achaeans to Assembly. The heralds cried their summons and the soldiers speedily trooped in. But first he called a meeting of the Royal Council beside the ship of Nestor, King of Pylos, and when he had gathered them together, unfolded a subtle plan to his Councillors.

'Friends,' he began, 'I was visited in my sleep by a Dream from Heaven, which came to me through the solemn night, and in its looks, its stature and its bearing resembled my lord Nestor most exactly. It stood beside me and addressed me by my royal titles. "Are you asleep?" it said. "It is not right for a ruler who has the nation in his charge, a man with so much on his mind, to sleep all night. Listen to me carefully, and understand that I come to you from Zeus, who, far off as he is, is much concerned on your behalf and pities you. He wishes you to prepare your long-haired troops for battle instantly. Your chance of capturing the spacious city of Troy has come. For the immortals that live on Olympus are no longer divided on that issue. Here's pleading has converted them all, and the Trojans' doom is sealed by Zeus. Remember what I have said." With that it flew away and I woke up. So now we must take steps to get our forces into battle order. But first, as is legitimate for me, I am going to test them by a speech in which I shall invite them to take to their well-found ships and sail for home. From your several stations, you must then speak out and urge them to remain.'

Agamemnon sat down, and Nestor, who was King of Sandy Pylos, got up to speak, and gave them his opinion as a loyal counsellor. 'My friends,' he said, 'Captains and Counsellors of the Argives, if any other of our countrymen had told us of a dream like this, we should have thought it false and felt anything but eagerness to exploit it. But as it is, the man who had the dream is our Commander-in-Chief; so I propose that we take steps at once to get the troops under arms.'

Nestor had no sooner finished than he made a move to break up the Council. The other sceptred kings took their cue from the venerable chieftain and also left their seats. They were met by the incoming troops, who had issued, tribe on tribe, from their ships and huts by the wide sea-sands to march in battalions to the meeting-place, like buzzing swarms of bees that come out in relays from a hollow rock and scatter by companies right and left, to fall in clusters on the flowers of spring. Rumour, the Messenger of Zeus, spread through them like fire, driving them on till all were gathered together. And now the meeting-place became the scene of turmoil. As they took their seats, the earth groaned beneath them, and above all the noise, the shouting of nine heralds could be heard, doing their utmost to make them stop their din and attend to their royal masters. When, after much ado, they had found their seats on the benches and had all been induced to settle down and cease from chatter, King Agamemnon rose, holding a staff which Hephaestus himself had made. Hephaestus gave it to Zeus the Royal Son of Cronos, and Zeus to Hermes the Guide and Slayer of Argus. The Lord Hermes presented it to Pelops the great charioteer, and Pelops passed it on to Atreus, Shepherd of the People. When Atreus died, he left it to Thyestes rich in flocks; and he in his turn bequeathed it to Agamemnon, to be held in token of his empire over many islands and all the Argive lands. This was the staff that Agamemnon now leant on as he addressed his Argive troops.

'I must announce to you, my gallant friends and Danaan men-at-arms, that Zeus the great Son of Cronos has dealt me a crushing blow. The cruel god, who once solemnly assured me that I should never sail home till I had brought the towers of Ilium tumbling down, has changed his mind, and now to my bitter disappointment bids me retreat to Argos in disgrace, with half my army lost. It appears that unconquerable Zeus, who has brought down the high towers of many a city and will destroy others yet, has decided thus in his omnipotence. But what a scandal, what a tale for our descendants' ears, that such a large and excellent force as ours should be engaged so ineffectually, with no decision in sight, in an unsuccessful struggle with a weaker enemy. I say weaker, because, if we and the Trojans made a truce and each side held a count, the enemy reckoning only native Trojans and we Achaeans numbering off in tens, with the idea that each of our squads should have a Trojan to pour out its wine, many a squad would go without a steward. Such I believe to be the odds that we enjoy against the Trojans in the city itself. Unfortunately, they have numerous and well-equipped allies from many towns, who thwart me and defeat all my efforts to bring down the great stronghold of Ilium. Nine fateful years have passed. The timbers of our ships have rotted and their rigging has perished. Our wives and little children sit at home and wait for us. Meanwhile the task we set ourselves when we came here remains undone. So now let every man of you take his cue from me. Aboard the ships, I say, and home to our own country! Troy with its broad streets will never fall to us.'

Agamemnon's words went straight to the heart of every man in the crowd except those who had attended the Council, and the whole Assembly was stirred like the waters of the Icarian Sea when a southeaster falls on them from a lowering sky and sets the great waves on the move, or like deep corn in a tumbled field bowing its ears to the onslaught of the wild West Wind. They raised a mighty roar and made a dash for

the ships. The dust they kicked up with their feet hung high
overhead. They shouted to each other to get hold of the ships
and drag them down into the friendly sea. They cleared the
runways out. They even started shifting the props from under
the hulls, and in their scramble to be off they made a din that
struck high heaven.

It was a word from Here to Athene that saved the Argives
from this unpredestined dash for home. 'Unsleeping Daughter
of aegis-bearing Zeus,' she said to her, 'here is a sorry state of
affairs. Are we to let these people run away and sail home over
the high seas to Argos without Argive Helen? Is she, for whom
so many of her countrymen have died on Trojan soil, far
from their motherland, to be left for Priam and the Trojans to
boast about? Bestir yourself; go down among these bronze-
clad Achaeans and use your eloquence to stop them. Deal
with them man by man. Don't let them drag the curved ships
down into the sea.'

The bright-eyed goddess Athene was nothing loath. She
swooped down from the Olympian heights and quickly
reaching the Achaean ships found Odysseus in his godlike
wisdom standing fast. He had not even touched his good black
ship: he was broken-hearted. Athene of the Flashing Eyes
went up to him and said: 'Royal son of Laertes, Odysseus
of the nimble wits, are you all going to run off like this,
tumbling aboard your galleys to get home, and leaving Helen
for Priam and his men to boast about, Argive Helen, for whom
so many of her countrymen have died far from their mother-
land on Trojan soil? Come, do not loiter here, but move about
among the troops. Use all your eloquence to stop them. Deal
with them man by man. Don't let them drag their curved
ships down into the sea.'

Odysseus recognized the voice of the goddess and set out
at a run, throwing off his cloak to be gathered up by the herald
Eurybates, his Ithacan squire. He went straight to King
Agamemnon, borrowed from him the everlasting sceptre of
the House of Atreus, and with this in his hand went down
among the ships and the bronze-clad troops. When he came

upon anyone of royal birth or high rank, he went up to him
and made courteous attempts to restrain him. 'I should not
think it right,' he said, 'to threaten you, sir, as I should a com-
mon man. But I do beg you to stand fast yourself and to make
your followers do the same. You do not really know what
King Agamemnon has in mind. This is only an experiment
with the men; they will soon feel his fist. Did we not all of us
hear what he said at the Council? I am afraid he may be angry
with the troops and punish them for this. Kings are divine and
they have their pride, upheld and favoured as they are by the
Counsellor Zeus.'

With the rank and file he had a different way. When he
caught any of them giving tongue, he struck the offender with
his staff and rated him severely. 'You there,' he said, 'sit still
and wait for orders from your officers, who are better men
than you, coward and weakling that you are, counting for
nothing in battle or debate. We cannot all be kings here; and
mob rule is a bad thing. Let there be one commander only,
one King, set over us by Zeus the Son of Cronos of the
Crooked Ways.'

Thus restoring order, Odysseus brought the men to heel;
and now they all flocked back to the meeting-place from the
ships and huts, with a noise like that of the roaring sea when
the surf is thundering on a league-long beach and the deep
lifts up its voice.

They all sat down, and quiet was established on the benches,
but for one man who refused to hold his tongue. This was the
irrepressible Thersites, who, when he felt inclined to bait his
royal masters, was never at a loss for some vulgar quip, empty
and scurrilous indeed, but well calculated to amuse the troops.
He was the ugliest man that had come to Ilium. He had a
game foot and was bandy-legged. His rounded shoulders
almost met across his chest; and above them rose an egg-shaped
head, which sprouted a few short hairs. Nobody loathed the
man more heartily than Achilles and Odysseus, who were his
favourite butts. But now it was against the noble Agamemnon
that he raised his shrill voice in a torrent of abuse, choosing

the moment when the exasperated soldiers were hot with indignation against him.

'My lord,' he shouted at the King in his loud and nagging way, 'what is your trouble now? What more do you want? Your huts are full of bronze, and since we always give you the first pick when a town is sacked, you have plenty of the choicest women in them too. Maybe you are short of gold, the ransom that some Trojan lord may come along with from the city to free a son of his who has been tied up and brought in by myself or another of the men? Or one more girl, to sleep with and to make your private property, though it ill becomes you as our general to lead the army into trouble through such practices. As for you, my friends, poor specimens that you are, Achaean women – I cannot call you men – let us sail for home by all means and leave this fellow here to batten on his spoils and find out how completely he depends on the ranks. Why, only a little while ago he insulted Achilles, a far better man than he is. He walked off with his prize and kept her for himself. But it needs more than that to make Achilles lose his temper. He takes things lying down. Otherwise, my lord, that outrage would have been your last.'

No sooner had Thersites launched this diatribe against Agamemnon, the Commander-in-Chief, than he found the great Odysseus standing by him with a grim look in his eye. Odysseus rated the man soundly. 'Thersites,' he began, 'this may be eloquence, but we have had enough of it. You drivelling fool, how dare you stand up to the kings? It is not for you – the meanest wretch, in my opinion, of all that followed the Atreidae to Ilium – to hold forth with the kings' names on your tongue, and to slander them with an eye to getting home. Nobody here knows exactly how this business will end – we may return in triumph; we may not. And all you do is to sit there and abuse King Agamemnon, our Commander-in-Chief, enlarging in your insolent way on the liberality that our gallant leaders show him. Now mark my words – and I make no idle threats. If I catch you once again playing the fool like this, let my head be parted from my shoulders and Telemachus be called no son of mine, if I don't lay my hands on you and strip you of your clothes, cloak, tunic, all that hides your nakedness, and then thrash you ignominiously and throw you out of the Assembly to go and blubber by the ships.'

As he finished, Odysseus struck him on the back and shoulders with his staff. Thersites flinched and burst into tears. A bloody weal, raised by the golden studs on the rod, swelled up and stood out on the man's back. He sat down terrified, and in his pain looked round him helplessly and brushed away a tear. The rest, disgruntled though they were, had a hearty laugh at his expense. 'Good work!' cried one man, catching his neighbour's eye and saying what they all were feeling. 'There's many a fine thing to Odysseus' credit, what with the sound schemes he has put forward and his leadership in battle. But he has never done us a better turn than when he stopped the mouth of this windy ranter. I do not think Thersites will be in a hurry to come here again and sling insults at the kings.'

Such was the verdict of the gathering. And now Odysseus, sacker of cities, rose to speak with the staff in his hand. Athene of the Flashing Eyes, disguising herself as a herald, stood beside him and called the Assembly to order, so that the farthest rows of Achaeans, as well as those in front, might hear his words and understand their purport. Odysseus had their interests at heart, and it was in this spirit that he now harangued them. 'My lord Agamemnon,' he began, 'it seems that the Achaeans are determined to render you, their King, an object of contempt to the whole world, breaking the promise they made you on the voyage here from Argos where the horses graze, the promise that you should never sail home till you had brought down the towers of Ilium. Hear how they whimper to each other about getting back! They might be little boys or widowed wives. Not that I deny that our labours here have been enough to send a man away disheartened. A sailor in a well-found ship will fret and fume when the winter gales and rising seas have cooped him up and kept him from

his wife for even a month; whereas *we* have hung on here for
nine long years. Small blame then to the troops for moping
by the ships. Yet what a shameful thing it would be after
staying so long to go home empty-handed! Be patient, my
friends. Hold out a little longer, till we discover whether
Calchas prophesies the truth or not. You all know what I
mean; in fact you saw the thing yourselves, though since then
death has thinned your ranks. It happened in Aulis (not, after
all, so very long ago), when the Achaean fleet was gathering
there with its load of trouble for Priam and the Trojans. We
were sacrificing to the gods on their holy altars round a
spring under a fine plane-tree, at the foot of which the spark-
ling stream gushed out, when a momentous thing occurred.
A snake with blood-red markings on his back, a fearsome
animal whom Zeus himself must have driven from his lair,
darted out from below an altar and made straight for the tree.
There was a brood of young sparrows on the highest branch,
poor little creatures nestling under the leaves – eight birds in
all, or nine counting the mother of the hatch. All of them,
cheeping piteously and with their mother fluttering round and
wailing for her little ones, were eaten by the snake. He got the
mother too; he coiled himself up and seized her by the wing
as she came screaming by. But when he had devoured them
all, mother and young, the god who had caused him to come
out transformed him – he was turned into stone by the Son of
Cronos of the Crooked Ways. And we stood gaping at the
miracle. What could be meant by the intrusion on our holy
rites of this portentous beast? Calchas interpreted the omen
then and there. "Why are you dumbfounded," he said,
"Achaeans of the flowing locks? It was for us that Zeus the
Thinker staged this prophetic scene. We have waited for it
long, and we shall have to wait for the sequel; but the memory
of this day will not die. There were eight young sparrows,
making nine with their mother, and all of these, mother and
hatch, were eaten by the snake. Nine, then, is the number of
years that we shall have to fight at Troy, and in the tenth its
broad streets will be ours." That is what Calchas prophesied;

and all he said is coming true. Soldiers and fellow-country-men, I call upon you all to stand your ground till we capture Priam's spacious town.'

When he finished, the Achaeans gave a great shout to show how well they had liked this speech from the godlike Odysseus – a shout that the ships around them echoed with a sullen roar. But Nestor the Gerenian charioteer also had something to say to his countrymen. 'Upon my word,' he exclaimed, 'you might be little boys with no interest in war, to judge by all this talk. What has become of our compacts and our oaths? You behave as though the warlike plans that we matured together, the loyalties we ratified in wine and pledged with our right hands, were so much rubbish. Words are the only weapons we are using now; and *they* will not get us anywhere, however long we stay and talk. My lord Agamemnon, be true as always to your firm resolve, and lead the Argives into action. If there are one or two traitors among us, scheming to sail for home before they find out whether Zeus was telling us the truth, leave them to rot. In any case they will not succeed. For I am convinced that the almighty Son of Cronos said "Yes" to us, that day we got aboard our ships of war to bring death and destruction to the Trojans. There was a flash of lightning on our right: he meant that all would be well. Let there be no scramble to get home, then, till every man of you has slept with a Trojan wife and been paid for the toil and groans that Helen caused him. Anyone who hankers to be off has only to touch his good black ship to find himself a dead man before all the rest.

'And now, my lord, make certain that your own plans are sound, and take advice from others. Here is my own: I am sure it will not be lost on you. Sort your men out, Agamemnon, into their tribes and clans, so that clan may help clan and the tribes support each other. Such dispositions, if the troops adhere to them, will show you what cowards you may have among the officers or in the ranks, and what good men. For each man will be fighting at his brothers' side, and you will soon find out whether it is God's will that stands between you and the sack of Troy, or the cowardice of your soldiers and their incompetence in war.'

King Agamemnon complimented Nestor on his speech. 'One more debate,' he said, 'where you, my venerable lord, have carried all before you! Ah, Father Zeus, Athene and Apollo, give me ten counsellors such as this, and King Priam's town, captured and sacked by Achaean hands, would soon be tottering. But Zeus the Son of Cronos *will* torment me. He entangles me in fruitless broils and squabbles. Look at my quarrel with Achilles over a girl, when each of us insulted the other, though it was I who lost my temper first. If ever he and I see eye to eye once more, there will not be a day's reprieve for the Trojans.

'However, the first thing for you all is to have a meal – and then to battle. Sharpen all spears; adjust your shields; see that your good horses have their fodder, and overhaul your chariots for action – in a grim pitched battle that will last all day. There will be no respite, none at all, till night parts us in our fury. The straps of your man-covering shields will be soaked with sweat on your breasts; your hands will weary on your spears; the horses tugging at your polished chariots will sweat. And as for any shirker I may find disposed to linger by the beaked ships, nothing can save him: he is for the dogs and birds of prey.'

The Argives welcomed Agamemnon's speech with a great roar, like the thunder of the sea on a lofty coast when a gale comes in from the South and hurls the waves against a rocky cape which they never leave at peace whatever wind is blowing. They broke up the Assembly at once and dispersed among the ships, where they lit fires in their huts and ate a meal. Each man as he made his offerings to his favourite among the everlasting gods prayed that he might come through the ordeal with his life. King Agamemnon himself sacrificed a fatted five-year-old ox to the almighty Son of Cronos and invited the leading chieftains of the united Achaeans to attend – Nestor first of all, then King Idomeneus; Aias and his namesake; Diomedes son of Tydeus; and for a sixth, Odysseus, whose thoughts were like the thoughts of Zeus. There was no need for him to invite his brother, Menelaus of the loud war-cry, who knew how heavy Agamemnon's burden was, and came of his own accord. Standing round the victim, they took up the sacrificial grains and heard King Agamemnon pray: 'Most glorious and mighty Zeus, god of the Black Cloud, Lord of High Heaven, grant that the sun may not set and dark-ness fall before I bring down Priam's palace, blackened with smoke, send up his gates in flames, and rip the tunic on the breast of Hector with my bronze. And at his side let plenty of his friends be felled and bite the dust.' Thus Agamemnon prayed, but Zeus was not prepared to grant him what he wished. He accepted his offering, but in return he sent him doubled tribulation.

When they had made their petitions and scattered the grain, they drew back the victim's head, slit its throat, and flayed it. Then they cut out slices from the thighs, wrapped them in folds of fat and laid raw meat above them. These pieces they burnt up on faggots stripped of leaves, then put the inner parts on spits and held them over the flames. When the thighs were burnt up and they had tasted the entrails, they carved the rest into small pieces, pierced them with skewers, roasted them thoroughly, and drew them all off.

Their work done and the food prepared, they fell to with a good will on the meal, in which all had equal shares; and when their hunger and thirst were satisfied, the Gerenian charioteer Nestor took the lead and said: 'Your majesty, Agamemnon King of Men; let us prolong this meeting no further, nor put off the work that God has set our hands to. Come, let the heralds of the bronze-clad Achaeans go the round of the ships and call out all the troops. Then we com-manders could inspect the whole army together and soon work up a fighting spirit in the men.'

King Agamemnon accepted his advice and gave immedi-ate orders to his clear-voiced heralds to call the long-haired Achaeans to battle. They cried their summons and the men quickly fell in. The royal chieftains of the King's Council bustled about, marshalling the troops, and with them went Athene of the Flashing Eyes, wearing her splendid cloak, the unfading everlasting aegis, from which a hundred golden tassels flutter, all beautifully made, each worth a hundred head of cattle. Resplendent in this, she flew through the ranks, urging the men forward; and in each one she inspired the will to carry on the war and fight relentlessly. Before long they were more enamoured with the thought of fighting than with that of sailing away to their own country in their hollow ships.

As they fell in, the dazzling glitter of their splendid bronze flashed through the upper air and reached the sky. It was as bright as the glint of flames, caught in some distant spot, when a great forest on a mountain height is ravaged by fire.

Their clans came out like the countless flocks of birds – the geese, the cranes or the long-necked swans – that foregather in the Asian meadow by the streams of Cayster, and wheel about, boldly flapping their wings and filling the whole meadow with harsh cries as they come to ground on an advancing front. So clan after clan poured out from the ships and huts onto the plain of Scamander, and the earth resounded sullenly to the tramp of marching men and horses' hooves, as they found their places in the flowery meadows by the river, innumerable as the leaves and blossoms in their season.

Thus these long-haired soldiers of Achaea were drawn up on the plain, facing the Trojans with slaughter in their hearts, as many and as restless as the unnumbered flies that swarm round the cowsheds in the spring, when pails are full of milk.

And now, with the practised ease with which goatherds sort out their wandering flocks when they have mingled in the pastures, the captains brought their companies into battle order; and in among them moved King Agamemnon, with head and eyes like Zeus the Thunderer, with a waist like the War-god's waist, and a breast like Poseidon's. As a bull stands out from the cattle in a herd, conspicuous among the grazing cows, so on that day Zeus made the son of Atreus stand out from the crowd and eclipse his fellow kings.

Tell me now, you Muses that live on Olympus, since you

are goddesses and witness all that happens, whereas we men know nothing that we are not told – tell me who were the captains and chieftains of the Danaans. As for the rank and file that came to Ilium, I could not name or even count them, not if I had ten tongues, ten mouths, a voice that could not tire, a heart of bronze, unless you Muses of Olympus, Daughters of aegis-bearing Zeus, would serve me as remembrancers. Here then are the captains of the fleet, and here are the ships from first to last.

First the Boeotians, with Peneleos and Leitus, Archesilaus, Prothoenor and Clonius in command. They came from Hyrie and Stony Aulis, from Schoenus and Scolus; from Eteonus, where the hills run high; from Thespeia and Graia and the spreading lawns of Mycalessus. With them were those from Harma, from Eilesion and from Erythrae. Eleon and Hyle too, and Peteon sent their men. So did Ocalea and the stronghold of Medeon; Copae and Eutresis; and Thisbe rich in doves. They came from Coronea too; from grassy Haliartus, Plataea, Glisas, and the strong town of Lower Thebes; from holy Onchestus, with Poseidon's sacred wood; from Arne, where the grapes hang thick; from Mideia and holy Nisa, and from Anthedon on the borders of beyond. All these in fifty ships, with a hundred and twenty young Boeotians in each.

The men from Aspledon and Minyaean Orchomenus were led by Ascalaphus and Ialmenus, sons of Ares, whom Astyoche conceived in the palace of Actor son of Azeus, where the gentle maiden went in secret to an upper room and slept with the mighty War-god. They had brought a squadron of thirty hollow ships.

Schedius and Epistrophus, sons of the magnanimous Iphitus son of Naubolus, commanded the men from Phocis, who lived in Cyparissus and in Rocky Pytho; in sacred Crisa, in Daulis and in Panopeus; round Anemoreia and Hyampolis, the lovely waters of Cephisus, and Lilaea, where Cephisus rises. Forty black ships travelled with these two, under whose command the Phocians fell in and took their battle stations by the Boeotians on the left.

Leading the Locrians came the fleet-footed son of Oïleus, the lesser Aias – not such a man as Telamonian Aias, indeed inferior by far. He was short, and wore a linen corslet; but not a Hellene or Achaean was his equal in spearmanship. His following had come from Cynus, Opus and Calliarus; from Bessa, Scarphe and beautiful Augeiae; from Tarphe and Thronion and the banks of the River Boagrius. Forty black ships had set out under him, manned by the Locrians who live across the straits from holy Euboea.

Euboea itself sent the fiery Abantes, the men of Chalcis, Eiretria, and Histiaea rich in vines; of seaside Cerinthus and the high fortress of Dius; and those who had their homes at Styra and Carystus. These were all captained by Elephenor, offshoot of the War-god, son of Chalcodon and chieftain of the gallant Abantes. His followers were quick on their feet; they wore their hair in locks at the back; they carried ashen spears and wished for nothing better than to lunge with them and tear the corslets on their enemies' breasts. Forty black ships came under Elephenor's command.

Next the Athenians from their splendid citadel in the realm of the magnanimous Erechtheus, a child of the fruitful Earth who was brought up by Athene Daughter of Zeus and established by her at Athens in her own rich shrine, where bulls and rams are offered to him yearly in due season by Athenian youths. These were commanded by Menestheus son of Peteos. He had no living rival in the art of handling infantry and horse, excepting Nestor, who was an older man. Fifty black ships had come across with him.

From Salamis, Aias had brought twelve ships, and beached them where the Athenian force was stationed.

The citizens of Argos and Tiryns of the Great Walls; the men of Hermione and Asine, towns that embrace a deep gulf of the sea; and those from Troezen, from Eionae, and from vine-clad Epidaurus, with the Achaean youth of Aegina and Mases, were led by Diomedes of the loud war-cry and by Sthenelus, son of the far-famed Capaneus. Highborn Euryalus, son of King Mecisteus son of Talaus, had come with them as third in command. But the warlike Diomedes was in charge of the whole force, and eighty black ships set sail under him.

The troops that came from the great stronghold of Mycenae, from wealthy Corinth and the good town of Cleonae; the men who lived in Orneiae and in lovely Araethyrea; in Sicyon, where Adrestus reigned in early years; in Hyperesie and in steep Gonoessa; in Pellene and round Aegion; in all the length of the coast and the broad lands of Helice – these, in their hundred ships, King Agamemnon son of Atreus led. His following was by far the finest and most numerous. He was a proud man as he took his stand among his people, armed in gleaming bronze, the greatest captain of them all, in virtue of his rank and as commander of by far the largest force.

The men from the rolling lands of Lacedaemon deep in the hills; from Pharis and Sparta and Messe rich in doves; from Bryseiae and beautiful Augeiae; those from Amyclae and the seaside fort of Helos; the villagers of Oetylus and Laas – all these came under the King's brother, Menelaus of the loud war-cry, with sixty ships, and had their separate station. Menelaus strode among them, in all the confidence of his own gallantry, and urged them to battle; for nobody was more eager than he to avenge himself for the toil and groans that Helen had caused him.

Next came the men from Pylos and lovely Arene; from Thryon, where the Alpheus is forded; from handsome Aepy; from Cyparisseis, Amphigeneia, Pteleus and Helos; and from Dorion, where the Muses met Thamyris the Thracian as he was on his way from Oechalia and the home of Oechalian Eurytus. Thamyris had boasted that he would win in a singing-match with the Muses themselves, Daughters of aegis-bearing Zeus. This angered them. They struck him blind; they robbed him of the divine gift of song, and caused him to forget his harping. The Gerenian charioteer Nestor was in command of these men. His squadron numbered ninety hollow ships.

Then the Arcadians, from the lands where Mount Cyllene lifts its peak and Aepytus was buried, where men are trained in hand-to-hand fighting; from Pheneus, from Orchomenus rich in sheep, from Rhype and Stratie and windy Enispe; from Tegea and the pleasant town of Mantinea, and from Stymphelus and Parrhasie. They were led by King Agapenor son of Ancaeus, in sixty ships, each with its complement of trained Arcadian warriors. Agamemnon King of Men had himself given Agapenor the well-found ships in which to cross the wine-dark sea, as the Arcadians knew nothing of sea-faring.

The men from Buprasion and as much of the kindly land of Elis as lies between Hermine, Myrsinus of the Marches, the Olenian Rock and Alision, came under four commanders, each with a squadron of ten fast ships filled with Epean troops. Two of their companies were led by Amphimachus son of Cteatus and Thalpius son of Eurytus, both of the House of Actor; a third by the stalwart Diores son of Amarynceus; and the fourth by Prince Polyxeinus, the son of King Agasthenes, Augeas' son.

Those from Dulichium and the sacred Echinean Islands, across the sea from Elis, were led by Meges, the warrior son of Phyleus, a charioteer whom Zeus had loved and who had parted from his father once upon a time in anger and migrated to Dulichium. Forty black ships made up his company.

Odysseus next, leading the proud Cephallenians, masters of Ithaca and the wooded peak of windswept Neriton, and those from Crocyleia and rugged Aegilips; from forested Zacynthus too, and Samos and the mainland opposite the islands. These were the forces of Odysseus, whose wisdom rivalled that of Zeus. Twelve ships with crimson-painted bows came under him.

Thoas, Andraemon's son, captained the Aetolians, from Pleuron and Olenus, Pylene, Chalcis by the sea, and rocky Calydon. For the sons of Oeneus the Magnificent were no more; Oeneus himself was dead; and so was red-haired Meleager, on whom kingship over all the Aetolians had devolved. Thoas had forty black ships under him.

The illustrious spearman Idomeneus led the Cretans: the men from Cnossus, from Gortyn of the Great Walls, from

Lyctus, Miletus, chalky Lycastus, Phaestus and Rhytion, fine cities all of them; and the other troops that had their homes in Crete of the Hundred Towns. All these were led by the great spearman Idomeneus and by Meriones, a compeer of the man-destroying War-god. Eighty black ships came under their command.

Tlepolemus, the tall and handsome son of Heracles, had brought from Rhodes nine shiploads of lordly Rhodians, whose three tribes occupy three separate parts of the island, Lindus, Ielysus and Cameirus on the chalk. These were the forces of the famous spearman Tlepolemus, son of the mighty Heracles by Astyocheia, whom he carried off from Ephyre and the River Selleïs, sacking many strongholds held by warrior chiefs. Tlepolemus, when he had grown to manhood in the palace, killed his own father's uncle, Licymnius, off-shoot of the War-god, who was an old man by then. He quickly built some ships, gathered a large following and fled overseas, menaced as he was by the other sons and the grandsons of the mighty Heracles. Thus, as a fugitive and after many hard-ships, he reached Rhodes, where his people settled in three districts, according to their tribes, and enjoyed the smiles of Zeus the Son of Cronos, King of gods and men, who filled their treasuries with untold wealth.

Next there was Nireus with three trim ships from Syme, Nireus son of Aglaia and King Charopus, Nireus the hand-somest Danaan that came to Ilium, excepting only the flawless son of Peleus. And yet he was a weakling and his following was small.

The men from Nisyrus, Crapathus and Casus, from Cos, the city of Eurypylus, and the Calydnian Isles, were led by Pheidippus and Antiphus, the two sons of King Thessalus son of Heracles. They had a squadron of thirty hollow ships.

We come now to the men that lived in Pelasgian Argos, in Alus and Alope, in Trachis, Phthia, and Hellas, land of lovely women, bearing the names of Myrmidons and Hellenes and Achaeans. These had sailed, in their fifty ships, under Achilles' command. But now the sound and fury of war did not concern them at all. There was no one to draw them up in battle order; for the great Achilles of the nimble feet was lying by his ships, sick at heart for the gentle girl Briseis, whom he had won from Lyrnessus by the sweat of his brow when he sacked Lyrnessus itself and stormed the walls of Thebe, and brought down the sturdy spearmen Mynes and Epistrophus, the sons of King Euenus, Selepus' son. This was the girl he grieved for as he lay there. But he was not destined to lie idle long.

The men that lived in Phylace and flowery Pyrasus, Demeter's sanctuary; in Iton, mother of sheep; in Antron by the sea, and Pteleus deep in grass, were led by the warlike Protesilaus while he lived. But by now the black earth had received him in her bosom. He had been the first of the Achaeans to leap ashore, but he fell then and there to a Dardanian foe, leaving his wife in Phylace with lacerated cheeks, and his house half-built. His followers grieved for their leader, but they were not left without a chief. They were commanded by Podarces, offshoot of the War-god and son of Phylacus' son Iphiclus, the lord of many sheep. Podarces was a brother of the great-hearted Protesilaus, a younger brother, the noble warlike Protesilaus being both the older and the better man. So their troops did not lack a leader, though they mourned the gallant dead. Forty black ships had come under his command.

The men that lived in Pherae by the Boebeian Lake, in Boebe, Glaphyrae and lovely Iolcus, were led in their eleven ships by Admetus' son, Eumelus, whom queenly Alcestis, Pelias' most beautiful daughter, had borne to Admetus.

Those from Methone, Thaumacie, Meliboea and rugged Olizon were brought by the great archer Philoctetes in seven ships, each manned by fifty oarsmen trained to go into battle with the bow. But their commander lay in agony on the lovely isle of Lemnos, where the Achaean army had left him, suffering from the poisonous bite of a malignant water snake. So he lay there pining, though the Argives by their ships were destined before long to think once more of King Philoctetes. Meanwhile, though his followers missed their leader, they were not left without a chief. They were commanded by Medon, the bastard son of Oïleus, whom Rhene bore to Oïleus sacker of towns.

The men from Tricce, from Ithome with its terraced hills, and from Oechalia, the city of Oechalian Eurytus, were led by the two sons of Asclepius, the admirable physicians Podaleirius and Machaon. Thirty hollow ships came under their command.

Those from Ormenion and the spring of Hypereia, from Asterion and the white towers of Titanus, were led by Eurypylus, Euaemon's highborn son, with forty black ships under him.

Of those that dwelt in Argissa and Gyrtone, Orthe, Helone, and the white town of Oloosson, the dauntless Polypoetes was in command. He was a son of Peirithous, son of immortal Zeus. Far-famed Hippodameia had conceived him for Peirithous on the day when he took his revenge on the shaggy people of the wilds, expelled them from Pelion and drove them into the hands of the Aethices. Polypoetes was not alone, but shared his command with Leonteus, offshoot of the Wargod and son of proud Coronus son of Caeneus. Their squadron numbered forty black ships.

Gouneus from Cyphus brought two-and-twenty ships. He led the Enienes and the dauntless Peraebians, who had pitched their homes round wintry Dodona and tilled the fields by the delectable Titaresius, which pours its lovely stream into the Peneus, yet does not mingle with the silver eddies of Peneus but floats along on top of them like oil, being a part of the formidable waters of Styx, the river of the oath.

Prothous son of Tenthredon commanded the Magnetes who lived by the Peneus and by Mount Pelion of the trembling leaves. These were the men that the dashing Prothous led. Forty black ships came under his command.

These then were the captains and commanders of the Danaans. Now tell me, Muse, of all the men and horses that crossed with the Atreidae, which were the first and foremost?

Of the horses, the best by far were those of Admetus, which his son Eumelus drove. Swift as birds, they were alike in coat and age, and were matched to a plumb-line all along their backs. Both were mares and had been reared in Peraea by Apollo of the Silver Bow to carry panic through the ranks.

Of the men, Telamonian Aias was by far the best, but only while Achilles was in dudgeon, since he, the peerless son of Peleus, was the finest man of all and drove the finest horses. But he was lying now by his beaked seagoing ships, nursing his quarrel with the Commander-in-Chief, Agamemnon son of Atreus. Meanwhile on the sea beach his people passed the time in archery, in throwing disks and casting javelins; the horses stood idle, each by its own chariot, munching clover and parsley from the marsh; their masters' chariots lay covered up inside the huts; and the men themselves, who missed their battle-loving chief, strolled aimlessly about the camp and did no fighting.

But the rest marched on, and the whole plain seemed to be consumed by fire. Earth groaned beneath them as it does for Zeus the Thunderer in his anger, when he lashes the ground above Typhoeus in the Arimean Mountains, where people say Typhoeus lies abed. Thus earth reverberated to their marching feet as they came swiftly on across the plain.

Meanwhile, fleet Iris of the Whirlwind Feet was sent to the Trojans by aegis-bearing Zeus to bring them the portentous news. They had all foregathered, young and old alike, for a conference at Priam's doors. Iris of the Nimble Feet came up to them and spoke in a voice like that of Priam's son Polites, who was posted as a lookout for the Trojans on the top of old Aesyetes' tomb, ready to dash home at the first sign of a sortie from the Achaean ships. Iris looked exactly like this man as she addressed herself to Priam.

'Sire,' she said, 'I see that you are still as fond of interminable talk as you were in peace-time, though the death-struggle is upon us. Indeed, I have taken part in many battles, but never have I seen so great and formidable a force. They are rolling over the plain to fight at the city walls like the leaves of the forest or the sands of the sea. Hector, I urge you above all to do as I say. In his great city, Priam has many allies. But these foreigners all talk different languages. Let their own captains in each case take charge of them, draw up their countrymen, and lead them into battle.'

Hector did not fail to recognize the goddess' voice and immediately dismissed the meeting. They rushed to arms. The gates were all thrown open and with a great din the whole army, infantry and horse, poured out.

Outside the town and some way off in the plain, there is a high mound, with open ground on every side, which men call Thorn Hill, but the immortals know as the tomb of dancing Myrine. It was here that the Trojans and their allies now formed up in battle order.

Priam's son, the great Hector of the flashing helmet, led the Trojans. With him marched by far the finest and most numerous force, keen spearmen all of them.

The Dardanians were led by Anchises' admirable son Aeneas, whom Aphrodite conceived for Anchises when she clasped the man in her divine embrace, on the slopes of Mount Ida. Aeneas was not in sole command, but was supported by Antenor's two sons, Archelochus and Acamas, both experienced in all kinds of fighting.

The men that lived in Zeleia, under the lowest spurs of Ida, and drank the dark water of Aesepus – a prosperous Trojan clan – were led by the famous son of Lycaon, Pandarus, who owed his skill with the bow to Apollo himself.

Those from Adresteia and the land of Apaesus, from Pityeia and the steep slopes of Tereia, were led by Adrestus and Amphius in his linen corslet, the two sons of Merops of Percote, who was a seer of surpassing skill and had done his best to dissuade his sons from hazarding their lives in the war. But they would not listen to him: black Death enticed them to their fate.

The men from Percote and Practius; from Sestus, Abydus and holy Arisbe, were led by Asius son of Hyrtacus – the lordly Asius, whom his big and glossy horses had brought from Arisbe and the River Selleïs.

Hippothous was in command of the tribes of Pelasgian spearmen who lived in deep-soiled Larissa. These men followed Hippothous and Pylaeus, offshoot of Ares, the two sons of Pelasgian Lethus son of Teutamus.

Acamas and the noble Peiros led the Thracians whose lands are bounded by the swift-flowing Hellespont; while Euphemus, son of King Troezenus son of Ceas, led the warlike Cicones.

Pyraechmes commanded the Paeonians with their curving bows. They had come from far, from Amydon and the banks of the broad River Axius – the Axius, whose waters are the most beautiful that flow over the earth.

Pylaemenes of the shaggy breast led the Paphlagonians, from the lands of the Eneti, from which the wild mules come. They lived in Cytorus, round Sesamon, in pleasant homesteads by the River Parthenius, in Cromna, and Aegialus, and lofty Erythini.

Odius and Epistrophus led the Alizones, from distant Alybe, the native place of silver.

Of the Mysians, Chromis and Ennomus were in command. Ennomus was an augur. But all his bird-lore did not save him from the black hand of Death. He fell a victim to the great runner Achilles, in the river-bed, when he made havoc of the Trojans and their allies.

Phorcys and Prince Ascanius led the Phrygians, eager for battle, from remote Ascania; while the Maeonians were led by Mesthles and Antiphus, the sons of Talaemenes, whose mother was the Gygaean Lake. These two led the Maeonians, whose native land is under Tmolus.

Nastes led the Carians, men of uncouth speech, who possessed Miletus, Mount Phthires of the myriad leaves, the streams of Maeander and the steep crest of Mycale. These were the men whom Amphimachus and Nastes brought – Nastes and Amphimachus, the noble sons of Nomion. And what a fool Amphimachus was! He went into battle like a girl, decked

in gold. Not that it saved him from a dreadful end. He fell to
Achilles the great runner, there in the river-bed, and the
provident Achilles made off with the gold.

Last, Sarpedon and the peerless Glaucus led the Lycians,
from distant Lycia and the swirling streams of Xanthus.

III

A TRUCE AND A DUEL

When all were drawn up, each company under its own commander, the Trojans advanced with a shouting and a din like that of birds. They filled the air with clamour, like the cranes that fly from the onset of winter and the sudden rains and make for Ocean Stream with raucous cries to bring death and destruction to the Pigmies, launching their wicked onslaught from the morning sky. But the Achaeans moved forward in silence, breathing valour, and filled with the resolve to stand by one another.

In their swift advance across the plain, their marching feet had raised a cloud of dust, dense as the mist that the South Wind wraps round the mountain-tops, when a man can see no farther than he can heave a rock, and shepherds grumble, while the thief, who finds it better than the night, rejoices.

The two forces were about to clash, when the godlike Paris stepped out from the Trojan ranks and offered single combat. He had a panther's skin on his back, and a curved bow and a sword were slung from his shoulders. Brandishing a couple of bronze-headed spears, he challenged any Argive champion to meet him man to man and fight it out.

When the veteran Menelaus saw him striding towards him in front of the crowd, he was as happy as a hungry lion when he finds the great carcass of an antlered stag or a wild goat and devours it greedily in spite of all the efforts of the sturdy huntsmen and the nimble hounds to drive him off. Thus Menelaus rejoiced when his eye fell on Prince Paris, for he thought his chance had come of paying out the man who had wronged him. He leapt down at once from his chariot to the ground with all his arms.

But when royal Paris saw that it was Menelaus who had

taken up his challenge, his heart failed him completely, and he slipped back into the friendly ranks in terror for his life, like a man who comes on a snake in a wooded ravine, recoils, and with pale cheeks and trembling limbs goes back the way he came. Thus royal Paris slunk back among the lordly Trojans in his terror of Atreides.

Hector had observed his brother and fell foul of him at once. 'Paris, you pretty boy,' he shouted at him, 'you woman-struck seducer; why were you ever born? Why weren't you killed before your wedding day? Yes, I could wish it so. Far better that than to be a disgrace to the rest of us, as you are, and an object of contempt. How the long-haired Achaeans must laugh when they see us make a champion of a prince because of his good looks, forgetting that he has no strength of mind, no courage. When I look at you to-day, can *you* be the man, I ask, who picked yourself a crew of friends, sailed overseas in your much-travelled ships, hobnobbed with foreigners and carried off a beautiful woman from a distant land and warlike family, to be a curse to your father, to the city and to the whole people, to cause our enemies to rejoice, and you to hang your head in shame? And now are you too cowardly to stand up to the brave man whom you wronged? You would soon find out the kind of fighter he is whose lovely wife you stole. Your lyre would not help you at all, nor Aphrodite's gifts, those locks of yours and your good looks, when he had made you bite the dust. But the Trojans are too soft. Otherwise you would have been stoned to death long ago for the evil you have done.'

'Hector, your taunts are justified,' replied the noble Paris; 'you have not said a word too much. How like your indomit-able spirit! Your tireless energy puts me in mind of an axe in a carpenter's hands, hacking its way through a log and giving him the power to shape the timbers for a ship. But there is something you must not reproach me for – the lovely gifts I have from Golden Aphrodite. The precious gifts that the gods lavish on a man unasked are not to be despised, even though he might not choose them if he had the chance.

However, if you insist on my undertaking this duel, make all the troops sit down and let me meet the formidable Menelaus between the two armies and fight him for Helen and her wealth. The one who wins and proves himself the better man can carry off the lady to his own house, goods and all, while the rest make a treaty of peace, by which we stay in deep-soiled Troy and the enemy sail home to Argos where the horses graze and Achaea land of lovely women.'

This delighted Hector. He stepped out into no-man's-land, and grasping his spear by the middle thrust back the Trojans' line. They all sat down; but the long-haired Achaeans kept up their archery, making Hector the target for their arrows and stones. King Agamemnon had to intervene. 'Argives, enough!' he shouted. 'Men, cease shooting. Hector of the flashing helmet is trying to make himself heard.'

The troops abandoned their attack and silence was established promptly. Then Hector spoke between the two armies. 'Trojans,' he said, 'and Achaean men-at-arms; hear from me what Paris, who began this trouble, now proposes. He suggests that all the troops should ground their arms while he and the warrior Menelaus fight a duel, between the two armies, for Helen and her wealth. The one who wins and proves himself the better man shall have the lady, goods and all, and take them home with him, while the rest of us make a treaty of peace.'

Hector's speech was received in complete silence. At last Menelaus of the loud war-cry spoke up. 'Listen now to me,' he said. 'I am the chief sufferer, and I think that the Argives and Trojans can now part in peace, having had quite enough to bear as a result of this feud between myself and Paris, who began it. One of us must die – Fate has already marked him out for death – and then the rest of you will soon be reconciled. Bring a couple of sheep, a white ram and a black ewe, for Earth and the Sun; and we will bring one for Zeus. And let King Priam be fetched, so that he can take the oaths himself, since he has arrogant and unscrupulous sons, and we do not want to see a solemn treaty wrecked by treachery. Young men are for the most part unstable, whereas when an old man takes a hand in such affairs, he considers the future as well as the past and does the very best for both parties.'

Menelaus' pronouncement was welcomed by Trojans and Achaeans alike as a reprieve from the painful business of fighting. The charioteers fell back on the infantry, got down from their chariots and discarded their equipment, which they laid on the ground in separate heaps at close intervals. Hector despatched two messengers at all speed to the city, to fetch the sheep and to summon Priam; and King Agamemnon sent Talthybius off to the hollow ships and told him to bring back a lamb. Talthybius hastened to carry out his sovereign's orders.

Meanwhile Iris brought the news to white-armed Helen, disguising herself as Helen's sister-in-law, Laodice, the most beautiful of Priam's daughters, who was married to the lord Helicaon, Antenor's son. She found Helen in her palace, at work on a great purple web of double width, into which she was weaving some of the many battles between the horse-taming Trojans and the bronze-clad Achaeans in the war that had been forced upon them for her sake. Iris of the Nimble Feet went up to her and said: 'My dear sister, come and see how strangely the Trojan and Achaean soldiers are behaving. A little while ago they were threatening each other with a terrible battle in the plain and looked as though they meant to fight to the death. But now the battle is off, and they are sitting quietly there, leaning on their shields, with the long javelins stuck on end beside them, while Paris and the redoubtable Menelaus are to fight a duel for you with their great spears, and the winner is to claim you as his wife.'

This news from the goddess filled Helen's heart with tender longing for her former husband and her parents and the city she had left. She wrapped a veil of white linen round her head, and with the tear-drops running down her cheeks set out from her bedroom, not alone, but attended by two waiting-women, Aethre daughter of Pittheus, and the ox-eyed lady Clymene. In a little while they reached the neighbourhood of the Scaean Gate.

At this gate, Priam was sitting in conference with the Elders of the city, Panthous and Thymoetes, Lampus and Clytius, Hicetaon, offshoot of the War-god, and his two wise counsellors, Ucalegon and Antenor. Old age had brought their fighting days to an end, but they were excellent speakers, these Trojan Elders, sitting there on the tower, like cicadas perched on a tree in the woods chirping delightfully. When they saw Helen coming to the tower, they lowered their voices. 'Who on earth,' they asked one another, 'could blame the Trojan and Achaean men-at-arms for suffering so long for such a woman's sake? Indeed, she is the very image of an immortal goddess. All the same, and lovely as she is, let her sail home and not stay here to vex us and our children after us.'

Meanwhile, Priam had called Helen to his side. 'Dear child,' he said, 'come here and sit in front of me, so that you may see your former husband and your relatives and friends. I bear you no ill will at all: I blame the gods. It is they who brought this terrible Achaean war upon me. And now you can tell me the name of that giant over there. Who is that tall and handsome Achaean? There are others taller by a head, but I have never set eyes on a man with such good looks or with such majesty. He is every inch a king.'

'I pay you homage and reverence, my dear father-in-law,' replied the gracious lady Helen. 'I wish I had chosen to die in misery before I came here with your son, deserting my bridal chamber, my kinsfolk, my darling daughter and the dear friends with whom I had grown up. But things did not fall out like that, to my unending sorrow. However, I must tell you what you wished to know. The man you pointed out is imperial Agamemnon son of Atreus, a good king and a mighty spearman too. He was my brother-in-law once, shameless creature that I am – unless all that was a dream.'

When he heard this the old man gazed at Agamemnon with envious admiration. 'Ah, lucky son of Atreus,' he exclaimed, 'child of fortune, blessed by the gods! So you are the man whom all these thousands of Achaeans serve! I went to

Phrygia once, the land of vines and galloping horses, and learnt how numerous the Phrygians are when I saw the armies of Otreus and King Mygdon encamped by the River Sangarius. I was their ally and I bivouacked with them that time the Amazons, who fight like men, came up to the attack. But even they were not as many as these Achaeans with their flashing eyes.'

The old man, noticing Odysseus next, said: 'Tell me now, dear child, who that man is. He is shorter than King Agamemnon by a head, but broader in the shoulders and the chest. He has left his armour lying on the ground, and there he goes, like a bellwether, inspecting the ranks. He reminds me of a fleecy ram bringing a great flock of white sheep to heel.'

'That,' said Helen, child of Zeus, 'is Laertes' son, Odysseus of the nimble wits. Ithaca, where he was brought up, is a poor and rocky land; but he is a master of intrigue and stratagem.'

The wise Antenor added something to Helen's picture of Odysseus. 'Madam,' he said, 'I can endorse what you say, for Odysseus has been here. He came with Menelaus on an embassy in your behalf, and I was their host. I entertained them in my own house, and I know not only what they look like but the way they think. In conference with the Trojans, when all were standing, Menelaus with his broad shoulders overtopped the whole company; but Odysseus was the more imposing of the two when both were seated. When their turn came to express their views in public, Menelaus spoke fluently, not at great length, but very clearly, being a man of few words who kept to the point, though he was the younger of the two. By contrast, when the nimble-witted Odysseus took the floor, he stood there with his head bent firmly down, glancing from under his brows, and he did not swing his staff either to the front or back, but held it stiffly, as though he had never handled one before. You would have taken him for a sulky fellow and no better than a fool. But when that great voice of his came booming from his chest, and the words poured from his lips like flakes of winter snow, there was no man alive who could compete with Odysseus. When we looked at him then, we were no longer misled by appearances.'

Aias was the third man whom the old king noticed and enquired about. 'Who is that other fine and upstanding Achaean,' he asked, 'taller than all the rest by a head and shoulders?'

'That,' said the gracious lady Helen of the long robe, 'is the huge Aias, a tower of strength to the Achaeans. And there on the other side is Idomeneus, standing among the Cretans like a god, with his Cretan captains gathered round him. My lord Menelaus often entertained him in our house, when he paid us a visit from Crete. And now I have picked out all the Achaeans whom I can recognize and name, except two chieftains whom I cannot find, Castor the tamer of horses and Polydeuces the great boxer, my own brothers, borne by the same mother as myself. Either they did not join the army from lovely Lacedaemon, or if they crossed the seas and came here with the rest, they are unwilling to take part in the fighting on account of the scandal attached to my name and the insults they might hear.'

She did not know, when she said this, that the fruitful Earth had already received them in her lap, over there in Lacedaemon, in the country that they loved.

Heralds, meanwhile, were bringing through the town the wherewithal for the treaty of peace, two sheep and a goatskin bottle full of mellow wine, the fruit of the soil. The herald Idaeus, who carried a gleaming bowl and golden cups, came up to the old king and roused him to action. 'Up, my lord,' he said. 'The commanders of the Trojan and Achaean forces are calling for you to come down onto the plain and make a truce. Paris and the warrior Menelaus are going to fight each other with long spears for Helen. The winner is to have the lady, goods and all, while the rest make a treaty of peace, by which we stay in deep-soiled Troy, and the enemy sail home to Argos where the horses graze and Achaea land of lovely women.'

The old man shuddered when he heard this; but he told

his men to harness horses to his chariot, and they promptly obeyed. Priam mounted and drew back the reins, Antenor got into the splendid chariot beside him, and they drove their fast horses through the Scaean Gate towards the open country.

When they reached the assembled armies, they stepped down from their chariot onto the bountiful earth and walked to a spot midway between the Trojans and Achaeans. King Agamemnon and the resourceful Odysseus rose at once; and stately heralds brought the victims for the sacrifice together, mixed wine in the bowl, and poured some water on the kings' hands. Then Agamemnon drew the knife that he always carried beside the great scabbard of his sword, and cut some hair from the lambs' heads. The hair was distributed among the Trojan and Achaean captains by the heralds. And now Agamemnon lifted up his hands and prayed aloud in the hearing of all: 'Father Zeus, you that rule from Mount Ida, most glorious and great; and you, the Sun, whose eye and ear miss nothing in the world; you Rivers and you Earth; you Powers of the world below that make the souls of dead men pay for perjury; I call on you all to witness our oaths and to see that they are kept. If Paris kills Menelaus, let him keep Helen and her wealth, and we shall sail away in our seagoing ships. But if red-haired Menelaus kills Paris, the Trojans must surrender Helen and all her possessions, and compensate the Argives suitably, on a scale that future generations shall remember. And if, in the event of Paris' death, Priam and his sons refuse to pay, I shall stay here and fight for the indemnity until the war is finished.'

Agamemnon now slit the lambs' throats with the relentless bronze and dropped them gasping on the ground, where the life-force ebbed and left them, for the knife had done its work. Then they drew wine from the bowl in cups, and as they poured it on the ground they made their petitions to the gods that have been since time began. The watching Trojans and Achaeans prayed as well – the same prayer served them both. 'Zeus, most glorious and great, and you other immortal gods; may the brains of whichever party breaks this treaty be poured out on the ground as that wine is poured, and not only theirs but their children's too; and may foreigners possess their wives.' Such were their hopes of peace, but Zeus had no intention yet of bringing peace about.

Dardanian Priam now made himself heard. 'Trojans and Achaean men-at-arms,' he said, 'attend to me. I am going back to windy Ilium, since I cannot bear to look on while my own son fights the formidable Menelaus. All I can think is that Zeus and the other immortal gods must know already which of the two is going to his doom.'

With these words, the venerable king put the lambs in the car and himself mounted and drew back the reins. Antenor took his place beside him in the splendid chariot, and the two drove off on their way back to Ilium.

Priam's son Hector and the admirable Odysseus proceeded to measure out the ground, and then to cast lots from a metal helmet to see which of the two should throw his bronze spear first. The watching armies prayed, with their hands raised to the gods – the same prayer served them both. 'Father Zeus, you that rule from Mount Ida, most glorious and great; let the man who brought these troubles on both peoples die and go down to the House of Hades; and let peace be established between us.'

They made their prayers; and now great Hector of the flashing helmet shook the lots, turning his eyes aside. One of the lots leapt out at once. It was that of Paris.

The troops sat down in rows, each man by his high-stepping horses, where his ornate arms were piled; and Prince Paris, husband of Helen of the lovely hair, put on his beautiful armour. He began by tying round his legs a pair of splendid greaves, which were fitted with silver clips for the ankles. Next he put a cuirass on his breast. It was his brother Lycaon's and he had to adjust it. Over his shoulder he slung a bronze sword with a silver-studded hilt, and then a great thick shield. On his sturdy head he set a well-made helmet It had a horse-hair crest, and the plume nodded grimly from the top. Last, he took up a powerful spear, which was fitted to his grip.

Battle-loving Menelaus also equipped himself in the same way; and when both had got themselves ready, each behind his own front line, they strode out between the two forces, looking so terrible that the spectators were spellbound, horse-taming Trojans and Achaean men-at-arms alike. The two men took their stations not far from one another on the measured piece of ground, and in mutual fury brandished their weapons. Paris was the first to hurl his long-shadowed spear. It landed on the round shield of Menelaus. But the bronze did not break through; the point was bent back by the stout shield. Then Menelaus son of Atreus brought his spear into play, with a prayer to Father Zeus: 'Grant me revenge, King Zeus, on Paris, the man who wronged me in the beginning. Use my hands to bring him down, so that our children's children may still shudder at the thought of injuring a host who has received them kindly.'

With that, he balanced his long-shadowed spear and hurled it. The heavy weapon struck the round shield of Priam's son. It pierced the glittering shield, forced its way through the ornate cuirass, and pressing straight on tore the tunic on Paris' flank. But Paris swerved, and so avoided death. Menelaus then drew his silver-mounted sword, swung it back, and brought it down on the ridge of his enemy's helmet. But the sword broke on the helmet into half a dozen pieces and drop-ped from his hand. Menelaus gave a groan and looked up at the broad sky. 'Father Zeus,' he cried, 'is there a god more spiteful than yourself? I thought I had paid out Paris for his infamy, and now my sword breaks in my hand, when I have already cast a spear for nothing and never touched the man!'

With that he hurled himself at Paris, seized him by the horsehair crest, and swinging him round, began to drag him into the Achaean lines. Paris was choked by the pressure on his tender throat of the embroidered helmet-strap, which he had fitted tightly round his chin; and Menelaus would have hauled him in and covered himself with glory, but for the quickness of Aphrodite Daughter of Zeus, who saw what was happening and broke the strap for Paris, though it was made of leather from a slaughtered ox. So the helmet came away empty in the great hand of the noble Menelaus. He tossed it, with a swing, into the Achaean lines, where it was picked up by his own retainers, and flung himself at his enemy again in the hope of despatching him with his bronze-pointed spear. But Aphrodite used her powers once more. Hiding Paris in a dense mist, she whisked him off – it was an easy feat for the goddess – and put him down in his own perfumed fragrant bedroom. Then she went herself to summon Helen.

She found Helen on the high tower, surrounded by Trojan women. Aphrodite put out her hand, plucked at her sweet-scented robe, and spoke to her in the disguise of an old woman she was very fond of, a wool-worker who used to make beautiful wool for her when she lived in Lacedaemon. 'Come!' said the goddess, mimicking this woman. 'Paris wants you to go home to him. There he is in his room, on the inlaid bed, radiant in his beauty and his lovely clothes. You would never believe that he had just come in from a duel. You would think he was going to a dance or had just stopped dancing and sat down to rest.'

Helen was perturbed and looked at the goddess. When she observed the beauty of her neck and her lovely breasts and sparkling eyes, she was struck with awe. But she made no pretence of being deceived. 'Lady of mysteries,' she said, 'what is the object of this mummery? Now that Menelaus has beaten Paris and is willing to take home his erring wife, you are plotting, I suppose, to carry me off to some still more distant city, in Phrygia or in lovely Maeonia, for some other favourite of yours who may be living in those parts? So you begin by coming here, and try to lure me back to Paris. No; go and sit with him yourself. Forget that you are a goddess. Never set foot in Olympus again, but devote yourself to Paris. Pamper him well, and one day you may be his wife – or else his slave. I refuse to go and share his bed again – I should never hear the end of it. There is not a woman in Troy who would not curse me if I did. I have enough to bear already.'

The Lady Aphrodite rounded on her in fury. 'Obstinate

wretch!' she cried. 'Do not provoke me, or I might desert you in my anger, and hate you as heartily as I have loved you up till now, rousing the Trojans and Achaeans to such bitter enmity as would bring *you* to a miserable end.'

Helen was cowed, child of Zeus though she was. She wrapped herself up in her white and glossy robe, and went off without a sound. Not one of the Trojan women saw her go: she had a goddess to guide her.

When they reached the beautiful house of Paris, the maids in attendance betook themselves at once to their tasks, while Helen, the great lady, went to her lofty bedroom. There the goddess herself, laughter-loving Aphrodite, picked up a chair, carried it across the room and put it down for her in front of Paris. Helen, daughter of aegis-bearing Zeus, sat down on it, but turned her eyes aside and began by scolding her lover: 'So you are back from the battlefield – and I was hoping you had fallen there to the great soldier who was once my husband! You used to boast that you were a better man than the mighty Menelaus, a finer spearman, stronger in the arm. Then why not go at once and challenge him again? Or should I warn you to think twice before you offer single combat to the red-haired Menelaus? Do nothing rash – or you may end by falling to his spear!'

Paris had his answer ready. 'My dear,' he said, 'do not try to put me on my mettle by abusing me. Menelaus has just beaten me with Athene's help. But I too have gods to help me, and next time I shall win. Come, let us go to bed together and be happy in our love. Never has such desire overwhelmed me, not even in the beginning, when I carried you off from lovely Lacedaemon in my seagoing ships and we spent the night on the isle of Cranae in each other's arms – never till now have I been so much in love with you or felt such sweet desire.'

As he spoke, he made a move towards the bed, leading her to it. His wife followed him; and the two lay down together on the well-made wooden bed.

Meanwhile Menelaus was prowling through the ranks like

a wild beast, trying to find Prince Paris. But not a man among the Trojans or their famous allies could point him out to the warrior Menelaus. Not that if anyone had seen him he would have hidden him for love: they loathed him, all of them, like death. In the end King Agamemnon made a pronouncement: 'Trojans, Dardanians and allies, listen to me. The great Menelaus has won: there is no disputing that. Now give up Argive Helen and her wealth, and compensate me suitably on a scale that future generations shall remember.'

Atreides had spoken. The Achaeans all applauded.

IV

PANDARUS BREAKS THE TRUCE

THE gods, meanwhile, had sat down for a conference with
Zeus in the Hall of the Golden Floor. The Lady Hebe, acting
as their cupbearer, served them with nectar, and they drank
each other's health from tankards of gold as they looked out
on the city of Troy.

By way of tormenting Here, the Son of Cronos opened in a
sarcastic vein. 'Two of the goddesses,' he slyly observed, 'are
on Menelaus' side, Here of Argos and Alalcomenean Athene.
But I note that they sit idle here and are content to watch;
whereas laughter-loving Aphrodite always keeps close to
Paris and shields him from calamity. Only a moment ago she
whisked him off when he thought his end had come. Never-
theless, victory has certainly gone to Menelaus favourite of
Ares, and it remains for us to consider what shall happen next.
Are we to stir up this wicked strife again, with all the sound
and fury of war; or shall we make the Trojans and Achaeans
friends? Subject to your approval this would mean that King
Priam's city would survive and Menelaus take Argive Helen
back.'

This speech drew muttered protests from Athene and Here,
who were sitting together, plotting evil for the Trojans. How-
ever, Athene held her tongue, for all her annoyance with her
Father, Zeus. She made no rejoinder, though she seethed with
indignation. But Here could not contain her rage, and burst
into speech. 'Dread Son of Cronos, what you propose is
monstrous! How can you think of making all my labour null
and void, the pains I took, the sweat that poured from me
while my horses toiled around as I was gathering the clans to
make trouble for Priam and his sons? Do as you please; but do
not imagine that all the rest of us approve.'

Zeus the Cloud-gatherer fiercely resented this. 'Madam,' he said, 'what injury can Priam and his sons have done you to account for the vehemence of your desire to sack the lovely town of Troy? Will nothing satisfy your malice but to storm the gates and the long walls and eat up Priam and his sons and all his people raw? Act as you see fit – I do not wish this difference of ours to grow into a serious breach. But there is one condition that I make – remember it. When it is *my* turn to desire the downfall of a town and I choose one where friends of yours are living, make no attempt to curb my anger, but let me have my way, since I have given in to you this time of my own accord, though much against my inclination. For of all the cities that men live in under the sun and starry sky, the nearest to my heart was holy Ilium, with Priam and the people of Priam of the good ashen spear. Never at their banquets did my altar go without its proper share of wine and fat, the offerings that we claim as ours.'

'The three towns *I* love best,' the ox-eyed Queen of Heaven replied, 'are Argos, Sparta, and Mycenae of the Broad Streets. Sack those, if ever they become obnoxious to you. I shall not grudge you their destruction nor make a stand on their behalf. Even if I do object and meddle with your plans, I shall achieve nothing – you are far too strong for me. And yet my enterprises ought not to be thwarted any more than yours. For I too am divine and our parentage is one. Of all the children of Cronos of the Crooked Ways, I take precedence, both by right of birth and because I am your Consort and you are King of all the gods. However, by all means let us yield to one another in this matter, I to you and you to me, and the rest of the immortal gods will follow us. All I ask you to do now is to tell Athene to visit the front and arrange for the Trojans to break the truce by an act of aggression against the triumphant Achaeans.'

The Father of men and gods did not demur, and at once made his wishes clear to Athene. 'Off with you to the front,' he said. 'Visit the armies and contrive to make the Trojans break the truce by attacking the Achaeans in their triumph.'

With this encouragement, Athene, who had already set her heart on action, sped down from the peaks of Olympus, like a meteor that is discharged by Zeus as a warning to sailors or some great army on the land, and comes blazing through the sky and tossing out innumerable sparks. Thus Pallas Athene flashed down to earth and leapt into their midst. Horse-taming Trojans and Achaean men-at-arms were awestruck at the sight. Every man looked at his neighbour with a question on his lips: 'Does this mean war again with all its horrors? Or is Zeus, our arbiter in battle, making peace between us?'

While the Achaeans and Trojans were asking each other what was coming, Athene disguised herself as a man and slipped into the Trojan ranks in the likeness of a sturdy spear-man called Laodocus son of Antenor. She was trying to find the stalwart and admirable Pandarus, Lycaon's son, wherever he might be. And she succeeded. Prince Pandarus was stand-ing there beside the powerful shield-bearing force that had come under his command from the River Aesepus. She went up to him and made her purpose clear. 'Pandarus, my lord, will you use your wits and take a hint from me? If you could bring yourself to shoot Menelaus with an arrow, you would cover yourself with glory and put every Trojan in your debt, Prince Paris most of all. He would be the first to come forward with a handsome gift, if he saw the great Menelaus son of Atreus struck down by a shot from you and laid out on a funeral pyre. Come, shoot at Menelaus in his glory; and pray to the Archer-King Apollo, your own Lycian god. Promise him a splendid sacrifice of firstling lambs when you get home to your sacred city of Zeleia.'

Athene's eloquence prevailed upon the fool, and then and there he unsheathed his polished bow. It was made from the horns of an ibex that he himself had shot in the breast. He had lain in wait for the beast and caught it on the breast as it came out from a cleft in the rock, so that it tumbled back into the cleft. The horns on its head, measuring sixteen hands across, were worked up by a craftsman in horn, who fitted them together, made all smooth, and put a golden tip on the end. Pandarus strung the bow, slanting it against the ground, and laid it carefully down, while his gallant followers held their shields in front to protect him from attack by the fierce Achaeans till he had shot Menelaus, the battle-loving son of Atreus. Then he took off the lid of his quiver and picked out an arrow, feathered but as yet unused, and fraught with agony. He deftly fitted the sharp arrow to the string and offered up a prayer to the Archer-King Apollo, his own Lycian god, promising him a splendid sacrifice of firstling lambs when he should get home to his sacred city of Zeleia. And now, gripping the notched end and the ox-gut string, he drew them back together till the string was near his breast and the iron point was by the bow. When he had bent the great bow to a circle, it gave a twang, the string sang out, and the sharp arrow leapt into the air, eager to wing its way into the enemy ranks.

Ah but the happy gods that never die did not forget you, Menelaus – Athene above all, the Fighting Daughter of Zeus, who took her stand in front and warded off the piercing dart, turning it just a little from the flesh, like a mother driving a fly away from her gently sleeping child. With her own hand she guided it to where the golden buckles of the belt were fixed and the corslet overlapped. So the sharp arrow struck the fastened belt. It drove through the decorated belt and pressed on through the ornate cuirass, and through the apron that Menelaus wore as a last protection against flying weapons. This did more than all the rest to save him; yet the arrow sped on through the apron too. In the end, it made a shallow wound, and at once the dark blood came flowing from the cut. It was like the purple dye with which some Carian or Maeonian woman stains ivory to make a cheek-piece for a horse, a lovely ornament that is laid by in store, though every driver longs to see it on his horse, till one day it takes the fancy of a king, who buys it to adorn his horse and be a badge of honour for his charioteer. Thus, Menelaus, blood stained your comely thighs and legs and ran down to your shapely ankles.

King Agamemnon shuddered when he saw the dark blood

streaming from the cut. Indeed the veteran Menelaus was himself aghast, though when he observed that the binding and barbs of the arrow-head had not sunk in, he recovered his composure. But King Agamemnon gave a deep groan and seized him by the hand, while all his men expressed their consternation. 'My dear brother!' cried Agamemnon. 'It was your death, then, that I swore to when I made the truce and sent you out to fight alone for us against the Trojans, who have shot you now and trampled on their solemn pact. Yet a pact that has been ratified by our right hands and solemnized with wine and in the blood of lambs is not so easily annulled. The Olympian may postpone the penalty, but he exacts it in the end, and the transgressors pay a heavy price, they pay with their lives, and with their women and their children too. The day will come – I know it in my heart of hearts – when holy Ilium will be destroyed, with Priam and the people of Priam of the good ashen spear. Zeus, Son of Cronos, from his high seat in Heaven where he lives, will wave his sombre aegis over them all in his anger at this perjury of theirs. All this will happen without fail. Yet if you die, Menelaus, if your end has really come, how bitterly I shall lament you. And what a sorry figure I shall cut on my return to thirsty Argos! For the Achaeans will at once be set on getting home. We should be forced to leave Argive Helen here for Priam and his men to boast about, while the earth would rot your bones as you lay in Troyland with your task undone. I can already hear some Trojan braggart say, as he stamps on the tomb of illustrious Menelaus: "May every quarrel picked by Agamemnon end like this – a futile expedition, retreat in empty ships, and the sterling Menelaus left behind!" That is how they will talk – and I shall pray for the earth to swallow me.'

But red-haired Menelaus was able to comfort him. 'Courage!' he said. 'Say nothing to dispirit the men. The arrow did not reach a vital spot. Before it got so far, it was stopped by the metal of my belt, the corslet underneath, and the apron, with the bronze they put on it.'

'If only you are right, my dear Menelaus!' exclaimed King Agamemnon. 'But a physician shall examine the wound and apply ointments to relieve the pain.'

With that he turned to Talthybius, his noble squire. 'Talthybius,' he said, 'go as quickly as you can and fetch Machaon – you know the man – the son of the great physician Asclepius, to see my lord Menelaus. Some Trojan or Lycian archer who knows his business well has shot him with an arrow, to his own renown and our discomfiture.'

Agamemnon's squire obediently set out and made his way through the bronze-clad Achaean ranks, searching for the lord Machaon. He found him standing with his men, the powerful shield-bearing force that had come under his command from Tricce where the horses graze. He went up to him and delivered his message: 'Quick, my lord Machaon! King Agamemnon has sent for you to see our great captain, Menelaus. Some Trojan or Lycian archer who knows his business well has struck him with an arrow, to his own renown and our discomfiture.'

Stirred by the herald's news, Machaon set off with him and they threaded their way through the serried ranks of the great Achaean army. When they reached the spot where red-haired Menelaus lay wounded, with all the chieftains gathered round him in a circle, the admirable Machaon passed through the ring, went up to him and at once extracted the arrow from the fastened belt, though the pointed barbs broke off as the head was pulled out. Then he undid the glittering belt, the corslet underneath, and the apron that the coppersmiths had made. When he found the place where the sharp point had pierced the flesh, he sucked out the blood and skilfully applied a soothing ointment from the supply with which the friendly Cheiron had equipped his father.

While they were attending to Menelaus of the loud war-cry, the Trojan battle-lines advanced to the attack. So the Achaeans once more put on their armour and turned their thoughts to war.

Agamemnon now showed his mettle. He was at once alert.

There was no sign in him of nervous fears, no hesitation to give battle, nothing but eagerness for the fight and the glory he might win. He decided not to use his horses and his inlaid chariot. So the pair were led aside by his squire, snorting as they went. But Agamemnon was careful to instruct the man – it was Eurymedon son of Ptolemy – to keep them close at hand, in case he grew weary at any point in his long tour of the forces. Then he set out on foot to go the round of his army.

When he came upon any of his horse-loving Danaans who were up and doing, he stopped and encouraged them. 'Argives,' he said, 'you have the right spirit: do not forget it now. Perjurers will get no help from Father Zeus. The men who went back on their word and broke the truce are going to have their own smooth flesh devoured by vultures, while we carry off their little children and the wives they love, on board our ships, when we have sacked their stronghold.'

On the other hand, any that he found shrinking from the ugly business of war came in for a sharp rebuke and angry words. 'Contemptible creatures,' he exclaimed, 'brave only with the bow! Argives, is there no shame in you? Why do you stand there dazed like fawns that dash across the plain and stop when they are tired, because they have no spirit? That is what you look like, standing there in a trance instead of fighting. Are you waiting for the Trojans to threaten our good ships on the grey sea beach, in the hope that Zeus will put his hand out and protect you then?'

In this way Agamemnon went the rounds and impressed his will on the men. In his tour of the serried ranks he came upon the Cretans, the troops that paraded under the able Idomeneus. In the forefront was Idomeneus himself, brave as a boar; while Meriones commanded the company in the rear. Agamemnon King of Men was delighted when he saw them and was quick to compliment their leader. 'Idomeneus,' he said, 'of all my horse-loving Danaans there is not one I count on more than you, not only on the battlefield but off it. I show you this when we sit down to dine and the sparkling

wine of the elders is mixed in the bowl for our best men.
When the rest of the long-haired Achaeans have drunk up
their portion, your cup stands full, like mine, to drink from
as you wish. Off with you into battle, and be the man you
have always claimed to be!'

'My lord Atreides,' said Idomeneus, the Cretan King, 'you
can rely on my loyal support and the solemn assurance I gave
you when this business began. Rouse the rest of the long-
haired Achaeans, so that we may join battle at once, now that
the Trojans have broken their oath. As for them, they have
nothing to expect but death and disaster, since they went back
on their word and broke the truce.'

Well pleased with this reply, Atreides passed on and made
his way through the crowd to the two lords named Aias.
The pair were arming, and the massed infantry behind them
loomed like the cloud that a goatherd sees from a lookout
bearing down on him across the sea with the roaring West
Wind at its back. On it comes, over the sea, with the whirlwind
in its wake, darkening in the distance till it looks as black as
pitch. The goatherd shudders at the sight and drives his flock
into a cave. Thus the gallant youths behind the two Aiantes
moved into battle in their closed formations, dark as a cloud,
bristling with shields and spears. King Agamemnon rejoiced
when he saw them, and paid a signal tribute to the two
Aiantes, saluting them as leaders of his bronze-clad Argives.
'For you,' he said, 'I have no orders – exhortation would be
out of place. Your very leadership inspires your men to fight
their best. By Father Zeus, Athene and Apollo, that is the
temper I should like to find in all. King Priam's city, captured
and sacked by Achaean hands, would soon be tumbling
down.'

Leaving them with these words, Agamemnon passed on and
came to Nestor, the clear-voiced orator from Pylos, whom he
found preparing his men for the fight and marshalling them
under their officers, the sturdy Pelagon, Alastor and Chro-
mius, Prince Haemon and Bias the great captain. Nestor put
his charioteers with their horses and cars in the front; and at

the back a mass of first-rate infantry to serve as rearguard. In between, he stationed his inferior troops, so that even shirkers would be forced to fight. He told his charioteers, whom he instructed first, to hold in their horses and not to get entangled in the mêlée. 'Do not think,' he said, 'that his bravery and skill entitle a charioteer to break the ranks and fight the Trojans on his own. And don't let anybody drop behind and weaken the whole force. When a man in his own chariot comes within reach of an enemy car, it is time for him to try a spear-thrust. Those are the best tactics. This is the discipline and spirit that enabled our forefathers to take walled towns by storm.'

Thus the old man used the experience he had gained in battles long ago to inspire his troops. It warmed King Agamemnon's heart to watch him, and he told him what he felt. 'My venerable lord,' he said, 'how happy I could be if your admirable spirit were matched by the vigour of your limbs, and your strength were unimpaired. But age, which no one can escape, lies heavy on you. If only you could pass it on to someone else and join the ranks of youth!'

'My lord Atreides,' said Nestor the Gerenian Knight, 'I too could wish most heartily to be the man I was when I killed the great Ereuthalion. But the gods do not grant us all their favours at a single time. I was a young man then: now age oppresses me. Yet for all that I shall be with my charioteers, and in command. Their plans and orders come from me – it is the privilege of age – even if the handling of the spears is left to younger men than myself, with the vigour needed for the work.'

Content with what he had seen of Nestor, Agamemnon resumed his tour. The next he visited was Peteos' son, Menestheus tamer of horses. This man and his Athenian troops, whose battle-cry was famous, were standing idle; and close beside them was Odysseus of the nimble wits, with his Cephallenians, a substantial force, but also standing easy. The call to battle had not reached their ears, for the Trojan and Achaean regiments had only just begun to move into action.

So they stood and waited for some other Achaean battalion to advance against the Trojans and begin the fight. When he noticed this, King Agamemnon gave them a severe rebuke. 'You, sir,' he said, 'Menestheus, son of a royal father; and you, Odysseus, arch-intriguer, always looking to your own advantage; why are you hanging back like this and leaving others to advance? It is for you to take your stand in the front line and welcome the shock of battle. Are you not the first to get my invitation when a banquet for the leading captains is afoot? On such occasions you are quite content to take your fill of roasted meat and mellow wine. But now you seem content to watch while ten battalions of Achaeans fall on the enemy before you make a move.'

The resourceful Odysseus gave him a black look. 'My lord Atreides,' he replied, 'this is absurd. Can you maintain that in a pitched battle we ever loiter in the rear? You shall have your wish, if that is what is troubling you, and see the father of Telemachus at grips with the front rank of these horse-taming Trojans. Meanwhile, you are talking nonsense.'

When King Agamemnon saw that Odysseus had taken umbrage, he smiled at him and apologized: 'Royal son of Laertes, Odysseus of the nimble wits; I do not blame you over-much, and I shall spur you on no more. For I know that in your heart you are well disposed towards me. In fact, we see eye to eye. But enough. Later, I will make amends for anything uncivil I may have said just now. Let the gods wipe it out.'

With this he left them there and went in search of others. The next he came upon was Tydeus' son, the great-hearted Diomedes, who was standing in his well-made chariot, with the horses yoked. Sthenelus son of Capaneus stood close at hand. King Agamemnon looked at Diomedes and took him sharply to task.

'What does this mean?' he asked. 'The son of Tydeus, that dauntless charioteer, shirking the battle, watching the way it goes? It was not Tydeus' habit to shrink back, but to sally out in front of all his friends and come to grips. That is what people say who saw the man at work. They say he was superb.

But I never knew him or set eyes on him, though he did come to Mycenae once, not as an enemy but on a friendly visit, with Prince Polyneices in search of reinforcements. It was the time of their expedition against Thebes of the Sacred Walls. They begged our people very hard for adequate support, and we promised all they asked for. But Zeus made us change our minds by showing inauspicious omens; and they left Mycenae. When they had gone some way and reached the deep meadows and reedy banks of Asopus, the Achaean commanders sent Tydeus forward for a parley. He went to Thebes and found a large party of Cadmeians at dinner in the palace of Prince Eteocles. Now as a visitor, alone among a crowd of strangers, even the gallant Tydeus might have felt some qualms. But not at all – he challenged them to friendly matches, and won easily in every case, with Athene's generous help. That nettled the horse-racing Cadmeians, and when Tydeus left, they sent ahead and laid an ambush in his path – fifty men with two officers, Maeon son of Haemon, a man of rank, and a hardened bully called Polyphontes, whose father too had been a killer. But Tydeus dealt with them and brought them to an ugly end. He killed the whole party, but for one, whom he sent home. He had a warning from the gods and let Maeon off.

'That, sir, was Aetolian Tydeus. You are his son. But you do not fight as he did, though you may be better when it comes to talking.'

The staunch Diomedes made no reply to this harangue. He accepted the rebuke from the sovereign he revered. But the son of the illustrious Capaneus could not keep his peace. 'My lord,' he said, 'you know the facts: do not distort them. I claim that we are far better men than our fathers. We *did* succeed in capturing Seven-gated Thebes. With a weaker force, we stormed more powerful defences than they ever faced, because we put our faith in Zeus and the signs that the gods sent us; whereas they came to grief through their own presumption. So never talk to me about our fathers in the same breath as ourselves.'

'Be quiet, man, and take your cue from me,' Diomedes interposed with an angry glance at Sthenelus. 'I am not going to quarrel with Agamemnon, our Commander-in-Chief, for spurring on his troops to fight. It is he who will get the credit if the Achaeans beat the Trojans and capture holy Ilium; but at the same time, if the Achaeans are defeated, he will suffer most. Come; it is time for you and me to turn our thoughts to war.'

With that, he jumped down from his chariot in all his armour. As he leapt into action, the bronze rang grimly on the prince's breast. The stoutest heart might well have been dismayed.

And now battalion on battalion of Danaans swept relentlessly into battle, like the great waves that come hurtling onto an echoing beach, one on top of the other, under a westerly gale. Far out at sea their crests begin to rise, then in they come and crash down on the shingle with a mighty roar, or arch themselves to break on a cliff and send the sea foam flying. Each of the captains shouted his orders to his own command, but the men moved quietly. They obeyed their officers without a sound, and came on behind them like an army of the dumb. The metalled armour that they marched in glittered on every man.

It was otherwise with the Trojans. They were like the sheep that stand in their thousands in a rich farmer's yard yielding their white milk and bleating incessantly because they hear their lambs. Such was the babel that went up from the great Trojan army, which hailed from many parts, and being without a common language used many different cries and calls.

Ares, the god of War, spurred on the Trojan forces; Athene of the Flashing Eyes, the Achaeans. Terror and Panic were at hand. And so was Strife, the War-god's Sister, who helps him in his bloody work. Once she begins, she cannot stop. At first she seems a little thing, but before long, though her feet are still on the ground, she has struck high heaven with her head. She swept in now among the Trojans and Achaeans, filling them with hatred of each other. It was the groans of dying men she wished to hear.

At last the armies met, with a clash of bucklers, spears and bronze-clad fighting men. The bosses of their shields collided and a great roar went up. The screams of the dying were mingled with the vaunts of their destroyers, and the earth ran with blood. So, in winter, two mountain rivers flowing in spate from the great springs higher up mingle their torrents at a watersmeet in some deep ravine, and far off in the hills a shepherd hears their thunder. Such was the tumult and turmoil as the two armies came to grips.

Antilochus was the first to kill his man, Echepolus son of Thalysius, who was fighting in full armour in the Trojan front. With the first cast he struck this man on the ridge of his crested helmet. The spear-point, landing in his forehead, pierced the bone; darkness came down on his eyes, and he crashed in the mêlée like a falling tower. He was scarcely down when Prince Elephenor son of Chalcodon and leader of the fiery Abantes seized him by the feet and tried to drag him quickly out of range to spoil him of his armour – an enterprise he did not carry far, for the valiant Agenor saw him dragging the corpse away. With his bronze-headed shaft Agenor caught him on the flank, which the shield had left exposed as Elephenor stooped. The man collapsed, and over his lifeless body a grim struggle ensued between Trojans and Achaeans. They leapt at each other like wolves, and men tossed men about.

It was now that Telamonian Aias struck down Anthemion's son, Simoisius. This sturdy youngster took his name from the River Simoïs, beside which he was born when his mother was returning from Mount Ida, where her father and mother had taken her to see their sheep. His life was too short for him to repay his parents for their loving care, for it ended when he met the great Aias' spear. He had scarcely sallied out when Aias struck him in the breast by the right nipple. The bronze spear went clean through his shoulder and he came down in the dust, felled like a slender poplar with a bushy top that has shot up in the big meadows by a stream and is cut down by a

wainwright with his gleaming axe. Later, the man will make
felloes from it for the wheels of a beautiful chariot; but he
leaves it now to lie and season on the bank. Thus King Aias
felled Simoisius, Anthemion's son.

And now Priam's son Antiphus in his shimmering cuirass
aimed a sharp javelin across the crowd at Aias himself.
Antiphus missed his man, but he made a hit, for he caught
Leucus, one of Odysseus' comrades, in the groin, as he was
dragging Simoisius away. The body fell from Leucus' hands
and he himself came crashing down on it. Odysseus was in-
furiated when he saw Leucus killed. In his glittering bronze
equipment he made his way through the front ranks right up
to the enemy line, where he took his stand and after one look
round let fly with his shining lance. The Trojans leapt back
when they saw it coming. But Odysseus had not cast in vain.
He struck Democoön, a bastard son of Priam's, who had
joined him from his stud-farm at Abydus, only to fall to the
spear that Odysseus cast in his anger at his comrade's death.
The bronze point struck Democoön on one temple and came
out at the other. Night descended on his eyes; he fell with a
thud, and his armour rang out. Illustrious Hector and the
whole Trojan front fell back, while the Argives shouted in
triumph, dragged the corpses in, and advanced still farther.

This filled Apollo, who was watching from Pergamus,
with indignation, and he called aloud to the Trojans: 'On with
you, Trojan charioteers! Never give Argives best in battle.
They are not made of stone or iron. Their flesh cannot keep
out the penetrating bronze when they are hit. And what is
more, the son of Thetis of the Lovely Locks, Achilles, is not
fighting. He is sulking by the ships.' Thus the redoubtable
god encouraged them from the citadel, while the Achaeans
were emboldened by Athene Daughter of Zeus, the august
Lady of Triton, who went through the ranks herself and
spurred on any laggards that she saw.

And now Diores son of Amarinceus was caught in the
toils of Fate. He was hit by a jagged stone on the right leg
near the ankle. The man who threw it was the Thracian

captain, Peiros son of Imbrasus, who came from Aenus. The brutal rock shattered the two sinews and the bones; and Diores fell backwards in the dust, stretching his hands out to his friends and gasping for breath. But Peiros, the man who had hit him, ran up and struck him by the navel with his spear. His entrails poured out on the ground and night descended on his eyes.

As Peiros sprang away, Aetolian Thoas hit him in the chest with a spear, below the nipple, and the bronze point sank into the lung. Thoas came up to him, pulled the heavy weapon from his breast, and drawing his sharp sword struck him full in the belly. He took Peiros' life, but he did not get his armour. For Peiros' men, the Thracians with the topknots on their heads, surrounded him. They held their long spears steady in their hands and fended Thoas off, big, strong and formidable though he was. Thoas was shaken and withdrew.

So these two, Peiros and Diores, were stretched in the dust at each other's side, both of them chieftains, one of the Thracians, the other of the bronze-clad Epeans. But they were not the only people killed. Indeed this was no idle skirmish. A newcomer as yet unhit would soon have found that out, had Athene shielded him from the hail of missiles and led him by hand into the thick of the fray. It was a day when many Trojans and Achaeans bit the dust and were stretched out side by side.

V

DIOMEDES FIGHTS THE GODS

PALLAS ATHENE now inspired Diomedes son of Tydeus with audacity and resolution, so that he might eclipse all his comrades-in-arms and cover himself with glory. She made his shield and helmet glow with a blaze as steady as the Star of Summer when he rises from his bath in Ocean to outshine all other stars. Such was the fire that she caused to stream from his head and shoulders as she thrust him into the very heart of the battle.

There was a Trojan called Dares, a wealthy citizen of good repute, who was priest of Hephaestus. He had two sons, Phegeus and Idaeus, both trained in every kind of fighting. These two detached themselves from the rest and advanced against Diomedes in their chariot, while he went to meet them on foot. When they had come within range, Phegeus began the fight by hurling his long-shadowed spear. But the spear-point passed over Diomedes' left shoulder and did not touch him. It was now Diomedes' turn to cast, and his weapon did not leave his hand for nothing. It struck Phegeus in the middle of the breast and tumbled him out of the well-made chariot, which Idaeus then deserted also, with a leap to the rear, not daring to bestride his brother's corpse. And Black Fate would have got him too if Hephaestus had not come to the rescue and wrapped him in night, saving him so that his aged priest might not be utterly broken by grief. The magnificent Diomedes drove the men's horses off and told his followers to take them back to the hollow ships.

When the Trojans saw what had happened to Dares' sons, how one was killed beside his chariot and the other put to flight, they were dismayed, for all their bravery. Moreover it was at this point that Athene of the Bright Eyes interposed and laid a restraining hand on the arm of the fierce War-god. 'Ares,' she cried, 'murderous Ares, Butcher of Men and Sacker of Towns; is it not time for us to let the Trojans and Achaeans fight it out and see whom Father Zeus intends to win? Let us two leave the field before we make him angry.' With this, Athene led the impetuous War-god out of the fight, and made him sit down on the grassy bank of Scamander.

As a result, the Danaans thrust back the Trojan line and each of their leaders killed his man. Agamemnon King of Men began by hurling the great Odius, chieftain of the Alizones, from his chariot. Odius had been the first to fly, and as he turned, Agamemnon caught him in the back with his spear, midway between the shoulders, and drove it through his breast. He fell with a thud and his armour rang about him.

Next, Idomeneus killed Phaestus son of Maeonian Borus, who had come from the fertile lands of Tarne. As Phaestus was getting into his chariot the great spearman pierced his right shoulder with a long javelin. Phaestus crashed down from his car, and hateful night engulfed him. Idomeneus' retainers stripped his corpse.

Then Menelaus son of Atreus with his sharp-pointed spear killed the hunter Scamandrius son of Strophius. He was a great man for the chase, who had been taught by Artemis herself to bring down any kind of wild game that the mountain forest yields. But Artemis the Mistress of the Bow was of no help to him now, nor were the long shots that had won him fame. For as Scamandrius fled before him, the glorious spearman Menelaus son of Atreus struck him with his lance in the middle of the back between the shoulders and drove it through his chest. He fell face downward and his armour clanged upon him.

Next, Meriones killed Phereclus son of Tecton, Harmon's son, a carpenter who could turn his hand to any kind of curious work. Pallas Athene had no greater favourite. It was he who had built for Paris those trim ships that had started all the trouble and proved a curse to the whole Trojan people – and to himself, since he knew nothing of the oracles. Meriones ran after him, and when he caught him up, struck him on the right buttock. The spear-head passed clean through to the bladder under the bone. He dropped on his knees with a scream, and Death enveloped him.

Then Meges killed Pedaeus, an illegitimate son of Antenor's, whom, to please her husband, the gracious lady Theano had brought up like a child of her own. Meges the mighty spear-man caught up this man and struck him with his sharp lance on the nape of the neck. The point came through between his jaws and severed his tongue at the root. He fell down in the dust and bit the cold bronze with his teeth.

Meanwhile Eurypylus, Euaemon's son, killed the noble Hypsenor, son of the proud Dolopion, who served as priest to the River-god Scamander and was worshipped by the Trojan people. As he fled before him, Eurypylus, Euaemon's high-born son, gave chase and slashed at Hypsenor's shoulder with his sword. The man's great arm was shorn off and fell bleeding to the ground. Fate set her seal on him, and the shadow of Death fell over his eyes.

Such was the execution done by the Danaan front line in this assault. As for Diomedes himself, you could not have told to which army, Trojan or Achaean, he belonged. He stormed across the plain like a winter torrent that comes tearing down and flattens out the dykes. Against its sudden onslaught, backed by the heavy rains, nothing can stand, neither the dykes that were meant to hem it in, nor the stone walls round the vineyards and their sturdy trees. It has its way, and far and wide the farmers see the wreckage of their splendid work. Thus the Trojans in their serried lines collapsed before the son of Tydeus, unable for all their numbers to withstand him.

When the noble Pandarus, Lycaon's son, saw Diomedes storming across the plain, and driving companies before him, he lost no time, but bent his crooked bow, took aim at him, and struck him as he forged ahead, in the right shoulder on a plate of his cuirass. Piercing the plate, the sharp arrow pressed straight on, and blood spread over the cuirass. Pandarus raised a great shout of triumph over Diomedes. 'Trojans,' he cried, 'forward and at them! Forward, charioteers! The best man they have got is badly wounded. And he won't last much longer, if King Apollo was in earnest when he sent *me* here from Lycia.'

Pandarus could boast, yet Diomedes was not beaten by the bitter dart. He fell back, but came to a halt by his horses and chariot, and called to Sthenelus son of Capaneus: 'Quick, my dear Sthenelus, get down from the chariot and draw this wretched arrow from my shoulder.'

Sthenelus leapt from the chariot to the ground, came over to him, and pulled out the arrow, clean through his shoulder. The blood came gushing through his knitted tunic, and Diomedes of the loud war-cry offered up a prayer to Athene: 'Listen to me, unsleeping Child of Zeus who wears the aegis. If ever in the past you wished us well and stood by my father or myself in the heat of action, be kind to me again, Athene. Let me kill Pandarus. Bring me within spear-cast of the man who shot me. I never had a chance. And now he's telling people I'm as good as dead.'

Diomedes' prayer came to the ears of Pallas Athene, and she made a new man of him. She came and stood by him too and spoke momentous words: 'Now, Diomedes, you can fight the Trojans fearlessly. I have filled your heart with the audacity of your father Tydeus, the great shield-bearing charioteer. Also I have swept the mist from your eyes and made you able to distinguish gods from men. And I tell you now, in case a god comes here to put you to the test, that you must not fight against the immortals, with one exception only. If Aphrodite Daughter of Zeus comes into the battle, use your sharp bronze and wound her.'

With that, bright-eyed Athene disappeared, and the son of Tydeus went and took his place once more in the front line. Even without Athene he had been determined to fall on the enemy again. And now he was three times as bold as he had been before, like a lion that a shepherd in charge of the woolly sheep on an outlying farm has wounded as he leapt into the yard, but failed to kill. He has only roused him to greater fury; and now he cannot keep him off, but hides in the stables, deserting the sheep in their panic. They are mown down in heaps, and the lion, furious still, jumps the high wall and so gets out of the yard. It was with such fury that the mighty Diomedes charged the Trojan line.

He began by killing Astynous and a chieftain called Hypeiron. He struck the one above the nipple with his bronze-pointed spear, and the other with his great sword on the collar bone by the shoulder, so that the shoulder was severed from the neck and back. He left them lying there, and went in chase of Abas and Polyeidus, the sons of Eurydamas, an old man who believed in dreams. But he had had no dreams to expound to these two when they set out for the front, and the mighty Diomedes killed them both. Then he went after Xanthus and Thoön, sons of Phaenops, a pair of striplings whose father, by now an old and ailing man, had got no other son to whom he could bequeath his wealth. They were the next to fall. Diomedes slew them both, leaving their father broken-hearted. He never saw them in the flesh again, home from the war. It was their cousins who stepped into the estate.

Diomedes' next victims were two sons of Dardanian Priam, Echemmon and Chromius, who were riding in the same chariot. Like a lion who pounces on cattle feeding in a glade and breaks an ox's or a heifer's neck, the son of Tydeus tumbled them rudely out of their chariot, without so much as 'by your leave', then stripped them of their arms and gave their horses to his men to drive to the ships.

Aeneas, seeing what havoc Diomedes was making of the Trojan lines, set out through the mêlée and the rain of missiles in search of Prince Pandarus. When he found the noble and stalwart son of Lycaon, he went up to him at once. 'Pandarus,' he said, 'what are you doing with your bow and your winged arrows? Are you not supposed to be an archer, the best that Lycia can boast, better than anyone we have in Troy? For Heaven's sake, man, put up a prayer to Zeus and let fly at that fellow over there. I don't know who it is, but he is having it all his own way and has done us too much harm already, and brought many of our best men down. Yet be careful – he may be one of the immortals, annoyed with us for some shortcoming in our rites. Perhaps we are being punished by an angry god.'

Lycaon's noble son saluted Aeneas with the respect due to a Trojan Councillor. 'If you ask me,' he said, 'the man is Diomedes to the life. I recognize him by his shield and the vizor of his helmet. I know his horses too when I see them. And yet I cannot swear that he is not a god. But if he is the man I take him for, the formidable Diomedes, I see the hand of Heaven in this mad attack of his. Some god must surely have been standing by him, wrapped in haze, to have made my arrow swerve as it hit him. For I *have* shot at him; and I hit him in the right shoulder, clean through the plate of his cuirass. I certainly thought I had seen him off to Hades. And yet I did not kill him. So perhaps it *is* some angry god. And here am I, without a chariot and pair to carry me, while all the time I have eleven splendid chariots at home, fresh from the wainwright's hands, with cloths spread over them, and a couple of horses standing by each, munching white barley and rye. There in the palace before I left for the front, my father Lycaon, the old spearman, told me time and again that I ought to lead the men from a chariot and pair when we engaged the enemy. But I would not listen to him – better for me if I had. I thought of my horses, who had always had enough to eat, and was afraid that fodder might run short in the congested city. So I left and came to Ilium on foot, relying on archery. Not that archery was going to do me any good. For I have already shot at a couple of their best men, Diomedes and Menelaus, and in each case I scored a hit and drew blood – there is no doubt about it. But I only roused them to greater efforts. Yes, I did an unlucky thing when I took my crooked bow from its peg, that day I set out with my company for your lovely town to please Prince Hector. But if ever I get home again and set eyes on my own country and my wife and the high roof of my great house, I shall be ready to let anybody cut my head off then and there, if I don't smash this

bow with my own hands and throw it in the blazing fire.
The thing is of no earthly use to me.'

'Don't talk like that,' said the Trojan commander Aeneas.
'Yet it is true enough that nothing can be done to stop the
man till you and I get into a chariot and attack him with other
weapons. Come, mount my car, and you will see what horses
of the breed of Tros are like, and how quickly mine can cover
the ground. It makes no odds which way you drive them, in
flight or in pursuit. We can rely on them to get us safely into
Troy, if Zeus gives Diomedes son of Tydeus yet another
victory. Come now, take the whip and reins, and when the
time comes I will dismount and do the fighting. Or let me
take care of the horses, leaving you to stand up to the man.'

'Aeneas, take the reins yourself and drive your own horses,'
Lycaon's noble son replied. 'They will pull the chariot better
with their usual driver behind them, if presently we have to
run away from Tydeus' son. They might take fright and jib,
when they missed your voice, and refuse to take us off the
field. Then the indomitable Diomedes would close in, finish
us off, and drive away our horses. So handle your own chariot
and pair, and when the man comes up I will receive him with
my spear.'

This point decided, they mounted the decorated car and
resolutely drove their fast pair in Diomedes' direction. Sthe-
nelus the noble son of Capaneus saw them, and promptly
warned Tydeides. 'My lord,' he said, 'my dearest Diomedes,
here come two stalwarts bent on fighting you – a really for-
midable pair. One is the bowman Pandarus, who calls him-
self Lycaon's son. The other is Aeneas, who can name the
lord Anchises as his father and Aphrodite as his Mother.
Quick, let us fall back in the chariot. I beg you not to storm
about in the front line any more, or you may lose your life.'

The mighty Diomedes gave him an angry look. 'Don't
talk to me of flight,' he said. 'You will not persuade me. It
is not in my nature to evade a fight or run away. I am as
strong as ever and decline to use the chariot: I will go to meet
them as I am. Pallas Athene lets me show no cowardice. As

for those two, their horses may be fast, but they will not save
both of them from us and get them home, even if one escapes.
Now listen; and do not forget what I say. If Athene in the
fullness of her wisdom lets me win and kill them both, leave
our own horses here – you can tie the reins to the rail – and
concentrate on the horses of Aeneas. Seize *them* and drive them
out of the Trojan lines into our own. For I tell you, they are
bred from the same stock as those that all-seeing Zeus gave
Tros in return for his boy Ganymedes; and *they* were the best
horses in the world. Later, Prince Anchises stole the breed by
putting mares to them without Laomedon's consent. The mares
foaled in his stables, and of the six horses that he got from them
he kept four for himself and reared them at the manger, but
gave these two to Aeneas for use in battle. If we could capture
them we should cover ourselves with glory.'

While they were talking, the other two, driving this pair of
thoroughbreds, came up to them at a gallop, and Pandarus,
the noble son of Lycaon, called across to them: 'So the stub-
born Diomedes has survived my shot and braves it out. A son
of the haughty Tydeus is not to be brought down by an arrow!
Well, I shall try him with a spear this time and see what that
will do.'

With this, he poised and hurled his long-shadowed javelin
and struck Tydeides' shield. The bronze head pierced the
shield and reached the man's cuirass. Lycaon's noble son raised
a shout of triumph over him. 'A hit,' he cried, 'clean through
the flank. You won't stand up to that for long. And what a
triumph I shall have to thank you for!'

'A miss! You never touched me,' said the powerful Dio-
medes, unperturbed. 'And what is more, I fancy that before
you two have done, one or the other is going to have a fall
and glut the stubborn god of battle with his blood.'

With that, Diomedes cast. His spear, guided by Athene,
struck Pandarus on the nose beside the eye and passed through
his white teeth. His tongue was cut off at the root by the
relentless bronze, and the point came out at the base of his
chin. He crashed from the chariot. His burnished, scintillating

armour rang out upon him, and the horses shied, thorough-
breds though they were. This was the end of Pandarus.

Aeneas leapt down from the chariot with his shield and his
long spear, fearing that the Achaeans might try to rob him of
the corpse. He now bestrode it like a lion in the pride of his
power, covering it with his spear and his round shield, deter-
mined to kill all comers and uttering his terrible war-cry.
Diomedes picked up a lump of rock. Even to lift it was a feat
beyond the strength of any two men bred to-day, but Dio-
medes handled it alone without an effort. With this he struck
Aeneas on the hip, where the thigh turns in the hip-joint – the
cup-bone as they call it. He crushed the cup-bone, and he
broke both sinews too – the skin was lacerated by the jagged
boulder. The noble Aeneas sank to his knees and supported
himself with one great hand on the ground; but the world
went black as night before his eyes. Indeed the prince would
have perished there and then, but for the quickness of his
Mother, Zeus' Daughter Aphrodite, who had conceived him
for Anchises when he was looking after the cattle. Seeing
what had happened, she threw her white arms round her
beloved son, and drew a fold of her shimmering robe across
him, to protect him from flying weapons and a fatal spear-cast
in the breast from the Danaan charioteers.

While Aphrodite was rescuing her son from the field,
Sthenelus, not forgetting the instructions he had had from
Diomedes of the loud war-cry, tied his horses' reins to the
chariot rail, left them kicking their heels some way from the
scene of turmoil, and made a dash for Aeneas' long-maned
pair. Seizing these, he drove them out of the Trojan into the
Achaean lines, where he handed them over to Deipylus, a
comrade-in-arms whom he liked and trusted more than any
man of his own age, and who had often proved his loyalty.
After telling Deipylus to drive the pair back to the hollow
ships, the gallant Sthenelus mounted his chariot, grasped the
shining reins, and drove his own powerful horses off at a
gallop in quest of Diomedes, whom he was eager to rejoin.

Diomedes himself had gone in relentless pursuit of Cyprian

Aphrodite, realizing that this was some timid goddess, and not one of those that play a dominating part in the battles of mankind, such as Athene or Enyo, Sacker of Towns. After a long chase through the crowd, the son of the great-hearted Tydeus came up with his quarry and leapt to the attack. He made a lunge at her and with his sharp spear cut her gentle hand at the base of the palm. The point, tearing the imperishable robe which the Graces had made for her, pierced the flesh where the palm joins the wrist. Out came the goddess's immortal blood, the ichor that runs in the veins of the happy gods, who eat no bread nor drink our sparkling wine and so are bloodless and are called immortals. Aphrodite gave a piercing scream and dropped her son, whom Phoebus Apollo took into his arms and wrapped in a dark blue cloud, to save him from a fatal spear-cast in the breast from the Danaan charioteers.

Diomedes of the loud war-cry raised a great shout of triumph over Aphrodite. 'Daughter of Zeus,' he cried, 'be off from this battle and leave war alone. Is it not enough for you to set your traps for feeble womenfolk? If you persist in joining in the fight, you will be taught to tremble at the very name of war.'

Cowed by his threatening attitude and distraught with pain, Aphrodite withdrew. Her lovely skin was stained with blood and the wound was smarting grievously; but Iris of the Whirlwind Feet took charge of her and led her out of the turmoil. To the left of the battlefield, Aphrodite found the turbulent War-god, seated on the ground, with his spear and his fast horses resting on a cloud. Sinking to her knees, she implored her Brother for the loan of his horses with the golden harness on their heads. 'See me safe, my dear Brother,' she said. 'Let me have your horses, to get me to Olympus where the immortals live. I am in great pain from a wound that was given me by a mortal man, the son of Tydeus, who is in a mood now to fight with Father Zeus himself.'

Ares lent her the horses with the golden harness, and Aphrodite mounted the chariot in great distress. Iris got in beside her, took the reins in her hands and flicked the horses with the whip to make them start. The willing pair flew off; and before long they reached the steep heights of Olympus, where the gods have their home. There, fleet Iris of the Whirlwind Feet brought the horses to a halt, unyoked them from the car, and threw ambrosial fodder down beside them, while lovely Aphrodite went to her Mother Dione and sank down at her knees. Dione took her Daughter in her arms and spoke to her fondly as she stroked her with her hand. 'Dear Child!' she said. 'Which of the Heavenly Ones has hurt you now like this, out of mere spite, as though you were a branded felon?'

Laughter-loving Aphrodite told her tale. 'That bully Diomedes son of Tydeus wounded me because I was rescuing my own beloved son Aeneas, my favourite, from the battlefield. This war has ceased to be a struggle between Trojans and Achaeans: the Danaans are fighting now against the gods themselves.'

To this the gracious goddess Dione replied: 'Endure, my Child, and face your troubles gallantly. Many of us that live here on Olympus have suffered at the hands of men, in our attempts to injure one another. Ares, for one, had to suffer when Otus and the mighty Ephialtes, the children of Aloeus, threw him into chains. He spent thirteen months trussed up in a bronze jar. And that would have been the end of Ares and his appetite for war, if the beautiful Eriboea, the young giants' step-mother, had not told Hermes what they had done. Ares' strength was on the point of giving out when Hermes spirited him away – the fetters nearly proved too much for him. Here suffered too, when the powerful Heracles, Amphitryon's son, struck her with a three-barbed arrow in the right breast – she was in agony. And the monstrous Hades himself was wounded by an arrow, and had to bear it like the rest, when that same man, the son of aegis-bearing Zeus, shot him at the Gate of Hell among the dead, and left him to his anguish. Sick at heart and in excruciating pain, Hades found his way to high Olympus and the Palace of Zeus. The arrow had driven into his shoulder muscles and was draining his strength. However, Paeeon the Healer spread soothing ointments on the wound and cured him; for after all he was not made of mortal stuff. But think of the audacity, think of the savagery of the man, who cared so little what wickedness he set his hand to that he plagued the very gods of Olympus with his bow! As for your trouble, it was Athene of the Flashing Eyes who told the man to chase you. But Diomedes is a fool. He does not know how short life is for the man who fights against immortals. For him, there is no home-coming from war and its horrors, no little children gathering at his knees to call him father. So let Tydeides, strong man as he is, take care that no one more formidable than you comes out to fight him, or one day Aegialea, the wise daughter of Adrestus and gallant wife of this horse-taming Diomedes, will hear that she has lost her husband, the best of the Achaeans, and wake her household from their sleep with her lamentations.'

As she spoke, Dione wiped the ichor from her Daughter's hand with both her own. The wound healed, and the sting was taken out of the pain.

Athene and Here had missed nothing of this scene, and they seized the occasion to repay Zeus for his sarcasm. The bright-eyed goddess Athene undertook the task. 'Father Zeus,' she said, 'I hope you will not take it amiss when I suggest that your Cyprian Daughter must have been at work again, luring Achaean women into the arms of the Trojans whom she loves so dearly. One of these ladies evidently wears a golden brooch, and Aphrodite scratched her dainty hand on it when she was fondling her.'

This only drew a smile from the Father of men and gods. But he called Golden Aphrodite to his side and said: 'Fighting, my child, is not for you. *You* are in charge of wedlock and the tender passions. We will leave the enterprising War-god and Athene to look after military affairs.'

While this talk was going on in heaven, Diomedes of the loud war-cry flung himself once more at Aeneas. He knew that Apollo himself had taken him under his protection, but he cared nothing even for that great god, and persisted in his

efforts to kill Aeneas and spoil him of his splendid armour.
Three times he leapt at him in his murderous fury, and thrice
Apollo thrust his bright shield back. But when he charged
like a demon for the fourth time, the Archer-god checked him
with a terrible shout: 'Think, Tydeides, and give way! Do
not aspire to be the equal of the gods. The immortals are not
made of the same stuff as men that walk on the ground.'

When he heard this Tydeides fell back a little to avoid the
wrath of the Archer-god; and Apollo removed Aeneas from
the battlefield to the holy citadel of Pergamus where his
temple stood. There, in the spacious sanctuary, Leto and Arte-
mis the Archeress not only healed him but made him more
splendid than ever.

Meanwhile Apollo of the Silver Bow created a phantom
which looked exactly like Aeneas and was armed as he was.
Round this phantom, the Trojans and the brave Achaeans
hacked at each other's leather shields – the great round bucklers
or the light targets that they held across their breasts. But now
Phoebus Apollo intervened with an appeal to the tempestuous
War-god. 'Ares,' he cried, 'murderous Ares, Butcher of Men
and Sacker of Towns; I call on you to take a hand and drive
this man Tydeides from the field. He is in a mood to fight
Father Zeus himself. He began by closing with Aphrodite
and wounding her in the wrist, and then he flung himself,
like a demon, at me.'

With that, Apollo withdrew and sat down on the heights of
Pergamus, while Ares the Destroyer disguised himself as
Acamas, the fiery Thracian captain, and slipped in among the
Trojans to put new heart in them. He began by exhorting the
royal sons of Priam, crying: 'Princes of the royal blood, how
much longer are you going to let your men be slaughtered
by the Achaeans? Till they are storming at the city gates?
See where Aeneas, son of the proud Anchises, lies – a man
whom we looked up to as we do to my lord Hector. Come
on now, and rescue our gallant comrade from this seething
mass.'

With such words as these he roused the fighting spirit in

one and all. Sarpedon too joined in, and rebuked the admirable Hector roundly. 'Hector,' he said, 'where is the spirit you used to show? You talked of holding the city without troops or allies, single-handed but for your brothers and your sisters' husbands. And what has become of *them*? I cannot see a single one. They are cowering like hounds before a lion, while we do the fighting, though we came in only as your allies. And it was a long, long journey that *I* made to reinforce you. It's a far cry from Lycia and the eddying Xanthus, where I left my dear wife and my baby son, and great possessions too, which many a poor neighbour is itching to get hold of. Nevertheless, I make my Lycians fight, and am not slow myself to meet my man in battle, though I own nothing here, livestock or goods, that the Achaeans could carry off. Meanwhile you stay there and do not even tell your men to make a stand and fight for their womenfolk. Take care that you and they do not get caught like fish in the meshes of a dragnet and fall an easy prey to the enemy, who may be sacking your fine city any day. You should be thinking of all this, day and night, and begging the leaders of your glorious allies to make a determined stand. That should be your answer to the hard things that are said about you.'

Hector was stung by Sarpedon's rebuke. He jumped down from his chariot at once in all his armour, and swinging a pair of sharp spears in his hand went everywhere among his men, driving them on to fight and rousing their martial spirit. As a result, the Trojans turned about and faced the Achaeans. But these too held their ground. They closed their ranks and were by no means put to flight. Indeed, as the infantry came to grips again and the chariots wheeled to withdraw, the dust that the horses' hooves kicked up among them into the copper sky settled down on the Achaeans and whitened them, like chaff-heaps whitened by the falling dust when men are winnowing and the chaff is blown across the sacred threshing-floor by the wind that auburn-haired Demeter sends to separate it from the grain. So steadily did the Achaeans meet the shock.

But now the fierce War-god, ranging everywhere, threw a veil of darkness over the battle to help the Trojans. He was carrying out the orders he had had from Phoebus Apollo of the Golden Sword. Phoebus had told him to put fresh heart into the Trojans, when he saw Pallas Athene, who was on the Danaans' side, withdraw. Moreover, Phoebus himself made Aeneas leave the rich shrine where he had taken sanctuary, and filled the great captain with fresh valour. So Aeneas took his place once more among his comrades, who were happy to find him still alive and see him come back sound of limb and in good heart. Not that they questioned him at all: they were kept far too busy by Apollo of the Silver Bow, Ares Killer of Men, and Strife in her unquenchable fury.

The Danaans, on their side, were spurred on to fight by the two Aiantes, with Odysseus and Diomedes. They needed little encouragement. No onslaught of the Trojans shook them, however hard it was pressed home. They stood their ground like the motionless clouds with which the Son of Cronos caps the mountains in calm weather, when angry Boreas and all his boisterous friends are sleeping and there are no blustering winds to send the dark clouds flying. Thus the Danaans held firm against the Trojans and did not flinch. Agamemnon strode through the ranks and gave them every exhortation. 'My friends,' he said, 'be men. Have a stout heart, and in the field fear nothing but dishonour in each other's eyes. When soldiers fear disgrace, then more are saved than killed. Neither honour nor salvation is to be found in flight.'

As he finished, he made a swift cast with a javelin and struck a Trojan officer in Prince Aeneas' company called Deicoön son of Pergasus, whose habitual gallantry in the front line had made the Trojans honour him like one of Priam's sons. King Agamemnon hit him on the shield, which failed to keep the weapon off. The bronze point pierced it and pressed on through the belt into his abdomen. He fell with a thud, and his armour rang upon him.

Aeneas replied by killing two champions on the Danaan side, the sons of Diocles, Crethon and Orsilochus, whose father lived in the fine town of Phere. Diocles was a man of substance, tracing his descent from the god of the River Alpheus, which flows as a broad stream through Pylian territory. The first Orsilochus, a powerful chieftain, was a son of this River. Then came the great-hearted Diocles, who in his turn had these twin sons, Crethon and Orsilochus. He trained them in all arms, and when they were of age they embarked with the Argives in their black ships for Troy the land of horses to seek satisfaction for the Atreidae, Agamemnon and Menelaus. But there the adventure ended – in their death. As a pair of lions are brought up by their mother in the mountain jungle to plunder the farmers' yards and prey on the cattle and the sturdy sheep till they themselves fall victims to the bronze of man, the pair met their conqueror and were felled, like tall pine-trees, by the hands of Aeneas.

The gallant Menelaus was filled with pity at their fate, and dashed up through the front rank in his glittering bronze equipment, brandishing his spear. He was emboldened by Ares, who wished for nothing better than to see him fall to Aeneas. But Antilochus, the great King Nestor's son, saw what Menelaus was doing and followed him into the front line, fearing that some calamity might overtake their leader and bring the whole expedition to grief. Menelaus and Aeneas were already offering fight and aiming their sharp spears at one another as Antilochus came up to his commander and took his place beside him; and when Aeneas saw the two men making this united stand, he felt unable to face them, for all the daring he had shown before. So Menelaus and Antilochus dragged back their dead into the Achaean lines, and after handing over the ill-starred couple to their men, went back and fought in the front rank once more.

Their next victim was the redoubtable Pylaemenes, commander of the gallant Paphlagonian infantry. He was standing still when the great spearman Menelaus son of Atreus struck him with a javelin, which landed on his collar bone. Meanwhile Antilochus was dealing with his squire and charioteer, Mydon the brave son of Atymnius, who was wheeling his powerful horses round. He hit him full on the elbow with a lump of rock, and the reins, white with their ivory trappings, dropped from his hands and fell down in the dust. Antilochus dashed in and drove his sword into the man's temple. With a gasp he fell headlong from the well-made chariot, and buried his head and shoulders in the dust. For a little while he stuck there, for the sand happened to be deep. Then his horses kicked him down and laid him flat on the ground. Antilochus gave them a touch of the whip and sent them off into the Achaean lines.

Across the ranks, Hector had observed these two and now made towards them with a great cry. He was supported by a powerful following of Trojans, who were led on by Ares himself and the goddess Enyo, with shameless Panic in her train. Ares brandished in his hand a spear of monstrous size, and strode, now in front of Hector, now behind him.

When Diomedes of the loud war-cry saw Ares he was filled with dismay, like the improvident traveller who, after a long journey over the plain, finds his way barred by the estuary of a fast-flowing river, takes one look at the seething foam, and turns back in his tracks. Thus Tydeides fell back, but not without warning his men. 'My friends,' he said, 'no wonder we have been impressed by my lord Hector's spearmanship and daring: he always has a god with him to save his skin. See, there is Ares with him now, disguised as a man. Retreat; but keep your faces to the enemy. We must not offer battle to the gods.'

No sooner had he given this order than the Trojans were on them and Hector killed two men, Menesthes and Anchialus, both veterans, who were riding in one chariot. The great Telamonian Aias was filled with pity when he saw them fall. Taking his stand close by them, he let fly with a glittering javelin and struck Amphius son of Selagus, a rich man, who lived in Paesus and owned many cornfields. But Destiny had taken him away from them to serve as an ally to Priam and his sons. Telamonian Aias struck him on the belt; the long spear stuck in his abdomen, and he fell with a crash. But when illustrious Aias ran up to strip him of his arms, the Trojans met him with a volley of glittering javelins, many of which he took on his shield. Nevertheless, he planted his foot on the corpse and dragged his bronze spear out. But he could not get the man's own arms and armour off his back – the javelins were too much for him. Moreover he was afraid of being surrounded and overpowered by the eager Trojans, who faced him in formidable numbers with their spears at the ready. So they managed to drive him off. Big, sturdy and redoubtable though he was, Aias was shaken, and retreated.

Such was the struggle where the fight was hottest. Meanwhile Tlepolemus, the tall and handsome son of Heracles, was brought by the stern hand of Fate into conflict with the godlike Sarpedon. These two, a son and a grandson of Zeus the Cloud-compeller, made at one another; and when they had come within range, Tlepolemus challenged his man: 'Sarpedon, Counsellor of the Lycians, what makes you come here and then hide yourself? You do not know what a battle is. They are wrong when they call you son of aegis-bearing Zeus: you are nothing like the sons he used to have. How different, by all accounts, from the mighty Heracles, my all-daring, lion-hearted father, who once came here for Laomedon's mares, with only six ships and a smaller force than ours, yet sacked Ilium and widowed its streets. Now *you* are a coward and your army is wasting away. You may be a strong man yourself and you have come all the way from Lycia to bolster up the Trojans. But much good you'll do them! You are going to fall to me and pass through the Gates of Hades.'

'Tlepolemus,' replied Sarpedon, leader of the Lycians, 'you know well enough that Heracles would never have sacked holy Ilium but for the stupidity of one man, the haughty Laomedon, who repaid his services with insults and refused to let him have the mares he had come so far to get. As for you, I say that here and now you are going to meet your doom and die at my hands. Conquered by my spear, you will yield your life to Hades of the Fabled Horse, and the glory to me.'

By way of reply to Sarpedon, the other raised his ashen shaft, and the long javelins leapt from both men's hands at one and the same time. Sarpedon struck Tlepolemus in the middle of the neck. The deadly spear-point passed right through, and the nether darkness came down on his eyes. At the same moment Tlepolemus' long spear hit Sarpedon in the left thigh. The point pressed furiously on and grazed the bone; but for a while his Father saved him from destruction.

The heroic Sarpedon was carried from the fight by his loyal followers. The great spear weighed him down as it was dragged along, for in their haste not one of them had noticed it or thought of pulling the ashen shaft from his thigh so that he could use his legs. They had their work cut out to see him safe.

On his side, Tlepolemus was removed from the field by the bronze-clad Achaeans. The excellent Odysseus had observed his fall, but was not to be dismayed. Indeed, it lashed him into fury, though he was uncertain what to do and for a moment debated whether he should start in pursuit of the son of Zeus the Thunderer or do further execution among the Lycians. But Fate did not intend the stalwart son of Zeus to fall to the sharp bronze of the brave Odysseus, and so Athene turned his fury on the Lycian ranks. Then and there he killed Coeranus, Alastor and Chromius, Alcander and Halius, Noemon and Prytanis. Indeed, the noble Odysseus would have gone on to kill yet more of the Lycians, but for the quick eye of Hector of the glittering helmet, who, when he saw what was afoot, hastened to the forefront in his armour of resplendent bronze, striking terror into the Danaans. His arrival was most welcome to Sarpedon son of Zeus, who appealed to him in his distress: 'Prince Hector, rescue me and do not leave me lying here at the mercy of the Danaans. Then I shall be content to die in your city if I must. For it is clear that I am not meant to see my country and my home again, and to bring happiness to my wife and little son.'

Hector of the bright helmet gave him no answer, but darted by. He made it his first business to thrust the Argives back and kill as many of them as he could. But the godlike Sarpedon was removed by his trusty men and laid under a fine oak-tree sacred to aegis-bearing Zeus, where the stalwart Pelagon, his own squire, extracted the ashen spear from his thigh. A mist descended on Sarpedon's eyes and he fainted. But presently he came to. The North Wind played about him and revived him from his swoon.

Meanwhile the Argives, faced by Ares and Hector in his arms of bronze, neither fled to their black ships nor counter-attacked, but fell back steadily, as they became aware of Ares' presence on the Trojan side. And who were the first and last of them to fall to Hector son of Priam and to Brazen Ares? Prince Teuthras was the first; then Orestes, tamer of horses; Trechus, an Aetolian spearman; Oenomaus; Oenops' son Helenus; and Oresbius of the flashing belt, who lived in Hyle on the shores of Lake Cephisis, where he looked after his rich estate, with other Boeotians for neighbours in a fertile countryside.

When the white-armed goddess Here saw them slaughter-ing Argives right and left, she could not conceal her feelings from Athene. 'Unsleeping Child of aegis-bearing Zeus,' she said, 'this is disastrous. If we let the maniac Ares run amuck like this, what of the promise that we made to Menelaus when we told him he would bring down the walls of Troy before he left? Come; it is time for you and me to throw ourselves into the battle.'

Athene of the Flashing Eyes was nothing loath. So Here, Queen of Heaven and Daughter of mighty Cronos, went off to put the golden harness on her horses, while Hebe deftly got her chariot ready by fixing the two bronze wheels, each with eight spokes, on the ends of the iron axle-tree. The felloes of these wheels are made of imperishable gold, with bronze tyres fitted on the rims – a wonderful piece of work – while the naves that rotate on each axle are of silver. The car itself has a platform of gold and silver straps tightly interlaced, with a double railing round it, and a silver shaft running out from the front. To the end of this pole, Hebe tied the beautiful

golden yoke and attached the fine gold breast-straps. And
Here, all agog for the hurly-burly of war, led her fast horses
under the yoke.

Meanwhile, on her Father's threshold, Athene Daughter of
aegis-bearing Zeus shed her soft embroidered robe, which
she had made with her own hands, put on a tunic in its place,
and equipped herself for the lamentable work of war with the
arms of Zeus the Cloud-compeller. She threw round her
shoulders the formidable tasselled aegis, which is beset at
every point with Fear, and carries Strife and Force and the
cold nightmare of Pursuit within it, and also bears the ghastly
image of a Gorgon's head, the grim and redoubtable emblem
of aegis-bearing Zeus. On her head she put her golden helmet,
with its four plates and double crest, adorned with fighting
men of a hundred towns. Then she stepped into the flaming
chariot, gripping the huge long spear with which she breaks
the noble warriors' ranks when she, the almighty Father's
Child, is roused to anger.

Here lost no time. She flicked the horses with her whip, and
the Gates of Heaven thundered open for them of their own
accord. They are kept by the Hours, the Wardens of the
broad sky and of Olympus, whose task it is to close the
entrance or to roll away the heavy cloud. Through these
gates the goddesses drove their patient steeds.

They found the Son of Cronos sitting aloof from the other
gods on the topmost of Olympus' many peaks. The white-
armed goddess Here brought her pair to a halt and had a
word with Zeus the Son of Cronos, the Lord Supreme.
'Father Zeus,' she said, 'are you not moved to indignation by
the violence of Ares and the sight of all these gallant Achaeans
whom he has slaughtered without rhyme or reason? I cannot
bear to watch. But your Cyprian Daughter and Apollo of the
Silver Bow appear to like it. In fact it suits them to have let
loose this savage who acknowledges no law. Father Zeus,
will you be angry with me if I give him a sound thrashing and
chase him from the field?'

'No; get to work!' said the Gatherer of the Clouds. 'And let our warrior Athene deal with him. No one is a better hand at twisting Ares' tail.'

The white-armed goddess Here had no fault to find with this. She flicked her horses with the whip, and the willing pair flew off on a course midway between the earth and starry sky. And since these horses of the gods with their high-thundering hooves cover at one bound the distance that a man can see into the haze as he looks out from a watchtower over the wine-dark sea, they soon reached Troy and its pair of noble rivers. There, at the watersmeet of Simoïs and Scamander, the white-armed goddess Here stopped her horses and released them from the yoke. She hid them in a mist, and Simoïs made ambrosia spring up for them to eat. Then the two goddesses set out on foot, strutting like pigeons in their eagerness to bring help to the Argive arms.

They made for that part of the field where the pick of the Achaeans had rallied round the great Diomedes tamer of horses and were standing at bay like flesh-eating lions, or like wild boars, who can be formidable too. There the white-armed goddess Here stopped and called aloud, mimicking the noble Stentor of the brazen voice, who could raise a shout like that of fifty men together. 'For shame, Argives! Contemptible creatures, splendid to look at! In the days when the great Achilles came out and fought, the Trojans never showed themselves in front of the Dardanian Gates: they were too fearful of his heavy spear. But now they are fighting far from the town and by your very ships.'

Thus she emboldened them and put fresh heart into every man. Meanwhile Athene of the Flashing Eyes had made straight for Diomedes son of Tydeus. She found the prince with his chariot and horses, airing the wound that Pandarus had given him with his arrow. Under the broad shoulder-strap of his round shield the sweat was irking him. Troubled by this and weakened in the arm, he had lifted up the strap and was wiping the dark blood away. The goddess laid her hand on his horses' yoke. 'Tydeus had a son,' she said, 'but how unlike himself! Tydeus was a little man, but what a fighter! He even fought when I had forbidden it and did not want him to show off – even when he was sent alone to Thebes to parley with a crowd of Cadmeians. I told him then to sit and eat his dinner quietly in the palace. And what must he do but challenge the young Cadmeians, like the lion-hearted man he was, and beat them all easily, with the help he had from me? How different from you! I stand beside you; I shield you from harm; and I tell you to fight the Trojans with my blessing. But you are exhausted and cannot lift a finger after all you have done! Or are you paralysed by fear? If that is the trouble, I no longer take you for a son of Tydeus and a grandson of the doughty Oeneus.'

'I recognize you, goddess,' said the stalwart Diomedes. 'You are the Daughter of aegis-bearing Zeus, and I can speak to you without reserve. I am not unmanned, either by fear or exhaustion. All I am doing is to keep in mind the limits you yourself imposed on me. You told me not to fight against the blessed gods, except for Aphrodite Daughter of Zeus. If *she* came into the fight you said I could wound her with my spear. But it is Ares who is carrying all before him. When I saw that, I fell back here and told the rest to rally round me.'

'My dearest Diomedes, true son of Tydeus!' cried Athene of the Flashing Eyes. 'I understand; but with me at your back, you need have no fear, either of Ares or of any other god. Quick now and at him! Drive up, and do not stop to think "This is the redoubtable War-god", but let him have it at short range. Look at the maniac over there! Do you know that only the other day that pestilential, double-dealing villain gave Here and myself his word to fight against the Trojans and help the Argives? And now he has forgotten all he said and is fighting on the Trojan side.'

As she spoke, she reached out, dragged Sthenelus back, and hustled him out of the chariot – he was only too glad to leap down. The eager goddess took his place in the car beside the noble Diomedes, and the beech-wood axle groaned aloud at the weight it had to carry, a formidable goddess and a mighty man of arms. Pallas Athene seized the reins and whip, and drove the horses straight off in the direction of Ares.

At the moment, Ares was despoiling the gigantic Periphas, the noble son of Ochesius and the best man in the Aetolian force. Spattered with blood, he was busy stripping the armour from his victim; and to conceal her approach from the redoubtable god, Athene had put a cap of invisibility on her head. But directly the Butcher Ares saw the gallant son of Tydeus, he left Periphas to lie where he had met his death, and made straight for Diomedes tamer of horses. When the two had come to close quarters, Ares began the fight with what he meant to be a mortal blow. He thrust at Diomedes with his bronze spear over the yoke and the horses' reins. But Athene of the Flashing Eyes, catching the shaft in her hand, pushed it up above the chariot, where it spent its force in the air. Diomedes of the loud war-cry then brought his spear into play, and Pallas Athene drove it home against the lower part of Ares' belly, where he wore an apron round his middle. There the blow landed, wounding the god and tearing his fair flesh. Diomedes drew out his spear, and Brazen Ares let forth a yell as loud as the war-cry of nine thousand or ten thousand battling men. The Achaeans and Trojans quaked with terror at that appalling cry from the god who never had his fill of war. Then, like the column of black air that issues from the clouds when a tornado springs up after heat, Diomedes son of Tydeus saw the Brazen War-god whirl up to heaven in a welter of haze.

Ares travelled rapidly, and directly he reached the gods' home on high Olympus he sat down by Zeus the Son of Cronos in a sorry frame of mind. He showed Zeus the immortal blood pouring from his wound, and told his story in a doleful voice. 'Father Zeus,' he said, 'does the sight of all this violence not stir your indignation? See what we gods have to suffer at each other's hands whenever it occurs to us to do mankind a favour. The fault is yours. We are all at loggerheads with you for having cursed the world with that crazy Daughter of yours, who is always up to some devilment or other. The rest of us, including every god on Olympus, bow to your will and stand in awe of you. But when it comes to her, you neither say nor do a thing to check the creature: you let her have her head, because she is a Child of your own, who was born for mischief. See how she has encouraged Tydeus' son, the insolent Diomedes, to run amuck among the immortal gods. He began by charging Aphrodite and cutting her wrist; and then he flung himself like a demon at *me*. Happily I am quick enough on my feet to have escaped. Otherwise I should have had a long and painful time there among the grisly dead, or should have come away crippled for life by his blows.'

Zeus the Cloud-gatherer gave Ares a black look. 'You turncoat,' he said, 'don't come to me and whine. There is nothing you enjoy so much as quarrelling and fighting; which is why I hate you more than any god on Olympus. Your Mother Here too has a headstrong and ungovernable temper – I have always found it hard to control her by word of mouth alone. I suspect it was she that started this business and got you into trouble. However, I do not intend to let you suffer any longer, since you are my own flesh and blood and your Mother is my Wife. But if any other god had fathered such a pernicious brat, you would long since have found yourself in a deeper hole than the Sons of Uranus.'

Thereupon, Zeus told Paeeon to heal him. Paeeon spread soothing ointment on the wound and healed it, for Ares was not made of mortal stuff. Indeed, he made the fierce War-god well in no more time than the busy fig-juice takes to thicken milk and curdle the white liquid as one stirs. Hebe bathed him then, and gave him lovely clothing to put on; and he sat down by Zeus the Son of Cronos with all his former self-esteem.

Meanwhile the two goddesses, Here of Argos and Alalco-menean Athene, came back to the palace of almighty Zeus. They had checked the Butcher in his murderous career.

VI

HECTOR AND ANDROMACHE

So the Trojans and Achaeans were left to carry on the grim struggle alone, and the battle kept swaying to and fro across the plain, with many a volley and counter-volley of bronze-headed spears, midway between Simoïs and the streams of Xanthus.

Telamonian Aias, bulwark of the Achaeans, was the first to break a Trojan company and give his friends new hope, when he struck the best fighter that the Thracians had, Acamas, the tall and splendid son of Eussorus. Aias let fly with his spear and hit this man on the ridge of his plumed helmet. The bronze point landed in his forehead, piercing the bone, and night came down on his eyes.

Next, Diomedes of the loud war-cry killed Axylus son of Teuthranus, who came from the pleasant town of Arisbe. He was a wealthy man, who lived well in his house by the roadside, and had made himself popular by entertaining all comers. But none of his friends came forward now to tackle the enemy for him and save him from a dreadful end. Diomedes killed the pair of them, him and his squire Calesius, who was serving as his charioteer, and they both went down to the world below.

Euryalus killed Dresus and Opheltius, and then sped after Aesepus and Pedasus, whom the Water-nymph Abarbarea had borne to the peerless Bucolion. Bucolion was a son of the haughty Laomedon, the first he had, the offspring of a secret love. He was shepherding his flocks when he met the Nymph and lay in her loving arms. She conceived and bore twin boys to him. It was these that fell now to Euryalus son of Mecisteus, who cut them off in their gallantry and strength, and stripped the armour from their shoulders.

Astyalus fell to the steadfast Polypoetes; Pidytes of Percote to the bronze spear of Odysseus; and the noble Aretaon to Teucer. Antilochus son of Nestor killed Ablerus with a glittering lance, and Agamemnon King of Men slew Elatus, who lived by the lovely waters of Satnioïs, in the hill town of Pedasus. The noble Leitus killed Phylacus, who had taken to his heels; and Eurypylus dispatched Melanthius.

Meanwhile Menelaus of the loud war-cry had captured Adrestus alive. This man's horses, bolting across the plain, had crashed into a tamarisk branch, snapped the shaft where it was fixed to the curved body of the chariot, and galloped off on their own towards the city, joining the rest in a wild stampede. Their master was tumbled out of the car, beside the wheel, flat on his face in the dust; and he soon had Menelaus son of Atreus standing over him with a long-shadowed spear in his hand. Adrestus threw his arms round Menelaus' knees and prayed to him: 'My lord Atreides, take me alive, and you shall have an ample ransom. My father is rich and has plenty of treasure in his house, bronze and gold and wrought iron. He would pay you a princely ransom if he heard that I had been taken alive to the Achaean ships.'

Thus he endeavoured to soften his captor's heart. And indeed Menelaus was just about to tell his squire to take him off to the Achaean ships, when Agamemnon came running up to remonstrate with his brother. 'My dear Menelaus,' he said, 'why are you so chary of taking men's lives? Did the Trojans treat you as handsomely as that when they stayed in your house? No; we are not going to leave a single one of them alive, down to the babies in their mothers' wombs – not even they must live. The whole people must be wiped out of existence, and none be left to think of them and shed a tear.'

The justice of this made Menelaus change his mind. He thrust Adrestus from him with his hand, and King Agamemnon struck him in the flank. The man collapsed; and Agamemnon put his foot on his chest and withdrew his ashen spear from the wound.

·Nestor then called to the Argives in a loud voice: 'Friends, Danaans, fellow soldiers; no looting now! No lingering behind to get back to the ships with the biggest share! Let us kill men. Afterwards, at your leisure, you can strip the corpses on the field.'

This put new heart and daring into every man; and it looked as though the Trojans, defeated and disheartened, would be thrust back into Ilium by the victorious Achaeans. But at this juncture, Priam's son Helenus, the best augur in Troy, sought out Aeneas and Hector and appealed to them. 'You two,' he said, 'are in supreme command. We put you there because you have never failed us in the council-chamber or in battle. Now prove us right. Make a stand here. Visit every part of the field yourselves, and check the troops before they reach the gates and in their panic fall into their women's arms and make the enemy happy men. When you have rallied every company, we will stand our ground and fight the Danaans here, exhausted as we are – we have no choice in the matter. Meanwhile, Hector, go into the city and speak to our mother. Tell her to collect the older women at the temple of Bright-eyed Athene on the Acropolis and unlock the doors of the shrine. Let her choose a robe from her palace, the loveliest and biggest she can find and the one she values most herself, and lay it on the Lady Athene's knees. And let her promise her to sacrifice in her temple a dozen yearling heifers untouched by the goad, if only she will have pity on the town and on the Trojans' wives and little children, and keep the savage spearman Diomedes, the mighty panic-maker, clear of holy Ilium. For he seems to me to have become our most redoubtable foe. We never were so terrified even of Achilles, prince of fighters though he was, and said to be a goddess' son. The fact is that Diomedes there has run amuck, and not a man can hold him.'

Hector acted promptly on his brother's advice. He leapt down from his chariot in all his armour, and swinging a pair of sharp spears in his hand went everywhere among his men, urging them to stand and rousing their fighting spirit. As a result, the Trojans turned about and faced the Achaeans, who now gave ground, and killed no more of the enemy. Indeed the Trojans rallied to such effect that the Argives thought some god must have come down from the starry sky to help them. And there was Hector crying aloud to his troops: 'Gallant Trojans; glorious allies; be men, my friends, and fight with the courage you have always shown, while I go into Ilium and tell our Elders and our wives to propitiate the gods and promise them a sacrifice.'

With this, Hector of the flashing helmet went off towards the town. As he walked, the dark leather rim of his bossed shield tapped him above and below, on the ankles and on the back of the neck.

Glaucus son of Hippolochus and Diomedes son of Tydeus now approached one another in the space between the two armies and offered battle. When they had come within range, Diomedes of the loud war-cry challenged the other. 'Whom have we here?' he asked. 'Give me your name, my good sir, if indeed you are a man. For I have never seen you till this moment in the field of honour. Yet in facing the long-shadowed spear in my hand you have shown far greater daring than any of your friends – the fathers of men who meet me in my fury are liable to weep. But if you are one of the immortals come down from the sky, I am not the man to fight against the gods of Heaven. Why, not even the powerful Lycurgus, Dryas' son, survived his quarrel with the gods of Heaven for very long. He chased the Nurses of the frenzied Dionysus through the holy hills of Nysa, and the sacred implements dropped to the ground from the hands of one and all, as the murderous Lycurgus struck them down with his ox-goad. Dionysus fled and found sanctuary under the salt sea waves, where Thetis took him to her bosom, trembling and completely cowed by the man's chastisement. But the immortals, easy livers as they are, resented what he had done – the Son of Cronos struck him blind. And he did not live long after that, with all the deathless gods against him. So you must not count on me if it comes to fighting with the Blessed Ones.

But if you are one of us mortals who plough the earth for food, come on, and you will meet your doom the sooner.'

'My gallant lord, Tydeides,' the noble son of Hippolochus replied, 'what does my lineage matter to you? Men in their generations are like the leaves of the trees. The wind blows and one year's leaves are scattered on the ground; but the trees burst into bud and put on fresh ones when the spring comes round. In the same way one generation flourishes and another nears its end. But if you wish to hear about my family, I will tell you the tale – most people know it already. There is a place called Ephyre in a corner of Argos where the horses graze. Here lived a man called Sisyphus, as cunning a rogue as ever was – Aeolus was his father's name. Sisyphus had a son called Glaucus; and Glaucus in his turn was father of the incomparable Bellerophon. It was Bellerophon's misfortune to be subject to King Proetus, a far more powerful nobleman than himself, who fell foul of him and expelled him from the Argive state. Queen Anteia, Proetus' wife, had fallen in love with the handsome youth, who was endowed with every manly grace, and begged him to satisfy her passion in secret. But Bellerophon was a man of sound principles and refused. So Anteia went to King Proetus with a lying tale. "Proetus," she said, "Bellerophon has tried to ravish me. Kill him, or die yourself." The King was enraged when he heard this infamous tale. He stopped short of putting Bellerophon to death – it was a thing he dared not do – but he packed him off to Lycia with sinister credentials from himself. He gave him a folded tablet on which he had traced a number of devices with a deadly meaning, and told him to hand this to his father-in-law, the Lycian king, and thus ensure his own death. Bellerophon's journey was forwarded by the gods in their own perfect way; and when he reached Lycia and the River Xanthus he was welcomed as an honoured guest by the king of those broad dominions. His host entertained him for nine days and slaughtered nine oxen for him. But the tenth day came, and then, in the first rosy light of Dawn, he examined him and asked to see what credentials he had brought him from his son-in-law Proetus.

'When he had deciphered the fatal message from his son-in-law, the King's first step was to order Bellerophon to kill the monstrous Chimaera, a creature whom the gods had foisted on mankind. She had a lion's head, a serpent's tail, and the body of a goat; and her breath came out in terrible blasts of burning flame. But Bellerophon let himself be guided by the gods, and succeeded in killing her. His second mission was to fight the famous Solymi – he spoke of that as the most terrific battle he had ever fought. And by way of a third task, he killed the Amazons who go to war like men. But the King had thought of something fresh, and set a cunning trap to catch him on his return from this adventure. He picked out the best men in all Lycia and stationed them in ambush. Not one of them came home – the incomparable Bellerophon killed them all. In the end the King realized that he was a true son of the gods. He pressed him to stay in Lycia, offered him his daughter's hand, and gave him half his kingdom, while the Lycians also made him the grant of a splendid estate with plenty of vineyards and cornfields for his private use.

'The princess bore three children to the doughty Bellerophon, Isander, Hippolochus, and Laodameia, who slept with Zeus the Counsellor and became the mother of Prince Sarpedon of the bronze mail. But the time came when Bellerophon incurred the enmity of all the gods, and wandered off in solitude across the Aleian Plain, eating his heart out and avoiding all contact with men. Ares, the insatiable War-god, had killed his son Isander in battle with the famous Solymi; and Artemis of the Golden Reins had slain Laodameia in anger. There remained Hippolochus – and I am his son. He sent me to Troy; and he used often to say to me, "Let your motto be *I lead*. Strive to be best. Your forefathers were the best men in Ephyre and Lycia. Never disgrace them." Such is my pedigree; that is the blood I claim as mine.'

Glaucus' tale delighted Diomedes of the loud war-cry. He

stuck his spear into the fruitful earth, and now addressed the Lycian prince in cordial terms. 'Surely,' he said, 'your family and mine are linked by old-established ties. Oeneus, my noble grandfather, once entertained the peerless Bellerophon in his palace and kept him there for twenty days, after which they gave each other the splendid gifts that host and guest exchange. Oeneus gave his friend a belt stained with a bright purple dye; and Bellerophon gave Oeneus a gold two-handled cup, which I left in my house when I set out. As for my father Tydeus, I don't remember him, as I was only a baby when he joined the Achaean expedition that came to grief at Thebes. But I have said enough to show that in me you will now have a good friend in the heart of Argos, and I shall have you in Lycia, if ever I visit that country. So let us avoid each other's spears, even in the mêlée, since there are plenty of the Trojans and their famous allies for me to kill, if I have the luck and speed to catch them, and plenty of Achaeans for you to slaughter, if you can. And let us exchange our armour, so that everyone may know that our grandfathers' friendship has made friends of us.'

With no more said, they leapt from their chariots, shook hands and pledged each other. But Zeus the Son of Cronos must have robbed Glaucus of his wits, for he exchanged with Diomedes golden armour for bronze, a hundred oxen's worth for the value of nine.

Meanwhile Hector had reached the oak-tree at the Scaean Gate and was at once besieged by Trojan wives and daughters, asking about their sons and brothers, their husbands and their friends. Recommending them all to pray to the gods, he dismissed them one after the other – but not before many of them had heard grievous news. Then he made his way to Priam's palace. This magnificent house was fronted with marble colonnades, and in the main building behind there were fifty apartments of polished stone, adjoining each other, where Priam's sons slept with their wives. His daughters had separate quarters, on the other side of the courtyard, where twelve adjoining bedrooms had been built for them, of

polished stone and well roofed in. Priam's sons-in-law slept
with their loving wives in these.

Hector was met at the palace by his gracious mother, who
was coming in with Laodice, the most beautiful of her
daughters. 'Hector!' she cried, putting her hand in his.
'Why have you come here, my child, in the middle of a
pitched battle? It is true then that those abominable Achaeans
are wearing us down and storming at the city walls. And the
spirit moved you to come in and lift your hands in prayer to
Zeus on the Acropolis. But wait a moment while I fetch you
some mellow wine, so that you may first make a libation to
Father Zeus and the other immortals and then, if you like,
enjoy a drink yourself. Wine is a great comfort to a weary
man; and you must be exhausted after fighting so hard for
your dear ones.'

'My lady mother,' replied the great Hector of the glittering
helmet, 'bring me no wine, or you will rob me of the use of
my legs and leave me feeble and unmanned. Nor should I
care to offer sparkling wine to Zeus with unwashed hands.
A man cannot pray to the Son of Cronos, the Lord of the
Black Cloud, when he is bespattered with blood and filth.
It is you who must pray. Collect the older ladies, and go with
offerings to the temple of Athene the Warrior. Take a robe,
the loveliest and biggest you can find in the house and the
one you value most yourself, and lay it on the Lady Athene's
knees. Promise her to sacrifice in her shrine a dozen yearling
heifers, untouched by the goad, if only she will have pity on
the town and on the Trojans' wives and little children, and
will keep that savage spearman Tydeus' son, the mighty panic-
maker, clear of sacred Ilium. Go, then, to Athene the Warrior's
shrine, while I go after Paris and order him out, though I
doubt whether he will listen to me. Indeed I wish the earth
would open and swallow him up. The gods brought him to
manhood only to be a thorn in the flesh for the Trojans and
my royal father and his sons. If I could see him bound for
Hades' Halls, I should say good riddance to bad rubbish.'

Hector's mother went into the palace and gave instructions to her maids. While these were going round the town to collect the older women, she went down to the scented storeroom where she kept her embroidered robes. These were the work of Sidonian women whom Prince Paris himself had shipped across the sea from Sidon, when he was on the cruise that brought him home with highborn Helen. From her wardrobe, Hecabe picked out the longest and most richly decorated dress as a gift for Athene. It had lain underneath all the rest, and now glittered like a star. With this she set out, and a number of the older ladies hurried along at her side.

When they reached the temple of Athene in the Acropolis, the doors were opened for them by Theano of the lovely cheeks, daughter of Cisseus and wife of Antenor the charioteer, who had been made priestess of Athene by the Trojans. With a loud cry, in which all joined, the women lifted their hands to Athene, while Theano of the lovely cheeks took the robe, laid it on the knees of the Lady goddess, and prayed to the Daughter of almighty Zeus: 'Lady Athene, mighty goddess, Protectress of Cities; break Diomedes' spear. Bring him crashing down in front of the Scaean Gate. And we will sacrifice to you here and now in your shrine twelve yearling heifers that never felt the goad, if you take compassion on the city and the Trojans' wives and little children.' Thus Theano prayed; but for answer Pallas Athene shook her head.

While the women were praying to the Daughter of almighty Zeus, Hector made his way to the splendid house where Paris lived. Paris had built this himself with the best workmen to be found in the fertile land of Troy. They built it for him, complete with sleeping-quarters, hall and court-yard, close to Priam's and Hector's houses in the Acropolis. The royal Prince Hector stepped indoors. He was carrying a spear eleven cubits long. The bronze point glittered in front of him, and there was a gold ring round the top of the shaft.

He found Paris in his bedroom attending to his beautiful armour, his shield and cuirass, and examining his curved bow, while Argive Helen sat beside him with her ladies-in-waiting and superintended their fancy-work. Directly he saw Paris,

Hector took him sharply to task. 'Sir,' he said, 'you disgrace yourself by sulking like this, while our men are falling in action round the town and at the very walls. It is your fault that this city is invaded by the sounds of battle, and you would be the first to quarrel with anyone else whom you found shirking his duty in the field. Off with you now, before the town goes up in flames!'

'Hector, you have every right to rebuke me,' said Paris; 'I admit it. But listen. I must explain that I am not sulking. I have no grudge against the Trojans, but came and sat down in my room to indulge my own chagrin. However, my wife has just been urging me, not without eloquence, to return to the front. And I think she is right – the same man does not always win. So give me a moment while I arm for battle; or else go on ahead, and I will follow. I can soon catch you up.'

This speech drew no reply from Hector of the flashing helmet, whom Helen now made a gracious effort to placate. 'Brother,' she said, 'I am indeed a shameless, evil-minded and abominable creature. Ah how I wish that on the very day when my mother bore me the Storm-fiend had swept me off into the mountains or the roaring sea, and the waves had overwhelmed me before all this could happen. And next to that, since the gods have ordained things to this evil end, I wish I had found a better husband, one with some feeling for the reproaches and contempt of his fellow-men. But as it is, this husband I have got is an inconstant creature; and he will never change, though one day he will suffer for it, if I am not mistaken. However, come in now, my dear brother, and sit down on this chair. No one in Troy has a greater burden to bear than you, all through my own shame and the wickedness of Paris, ill-starred couple that we are, tormented by Heaven to figure in the songs of people yet unborn.'

'Helen, you are kind,' said the great Hector of the flashing helmet; 'but do not ask me to sit down. I can only refuse, for I am late already and anxious to return and help the Trojans, who miss me terribly when I am gone. What you can do is to speed this fellow up. And he had better look sharp himself.

Then he could catch me up before I leave the town, since I intend to look in at my own house, to see my servants and my wife and little boy. For I cannot tell whether I shall ever come back to them again, or am doomed to fall to the Achaeans this very day.'

With this, Hector of the glittering helmet took his leave and soon reached his own well-built house. But he did not find his white-armed wife Andromache at home. She had climbed up on the city wall with her child and a lady attendant, and was standing there in tears and misery. Failing to find his good wife in the house, Hector went to the threshold to make inquiries of the maidservants. 'Maids,' he said, 'tell me what has happened. Where has the lady Andromache disappeared to from the house? Is she visiting one of my sisters or my noble brothers' wives? Or has she gone to Athene's shrine, where the rest of the Trojan ladies are interceding with the august goddess?'

'Hector,' said one of his busy maids, 'since you want to know the truth, she is not visiting your sisters or your noble brothers' wives, and she has not gone to Athene's shrine with the rest of the ladies to pray to the august goddess. She has climbed the great Tower of Ilium. She had heard that our men were being worn down and that the Achaeans had won a great victory. So she rushed off to the walls, like one distraught. And the nurse followed her with the baby in her arms.'

When Hector heard this, he rushed from the house and retraced his steps down the well-built streets. He had crossed the great city and had reached the Scaean Gate, by which he meant to go out on the plain, when Andromache herself, his richly dowered wife, came running up to meet him. Andromache was the daughter of the great-hearted Eëtion, the Cilician king, who lived below the wooded hill of Placus in Thebe-under-Placus. She came to meet her bronze-clad husband with a maid carrying a little boy in her arms, their baby son and Hector's darling, lovely as a star, whom Hector called Scamandrius, but the rest 'Astyanax', because his father was the one defence of Ilium.

Hector looked at his son and smiled, but said nothing. Andromache, bursting into tears, went up to him and put her hand in his. 'Hector,' she said, 'you are possessed. This bravery of yours will be your end. You do not think of your little boy or your unhappy wife, whom you will make a widow soon. Some day the Achaeans are bound to kill you in a massed attack. And when I lose you I might as well be dead. There will be no comfort left, when you have met your doom – nothing but grief. I have no father, no mother, now. My father fell to the great Achilles when he sacked our lovely town, Cilician Thebe of the High Gates. But though Achilles killed Eëtion, he was too chivalrous to despoil him. He burnt him in his decorated arms and built a mound above him; and the mountain Nymphs, Daughters of aegis-bearing Zeus, planted elms around it. I had seven brothers too at home. In one day all of them went down to Hades' House. The great Achilles of the swift feet killed them all, among their shambling cattle and their white sheep. As for my mother, who was Queen in Thebe under the woods of Placus, Achilles brought her here with the rest of his spoils but freed her for a princely ransom, and she was killed by Artemis the Archeress in her father's house.

'So you, Hector, are father and mother and brother to me, as well as my beloved husband. Have pity on me now; stay here on the tower; and do not make your boy an orphan and your wife a widow. Rally the Trojans by the fig-tree there, where the wall is easiest to scale and the town most open to attack. Three times already, their best men, under the two Aiantes and the famous Idomeneus, the Atreidae and the formidable Diomedes, have assaulted that point and tried to break in. Someone who knows the oracles must have told them its history, or else they have their own reasons for attacking there.'

'All that, my dear,' said the great Hector of the glittering helmet, 'is surely my concern. But if I hid myself like a coward and refused to fight, I could never face the Trojans and the Trojan ladies in their trailing gowns. Besides, it would go against the grain, for I have trained myself always, like a good soldier, to take my place in the front line and win glory for my father and myself. Deep in my heart I know the day is coming when holy Ilium will be destroyed, with Priam and the people of Priam of the good ashen spear. Yet I am not so much distressed by the thought of what the Trojans will suffer, or Hecabe herself, or King Priam, or all my gallant brothers whom the enemy will fling down in the dust, as by the thought of you, dragged off in tears by some Achaean man-at-arms to slavery. I see you there in Argos, toiling for some other woman at the loom, or carrying water from an alien well, a helpless drudge with no will of your own. "There goes the wife of Hector," they will say when they see your tears. "He was the champion of the horse-taming Trojans when Ilium was besieged." And every time they say it, you will feel another pang at the loss of the one man who might have kept you free. Ah, may the earth lie deep on my dead body before I hear the screams you utter as they drag you off!'

As he finished, glorious Hector held out his arms to take his boy. But the child shrank back with a cry to the bosom of his girdled nurse, alarmed by his father's appearance. He was frightened by the bronze of the helmet and the horsehair plume that he saw nodding grimly down at him. His father and his lady mother had to laugh. But noble Hector quickly took his helmet off and put the dazzling thing on the ground. Then he kissed his son, dandled him in his arms, and prayed to Zeus and the other gods: 'Zeus, and you other gods, grant that this boy of mine may be, like me, pre-eminent in Troy; as strong and brave as I; a mighty king of Ilium. May people say, when he comes back from battle, "Here is a better man than his father." Let him bring home the bloodstained armour of the enemy he has killed, and make his mother happy.'

Hector handed the boy to his wife, who took him to her fragrant breast. She was smiling through her tears, and when her husband saw this he was moved. He stroked her with his hand and said: 'My dear, I beg you not to be too much distressed. No one is going to send me down to Hades before my proper time. But Fate is a thing that no man born of woman, coward or hero, can escape. Go home now, and attend to your own work, the loom and the spindle, and see that the maidservants get on with theirs. War is men's business; and this war is the business of every man in Ilium, myself above all.'

As he spoke, glorious Hector picked up his helmet with its horsehair plume, and his wife set out for home, shedding great tears and with many a backward look. She soon got home, and there in the palace of Hector killer of men she found a number of her women-servants and stirred them all to lamentation. So they mourned for Hector in his own house, though he was still alive, thinking that he would never survive the violence and fury of the Achaeans and come home from the battlefield.

Paris had also been quick and had not lingered in his lofty house. Directly he had put on his splendid armour with its trappings of bronze, he hurried off through the town at full speed, like a stallion who breaks his halter at the manger where they keep and fatten him, and gallops off across the fields in triumph to his usual bathing-place in the delightful river. He tosses up his head; his mane flies back along his shoulders; he knows how beautiful he is; and away he goes, skimming the ground with his feet, to the haunts and pastures of the mares. So Paris, Priam's son, came down hotfoot from the citadel of Pergamus, resplendent in his armour like the dazzling sun, and laughing as he came.

He soon caught up his noble brother Hector, just as he was leaving the spot where he had talked with his wife. Before Hector could speak, Prince Paris began to excuse himself. 'My dear brother,' he said, 'I am afraid I have been too leisurely and kept you waiting when you wanted to be off. I have not been as punctual as you wished.'

'Sir,' said Hector of the glittering helmet, 'no reasonable man could make light of your achievements in battle: you have plenty of courage. But you are too ready to give up when it suits you, and refuse to fight. And I find it mortifying to hear you abused by the Trojans, whom you yourself have brought to this pass. But let us be off. Later I will make up for anything I may have said, if Zeus ever lets us drive the Achaeans from our soil and celebrate our deliverance with drink-offerings in the palace to the everlasting gods of Heaven.'

VII

AIAS FIGHTS HECTOR

PRINCE HECTOR said no more, but quickly passed out through the gate with his brother Paris. Both were eager for the fight, and to the expectant Trojans their reappearance was as welcome as a breeze from heaven to sailors numbed in leg and arm by the toil of smiting the sea-water with their blades of polished pine.

A victim fell at once to each. Paris killed Menesthius, who lived at Arne and was the son of King Areïthous the Maceman and the ox-eyed lady Phylomedusa. Hector, with his sharp spear, hit Eïoneus in the neck under the bronze rim of his helmet, and brought him down. Meanwhile Glaucus son of Hippolochus, the Lycian captain, casting a spear across the crowd, struck Iphinous son of Dexius on the shoulder, just as he was mounting behind his fast mares. He fell from his chariot to the ground and crumpled up.

When the bright-eyed goddess Athene saw them slaughtering Argives in this fierce assault, she sped down from the peaks of Olympus to sacred Ilium. But Apollo, who desired a Trojan victory, saw her from Pergamus and started out to intercept her. They met by the oak-tree and King Apollo son of Zeus at once accosted Athene. 'Daughter of almighty Zeus,' he said, 'why have you come down from Olympus in such haste? With what high purpose in your mind? Since the destruction of the Trojans moves you not at all, I take it that you have come to throw your weight into the scales and make the Danaans win. But listen to me – I have a better plan. Let us stop the fighting for the moment. Another day they can fight again and go on till they reach their goal in Ilium, since you goddesses will not be happy till you have razed this city to the ground.'

'So be it, Archer-King,' said Athene of the Flashing Eyes. 'That is what I too had in mind when I came from Olympus to visit the battlefield. But how do you propose to stop the men from fighting?'

King Apollo Son of Zeus replied: 'We could rouse the fighting spirit in horse-taming Hector and make him challenge one of the Danaans to mortal combat. The bronze-clad Achaeans would be on their mettle and put up a champion to fight a duel with Prince Hector.' This was Apollo's plan, and Athene, goddess of the Flashing Eyes, made no demur.

Priam's son Helenus was able to divine what these gods had agreed to do, and he went straight to his brother Hector. 'Prince Hector,' he said, 'will you, in your wisdom, allow yourself to be guided by your brother? I suggest that you should make the Trojans and Achaeans sit down, and challenge an Argive champion to meet you man to man. You need have no fears for your life – your time has not yet come. I have this from the deathless gods themselves.'

Hector was delighted. He stepped out into no-man's-land, and grasping his spear by the middle thrust back the Trojan lines. They all sat down, and Agamemnon made the Achaean soldiers do the same. Athene and Apollo of the Silver Bow also sat down, in the form of vultures, on the tall oak sacred to aegis-bearing Zeus. They enjoyed the sight of all these Trojan and Achaean warriors sitting there on the plain, rank upon rank, bristling with shields, helmets and spears, like the darkened surface of the sea when the West Wind begins to blow and ripples spread across it.

Hector stood between the two armies and said: 'Trojans and Achaean men-at-arms, hear a proposal that I wish to make. Zeus, from his high seat in Heaven, has not allowed our truce to last. It is clear that he means us all to go on suffering till the day when you bring down the towers of Troy, or succumb to us yourselves by your much-travelled ships. Now you have in your army the finest men of all Achaea. Is one of these prepared to fight me? If so, let him step forward from among his friends as your champion against Prince Hector.

And here are the conditions I lay down, with Zeus for witness.
If your man kills me with his long-pointed spear, he can strip
me of my arms and take them to your hollow ships; but he
must let them bring my body home, so that the Trojans and
their wives may burn it in the proper manner. If Apollo lets me
win and I kill your man, I shall strip his armour off and bring
it into sacred Ilium, where I shall hang it on the wall of the
Archer-King's shrine; but I shall send back his corpse to your
well-found ships, so that the long-haired Achaeans may give
him burial rites and make a mound above him by the broad
Hellespont. Then one day some future traveller, sailing by in
his good ship across the wine-dark sea, will say: "This is the
monument of some warrior of an earlier day who was killed
in single combat by illustrious Hector." Thus my fame will be
kept alive for ever.'

Hector's speech was received by the enemy in silence. They
were ashamed to refuse his challenge, but shrank from accept-
ing it. At last Menelaus, after many an inward struggle, rose
to his feet and reproached them bitterly. 'What does this
mean, you women of Achaea – I cannot call you men – who
used to be so ready with your threats? Not a single Danaan
willing to meet Hector? This is infamy, this is utter degrada-
tion! Very well then, sit there and rot, the whole crowd of
you, inglorious cowards to a man – and I will arm and fight
him myself. The issue lies with the gods above.'

He said no more, but began to put on his splendid armour.
And that, Menelaus, would have been the end of you, at
Hector's hands, since he was the better man by far, if the
Achaean kings had not leapt up and held you back, and if
Atreides himself, imperial Agamemnon, had not seized you
by the right hand and restrained you. 'You are mad, my lord
Menelaus,' he cried. 'There is no call for you to do this foolish
thing. Withdraw, however mortifying it may be. Do not let
ambition make you fight a better man. You would not be the
only one who has quailed before Prince Hector son of Priam.
Even Achilles feared to meet him in the field of honour, and
Achilles is a better man than you by far. So go back now and

sit down among your men; and the Achaeans will find some-
one else to fight for them against this man. He may be fear-
less and eager for his fill of trouble, but I think that even
Hector will be glad to take it easy, if he comes away alive
from the stern ordeal he has asked for.'

In the face of his brother's wise remonstrances, Menelaus
gave way; and with great relief his attendants took the armour
from his shoulders. Then Nestor rose to his feet and addressed
the Argives. 'This is enough,' he said, 'to make Achaea weep.
How Peleus the old charioteer would grieve, Peleus the great
orator and commander of the Myrmidons, who took such
delight, when I stayed with him once, in finding out from me
the parentage and pedigree of every Argive. If it came to his
ears that those same men were now all cowering before
Hector, he would lift up his hands to the gods and beg them to
let the spirit leave his flesh and go down to the House of
Hades. Ah, Father Zeus, Athene and Apollo, if only I could
be as young as I was when the Pylian levies were fighting with
the Arcadian spearmen at the swift River Celadon, below the
walls of Pheia, by the streams of Iardanus! We were chal-
lenged by their best man, Ereuthalion. He was like a god, and
he carried on his shoulders the armour of King Areïthous, the
great Areïthous, who was surnamed the Maceman by his
compatriots and their girdled wives, because he never fought
with a bow or a long spear but used to break the enemy ranks
with an iron mace. Lycurgus killed him, not by superior
strength, but by a stratagem. He caught him in a narrow
pass, where his iron mace could not save him. Before the
Maceman could bring it into play, Lycurgus was on him. He
pierced him through the middle with his spear, and brought
him crashing to the ground on his back. Then he stripped him
of the armour that Brazen Ares had given him, and after-
wards wore it himself when he went into battle. Later, when
Lycurgus had grown old in his palace, he let his squire Ereu-
thalion wear it; and so it came about that Ereuthalion chal-
lenged our champions in Areïthous' armour. And no one
dared to take the challenge up; they were all thoroughly

scared. But the spirit of adventure worked within me and I had the hardihood to take him on, though I was the youngest of them all. So we fought; and Athene gave me the victory. He was the tallest and strongest man I have ever killed – he looked like a giant as he lay sprawling there in all his breadth and height. Ah, if only I were still as young, with all my powers intact! Then Hector of the flashing helmet would soon have his fight. As it is, I see before me the best men in all Achaea – and not one that has the will to stand up to Hector!'

The old man's reproaches brought nine men to their feet. Agamemnon King of Men was the first to spring up. He was followed by the mighty Diomedes son of Tydeus; and these by the two Aiantes, full of martial valour; and these, again, by Idomeneus, and Idomeneus' squire Meriones, a peer of the man-killing War-god; and these by Eurypylus, Euaemon's highborn son. Thoas son of Andraemon got up too, and so did the good Odysseus. When all these had volunteered to fight Prince Hector, the Gerenian horseman Nestor rose again and said: 'You must decide by lot who is to have the honour, for the chosen man will not only render a service to Achaean arms but reap a rich reward in his own heart, if he escapes alive from the stern ordeal that awaits him.'

Each of them marked his own lot and cast it into the helmet of Agamemnon son of Atreus, while the troops raised their hands to the gods and prayed. 'Father Zeus,' they said, looking up into the broad sky, 'let it be Aias, or Diomedes, or the King of Golden Mycenae himself.'

As they prayed, Nestor the Gerenian charioteer shook the helmet, and Aias' lot leapt out – the very one they had hoped for. A herald carried it round the circle from left to right, showing it to each of the Achaean chieftains, and each in turn denied it when he failed to recognize his mark. At last, in the course of his tour, the herald with the lot came to the man who had marked it and put it in the helmet, illustrious Aias himself. Aias reached out. The herald came up to him and put the lot in his hand. Aias recognized his mark and rejoiced. He threw the lot on the ground at his feet and said: 'My friends, the lot is mine, and I am delighted, for I think I shall defeat Prince Hector. I only ask you, while I am arming for the fight, to pray to Zeus the Royal Son of Cronos. But let your prayers be silent, so that the Trojans may not overhear you. Or pray aloud! We are afraid of nobody whatever. No one is going to have his way with me and make me run, either by brute force or by skill. After all, I hope I too can fight and was not born and bred a fool in Salamis.'

So they prayed to King Zeus the Son of Cronos. They looked up into the broad sky and said: 'Father Zeus, you that rule from Mount Ida, most glorious and great; grant Aias a triumphant victory. But if you love Hector too and wish him well, let neither man be beaten, and the fight be drawn.'

While they prayed, Aias was putting on his flashing bronze. When all his armour was slung on, he sallied out, like the monstrous Ares when he joins embattled armies, hurled at each other by the Son of Cronos in soul-destroying hate. Thus the gigantic Aias, bulwark of Achaea, rose and went into battle, with a smile on his grim face, brandishing his long-shadowed spear as he strode forward. The Argives when they saw him were overjoyed, and there was not a Trojan whose knees did not tremble. Even Hector's heart fluttered in his breast. But it was too late for him to turn tail and slink back among his men: he was the challenger. And now Aias drew near, carrying a shield like a tower, made of bronze and seven layers of leather. Tychius the master-currier, who lived at Hyle, had made this glittering shield for him with the hides of seven big bulls, which he overlaid with an eighth layer of bronze. Holding this shield before his breast, Telamonian Aias went right up to Hector before halting to defy him. 'Hector,' he said, 'you are now going to discover, in single combat, what sort of champions the Danaans have at their disposal, even when they cannot count on Achilles, the lion-hearted breaker of men. At the moment he is lying idle by his beaked seagoing ships, nursing a quarrel with Agamemnon, our Commander-in-Chief. But for all that, we have men who can stand up to you – yes, plenty of them. So take the first cast and start the fight.'

To this the great Hector of the flashing helmet answered: 'Prince Aias, royal son of Telamon, do not try to scare me like a feeble child or a woman who knows nothing about warfare. To me, battle and slaughter are familiar things. I know well enough how to swing my toughened oxhide shield to right or left – the mark, to my mind, of the seasoned warrior. I know how to dash in when the chariots are on the move; and in close fighting I know all the steps of the War-god's dance. But enough; seeing the man you are, I do not want to play a sniper's part and steal a shot at you. So watch me cast – and may my cast go home!'

With this, he poised his long-shadowed javelin and cast. He struck the formidable, sevenfold shield of Aias on its metal sheath, the eighth and outermost layer. The untiring bronze tore through six layers, but was held up by the seventh hide. Then royal Aias in his turn launched his long-shadowed spear. The heavy weapon struck the round shield of Priam's son. It pierced the gleaming shield, forced its way through the ornate cuirass, and pressing straight on, tore the tunic on Hector's flank. But he had swerved, and so avoided death. And now the pair, when each had pulled his long spear out, fell on each other like flesh-eating lions, or like wild boars, whose strength is not to be despised. Hector struck Aias with a spear on the centre of his shield. But the bronze did not break through: the stout shield turned its point. Then Aias leaping in caught Hector on the shield. Hector was brought up short and the spear passed clean through his shield with force enough left to reach his neck and bring the dark blood gushing out. Yet even so, Hector of the flashing helmet did not give up the fight. He drew back a little and with his great hand picked up a large and jagged piece of black rock that was lying on the ground, hurled it at Aias' formidable sevenfold shield and struck it in the middle on the boss, making the bronze ring out. But Aias then picked up an even bigger rock, which he swung and hurled at Hector with such tremendous force that the great boulder crumpled his shield and swept him off his feet. Hector, jammed in the shield, lay stretched on his back. But Apollo quickly had him up again; and now they would have closed and hacked at one another with their swords, but for the heralds, those ambassadors of Zeus and men, a pair of whom, Talthybius on the Achaean side and Idaeus on the Trojan, had the wisdom to come up and intervene. They raised their staves between the combatants, and Idaeus, a herald of ripe experience, acting as their spokesman, said: 'Dear sons, give up now and break off the fight. Zeus the Cloud-gatherer loves you both, and you are both fine spearmen – we all of us know that. Also, it is nearly dark – another good reason for stopping.'

'Idaeus,' Telamonian Aias answered, 'it was Hector who asked for this duel: tell *him* to call it off. If he makes the first move, I will take my cue from him.'

'Aias,' said the great Hector of the flashing helmet, 'you are big, strong and able, and the best spearman on your side. Admitting that, I suggest that we cease fighting for the day, for we can always meet again and go on till the powers above decide between us. Also, the light is failing. We should do well to take the hint. The Achaeans would be very glad to see you back at the ships, your own friends and followers above all; while I should get a warm welcome in King Priam's city from the Trojans and the Trojan ladies in their trailing gowns, assembled for thanksgiving to the gods on my behalf. But first let us exchange gifts of honour, so that it may be said by Trojans and Achaeans alike that we two fought each other tooth and nail, but presently were reconciled and parted friends.'

With this he gave Aias his silver-studded sword, which he handed over with its scabbard and well-cut baldric; and Aias gave Hector his brilliant purple belt. So the two parted. Aias went back into the Achaean lines, while Hector rejoined the Trojan forces. His men were delighted when they saw him return to them alive and whole, safe from the fury and the unconquerable hands of Aias. They escorted him back to

the city like one they had given up for dead. Meanwhile, on
the other side, the Achaean men-at-arms conducted Aias to
King Agamemnon, elated by his victory.

When they reached the royal huts, Agamemnon King of
Men offered a five-year-old bull on their behalf to the al-
mighty Son of Cronos. They flayed and prepared it by cutting
up the carcass and deftly chopping it into small pieces. These
they pierced with spits, roasted carefully and then withdrew
from the fire. Their work done and the meal prepared, they
fell to with a good will on the food, which all shared alike,
though the noble son of Atreus, imperial Agamemnon, paid
Aias the honour of helping him to the long chine of the beast.
When their thirst and hunger were satisfied, a discussion was
opened by the old man Nestor, who had a proposal to lay
before them. His wisdom had often proved itself in the past;
he was their loyal counsellor; and it was in this spirit that he
now rose and addressed them. 'My lord Atreides, and you
other chieftains of the long-haired peoples of Achaea; we
have had heavy losses. The cruel War-god has darkened the
banks of Scamander with the blood of our dead, whose souls
have gone down to Hades. I suggest therefore that at dawn
you should announce a truce. Then let us get to work to-
gether, cart the bodies in here with oxen and mules, and burn
them not far from the ships, arranging in each case for friends
of the dead to bring the bones home to their children when
we return to our own country. Over the pyre, let us make
them a single barrow with such material as the plain provides.
Then, with this mound for a base, let us quickly build high
walls to protect the ships and ourselves, with strong gates
let into them, leaving carriage-way for the chariots. And a
little way outside, let us dig a deep trench parallel with the
walls, to serve as an obstruction to chariots and infantry, in
case the Trojans get out of hand some day and press us hard.'
Such was Nestor's scheme, to which the kings all indicated
their assent.

Meanwhile at the doors of Priam's palace in the Acropolis
of Ilium, the Trojans also held a meeting, but one that was

marred by an outburst of bitterness. It was the able Antenor who started the trouble. 'Trojans, Dardanians and allies,' he said, 'hear a proposal which I feel compelled to make. Let us have done now, and give Argive Helen back to the Atreidae, along with all her property. By fighting on as we are doing, we have made perjurers of ourselves. No good that I can see will ever come of that. We have no choice but to do as I say.'

With that, Antenor sat down, and Prince Paris, husband of the lady Helen, leapt to his feet. He dealt bluntly with the man. 'Antenor,' he said, 'I take exception to that speech of yours. You might have thought of something better. But if you mean what you say, and seriously propose this move, the gods themselves must have addled your brains, and it is time for me to let the gallant Trojans know what I feel. I declare outright that I will not give up my wife. At the same time I am willing to return all the goods I brought home with me from Argos and to add something of my own.'

Paris finished and sat down. He was followed by Dardanian Priam, who was as wise as the gods and now benevolently interposed. 'Trojans, Dardanians and allies,' he said, 'listen to my advice. For the moment, take your supper in the town as usual, not forgetting to mount guard and the need for every man to keep alert. At dawn let Idaeus go to the hollow ships and convey to my lords Agamemnon and Menelaus the offer we have heard from Paris, who started the quarrel. And there is another useful thing Idaeus can do. He can ask the Atreidae whether they are willing to refrain from hostilities till we have burnt our dead. Later we will fight again and go on till the powers above decide between us.'

The King's advice was well received, and they acted on it. The soldiers took their supper in their several messes; and at dawn Idaeus went to the hollow ships, where he found the Danaan war-chiefs in conference by the stern of Agamemnon's ship. He joined the circle and delivered his message with the clear enunciation of a herald. 'My lord Atreides, and other princes of the united Achaeans; Priam and the other Trojan

lords have instructed me to submit for your acceptance an
offer made by Paris, who started our feud. All the property
he brought away with him to Troy in his hollow ships – and
would to God he had perished first – he is willing to return,
with additions of his own. But he says that he will not give
up my lord Menelaus' wife, though the Trojans have urged
him to do so. Furthermore I am instructed to ask whether you
are willing to refrain from hostilities while we burn the dead.
Afterwards we can fight on, till the powers above decide be-
tween us.'

This pronouncement was received in complete silence by
the Achaean chiefs. At last Diomedes of the loud war-cry
spoke up. 'At this stage,' he said, 'let no one think of accepting
anything from Paris, or of taking Helen either. Any fool can
see that the Trojans' doom is sealed.'

The Achaean chieftains to a man applauded Diomedes
tamer of horses, and now King Agamemnon himself addressed
the herald. 'Idaeus,' he said, 'you have heard for yourself
what the Achaeans think. You have their answer: I concur in
it. The burning of the corpses is another matter. To that I
raise no objection. When men are dead and gone one cannot
grudge them the boon of quick cremation. A truce, then;
and let Zeus the Thunderer and Lord of Here witness it.'

As he spoke, he lifted up his sceptre for all the gods to see.
Idaeus then withdrew and made his way back to sacred Ilium,
where the Trojans and Dardanians had mustered and were all
seated in conference awaiting the herald's return. When
Idaeus reached them, he went to the centre of the gathering
and reported the result of his mission. Then they prepared
themselves at once for their double task, some to bring in the
dead, and others to fetch wood; while on the other side parties
of Argives were despatched on the same duties from their well-
found ships.

The Sun, climbing into the sky from the deep and quiet
Stream of Ocean, had already lit the fields with his first
beams when the Trojan and Achaean parties met. Even so,
they found it difficult to recognize their dead before they had

washed away the clotted blood with water. Then, as they lifted them onto the waggons, the hot tears flowed. King Priam had forbidden his men to cry aloud. So they heaped the corpses on the pyre in silent grief, and when they had consumed them in the flames they went back to holy Ilium. So too, on their side, the Achaean men-at-arms with heavy hearts piled up their dead on a pyre, and when they had burnt them in the flames returned to their hollow ships.

Before the following dawn, when the night still struggled with the day, a detachment of Achaean troops gathered by the pyre and set to work. Over the pyre, they made a single barrow with such material as the plain provided. Then, starting from this, they built a wall with high ramparts to protect the ships and themselves, fitting it with strong gates, so that the chariots could pass in and out. Outside and parallel with the wall, they dug a deep trench, and along this broad and ample ditch they planted a row of stakes.

The long-haired Achaeans toiling at this task were observed by the gods. These had sat down with Zeus, the Lord of the Lightning Flash, and were watching the great work of the bronze-clad warriors with amazement. It was Poseidon the Earthshaker who first voiced his feelings. 'Father Zeus,' he said, 'is there nobody left in the wide world with the decency to inform us of his plans? Have you seen that the long-haired Achaeans have thrown a wall round their ships and dug a trench along it, without offering the proper sacrifices to the gods? People will talk about this wall of theirs as far as the light of Dawn is spread; and the wall that I and Phoebus Apollo built with such labour for King Laomedon will be forgotten.'

Zeus the Cloud-compeller was indignant with him. 'Imperial Earthshaker,' he said, 'your misgivings are absurd. Leave it to other gods less powerful and resolute than you to be alarmed at this contraption; and rest assured that wherever the light of Dawn is spread, yours is the name that will be held in honour. Besides, what will there be to stop you, once the long-haired Achaeans have sailed for home? Why not break down the wall, scatter the fragments in the sea, and cover the long beach once more with sand? Then you could feel that the great Achaean works had been obliterated.'

While the gods were talking, the sun set and the Achaeans finished their task. They slaughtered some oxen in the huts and took their supper. A number of ships had put in from Lemnos with cargoes of wine – they came from Euneus, the son whom Hypsipyle had borne to Jason the great captain, and he had included a thousand gallons in the consignment as a special gift for the Atreidae, Agamemnon and Menelaus. From these, the long-haired Achaeans now supplied themselves with wine, some in exchange for bronze, some for gleaming iron, others for hides or live cattle, others again for slaves. It was a sumptuous meal that they sat down to. Right through the night the long-haired Achaeans feasted themselves, while in the city the Trojans and their allies did the same. But all night long Zeus the Thinker, brewing evil for them in his heart, kept thundering ominously. Their cheeks turned pale with fear, and they poured wine on the ground from their cups. Not a man dared drink before he had made a libation to the almighty Son of Cronos. But at last they lay down and enjoyed the boon of sleep.

VIII

THE TROJANS REACH THE WALL

As Dawn spread her saffron mantle over the world, Zeus, who delights in thunder, called the gods to a conference on the highest of Olympus' many peaks. He opened it himself, and all attended carefully. 'Listen,' he said, 'you gods and goddesses, while I tell you what I have resolved. I am determined to bring this business to a speedy close, and with that end in view I give you my ruling, which no god or goddess must defy – you must accept it, every one of you. If I find any god taking an independent course and going to the Trojans' or the Danaans' help, he shall be thrashed ignominiously and packed off to Olympus. Or I will seize him and hurl him into the gloom of Tartarus, far, far away, where the deepest of all chasms yawns below the world, where the Iron Gates are, and the Brazen Threshold, as far below Hades as the earth is under heaven. That will teach him by how much I am the most powerful of all the immortals. But perhaps you gods would like to put me to the test and satisfy yourselves? Suspend a golden rope from heaven and lay hold of the end of it, all of you together. Try as you may, you will never drag Zeus the High Counsellor down from heaven to the ground. But if I cared to take a hand and pulled in earnest from my end, I could haul you up, earth, sea and all. Then I should make the rope fast to a pinnacle of Olympus, and leave everything to dangle in mid-air. By so much does my strength exceed the strength of gods and men.'

Zeus finished, and they all held their tongues. He had spoken with tremendous force and left them dumbfounded. At last Athene, goddess of the Flashing Eyes, spoke up. 'Father of ours, Son of Cronos, Lord Supreme,' she said, 'we all know well enough that you are invincible. But we are sorry, none the less, for the Danaan spearmen, left as they will be to destruction and a miserable fate. However, we will refrain from fighting, as you say, and shall content ourselves with giving helpful advice to the Argives, so that they may not all come to grief through your anger.'

Zeus the Cloud-gatherer smiled at her as he replied: 'Have no fear, Lady of Trito and dear Child of mine. I was not in earnest, and I do not mean to be unkind to you.'

Zeus then harnessed to his chariot his two swift horses with their brazen hooves and flowing golden manes. He clothed himself in gold, picked up his splendid golden whip, mounted his chariot and started the horses with a flick. The willing pair flew off on a course midway between the earth and starry sky, and brought him to Gargarus, a peak of Ida of the many springs, the mother of wild beasts, where he has a precinct and a fragrant altar. There the Father of men and gods pulled up his horses, freed them from the yoke, and wrapped them in a dense mist. Then he sat down on the heights, exulting in his glory and looking out over the Trojan city and the Achaean ships.

Meanwhile the long-haired Achaeans ate a hasty breakfast in their huts and forthwith armed themselves; while on their side, in the city, the Trojans also prepared themselves for battle. There were fewer of them, yet for all that they were eager to grapple with the enemy, driven as they were by stern necessity to fight for their wives and children. The gates were all thrown open, and with a great din their whole army, infantry and horse, poured out.

Thus the two converging forces met once more with a clash of bucklers, spears and bronze-clad fighting men. The bosses of their shields collided and a great roar went up. The screams of the dying were mingled with the vaunts of their destroyers, and the earth ran with blood.

Right through the morning while the blessed light of day grew stronger, volley and counter-volley found their mark, and men kept falling. But at high noon the Father held out his golden scales, and putting sentence of death in either pan, on one side for the horse-taming Trojans, on the other for the bronze-clad Achaeans, raised the balance by the middle of the beam. The beam came down on the Achaeans' side, spelling a day of doom for them. Their sentence settled on the bountiful earth, while that of the Trojans went soaring up to the broad sky. Zeus thundered out from Ida and sent a flash of lightning down among the Achaean troops, who were confounded by it. Terror drained the colour from the cheeks of every man.

Then, neither Idomeneus nor Agamemnon had the heart to hold his ground. Nor did the two Aiantes stand, henchmen of Ares though they were. Gerenian Nestor, Warden of Achaea, was the only one who lingered, and that not of his own free will, but because his third horse was in trouble. Prince Paris, Lady Helen's husband, had hit him with an arrow on the top of the crown, where the mane starts to grow on a horse's head, a very deadly spot. In his agony he reared, for the point sank into his brain; and writhing round the dart he threw the other horses into confusion. Nestor rushed in with his sword and was slashing at the outrigger's reins, when Hector's horses came galloping up through the turmoil, with a redoubtable charioteer behind them, Hector himself. And the old man would then and there have lost his life, but for the quick eye of the veteran Diomedes, who saw the danger and gave Odysseus a resounding call for help. 'Odysseus,' he shouted, 'my noble and resourceful lord; where are you off to with your shield behind you like a coward in the crowd? Take care, or as you run away someone will catch you in the midriff with a spear. For Heaven's sake stop and help me keep that savage off the old man there.'

But the much-enduring, noble Odysseus did not hear him, and sped by on his way to the Achaeans' hollow ships. Left thus to his own resources, Diomedes none the less drove up to the point of attack, posted himself in front of Nestor's chariot, and brought reassurance to the old king. 'These young warriors,' he said, 'are proving too much for an old man like you, my lord, with all those years to carry. You are dead-beat.

That squire of yours is useless, and your horses are too slow. Come, get into my chariot and you will see what horses of the breed of Tros are like and how quickly mine can cover the ground, in flight or in pursuit, it makes no odds. I took them from Aeneas only the other day, these fighting thoroughbreds. Let our squires take charge of your horses, while you and I drive this pair at the Trojan charioteers and teach Hector that I too have a spear that is tingling in my hand.'

Nestor the Gerenian Knight was nothing loath. So their two gallant squires, Sthenelus and the gentle Eurymedon, took charge of Nestor's horses, while he and Diomedes both mounted Diomedes' chariot. Nestor took up the polished reins and started the horses with the whip. They were soon within range of Hector, and Tydeus' son let fly at him as he came charging up. He missed him, but instead got Hector's squire and charioteer, Eniopeus, a son of the proud Thebaeus. He hit him by the nipple on his breast, with the horses' reins in his hands. The man fell headlong from the car, making his horses shy, and died where he fell.

The death of his charioteer wrung Hector's heart, but sorry as he was for his comrade-in-arms, he left him lying there and went off in search of a dashing charioteer. His fast horses were not long without a driver. He soon found the daring Archeptolemus, Iphitus' son, made him get in behind the pair, and handed him the reins.

Irreparable disaster threatened the Trojans now, and they might have been driven into Ilium as lambs into a pen, if the Father of men and gods had not been alert and acted quickly. With a terrific thunderclap, he launched a dazzling bolt and guided it to earth in front of Diomedes' horses. The dreadful reek of burning sulphur filled the air. The horses shied and backed under the chariot. The polished reins dropped from Nestor's hands, and in his terror he turned to Diomedes and said: 'My lord Tydeides, wheel your horses round and fly. Do you not see that you can expect no help from Zeus? At the moment, the Son of Cronos is allowing Hector there to carry all before him. But only for the day. Another day our turn will come, if he is kind. However bold a man may be, he cannot run counter to the will of Zeus, who is far more powerful than we are.'

'All that, sir, is very true,' said Diomedes of the loud war-cry. 'And yet it cuts me to the quick to think of Hector holding forth and saying to the Trojans: "Tydeides ran from me. He didn't stop before he reached the ships." He is sure to brag like that, and when he does, may the earth swallow me up!'

'What nonsense, my dear sir, from the son of the doughty Tydeus!' replied Gerenian Nestor. 'Hector can dub you coward and milksop to his heart's content, but he will not convince the Trojans and Dardanians, nor those proud spearmen's wives whose loving husbands you have flung down in the dust.'

With no more said, he wheeled the horses round and drove them back in flight across the rout. Hector and the Trojans followed them up with a terrific roar and a hail of deadly missiles. And the great Hector of the glittering helmet raised a shout of triumph over Diomedes. 'Tydeides,' he cried, 'the Danaan horsemen used to honour you with the best seat at table, the first cut off the joint, and a never-empty cup. They will not think so well of you to-day. After all, you are no better than a woman. Off with you, wretched doll. No cowardice of mine is going to let you climb our walls or carry off our women in your ships. I shall see you off to Hades first.'

Tydeides, when he heard this, had half a mind to turn his horses and meet Hector face to face. Thrice he was on the point of doing so, and thrice the Counsellor Zeus thundered from Mount Ida as a sign to the Trojans that victory was theirs with help from him. And there was Hector calling aloud to his men: 'Trojans and Lycians and you Dardanians that like your fighting hand to hand! Be men, my friends; do justice to your valour. I am convinced that Zeus is on my side. He has assured me a triumphant victory, and disaster to the Danaans – fools that they are to have gone and made those flimsy, futile walls, which will not hold us up for an instant. As for the trench they have dug, our horses will jump that with ease. And once I get among the hollow ships, let your watchword be "Fire!" I want to see those ships go up in flames, and the Argives lurching about in the smoke and falling dead beside the hulls.'

Hector then turned to his horses, called them each by name and talked to them. 'Xanthus, and you, Podargus; Aethon, and my noble Lampus; repay me now for the attentions lavished on you by Andromache, a great king's daughter, who has always hastened to put honeyed wheat before you and mix you wine to drink at your pleasure, before she thought of serving me, who claim to be her loving husband. After them now at the gallop, and let us capture Nestor's shield, the talk of Heaven itself, of solid gold, they say, shield, bars, and all; or tear the inlaid breastplate that Hephaestus made for him from the shoulders of horse-taming Diomedes. If we could lay our hands on those two pieces, I should hope to make the Achaeans take to their fast ships this very night.'

Hector's vainglorious tone was resented by the Lady Here. With an impatient movement on her throne, which made high Olympus quake, she turned to the great god Poseidon and said: 'Imperial Earthshaker, I am distressed to see that even you can find no pity in your heart for the Danaans in their downfall. Yet at Helice and Aegae they make you many pleasing offerings. Can you not bring yourself to wish them victory? Why, if we who are on their side made up our minds to keep all-seeing Zeus from interfering and to thrust the Trojans back, what a sorry god he would be, sitting alone there on Ida!'

'Here,' replied the Lord of the Earthquake with the utmost indignation, 'these are wild words indeed, even from your unruly tongue. Far be it from me to join the others in a fight with Zeus the Son of Cronos, who is so much stronger than us all!'

While these two were talking to one another, the whole enclosure between the ships and the trench by the wall was filled

with a medley of chariots and armed men, penned in like
sheep by that peer of the impetuous War-god, Hector son of
Priam, now that Zeus had given him the upper hand. Indeed
he would have had the trim ships alight and going up in
flames, if the Lady Here had not put it into Agamemnon's
head to bestir himself and rally the Achaeans before it was too
late. He went along past huts and ships with a large purple
cloak gripped in his great hand and climbed up on the bulging
black hull of Odysseus' ship, which stood in the centre of the
line, so that a man's voice would carry to either end, to the
huts of Telamonian Aias, or to those of Achilles, who had had
confidence enough in their own bravery and strength to draw
up their trim ships on the extreme flanks. From this point
Agamemnon sent his voice ringing out to the whole Danaan
army. 'For shame, Argives,' he cried, 'contemptible creatures,
splendid only on parade! What has become of our assurance
that we were the finest force on earth? What of the idle
boasts you made that time in Lemnos as you gorged your-
selves on the beef of straight-horned cattle and drank from
bowls brimful of wine? You said that in a fight you could
each stand up to a hundred, nay, two hundred Trojans; where-
as to-day the whole crowd of us are no match for Hector
alone; and he, before long, will have the ships going up in
flames. Father Zeus, was a great king ever fooled by you like
this, and robbed of all his glory? Yet I can claim that on my
unhappy journey here in my ship of war I never overlooked a
single one of your fine altars. On every one of them I burnt
the fat and thighs of bullocks in my eagerness to bring down
the walls of Troy. Ah, Zeus, grant me this prayer at least. Let
us escape with our lives, if nothing else, and do not let the
Trojans overwhelm us like this.'

Thus Agamemnon prayed, and the Father was moved by
his tears. With a nod of his head he vouchsafed him the salva-
tion of his army, and at the same time sent out an eagle – best
of prophetic birds – with its talons in a fawn, the offspring of
some nimble doe. The eagle dropped the fawn by the splendid
altar of Zeus, where the Achaeans used to sacrifice to the

Father of Oracles; and when they realized that the bird came from Zeus, they fell on the Trojans with a better will and recalled the joy of battle.

Then, not one of the many Danaan charioteers could boast that he had raced Diomedes to the trench and driven out before him to engage the enemy. Diomedes was certainly the first to kill a Trojan man-at-arms. His victim, Agelaus son of Phradmon, had swung his horses round for flight. He had no sooner wheeled than Diomedes caught him in the back with his spear, midway between the shoulders, and drove it through his breast. He crashed from his chariot and his armour rang about him.

Diomedes was followed by the Atreidae, Agamemnon and Menelaus; these by the two Aiantes, dauntless and resolute; and these, again, by Idomeneus and Idomeneus' squire Meriones, a peer of the man-killing War-god; and these by Eurypylus, Euaemon's noble son. The ninth to sally out, bending his incurved bow, was Teucer, who took his usual place behind the shield of Aias son of Telamon. Aias would slowly move his shield aside. Teucer would peer about for a target in the crowd, and shoot. Then, as the man he hit dropped dead, Teucer, like a child running for shelter to its mother's skirts, took cover once again with Aias, who hid him under his glittering shield.

Who was the first of the Trojans to fall to the peerless Teucer? Orsilochus; then Ormenus and Ophelestes, Daetor and Chromius and the godlike Lycophontes; and Amopaon, Polyaemon's son, and Melanippus. All these in swift succession he brought down on the bountiful earth. Agamemnon King of Men was delighted when he saw what havoc Teucer was making in the Trojan ranks with his strong bow. He went up to him and said: 'Teucer son of Telamon, my beloved prince, shoot on as you are doing now, and you may well bring salvation to the Danaans and fame to your father Telamon, who took you under his roof and reared you though a bastard child. Repay him now with glory, far away as he is; and I tell you what I undertake to do. If aegis-bearing Zeus and

Athene ever let me sack the lovely town of Troy, I will hand you the first prize of honour after my own, a tripod, or a pair of horses with their chariot, or a woman to share your bed.'

'My noble lord, Atreides,' said the admirable Teucer, 'why flog a willing horse? I have been doing all I can, without a rest. From the moment when we thrust them back towards the town I have been watching for chances with my bow and picking men off. I have shot eight long-barbed arrows, and each has found its mark in the flesh of some fighting youngster over there. But here is a mad dog whom I cannot hit.'

As he spoke, he aimed at Hector, whom he yearned to bring down, and sent another arrow flying from his string. He missed him, but the arrow landed in the breast of one of Priam's noble sons, peerless Gorgythion, whose mother, the lovely Castianeira, with a figure like a goddess, had come from Aesyme to be married to the King. Weighed down by his helmet, Gorgythion's head dropped to one side, like the lolling head of a garden poppy, weighed down by its seed and the showers of spring.

Once more, in his eagerness to get him, Teucer aimed at Hector and sent an arrow flying from his string. He missed him this time too, for Apollo turned his dart aside, but he hit Archeptolemus, Hector's daring charioteer, by the nipple on his breast, as he was galloping into the fight. He crashed from his chariot, making his horses shy, and died where he fell.

The death of his charioteer wrung Hector's heart, but sorry as he was for his comrade-in-arms, he left him there, and called upon his brother Cebriones, who happened to be near, to take the horses' reins. Cebriones heard him and obeyed. Hector himself leapt to the ground from his resplendent chariot with a terrible shout, picked up a lump of rock and made straight for Teucer, whom he had determined to kill. Teucer had just taken a sharp arrow from his quiver and put it on the string. As he drew back the string and aimed at him, Hector of the flashing helmet struck his shoulder with the jagged stone on the weakest spot, where the clavicle leads over to the neck and breast. The bowstring snapped; his fingers and wrist were numbed; he sank down on his knees; and the bow dropped from his hand. But Aias did not disregard his brother's fall. Running up, he bestrode Teucer and covered him with his shield. Then two of their trusty men, Mecisteus son of Echius and the noble Alastor, lifted him from the ground and carried him off, groaning heavily, to the hollow ships.

Olympian Zeus now put fresh heart into the Trojans, and they drove the Achaeans right back to their own deep trench. Hector, resistless and elated, led the van. Like a hound in full cry after a lion or a wild boar, snapping at flank or buttock and following every twist and turn, he hung on the heels of the long-haired Achaeans, killing the hindmost all the time as they ran before him. They fled across the palisade and trench, suffering heavy losses at the hands of the Trojans; and they did not stop till they reached the ships. There they halted, calling to one another for help; and every man lifted up his hands and poured out prayers to all the gods. But there was Hector, wheeling his long-maned horses to and fro, and glaring at them with the eyes of Gorgo or the murderous War-god.

The white-armed goddess Here was sorry for them when she saw their plight and did not conceal her distress from Athene. 'Daughter of aegis-bearing Zeus,' she said to her, 'can you and I look on, without a final effort, while the Danaans perish? For that they will, and miserably too, mowed down by a single man. See what Hector has done to them already! And now there is no stopping him in his mad career.'

'Nothing could please me more,' said the bright-eyed goddess Athene, 'than to see that mad career cut short and have him killed on his native soil by Argive hands. But my Father is in a wicked mood, obstinate old sinner that he is, always meddling with my plans. He never thinks of the many times I went to his son Heracles' rescue when he was defeated by the tasks Eurystheus set him. Heracles had only to whimper to Heaven, and Zeus would send me speeding down to get him out of his difficulties. If my prophetic heart had warned me of

all this when Eurystheus sent him down to the House of Hades,
Warden of the Gates, to bring the Hound of Hell from Erebus,
he would never have re-crossed the cataracts of Styx. But now
Zeus hates me and is letting Thetis have her way, because she
kissed his knees and touched his chin with her hand when she
begged him to support Achilles sacker of towns. However,
the day will come when he will call me his darling of the
Flashing Eyes once more. Meanwhile, will you get our horses
ready, while I go into the palace of aegis-bearing Zeus and
arm for war? I want to see how pleased this son of Priam,
Hector of the flashing helmet, will be when we two show our-
selves athwart the ranks. It is now the Trojans' turn to fall
dead by the Achaean ships and glut the dogs and the birds of
prey with their fat and flesh.'

To this the white-armed goddess made no demur. So Here,
Queen of Heaven and Daughter of the mighty Cronos, went
off to put the golden harness on her horses, while, on her
Father's threshold, Athene Daughter of aegis-bearing Zeus
shed the soft, embroidered robe which she had made with her
own hands, put on a tunic in its place, and equipped herself
for the lamentable work of war with the arms of Zeus the
Cloud-compeller. Then she stepped into the flaming chariot,
gripping the huge, long spear with which she breaks the noble
warriors' ranks when she, the almighty Father's Child, is
roused to anger. And no sooner was she in than Here started
the horses with her whip.

The Gates of Heaven thundered open for them of their own
accord. They are kept by the Hours, the Wardens of the
broad sky and of Olympus, whose task it is to close the en-
trance or to roll away the heavy cloud. Through these gates the
goddesses drove their patient steeds.

When Father Zeus saw them from Ida, he was enraged and
at once told Iris of the Golden Wings to convey a message to
them. 'Off with you, Iris, fast as you can!' he said. 'Make
them turn back. Do not let them meet me face to face: it
would be a terrible thing for them to fight with Zeus. Tell
them from me, who make no idle threats, that I will hamstring

the horses they are driving, hurl them both from their chariot, and break the chariot up. Ten rolling years would pass, and they would not be healed of the wounds my thunderbolt would deal them. That will teach the Lady of the Flashing Eyes what it means to fight against her Father. As for Here, I am not so much hurt and angered by *her*. It is her instinct to defy me.'

Iris of the Whirlwind Feet sped off on her mission from the peaks of Ida to great Olympus; and there, on the rugged heights of Olympus, she met the two goddesses at the very gates, stopped them and delivered the message from Zeus. 'Whither away?' she said. 'What is the object of this mad adventure? The Son of Cronos forbids you to assist the Argives. Hear what he threatens – and you know that Zeus keeps his word. He will hamstring the horses you are driving, hurl you both from your chariot, and break the chariot up. Ten rolling years would pass, and you be left still suffering from the wounds his thunderbolt would deal you. That, Lady of the Flashing Eyes, will teach you what it means to fight your Father. It is not Here (who habitually defies his orders) that has hurt and angered him so much, as you and your graceless, brazen impudence – if you really dare to brandish that great spear of yours at Zeus.'

Her message delivered, Iris of the Fleet Foot took her leave, and Here turned to Athene in alarm. 'Daughter of aegis-bearing Zeus,' she said, 'I have changed my mind. We two will not go to war with Zeus on man's behalf. Let chance settle who is to die or live. Zeus must decide in his own mind between the Trojans and Danaans, as is only right.'

As she spoke she turned their chariot back. The Hours unyoked their long-maned horses for them, tethered them at their ambrosial mangers and tilted the chariot against the burnished wall by the gate, while the two goddesses rejoined the other gods in great chagrin and sat down on golden chairs.

Meanwhile Father Zeus had left Ida and was driving his fast chariot and horses to Olympus. He too was served when he reached the home of the gods. The illustrious Earthshaker unyoked his horses, put his chariot on its stand and covered it with a cloth. All-seeing Zeus himself sat down on his golden throne and great Olympus quaked beneath his feet.

Athene and Here, sitting by themselves away from Zeus, said not a word to him and asked him nothing. But he knew what was passing through their minds, and he said: 'Athene and Here, why are you so dejected? Not worn out, surely, by the glorious battle in which you killed so many of the Trojans whom you loathe? *I*, now, could never be turned from my path by all the gods in Olympus, such is the strength of my unconquerable hands. But you two were trembling in every limb before you even saw the battlefield and its horrors. Let me tell you what would have happened if you had not changed your minds. My thunderbolt would have wrecked you, and if you *had* got home to Olympus, it would have been in someone else's chariot.'

This sally drew mutterings from Athene and Here, where they sat together, still plotting trouble for the Trojans. However, Athene held her tongue, for all her annoyance with her Father, Zeus. She made no rejoinder, though she seethed with indignation. But Here could not contain her rage and burst into speech. 'Dread Son of Cronos, this is intolerable! We know as well as all the rest that your powers are not to be despised. But we cannot help being sorry for the Danaan spearmen, left as they will be to destruction and a miserable fate. However, if it is your wish, we will refrain from fighting and content ourselves with giving sound advice to the Argives, so that they may not all come to grief through your anger.'

To this the Cloud-compeller Zeus replied: 'Here, my ox-eyed Queen, you will have the opportunity at dawn to-morrow of seeing the almighty Son of Cronos do greater execution yet among the spearmen of the Argive force. For I tell you that the mighty Hector is going to give his enemies no rest till swift Achilles comes to life again beside the ships, when they are fighting at the very sterns, in desperate straits, over the body of Patroclus. That is decreed by Heaven. As for yourself, your annoyance leaves me calm. For all I care, you

can go to the bottomless pit and join Iapetus and Cronos, who
never enjoy the beams of Hyperion the Sun, nor any breezes,
sunk as they are in the depths of Tartarus. You can descend as
far as that, and your anger will still leave me unconcerned.
There are no limits to your impudence.'

This time, the white-armed goddess said not a word in
answer. And now the bright lamp of the Sun dropped into
Ocean, drawing black night in its train across the fruitful
earth. The Trojans had not wished the day to end, but to the
Achaeans, who had yearned for this relief, the dark came like a
tardy answer to their prayers.

Illustrious Hector withdrew the Trojans from the ships and
summoned a meeting in an open space beside the swirling
river, where the ground was clear of corpses; and they got
down from their chariots to hear what the King's son had to
say. He held a spear eleven cubits long; the bronze point
glittered in front of him; and there was a gold ring round the
top of the shaft. As he addressed his troops, he rested his weight
on the spear. 'Trojans, Dardanians and allies, listen to me,' he
said. 'I had hoped to destroy the ships and all the Achaeans
with them, before going home to windy Ilium. But the light
failed too soon. It was that more than anything that saved the
Argives and their fleet on the sea-shore. Now, we can only do
as night suggests and prepare for supper. Unyoke your long-
maned horses and put fodder by them. Then quickly go and
bring some cattle and fat sheep from the town, and supply
yourselves with mellow wine and bread from your houses.
Also, collect a quantity of wood, so that we can have plenty
of fires burning all night till dawn, and light up the whole
sky, in case the long-haired Achaeans make a dash for home,
in spite of the darkness, and take to the open sea. We must
certainly not leave them to embark at their leisure. Let us give
those fellows something to digest at home, an arrow or a sharp
spear in the back as they jump on board, to teach them and
other people too to think twice of the miseries of war before
they attack the horse-taming Trojans. In Troy itself, let our
sacred heralds call out the young lads and the grey-headed

old men to bivouac all round the town on the walls that the gods built us, while our womenfolk keep a big fire burning in every home. In addition, regular guards must be mounted, to see that the enemy do not steal into the city while the troops are away. Those, gallant Trojans, are my orders: let them be carried out.

'So much for the moment – I think that we can say "All's well". In the morning I will announce my further dispositions to the troops. I hope, and pray to Zeus and all the other gods, that I shall be able to drive away these hellhounds whom the Fates bring here in their black ships. It is night now: we must mount guard for ourselves as well. But at peep of dawn we will arm, and attack them fiercely at the hollow ships. Then I shall see whether the mighty Diomedes son of Tydeus can drive me back from the ships to the wall, or whether I shall bring him down with my sharp bronze and carry off his bloodstained arms. He will learn in the morning whether he has it in him to stand up against my spear. More likely, as tomorrow's sun goes up, he will lie bleeding in the battle-front, with half his company dead around their leader. I wish I were as sure of immortality and ageless youth and glory like Athene's or Apollo's, as I am that this day will prove disastrous to the Argives.'

The Trojans greeted this harangue from Hector with applause. They freed their sweating horses from the yokes and tethered them with thongs, each man by his own chariot. Then they went quickly to the town and brought out oxen and fat sheep, supplying themselves at the same time with mellow wine and bread from their homes. They also collected large quantities of wood; and presently the smell of roast meat was rising to high heaven on the breeze.

Thus all night long they sat, across the corridors of battle, thinking great thoughts and keeping their many fires alight. There are nights when the upper air is windless and the stars in heaven stand out in their full splendour round the bright moon; when every mountain-top and headland and ravine starts into sight, as the infinite depths of the sky are torn open to the very firmament; when every star is seen, and the shepherd rejoices. Such and so many were the Trojans' fires, twinkling in front of Ilium midway between the ships and the streams of Xanthus. There were a thousand fires burning on the plain, and round each one sat fifty men in the light of its blaze, while the horses stood beside their chariots, munching white barley and rye, and waiting for Dawn to take her golden throne.

IX

OVERTURES TO ACHILLES

WHILE the Trojans thus kept watch, the Achaeans were shuddering in the grip of Panic, who treads on the heels of Rout. All their captains knew the tortures of despair. Their hearts were storm-tossed, like the fish-delighting sea when Boreas and Zephyr, the winds that blow from Thrace, pounce on it with alternate squalls, and the black rollers lift their crests and pile up seaweed all along the beach.

Agamemnon, wandering about distraught by his grief, told his clear-voiced heralds to summon every man by name to a meeting, but not to call out loud; and he played a leading part in the work himself. They sat down to the Assembly in a sorry mood, and as Agamemnon rose to address them, he groaned heavily and the tears ran down his face like water trickling from a spring in dark streaks down a precipice. 'My friends,' he said, 'Captains and Counsellors of the Argives, Zeus the great Son of Cronos has dealt me a crushing blow. The cruel god, who once assured me solemnly that I should bring down the walls of Ilium before I left this spot, has changed his mind, and now to my bitter disappointment bids me retreat to Argos in disgrace, with half my army lost. It is clear that unconquerable Zeus, who has brought down the high towers of many a city and will destroy others yet, has decided thus in his omnipotence. So now let every man of you follow my lead. Aboard the ships, I say, and home to our own country! Troy, with its broad streets, will never fall to us.'

Agamemnon's outburst was received in complete silence by the Achaean soldiery. For a long time they sat in speechless dejection; but at last Diomedes of the loud war-cry rose to his feet. 'My lord Atreides,' he began, 'it is you, first and foremost, you and this imbecility of yours, that I fall foul of. I do so in open debate (where, as your majesty knows, we are privileged), and you must not be offended. You took it on yourself the other day to reprimand me in front of the troops. You said I was a milksop and a coward – every Argive young and old has heard the story. But has not Zeus in his wisdom withheld some gifts from *you*? He gave you the imperial sceptre and the homage it brings with it, but he did not give you courage – and courage is the secret of power. Sir, do you really believe the Achaeans to be the cowards and recreants that your words imply? If you, for one, have set your heart on getting away, why not be off? The road is clear, and your ships are standing by the sea, the whole great fleet of them that brought you from Mycenae. But the rest of the long-haired Achaeans are going to stay till we sack Troy. No; they too can take to the ships like you and scuttle home; and we two, I and Sthenelus, will fight on till we reach our goal in Ilium. It is by Heaven's will that we are here.'

The Achaeans were all delighted with Diomedes tamer of horses. They shouted their approval. And now the Charioteer Nestor rose to speak. 'Tydeides,' he said, 'you are a great man in a fight, and in debate you have no rival of your age. There is not one of us here who will cavil at your speech or gainsay a word of it. But you stopped too soon. The fact is that, although you talk sense to the Argive kings and were quite right in saying what you did, you are still rather young – indeed you might have been my youngest son. And I, who am so much older than yourself, am left to explain the implications of your speech and work them out in detail. When I come to do so, I shall count on everyone's support, even King Agamemnon's; for that man is indeed an enemy of his country, clan and hearth who enjoys the bitter taste of civil war. But enough for the moment. Let us take our cue from the dark night and prepare for supper. Sentries must be posted at intervals along the trench outside the wall. That is a duty I leave to the younger men. And after that, you, Atreides, as our overlord, must give us a lead. Invite the seniors to a banquet. It is a proper thing for you to do, and one that cannot hurt you. Day by day Achaean ships bring wine to you over the seas from Thrace. Your huts are full of it; and as the King of this great people, it is for you to offer hospitality. When you have gathered us all under your roof, you must listen to the man who can give you the best advice. And God knows we Achaeans need the best and cleverest we can get, with all these enemy fires so close to the ships. Nobody finds *them* a pleasant sight. This very night will make or mar the expedition.'

Nestor's advice was well received and promptly followed. Armed sentries went out at the double under the command of Prince Thrasymedes, Nestor's son; Ascalaphus and Ialmenus, children of the War-god; Meriones, Aphareus, and Deipyrus; and the noble Lycomedes, Creon's son. There were seven captains of the guard, and a hundred young men marched behind each, with long spears in their hands. They took their posts midway between the ditch and the wall, and there each party lit a fire and everyone prepared his supper.

Meanwhile Atreides led the whole party of senior commanders to his hut and had a savoury meal served up for them. They helped themselves to the good things spread before them, and when all had satisfied their hunger and thirst, the old man Nestor took the floor and expounded his idea. He had their interest at heart; and this was not the only time his wisdom won the day. 'Your majesty, Agamemnon son of Atreus, King of Men,' he said; 'with you my speech begins and it will end with you. You are King of a great people, for whose wise governance Zeus put the sceptre in your hands and entrusted you with the laws. So it behoves you, above all, both to give and listen to advice, and not only that, but to carry out the suggestions that others may feel bound to put forward in your interest. In any case, you will get the credit for whatever moves originate with *them*. And now I will tell you what I think is best, in the confidence that nobody will hit on a better remedy than mine. I long ago made up my mind, and I have not altered it; in fact, your majesty, not since the moment when you infuriated Achilles by taking the lady Briseis from his hut. We were all against it; and I, for one, did my utmost to dissuade you. But your arrogant temper got the better of you and you degraded a man of the highest distinction, whom the gods themselves esteem, by confiscating his prize, to your own profit. Which brings me to my point. Even at this late hour let us take steps to approach and placate him with peace offerings and a humble apology.'

'My venerable lord,' replied Agamemnon King of Men, 'the account of my blind folly that you have given us is wholly true. Blinded I was – I do not deny it myself. The man whom Zeus has taken to his heart and honours as he does Achilles, to the point of crushing the Achaeans for his sake, is worth an army. But since I did give in to a lamentable impulse and commit this act of folly, I am willing to go back on it and propitiate him with a handsome indemnity. Before you all, I will enumerate the splendid gifts I offer: – seven tripods, untarnished by the flames; ten talents of gold; twenty cauldrons of gleaming copper; and twelve powerful, prize-winning racehorses. Why, with nothing more than the prizes they have won for me, a man would not be badly off or short of precious gold. In addition, I will give him seven women, skilled in the fine crafts, Lesbians whom I chose for their exceptional beauty as my part of the spoils when he captured the city of Lesbos. These he shall have from me, and with them the woman I took from him, the daughter of Briseus. Moreover I shall give him my solemn oath that I have never been in her bed and slept with her, as a man does with a woman. All these gifts shall be put in his hands at once. Later, if the gods permit us to sack the great city of Priam, let him come in with us when we are sharing out the spoils, load his ship with gold and bronze to his heart's content, and pick out twenty Trojan women for himself, the loveliest he can find after Argive Helen. And if in due course we get back to Achaean Argos, the richest of all lands, he can become my son-in-law, and I will treat him as I do Orestes, my own beloved son, who is being brought up there in the lap of luxury. I have three daughters in my palace, Chrysothemis, Laodice and Iphianassa. Of these he shall choose for his own whichever he likes best, and take her to Peleus' house without making the usual gifts. Indeed, I will pay *him* a dowry, a generous one, bigger than anyone has ever given with his daughter. Not only that, but I will give him seven fine towns: Cardamyle, Enope and grassy Hire; holy Pherae and Antheia with its deep meadows; beautiful Aepeia and Pedasus rich in vines. They are all near the sea, in the farthest part of sandy Pylos. Their citizens are rich in flocks and cattle. They would do homage and pay tribute to him as though he were a god, acknowledging his sceptre and prospering under his paternal sway. All this I will do for him if he relents. Let him surrender. Why do we loathe Hades more than any god, if not because he is so adamantine and unyielding? Yes, let him submit himself to me, who am his senior by so much, both as a man and as a king.'

'Your majesty, Agamemnon son of Atreus, King of Men,' replied Nestor the Gerenian charioteer; 'nobody can say that your present offer to Prince Achilles is not generous. Very well then, let us send a deputation with all speed to the hut of Peleus' son. I am ready to nominate the men myself, and they must not refuse the duty. First of all the venerable Phoenix – he can go in advance – and after him the great Aias and the noble Odysseus. Of the heralds, Odius and Eurybates are the men to go with them. But first let someone fetch water for our hands and call for silence, so that we may pray to Zeus the Son of Cronos and implore his grace.'

Everyone was satisfied with Nestor's arrangements. Heralds hastened to pour water over their hands, while their squires filled the mixing-bowls to the brim with drink, and after pouring a little first in each man's cup, served them all with wine. When they had made their libations and drunk as much as they wished, the envoys set out from the hut of Agamemnon son of Atreus, after Nestor the Gerenian charioteer had given them full instructions, glancing from one man to another as he exhorted them to do their utmost to placate the peerless Achilles, but with his eye for the most part on Odysseus.

Aias and Odysseus walked together along the shore of the sounding sea, with many a prayer to the great Sea-god who girdles the world that the task of softening the proud heart of Achilles might not prove too hard. When they came to the Myrmidons' huts and ships, they found the prince beguiling the time with music. He was singing of famous men and accompanying himself on a tuneful lyre, a beautifully ornamented instrument with a silver crossbar, which he had chosen from the spoils when he destroyed Eëtion's city. He was alone but for Patroclus, who was sitting opposite with his eyes on Achilles, quietly waiting for him to stop singing. The two envoys drew near, the noble Odysseus leading, and halted in front of the prince. Surprised, Achilles sprang to his feet with the lyre in his hand and came forward from the chair in which he had been sitting. Patroclus too got up when he saw the men; and with a gesture of greeting, Achilles the great runner said: 'Welcome – to two dear friends! It was time that someone came; and angry as I am, there are no two Achaeans whom I love more than you.'

With this, the noble Achilles led them into his hut and seated them on chairs with purple coverings. Then he turned quickly to Patroclus, who was standing by, and said: 'Bring out a bigger bowl, my lord Patroclus, put less water in the wine, and give every man a cup. Here are my dearest friends under my own roof.'

Patroclus carried out his comrade's orders. He put down a big bench in the firelight, and laid on it the backs of a sheep and a fat goat and the chine of a great hog rich in lard. Automedon held these for him, while Achilles jointed them, and then carved up the joints and spitted the slices. Meanwhile, Patroclus, the royal son of Menoetius, made the fire blaze up. When it had burnt down again and the flames had disappeared, he scattered the embers and laid the spits above them, resting them on dogs, after he had sprinkled the meat with holy salt. When he had roasted it and heaped it up on platters, Patroclus fetched some bread and set it out on the table in handsome baskets; and Achilles divided the meat into portions. This done, he took a chair by the wall, opposite King Odysseus, and told his friend Patroclus to sacrifice to the gods. Patroclus threw the ritual pieces on the fire, and they all helped themselves to the good things spread before them. When their thirst and hunger were satisfied, Aias nodded to Phoenix. But Odysseus caught the signal, and having filled his cup with wine drank to Achilles and said:

'Your health, Achilles! With all these appetizing dishes to dispose of, we cannot complain of our rations, either in my lord Agamemnon's hut or here again in yours. But at the moment the pleasures of the table are far from our thoughts. We are confronted by a disaster, your highness, the magnitude of which appals us. Unless you rouse yourself to fight, we have no more than an even chance of saving our gallant ships or seeing them destroyed. The insolent Trojans and their famous allies are bivouacking close to the ships and wall. Their camp is bright with fires. They are convinced that there is nothing left to stop them now from swooping down on our black ships. Zeus the Son of Cronos has encouraged them, with lightning flashes on the right. Hector has run amuck, triumphant and all-powerful. He trusts in Zeus, and fears neither man nor god in the frenzy that possesses him. His one prayer is for the early coming of the gracious Dawn, for he is itching to hack the peaks from the sterns of our ships, to send up the ships themselves in flames, to smoke us out and to slaughter us by the hulls. And indeed I am terribly afraid that the gods may let him carry out his threats – that it may be our fate to perish here, far from Argos where the horses graze. Up with you then, if even at this late hour you want to rescue the exhausted troops from the Trojans' fury. If you refuse, you yourself will regret it later, for when the damage has been done there will be no mending it. Bestir yourself, before that stage is reached, to save the Danaans from catastrophe.

'My good friend, when your father Peleus sent you from Phthia to join Agamemnon, did he not admonish you in these words: "My son, Athene and Here, if they wish you well, are going to make you strong. What *you* must do is to keep a check on that proud spirit of yours; for a kind heart is a better thing than pride. Quarrels are deadly. Be reconciled at once; and all the Argives young and old will look up to you the more"? Those were the old man's precepts – which you have forgotten. Yet even so, it is not too late for you to yield. Give up this bitter animosity. Agamemnon is ready to make you ample compensation the moment you relent. If you will listen, I will enumerate the gifts he destined for you in his hut. Seven tripods, untarnished by the flames; ten talents of gold; twenty cauldrons of gleaming copper; and twelve powerful, prize-winning race-horses. He said that with nothing more than the prizes they had won for him, a man would not be badly off or short of precious gold. In addition, he will give you seven women, skilled in the fine crafts, Lesbians whom he chose for their exceptional beauty as his part of the spoils when you yourself captured the city of Lesbos. These you shall have from him, and with them the woman he took from you, the daughter of Briseus. Moreover, he will give you his solemn oath that he has never been in her bed and slept with her, as a man does, your highness, with a woman. All these gifts shall be put in your hands at once. Later, if the gods permit us to sack the great city of Priam, you must come in with us when we are sharing out the spoils, load your ship with gold and bronze to your heart's content, and pick out twenty Trojan women for yourself, the loveliest you can find after Argive Helen. And if in due course we get back to Achaean Argos, the richest of all lands, you can become his son-in-law, and he will treat you as he does Orestes, his own beloved son, who is being brought up there in the lap of luxury. He has three daughters in his palace, Chrysothemis, Laodice and Iphianassa. Of these you shall choose for your own whichever you like best and take her to Peleus' house without making the usual gifts. In fact, he will pay *you* a dowry, a generous one, bigger than anybody has ever given with his daughter. Not only that, but he will give you seven fine towns, Cardamyle, Enope and grassy Hire; holy Pherae and Antheia with its deep meadows; beautiful Aepeia, and Pedasus rich in vines. They are all near the sea, in the farthest part of sandy Pylos. Their citizens are rich in flocks and cattle. They would do homage and pay tribute to you as though you were a god, acknowledging your sceptre and prospering under your paternal sway. All this he will do for you, if you relent. But if your hatred of Atreides, gifts and all, outweighs every other consideration, do have some pity on the rest of the united Achaeans, lying dead-beat in their camp. They will honour you like a god. Indeed, you could cover yourself with glory in their eyes, for now is the time when you could get Hector himself. He fancies that he has no match among all the Danaans whom the ships brought here, and he may even venture near you, in his insensate fury.'

'Royal son of Laertes, Odysseus of the nimble wits,' replied Achilles the great runner; 'to save you from sitting there and taking it in turns to coax me, I had better tell you point-blank how I feel and what I am going to do. I loathe like Hell's Gates the man who thinks one thing and says another; so here I give you my decision. You can take it that neither my lord Agamemnon nor the rest of the Danaans are going to win me over, since it appears that a man gets no thanks for struggling with the enemy day in, day out. His share is the same, whether he sits at home or fights his best. Cowards and brave men are equally respected; and death comes alike to one who has done nothing and one who has toiled hard. All I have suffered by constantly risking my life in battle has left me no better off than the rest. I have been like a bird that brings every morsel she picks up to her unfledged chicks, however hard it goes with *her*. I have spent many a sleepless night and fought through many a bloody day – against men who, like us, are fighting for their womenfolk. I have captured twelve towns from the sea, besides eleven that I took by land in the deep-soiled realm of Troy. From each I got a splendid haul of loot, the whole of which I brought back every time and gave to my lord Agamemnon son of Atreus, who had stayed behind by the ships, and who, when I handed it over, gave a little of it out, in bits, but kept the lion's share. What he did give to the princes and kings in recognition of their rank is safe in their possession; and I am the only one he has robbed. It is not as though he had no wife. He *has* one, of his own choice. Let him sleep with her and be content.

'For that matter, what drove the Argives to make war on Troy? What did Atreides raise an army for and bring it here, if not for Helen of the lovely hair? And are the Atreidae the only men on earth who love their wives? Does not every decent and right-minded man love and cherish his own woman, as I loved that girl, with all my heart, though she was a captive of my spear? But now that he has snatched her from my arms and swindled me, don't let him try his tricks on me again. I know him too well. He will not succeed.

'No, Odysseus, he must look to you and the other kings if he wants to save the ships from going up in flames. He has already done marvels without me. He has built a wall, I see, and dug a trench along it, a fine broad trench, complete with palisade. But even so he cannot keep the murderous Hector out! Why, in the days when I took the field with the Achaeans, nothing would have induced Hector to throw his men into battle at any distance from the city walls. He came no farther than the Scaean Gate and the oak-tree, where he took me on alone one day, and was lucky to get home alive. But things have changed, and now I do not choose to fight with my lord Hector. So to-morrow I am going to sacrifice to Zeus and all the other gods, then lade and launch my ships. The very first thing in the morning, if you have the curiosity to look, you will see them breasting the Hellespont where the fishes play, and my men inside them straining at the oar. And in three days, given a good crossing by the great Sea-god, I should set foot on the deep soil of Phthia. I left a rich home there when I had the misfortune to come here; and now I shall enrich it further by what I bring back, the gold, the red copper, the girdled women, and the grey iron that fell to me by lot – everything, in fact, but the prize of honour that was given me and insultingly withdrawn by one and the same man, his majesty King Agamemnon son of Atreus.

'Tell him all I say, and tell him in public, so that the rest may frown on any further efforts he may make to overreach a Danaan prince, unconscionable schemer that he always is. And yet he would not dare to look me in the eye, for all his impudence. No; I will help him neither by my advice nor in the field. He has broken faith with me and played me false: never again shall I be taken in by what he says. So much for him. Let him go quietly to perdition. Zeus in his wisdom has already addled his brains.

'As for his gifts, I like them just as little as I like the man himself. Not if he offered me ten times or twenty times as much as he possesses or could raise elsewhere, all the revenues of Orchomenus or of Thebes, Egyptian Thebes, where the houses are stuffed with treasure, and through every one of a hundred gates two hundred warriors sally out with their chariots and horses; not if his gifts were as many as the grains of sand or particles of dust, would Agamemnon win me over. First he must pay me in kind for the bitter humiliation I endured.

'Again, I will not have any daughter of Agamemnon son of Atreus for my wife. She could be lovely as golden Aphrodite and skilful as Athene of the Flashing Eyes, and yet I would not marry her. He can choose some other Achaean, someone more royal than me and on a level with himself. If the gods allow me to get safely home, Peleus will need no help in finding me a wife. Up and down Hellas and Phthia there are plenty of Achaean girls, daughters of the noblemen in command of the forts. I have only to choose one and make her my own. There were often times at home when I had no higher ambition than to marry some suitable girl of my own station and enjoy the fortune that my old father Peleus had made. For life, as I see it, is not to be set off, either against the fabled wealth of splendid Ilium in the peaceful days before the Achaeans came, or against all the treasure that is piled up in Rocky Pytho behind the Marble Threshold of the Archer-King Apollo. Cattle and sturdy sheep can be had for the taking; and tripods and chestnut horses can be bought. But you cannot steal or buy back a man's life, when once the breath has left his lips. My divine Mother, Thetis of the Silver Feet, says that Destiny has left two courses open to me on my journey to the grave. If I stay here and play my part in the siege of Troy, there is no home-coming for me, though I shall win undying fame. But if I go home to my own country, my good name will be lost, though I shall have long life, and shall be spared an early death.

'One more point. I recommend all the rest of you to sail home too, for you will never reach your goal in the steep streets of Ilium. All-seeing Zeus has stretched out a loving hand above that city, and its people have taken heart. So leave me now and report to the Achaean lords in open council, as you seniors have the right to do – they must think out some better way of saving the ships and all the troops beside them, now that these overtures to me have met with blank refusal. But Phoenix can stay here and spend the night with us. Then he could embark for home with me in the morning – that is to say, if he wants to. There will be no compulsion.'

Achilles had finished. They were stunned by the down-rightness of his refusal, and a long silence ensued, which the old charioteer Phoenix was the first to break. He was in such terror for the Achaean ships that he burst into tears. 'My noble lord, Achilles,' he said, 'if you really think of sailing home and are so obsessed by anger that you refuse to save the gallant ships from going up in flames, what is to become of me without you, my dear child? How could I possibly stay here alone? Did not the old charioteer Peleus make me your guardian when he sent you off from Phthia to join Agamemnon? You were a mere lad, with no experience of the hazards of war, nor of debate, where people make their mark. It was to teach you all these things, to make a speaker of you and a man of action, that he sent me with you; and I could not bring myself to let you go, dear child, and stay behind, not if God himself undertook to strip me of my years and turn me into the sturdy youngster I was when I first left Hellas, the land of lovely women. I ran away because of a quarrel with my father, Amyntor son of Ormenus, and the reason why we were at daggers drawn was this. He was making love to a beautiful courtesan and was neglecting his wife, my mother, who kept entreating me to turn the woman's heart against the old man by forestalling him and spending a night in her arms. I consented, and did so. My father knew at once, and with solemn imprecations called on the avenging Furies to see to it that he should never have to take a son of mine on his lap; and as time showed, his curses were fulfilled by the gods, by Zeus of the Underworld and august Persephone. I was so enraged that my first instinct was to put my father to the sword. But one of the immortals restrained me. He made me think of public opinion, of the obloquy I should incur, and the horror of being called a parricide by my compatriots. Yet I could not bear the prospect of hanging about any longer in my angry father's house. Of course, the friends and kinsmen who had rallied round me were most importunate in their efforts to make me stay at home. Fat sheep and shambling cattle with crooked horns were slaughtered without end; many a fine fat hog was stretched across the flames to have his bristles singed; and many a jar of the old man's mellow wine was drunk. For nine nights they camped beside me, taking it in turn to go on guard, and keeping two fires burning, one under the colonnade of the walled yard, and the other in the fore-court, outside the door of the sleeping-quarters. But on the tenth night, which was pitch dark, I burst open the stout doors of my bedroom and escaped. I found it easy to climb the courtyard wall, and not one of the men on guard or the maid-servants saw me. Then I fled in earnest, right across Hellas and its spreading lawns, to deep-soiled Phthia, mother of sheep, where I presented myself to Peleus, the King. He took me to his heart and loved me as a father loves an only son, the cherished heir to a great estate. He made me a rich man by giving me a populous district to rule, and I settled down on the borders of Phthia as King of the Dolopes.

'Since then, most worshipful Achilles, all my loving devotion has gone to make you what you are. Do you remember how you would refuse to go out to dinner or touch your food at home with anyone but me; how I always had to take you on my knees and pamper you, by cutting titbits for you from my meat and holding my cup to your lips? You often soaked the front of my tunic with the wine that dribbled from your clumsy little mouth. Yes, I went through a great deal for you and worked hard. I felt that since Heaven was not going to send me a boy of my own, I had better make *you* my son, most worshipful Achilles, so that you could save me some day from a miserable end.

'Conquer your pride, Achilles. You have no right to be so stubborn. The very gods, for all their greater excellence and majesty and power, are capable of being swayed. Even they are turned from their course by sacrifice and humble prayers, libations and burnt-offerings, when the miscreant and sinner bend the knee to them in supplication. Do you not know that prayers are Daughters of almighty Zeus? They are wrinkled creatures, with a halting gait and downcast eyes, who make it their business to follow Sin about. But Sin is strong, and quick enough to leave them all behind. Stealing a march on them, she roams the world and brings mankind to grief. *They* come after and put the trouble right. The man who receives these Daughters of Zeus with humility when they approach him, is greatly blessed by them and has his own petitions granted. But when a man hardens his heart and rebuffs them, they go and pray to Zeus the Son of Cronos that he may himself be overtaken by Sin and punished through his fall. This applies to you, Achilles. You must give their due to the Daughters of Zeus by letting them placate you as they do all noble-hearted men. If my lord Agamemnon had not made you a generous offer, with the promise of more to come, but had persisted in his rancour, I should be the last person to bid you cast your anger to the winds and help the Argives, however great their need. But as it is, he is not only offering you a great deal now, but has pledged himself to future liberality, besides choosing as ambassadors to plead his cause the most distinguished men in the whole army, who are your own best friends among the Argives. Their pleas, their pilgrimage here, are things that you must not dismiss as trifles, though nobody can blame you for the resentment you have felt till now.

'We have heard many comparable tales of noblemen in olden times, who had worked themselves up into a passion, yet proved amenable to gifts and yielded to persuasion. Looking back a good many years, I can remember a case myself. We are all friends here, and I will tell you the story. The Curetes were fighting the warlike Aetolians at the city of Calydon. Losses were heavy on both sides. The Aetolians were defending their lovely town of Calydon, and the Curetes doing all they could to sack it. The trouble had started when Artemis of the Golden Throne took offence and let a monster loose on Calydon because King Oeneus had failed to make her any harvest-offering on the sacred hill in his estate. All the other gods enjoyed rich sacrifices; it was only this Daughter of almighty Zeus to whom he offered nothing. Perhaps he forgot her, perhaps he counted wrong – in either case he made a fatal mistake. For in her wrath, the Lady of the Bow sent him a creature of the gods, a ravenous wild boar, with flashing tusks, who settled down to ravage the royal lands. He strewed the ground with the tall fruit-trees he brought tumbling down, rooting them up, with the blossom on the twigs. But at last Oeneus' son Meleager killed him. He had to raise a force of huntsmen and hounds from many cities to do this; for the beast was far too powerful to be dealt with by a handful and brought a number of them to a wretched end. And even then, Artemis started a battle-royal over the carcass, setting the Curetes and the proud Aetolians at each other's throats for his head and shaggy hide.

'In the war that ensued, so long as the redoubtable Meleager played his part, things went badly for the Curetes, who were unable to sit down and besiege the city, for all their numbers. But many a sensible man is at times overmastered by passion, and that is what happened to Meleager now. Enraged with Althaea, his mother, he lay at home idle with his wife, the lovely Cleopatra, daughter of Marpessa of the slim ankles, herself the daughter of Euenus. Cleopatra's father, Idas, had in his time been the strongest man on earth and had actually faced Lord Phoebus Apollo with his bow for the sake of Marpessa, this lady with the lovely ankles. And later, in their home, Cleopatra's parents had given her the nickname Alcyone, in memory of her mother's life as a kingfisher and the plaintive calls she uttered when the Archer-god Apollo carried her off.

'Well, Meleager took to his bed, lay there with Cleopatra and nursed his soul-destroying wrath. It was his mother's curses that had embittered him. He had killed her brother, and she in her grief had importuned the gods to kill her son, falling on her knees, deluging her lap with tears, and beating the bountiful earth with her fists, as she called on Hades and august Persephone. And the Fury that walks in the dark and has inexorable thoughts heard her from Erebus.

'Before long the Curetes were storming at the city gates. One could hear them battering the walls. And now the Aetolian Elders tried to induce Meleager to come out and save the town. They sent him a deputation of the leading priests and promised him a liberal donation. They told him he could choose an estate of fifty acres for his own use, half vine-land and half open ploughland, to be carved out of the richest part of the lovely Calydonian plain. The old charioteer Oeneus added his prayers to theirs. He stood on the threshold of Meleager's lofty bedroom, and shook the solid wooden doors, begging and beseeching his son. His sisters and his lady mother earnestly adjured him too (though they only made him still more obstinate), and so did his comrades-in-arms, the dearest and most loyal friends he had. But he resisted all their entreaties till the very last moment, when the Curetes had scaled the walls and were firing the great city, and the missiles were hailing down on his very room. At that point Meleager's lovely wife approached him in tears. She pictured all the miseries that people suffer when their town is captured, the slaughter of the men, the city laid in dust and ashes by the flames, the alien enemy carrying off the children

and the women in their girdled gowns. Her sad recital
touched his heart, and he came out and donned his gleaming
armour. Thus he saved the Aetolians from disaster, at the dic-
tates of his own conscience. And that being so, they gave him
none of the splendid gifts they had offered. He saved them but
got nothing by it.

'My friend, do not think as he did or feel inspired to follow
his example. When the ships are already on fire, it will be
harder than ever to save them. No; come while the gifts are
still to be had, and the Achaeans will treat you like a god. If
you come in and risk your life in battle with no such induce-
ment, they will not think nearly so well of you, even though
you turn defeat into victory.'

Phoenix had done; and now Achilles the great runner spoke
again. 'My lord Phoenix,' he said, 'my dear old friend; I have
no use for the Achaeans' good opinion. I am content with the
approbation of Zeus, which will keep me by my beaked ships
as long as breath remains in my body and I can use my limbs.
What is more, I wish you to know that I object to your
currying favour with my lord Agamemnon by this attempt
to upset me with a display of maudlin emotion. Be careful
how you give that man your heart, or you may change my
love for you to hate. The right thing for you to do is to cross
the man who crosses me. I have decided, and these men shall
tell him so – I had rather give you half my kingdom than
relent. Meanwhile, stay here yourself – there's a comfortable
bed for you to sleep on – and at daybreak we will decide
whether to go home or not.'

As he finished, Achilles quietly signalled to Patroclus with a
movement of his eyebrows to make the bed for Phoenix, so
that the others might think of getting on their way as soon as
possible. It was Aias, the royal son of Telamon, who made the
first move. Turning to Laertes' son, he said: 'My lord Odysseus
of the nimble wits, let us go; for it seems to me that our
mission is doomed to failure, this time at any rate. Bad as the
news is, we must at once report it to the Danaans, who are no
doubt sitting up and awaiting us. But I cannot help reflecting

on the combination of rancour and arrogance that Achilles has displayed. Ruthlessness too. Not a thought for the affection of his comrades, who made him the idol of our camp! The inhumanity of it! After all, even in cases of murder it is quite common for a man to accept blood-money for a brother or maybe a son. The killer does not even have to leave the country if he pays up to the next of kin, whose pride and injured feelings are appeased by the indemnity. But you, Achilles – God knows why – have worked yourself up into this implacable fury over a girl, a single girl. And here are we, offering you seven of the very best, and a great deal more into the bargain. Be a little more forbearing. And remember your obligations as our host. We are under your roof; we were picked from the whole Danaan army; and we wish for nothing better than to remain your closest and your dearest friends of all the Achaeans that there are.'

'Your highness, Aias, royal son of Telamon,' Achilles the great runner answered; 'there is much in what you say. But my blood boils when I think of what happened, and the vile way in which Atreides treated me in public, like some disreputable outcast. Go now, and report my decision. I will not think again of bloodshed and war, until Prince Hector, son of the wise Priam, reaches the huts and ships of the Myrmidons, killing Argives as he comes, and destroys the fleet by fire. I have a notion that, however furious his attack may be, Hector will be brought up short, here by my own hut and my own black ship.'

When Achilles finished, his visitors, after each taking up a two-handled cup and offering a libation, made their way back along the line of ships, with Odysseus at their head. Patroclus told his men and the maidservants quickly to make a comfortable bed for Phoenix. When the women had carried out his orders and spread fleeces and a rug and a sheet of fine linen on the bedstead, the old man lay down on it and waited there for the blessed light of dawn. Achilles himself slept in a corner of his well-built wooden hut, with a woman he had brought from Lesbos at his side, the daughter of Phorbas, Diomede of the lovely cheeks. Patroclus slept in the corner opposite. He too had a companion, Iphis of the girdled robe, whom the noble Achilles had given him when he captured the high fortress of Scyros, the city of Enyeus.

The envoys reached Agamemnon's hut and were no sooner inside it than the Achaean lords leapt to their feet and were pledging them on every side with golden cups and bombarding them with questions. King Agamemnon was the most urgent of all. 'Illustrious Odysseus, flower of Achaean chivalry,' he said; 'tell me at once. Will he save the ships from being burnt; or is that proud spirit still implacable?'

The steadfast excellent Odysseus made his report: 'Your majesty, Agamemnon son of Atreus, King of Men; the man has no intention of relenting. In fact he is more virulent than ever. He repudiates you and your gifts. He says you can find out for yourself, with your friends' assistance, how to save the ships and men. Meanwhile, he threatens to drag his own curved ships into the sea at dawn. And he said he advised all the rest of us as well to sail for home. "You will never reach your goal," he said, "in the steep streets of Ilium. All-seeing Zeus has stretched out a loving hand above that city, and its people have taken heart." Those were his words. Of my fellow envoys, Aias and the two heralds (both reliable men) are here to bear me out. But the old man Phoenix is sleeping there. Achilles pressed him to stay, so that he could embark with him for home in the morning if he wished to, though he said he would not force him.'

Not a word was said when Odysseus had done. His message and the blunt way in which it was delivered left the Achaean lords aghast, and a long and gloomy silence followed, which was not broken till at last Diomedes of the loud war-cry ventured to speak. 'Your majesty,' he said, 'Agamemnon son of Atreus, King of Men; it is a thousand pities that you brought yourself to plead with my lord Achilles and make him such a princely offer. He is a proud man at the best of times; and now you have given him an even better conceit of himself. Well, we must let him be, whether he sails or stays. He'll fight again, when his own conscience speaks and the spirit moves him. And now I hope you will all follow my lead. For the moment, go to bed – you have enjoyed the food and wine that a man needs to keep up his strength and courage. But in the first fair light of Dawn, you, sir, must take action. Deploy your infantry and horse in front of the ships, and inspire them by your word of command, as well as by fighting in the front line yourself.'

The kings all expressed their approval of this advice from Diomedes of the loud war-cry. They made their libations and retired to their several huts, where they lay down and enjoyed the boon of sleep.

X

NIGHT INTERLUDE

THE chieftains of the united Achaeans spent the rest of the night by the ships in the soft arms of sleep. But Agamemnon son of Atreus, their Commander-in-Chief, had too much on his mind for easeful sleep. Groan after groan came up from the depths of his being, and his heart was shot through by fear, as the sky is pierced by lightning when the Lord of the Lady Here is brewing a hailstorm, or torrential rain, or a blizzard to mantle the fields with snow, or is about to unleash the dogs of war on some unhappy land. When he glanced out across the Trojan plain, he was confounded by the innumerable fires burning in front of Ilium, by the music of the flutes and reed-pipes, and the voices of the troops. And when he looked at the ships and his own army, he plucked the hair from his head by the roots for Zeus in heaven to see, and his proud heart came near to breaking. In the end he could think of nothing better than to go straight to Nestor son of Neleus in the hope that together they might hit upon some infallible way of saving the expedition from disaster. So he sat up on his bed and put on his tunic. He bound a stout pair of sandals on his comely feet, cast over his shoulders the glossy pelt of a great and tawny lion, which came down to his ankles, and then picked up his spear.

Menelaus was finding it as difficult as his brother to snatch a moment's sleep. He too was obsessed by anxiety for the Argives, who for his sake had unsheathed the sword and come to Troy across a wilderness of water. He cast a spotted leopard's skin round his broad shoulders, took up his bronze helmet and put it on his head, picked up a spear in his great hand, and set out to rouse his brother, the overlord of all the Argives, whom the people worshipped. He found him by the stern of his ship, slinging his armour on his shoulders. Agamemnon was delighted to see him; but Menelaus of the loud war-cry was the first to speak. 'My dear brother,' he said, 'why are you arming like this? Had you thought of sending a man out to spy on the Trojans? I am much afraid that you won't find anyone willing to accept the duty. It would take a stout heart indeed to venture out alone through the mysterious night and spy on the enemy camp.'

'Menelaus, my lord,' said King Agamemnon, 'what you and I must do is to rack our brains for some way of relieving the Argives and saving the ships, now that Zeus has turned against us. It is clear that Hector's offerings mean more to him than ours. That a single man – and he not a son of the gods – should do such damage in the course of a day as Hector has done to our arms is something quite outside my experience. But the fact remains that he has struck us blows which we shall feel to our cost for many a long day to come. However, I wish you now to run quickly by the ships and call Aias and Idomeneus, while I go to the excellent Nestor and tell him to get up. He might well pay a visit to the outposts, which are so important, and keep the sentries up to the mark. They will pay more attention to him than to anyone, for his own son and Idomeneus' squire Meriones are in command. We put them in charge of the whole detachment.'

'Very well,' said Menelaus of the loud war-cry; 'but what of myself? What exactly do you wish *me* to do? Shall I keep with them and wait for you to join us? Or am I to run back to you when I have given them their orders?'

'Keep with them,' said Agamemnon King of Men, 'or you and I may miss each other on the way – there are a great many paths across the camp. Give your man a shout in each case, and as you call him up, mention his lineage and his father's name. Let all of them have their dignities, and do not be proud. We too must work. Indeed Zeus seems to have picked us out for trouble from the moment we were born.'

Agamemnon dismissed his brother after carefully instructing him, and himself went in search of Nestor, the shepherd of the people, whom he found lying on a soft bed by his hut and his own black ship. At his side lay his ornate arms, a shield, two spears and a shining helmet; also the glittering belt that the old man put on when he prepared to lead his men into battle; for whatever the danger, he took no account of his age. Nestor, raising himself on his elbow and lifting his head, called out and challenged Atreides. 'Who goes there, wandering about the camp alone, close to the ships, at dead of night when everyone's asleep? Are you looking for a stray mule or one of your friends? Speak up, and don't advance on me before you answer. What is your business here?'

In reply to his challenge, Agamemnon King of Men said: 'Nestor son of Neleus, flower of Achaean chivalry; surely you recognize Agamemnon son of Atreus, the man whom Zeus has singled out for persecution as long as breath remains in his body and he can use his limbs. I am on the move as you see, because I am too much troubled about the war and the Achaeans' plight to enjoy a moment's sleep. My anxiety for my people is so acute that I am no longer master of myself. I am in torture. My heart is hammering as though it would burst from my breast, and my knees are trembling underneath me. I see that you can sleep no better than myself. If you want something to do, come with me and visit the sentries, to make sure that they have not been overcome by fatigue and fallen asleep, forgetting all about their duties. The enemy are sitting very close, and we know nothing of their plans. They might even launch a night attack.'

'Your majesty Atreides, Agamemnon King of Men,' replied the Gerenian horseman Nestor; 'I am quite sure that Zeus the Counsellor is not going to let Hector realize all the high hopes that he may be entertaining now. On the contrary, I fancy he will have more to worry him than ever, if Achilles sees fit to recover his temper. Of course I will go with you. But let us wake some of the others too – the gallant Diomedes and Odysseus, Aias the Runner, and the stalwart Meges. It would also be a good thing if someone could go along and call up the other two, Telamonian Aias and King Idomeneus, whose ships are at the end of the line and some way off. But what of Menelaus? I like and respect him, but I do blame him, and must say so even if it makes you angry, for sleeping at such a moment and leaving all the work to you. This is a time when he should be engaged with all the senior officers, imploring them to do their best. The situation is desperate.'

'Sir,' said King Agamemnon, 'there are times when I should indeed be glad to see you take him to task. He is often inclined to do nothing and let things slide, not through laziness or any lack of brains, but because he looks to me and depends on my initiative. To-night, however, he got up well before me and reported at my quarters. I have already sent him out to call up the two men you mentioned. So let us be going. We shall find them with the pickets outside the gates, where I told them to fall in.'

'If he is going to do as well as that,' said Nestor the Gerenian charioteer, 'no one will have a word to say against him or fail to respond to his leadership.'

As he spoke, he got into his tunic, then bound a pair of well-made sandals on his comely feet. Next he put on a purple cloak and fastened it with a brooch – it was a double cloak, with a thick nap on the wool, and he spread it out. Finally he picked up a strong spear with a sharp point of bronze, and set out on his way along the ships of the bronze-clad Achaeans.

The first man whom the Gerenian charioteer Nestor awakened was Odysseus, whose thoughts were like the thoughts of Zeus. He gave him a call, which woke him instantly. Odysseus came out of his hut and questioned his visitors: 'Why are you wandering about like this among the huts and ships at dead of night and unattended? What brings you here? It must be something serious.'

'Royal son of Laertes, Odysseus of the nimble wits,' answered Nestor the Gerenian charioteer, 'do not be annoyed with us. The Achaeans are indeed in serious trouble. But come along with us, and let us wake up some of the others whom we ought to consult before deciding whether to fight on or fly.'

When he heard this, Odysseus of the nimble wits went into his hut, slung his ornate shield on his back, and followed them. They went next to Diomedes son of Tydeus, and found him lying in the open outside his hut, with his armour. His men were sleeping round him with their shields for pillows. Their spears were stuck on end with the sharpened butts in the ground, and the bronze points flashed in the distance like lightning from Father Zeus. The prince was asleep, with the hide of a farmyard ox beneath him, and a glossy rug drawn under his head. Nestor the Gerenian charioteer went up to him, woke him with a touch of his foot, and flung a taunt at him to rouse him further. 'Wake up, Tydeides,' he said. 'Why should you sleep in comfort all night long? Has it escaped your notice that the Trojans are sitting on the plain above us, barely a stone's throw from the ships?'

Diomedes, who had woken and leapt up in a trice, replied with some feeling: 'You are a hard old man, sir, and you never take a moment's rest. Are there not younger men in the army to go the rounds and call up all the kings? There is no holding you down, my venerable lord.'

'My friend,' said Nestor the Gerenian horseman, 'I admit that you are right. I have my excellent sons, and I have troops in plenty, to go the rounds and call people up. But we are in a critical position. Our fate is balanced on a razor's edge – an appalling end for every man in the Achaean forces, or else salvation. However, if you are sorry for me – and you *are* the younger man – go yourself and wake Meges and Aias the Runner.'

Diomedes cast round his shoulders the glossy skin of a great lion, which reached to his feet, picked up his spear and went on his errand. When he had roused the two men in their huts, he brought them along with him.

The party then visited the outposts, but failed to catch any of the officers of the watch asleep. They were all sitting there with their weapons, on the alert, like dogs that keep uneasy watch over the sheep in a farmyard and think no more of sleep, because they have heard some savage animal coming down through the wooded hills with the hue and cry of men and hounds behind him. Thus the sentries kept watch through that evil night, banishing sleep from their eyes, and turning constantly towards the plain to catch the first sign of movement on the Trojans' part.

The old warrior was pleased with his inspection of the outposts, and gave them a word of encouragement: 'That is the style, my lads. Carry on; and let no one take a nap, or the enemy will swallow us up.'

He then passed quickly out across the trench, followed by the Argive kings who had been summoned to the council, and by Meriones and Nestor's noble son, whom they had invited to assist at their conference. Leaving the trench behind them, they sat down in an open place where the ground was not littered by the bodies of the dead. It was the very spot where the terrible Hector had paused in his slaughter of the Argives and turned back when night obscured the battlefield. After they had sat there for some time, exchanging their ideas, Nestor the Gerenian charioteer called for silence. 'My friends,' he said, 'I wonder if any man here has enough pluck and self-reliance to pay these arrogant Trojans a visit, on the chance of cutting off a straggler from the enemy? He might even overhear some talk about their plans and so find out whether they mean to stay in their advanced position by the ships, or to go back into the town, after their victory. If he discovered that and returned to us with a whole skin, there is not a man in the world who would not hear of his achievement. He will be well rewarded too. The leaders of the expedition will each give him a black ewe with its suckling lamb, a signal mark of honour, and he will be invited to all their feasts and ceremonial banquets.'

When Nestor had done, they all kept very quiet, all except Diomedes of the loud war-cry, who spoke up and said: 'Nestor, the adventure appeals to me. The Trojan camp is very near, and I will visit it. But I wish another man could go with me. I should feel more comfortable, and also more inclined to take a risk. Two men together seize advantages that one would miss; whereas a man on his own is liable to hesitate, if he does see a chance, and make stupid mistakes.'

At this, a number of others volunteered to go with Diomedes. Both the Aiantes, henchmen of Ares, wished to go. So did Meriones; and Nestor's son was eager. The famous spearman Menelaus son of Atreus also volunteered; and Odysseus too, the much-enduring Odysseus, said he would like to steal into the Trojan camp. Adventure was always dear to him.

Agamemnon King of Men now played his part. 'Diomedes son of Tydeus, my heart's delight,' he said, 'you shall have whatever companion you prefer, the best of the volunteers, of whom there are plenty. And you must not let respect for persons make you leave the better man and take the worse. Do not be influenced by a man's lineage, even if it is more royal than that of your choice.'

He said this in his terror for his red-haired brother Menelaus. But Diomedes of the loud war-cry soon came out with his decision: 'If it is really your pleasure that I should choose my companion myself, how could I overlook the godlike Odysseus, Pallas Athene's favourite, that gallant soul whom no adventure ever finds unready? Together, he and I could go through blazing fire and yet come home. He has the quickest brain of any man I know.'

'My lord Diomedes,' said the all-daring excellent Odysseus, 'there is no need for you to sing my praises, or to criticize me either, since you are talking to men who know me. Let us be off. The night is well advanced and dawn is near. The stars are past their zenith, and a good two-thirds of the night is gone, leaving us the third watch only.'

They said no more, but slung on their formidable arms. The veteran Thrasymedes gave Tydeides a two-edged sword, as his own had been left behind beside his ship, together with a shield. On his head he put an oxhide casque without peak or plume, of the sort called 'skull-cap', which young gallants wear to protect their heads. Meriones gave Odysseus a bow, a quiver and a sword, and set a leather helmet on his head. Inside it there was a strong lining of interwoven straps, under which a felt cap had been sewn in. The outer rim was cunningly adorned on either side by a row of white and flashing boars' tusks. This helmet originally came from Eleon, where Autolycus stole it from Amyntor son of Ormenus by breaking into his well-built house. Autolycus gave it to Amphidamas of Cythera to take to Scandaea; and Amphidamas gave it to Molus in return for hospitality. Molus, in his turn, gave it to his son Meriones to wear, and now it was Odysseus' head that it served to protect.

Armed in this formidable manner the pair set out, leaving all the chieftains there. Pallas Athene sent them a lucky omen, a heron close to their path on the right. The night was too dark for them to see the bird, but they heard it squawk, and Odysseus, pleased by the omen, offered a prayer to Athene: 'Hear me, Daughter of aegis-bearing Zeus, you that stand by my side in all my adventures – indeed I cannot make a move without your seeing me. To-night, Athene, show me your special favour, and grant that we may come back to the ships with some signal deed to our credit, which will make the Trojans sore.'

Diomedes of the loud war-cry followed him with a prayer of his own: 'Daughter of Zeus, Lady of Trito, hear me also. Be with me as you were with my noble father, Tydeus, when he went into Thebes as ambassador for the Achaeans, leaving their army on the banks of the Asopus. He went there with a friendly offer to the Cadmeians; but on his way back, he had a great and terrible thing to do, in which you helped him, Lady goddess, with your staunch support. Stand by me now and watch over me with the same devotion, and in return you shall have from me a yearling heifer, broad in the brow, whom no one yet has broken in and led beneath the yoke. She shall be sacrificed to you with gold foil on her horns.'

Thus they prayed; and Pallas Athene heard them. When their petitions to the Daughter of almighty Zeus were finished, they set out like a pair of lions through the black night, across the slaughter, picking their way among the corpses and the bloodstained arms.

The lordly Trojans too were given little time to sleep. Hector would not let them. He called together all the leading men, the Captains and Counsellors of the Trojans; and when he had gathered them round him, he told them of an idea that he had had. 'There is work to be done,' he said. 'Will anyone volunteer? A rich reward is offered, and I guarantee it to the man who does the job. Quite apart from the kudos he will win for himself, I will give the best chariot and pair of thoroughbreds in the Achaeans' camp to the man who dares to reconnoitre by the ships and find out whether the fleet is guarded as usual, or whether, as a result of their defeat at our hands, they are already discussing the possibility of flight, and are so utterly exhausted that they are not troubling to keep watch at night.'

Hector's challenge was at first received in complete silence. But among the Trojans present was a man called Dolon, the son of Eumedes, one of the sacred heralds – a rich man, with plenty of gold and bronze. His appearance, to be sure, was unattractive, but he was fast on his feet; and in a family of six he was the only son. This man came forward now and took the floor.

'Hector,' he said, 'the adventure appeals to me and I volunteer to reconnoitre for you by the ships. But first, will you hold up this staff and swear to give me the horses and inlaid chariot that the peerless Achilles drives? I promise you that I shall not be useless as a spy or fall below your expectations. For I mean to go right through the camp till I come to Agamemnon's ship, where I presume the senior officers will be deciding whether to retreat or fight on.'

Hector replied by taking the staff in his hands and giving Dolon his oath: 'Let Zeus himself, the Consort of Here and Lord of the Thundercloud, hear me swear that no other Trojan shall ride behind those horses, and that you shall rejoice in them for the rest of your days.'

Later events gave a twist that he had not expected to this promise of Hector's; but it served to send off Dolon, who at once slung his curved bow on his shoulders, threw the pelt of a grey wolf over it, put a ferret-skin cap on his head, and picking up a sharp javelin set out from the camp in the direction of the ships. Not that he was destined to come back from them with news for Hector. However, once he had put the camp behind him, crowded as it was with horses and men, he sped eagerly on his way.

King Odysseus saw him coming towards them and said to his companion: 'Here comes a man from the enemy, Diomedes, maybe to spy on our ships, or else to strip some of the corpses – one cannot say which. Shall we let him pass us by and go on a little way? Then we could make a dash and pounce on him. And if he is too fast for us, you must threaten him with your spear and head him off all the time towards the ships and away from the encampment, so that he may not slip through and reach the town.'

They decided to do this, and turned off among the dead beside the path. Dolon, in all innocence, passed by them at a run. When he had left them behind by as much as the width of fallow that mules plough in a day (and they are better than oxen at dragging a jointed plough through deep fallow), the two men gave chase. Dolon stopped when he heard the footsteps behind him, supposing that these were friends coming from the Trojans to turn him back, Hector having countermanded his mission. But when they were a spear-cast off or even less, he knew them for enemies and incontinently took to his heels. They were after him in a flash. Tydeides and Odysseus sacker of cities chased that man as relentlessly as a couple of sharp-toothed sporting dogs will hang on the heels of a roe or hare flying before them through wooded country and screaming as it goes. And the whole time they fended him off from his own people. In fact, fleeing as he was towards the ships, Dolon was just about to run into the outposts, when Athene gave Tydeides strength to make an extra spurt, so that none of the bronze-clad Achaeans should be able to boast that he had hit Dolon before Diomedes could reach him. Dashing up with his spear the mighty Diomedes gave him a shout. 'Stop,' he cried, 'or I get you with my spear; and I don't think it will be long before I lay you dead.'

As he spoke, he let fly, but missed the man on purpose. The head of the polished spear passed over his right shoulder and stuck in the ground. Dolon came to a halt, terrified. He was white with panic; he stuttered; and the teeth chattered in his mouth. His two pursuers came up panting and gripped his arms. Then he burst into tears and said: 'Take me alive, and I will ransom myself. I have bronze and gold and wrought iron at home, from which my father would be glad to pay you a fortune, if he heard that I had been taken alive to the Achaean ships.'

'Pull yourself together, man,' said the crafty Odysseus. 'Don't be troubled by the thought of death, but answer my questions, and see that you tell us the truth. What was your idea in leaving camp and coming to the ships alone at dead of night when everyone else is sleeping? Was it to strip some of the dead? Did Hector send you out to make a reconnaissance by the hollow ships? Or did you come on your own initiative?'

With quaking knees Dolon answered him: 'Hector dazzled me, against my better judgment, by promising me the splendid horses and inlaid chariot of the glorious Achilles. He wanted me to venture through the dark into the enemy's position and find out whether the ships are guarded as usual, or whether as a result of their defeat at our hands they are already discussing the possibility of flight and are so exhausted that they are not troubling to keep watch at night.'

Odysseus of the nimble wits smiled at the man. 'So you were itching,' he said, 'to lay your hands on the horses of that doughty prince, Achilles? A fine prize, to be sure! But they are hard to master and difficult to drive, at any rate for a mere man, or anyone but Achilles, whose Mother is a goddess. Now answer my questions, and let me have the truth. Where did you leave Hector, your Commander-in-Chief, when you came here just now? Where is his equipment lying? Where are his horses? How are the Trojans' sentries disposed, and where are the rest of them sleeping? And what are they planning to do next? Do they mean to hold their advanced position by the ships or to retire into the city after inflicting this defeat on the Achaeans?'

'I will answer all your questions truthfully,' said Dolon son of Eumedes. 'First, Hector is conferring with his advisers by the barrow of King Ilus, away from all the noise. Next, you inquired about our sentries, my lord. No special guard was mounted to watch the camp or keep a lookout. Each family has its fire, and the men detailed for duty stay awake and exchange hallooes to keep each other alert. As for the allies that have come to us from various parts, they are asleep. They leave it to us to keep watch: *their* women and children are not lying close at hand.'

But the shrewd Odysseus was not satisfied. 'How do you mean?' he asked. 'Are the allies sleeping in the same parts of the camp as the Trojan charioteers or somewhere else? Be precise: I want to know.'

'Once more, I can tell you everything,' said Eumedes' son Dolon. 'The Carians and the Paeonians with their crooked bows are lying over by the sea, with the Leleges, the Caucones and the excellent Pelasgi, whereas the Lycians, the lordly Mysians, the horse-taming Phrygians and the Maeonian charioteers were allotted ground in the direction of Thymbra. But why do you want me to go into all these details? If your idea is to raid our positions, what about the Thracians over there, newcomers, on their own, at the very end of the line? Rhesus, their king, the son of Eïoneus, is with them. That man has the loveliest and biggest horses I have ever seen. They are whiter than snow and they run like the wind. His chariot is beautifully finished with gold and silver; and he brought some huge pieces of golden armour with him too, a fantastic sight. Men really shouldn't wear such things; they are only fit for the immortal gods. Well now, will you take me to the ships or tie me up tight and leave me here while you go and satisfy yourselves about me? You'll soon find out whether I have told you the truth or not.'

But now the mighty Diomedes gave him a grim look. 'Dolon,' he said, 'you have given us excellent news, but do not imagine you are going to get away, now that you have fallen into our hands. If we set you free to-night, there is nothing to prevent your coming down once more to the Achaean ships, either to play the spy or to meet us in open fight. But if I lay my hands on you and take your life, you will never be a nuisance to the Argives again.'

Dolon, raising his great hand, was just about to touch his captor's chin and plead for mercy, when Diomedes fell on him with his sword and struck him full on the neck. He cut through both the sinews, and Dolon's head met the dust before he ceased to speak. They took the ferret-skin cap from his head, and stripped him also of the wolf's pelt, and his in-curved bow and long spear. Then the noble Odysseus held up the trophies in his hand for Athene, goddess of Spoil, to see, and prayed to her: 'Let these gladden your heart, goddess, for you were the first of all the immortals in Olympus whom we called on for help. Help us again, in our raid on the sleeping Thracians and their horses.'

As he finished his prayer, he raised the bundle clear of his head and dumped it in a tamarisk bush. Then he gathered a handful of reeds and fresh tamarisk twigs, and put them on top to mark the spot clearly, so that they should not miss it as they came back through the darkness of the night. And now the two went ahead, threading their way among the blood-stained arms, and before long reached the Thracian encamp-ment. The men were asleep, tired out by their exertions, and their fine equipment was neatly piled in three rows on the ground beside them. A pair of horses stood by each man. Rhesus slept in the centre, with his fast horses beside him, tied by the reins to the end of the chariot-rail. Odysseus saw him first and pointed him out to Diomedes. 'There's our man, Diomedes,' he said, 'and there are the horses that Dolon told us about before we killed him. Now put out all your strength. No need to stand there fumbling with your arms. Quick! Get the horses clear. Or kill the men yourself, and I'll look after the horses.'

And now Diomedes, filled with fury by Athene of the

Flashing Eyes, laid about him with his sword and killed them right and left. Hideous groans came up from the dying men, and the earth ran red with blood. The son of Tydeus dealt with those men from Thrace like a lion who has found some sheep or goats unshepherded and hurls himself on the flock with murder in his heart. He slaughtered twelve of them, and as he came to each and put him to the sword, Odysseus of the nimble wits seized the body by the foot from behind and dragged it out, with a view to leaving the way clear for the long-maned horses, who were unaccustomed to their new masters and might be frightened if they trod on a corpse. The thirteenth man whom Tydeides came upon was King Rhesus, who was breathing heavily when he robbed him of his sweet life. He was under the influence of an evil dream which had come to him that night and, through the machinations of Athene, had taken the form of Diomedes son of Tydeus.

Meanwhile the all-daring Odysseus unfastened the stamping horses from the car, tied them together with thongs and drove them out of the crowded space with a touch or two of his bow, for it had not occurred to him to pick up the shining whip that lay in the decorated chariot. Directly he was clear, he gave a whistle, to let King Diomedes know.

But Diomedes was in no hurry. In fact he was wondering what was the most outrageous thing he could do, whether to get hold of the chariot in which the ornamented armour lay and drag it out by the shaft or hoist it up and carry it off; or whether to do further execution among the Thracians. The noble Diomedes was still trying to make up his mind when Athene came down to his side with a word of warning. 'The son of the great-hearted Tydeus,' she said, 'would be well advised to think of getting home to the hollow ships, or he may reach them in full flight. There are other gods, and they might wake the Trojans up.'

When he heard this, Diomedes, who recognized the voice of the goddess, mounted at once; Odysseus struck the horses with his bow; and off they flew to the Achaean ships.

Now Apollo of the Silver Bow had also kept his eyes open, and not for nothing. When he saw how Athene was dancing attendance on Tydeides, he was enraged with her and descended on the great Trojan army, where he roused one of the Thracian leaders, Hippocoön, a noble kinsman of Rhesus. Waking suddenly, the man leapt up, and when he saw the empty places where the horses had stood, and the men gasping out their lives in hideous carnage, he gave a groan and called his friend by name. This brought the Trojans running up to the spot with a fearful hue and cry. And there they looked with amazement at the terrible things that the two men had done before escaping to the hollow ships.

When Odysseus and Diomedes reached the spot where they had killed Hector's spy, King Odysseus pulled up their cantering horses, and Tydeides jumped down and handed up the bloodstained arms to Odysseus. Then he mounted again and flicked the horses; and they flew on with a will towards the hollow ships, eager to reach their journey's end.

Nestor was the first to hear the distant sounds. 'My friends,' he said, 'Captains and Counsellors of the Argives; can I be mistaken, or am I right? I could swear, at all events, that I hear the sound of galloping horses. Think what it would be to see Odysseus and the mighty Diomedes come dashing in here with some fine horses from the Trojan camp! But I am horribly afraid that the Trojans are on the warpath and that our two best men are in trouble.'

The last words were not out of his mouth when the two arrived. They jumped down to the ground, and were welcomed by their friends with much shaking of hands and many exclamations of delight. No one was more eager to hear their story than Nestor the Gerenian charioteer. 'Tell me,' he said, 'illustrious Odysseus, flower of Achaean chivalry; how did you get hold of these horses? Did you go in and take them from the Trojan camp; or did some god meet you on the way and make you a present of them? They shimmer like the sunshine. I meet the Trojans constantly – in fact I can claim that I never stay behind by the ships, old as I am for a fighting man – but I have never seen or imagined horses like these. Come now; you met a god and he gave them to you? Zeus the Cloud-gatherer is very fond of you both, and so is his Daughter, Athene of the Flashing Eyes.'

'Nestor son of Neleus, whom the Achaeans love to honour,' replied Odysseus of the nimble wits; 'the gods have greater powers than men, and if one of them wished to make us a present he could easily produce an even finer pair. But to answer your question, my lord – these horses have only just arrived, and they are Thracian. The excellent Diomedes killed their master, and the twelve best men in his company beside him. We killed fourteen men in all, for we caught a spy near the ships, sent out to reconnoitre in our camp by Hector and the rest of the insolent Trojans.'

With that, he drove the thoroughbreds across the trench, laughing; and the other Achaeans followed him in a merry mood. When they reached Tydeides' comfortable hut, they tied up the pair with well-cut thongs at the mangers where Diomedes' own fast horses stood munching their honey-sweet barley. Odysseus put Dolon's bloodstained equipment in the after part of his ship, until such time as he could prepare his sacrifice for Athene. Then they went into the sea to wash all the sweat from their shins and necks and thighs. When the waves had removed the sweat from their bodies and they felt refreshed, they went and bathed themselves in polished baths. Then, after washing and rubbing themselves with olive-oil, they sat down to supper and from a full mixing-bowl drew mellow wine and made libations to Athene.

XI

ACHILLES TAKES NOTICE

When Dawn had risen from the bed where she sleeps with the Lord Tithonus to bring daylight to the immortals and to men, Zeus sent down the demon Strife to the Achaean ships with the banner of battle in her hands. She took her stand on the bulging black hull of Odysseus' ship, which lay in the centre of the line, so that a shout would carry to either end, to the huts of Telamonian Aias or to those of Achilles, who had had confidence enough in their own bravery and strength to draw up their trim ships on the extreme flanks. Standing there, the goddess uttered her great and terrible war-cry, thereby inspiring every Achaean heart with a firm resolve to carry on the war relentlessly. And soon enough they were more enamoured with the thought of fighting than with that of sailing away to their own country in their hollow ships.

Atreides in a loud voice gave his troops the order to prepare for battle, and himself put on his gleaming bronze. He began by tying round his legs a pair of splendid greaves which were fitted with silver clips for the ankles. Next he put on his breast the cuirass that Cinyras had once presented to him as a friendly gift. News had reached Cinyras in far-off Cyprus of the great Achaean expedition that was sailing for Troy, and he had sent this cuirass as a gracious offering to the King. It was made of parallel strips, ten of dark blue enamel, twelve of gold, and twenty of tin. On either side three snakes rose up in coils towards the opening for the neck. Their iridescent enamel made them look like the rainbow that the Son of Cronos hangs on a cloud as a portent to mankind below. Next, Agamemnon slung his sword from his shoulders. Golden studs glittered on the hilt, but the sheath was of silver, with a golden baldric attached. Then he took up his manly and man-covering shield, a nobly decorated piece, with its ten concentric rings of bronze, and twenty knobs of tin making a white circle round the dark enamel boss. The central figure on it was a grim Gorgon's head with awe-compelling eyes, and on either side of her, Panic and Rout were depicted. It was fitted with a silver baldric, round which a writhing snake of blue enamel twisted the three heads that grew from its single neck. On his head, Agamemnon put his helmet, with its four plates, its double crest and its horsehair plume nodding defiantly above; and finally he picked up a pair of strong and sharp bronze-headed spears. Beams from the bronze he wore flashed into the distant sky, and Athene and Here thundered in answer by way of salutation to the King of Golden Mycenae.

The charioteers all left their chariots in their drivers' charge with instructions to draw them up in proper order at the trench, while they themselves, with a bustle and din that smote the morning sky, fell in on foot at the double in their full equipment, with the result that they had formed their line along the trench some time before their drivers, though these were but a little way behind them. The Son of Cronos fanned the war-fever in their hearts, and from on high caused a bloody dew to fall out of the upper air, resolved as he was to send many a gallant soul to Hades.

On their side too the Trojans fell in, on the high ground of the plain, round the great Hector, peerless Polydamas, Aeneas, whom the Trojan people honoured like a god, and Antenor's three sons, Polybus, the noble Agenor and the young and godlike Acamas. Hector with his circular shield was conspicuous among their champions. Like a baleful star that at one moment shines out in all its splendour from behind a cloud and at the next is hidden by the mist, Hector was seen, now in the foremost company, now with the rearguard, spurring them on. In his panoply of bronze he flashed like the lightning that comes from aegis-bearing Father Zeus.

And now, like reapers who start from opposite sides of a rich man's field and bring the wheat or barley tumbling down in armfuls till their swathes unite, the Trojans and Achaeans fell upon each other to destroy. Their numbers were equal, and panic was unthinkable to either side. They rushed in like wolves, and Strife, the heart-breaker, rejoiced when she saw them. For it happened that she was the only one of the gods to witness this action, the rest not being on the battlefield, but taking their ease at home, each in his lovely house built on the folds of Olympus. They were all at loggerheads with the Son of Cronos, the Lord of the Black Cloud, because he wished to give the Trojans a victory. But the Father cared nothing for that. He had slipped away from them and sat down alone, exulting in his power, and looking down on the city of Troy and the Achaean ships, on the flashing bronze, and the killers and the killed.

Right through the morning, while the blessed light of day grew stronger, volley and counter-volley found their mark, and men kept falling. But about the time when a woodman felling the tall trees in a mountain dell grows weary in the arm, and feeling he has done enough, yields to the tempting thought of food and prepares himself a meal, the Danaans, calling to their friends across the ranks, put forth their strength and broke the enemy battalions. And in rushed Agamemnon, first of them all, and killed a Trojan captain, Bienor, and after him his comrade and driver, Oïleus. Oïleus had leapt down from his chariot to oppose him. But as he moved in to the attack, Agamemnon struck him on the forehead with a sharp spear. For all its weight of bronze the helmet failed to stop the spear, which pierced both the metal and the bone, and spattered the inside of the helmet with his brains. That was the end of Oïleus and his attack.

Agamemnon King of Men, after stripping off their tunics, left the dead men there with their breasts gleaming in the sun, and went on to kill Isus and Antiphus, two sons of Priam, one a bastard and the other legitimate, who were using one chariot. The bastard Isus was driving it; the noble Antiphus was the fighting-man beside him. This couple had once been caught by Achilles as they shepherded their flocks on the spurs of Ida. He had tied them up with pliant twigs of willow, but afterwards accepted ransom and released them. And now they met imperial Agamemnon son of Atreus. Isus, he hit with his spear above the nipple on his breast; Antiphus, he struck beside the ear with his sword and hurled him out of the chariot. Then with all speed he stripped the splendid armour from the pair, recognizing them as he did so, for he had seen them before by his own fast ships when Achilles the great runner had brought them in from Ida. All this was as easy for Agamemnon as it is for a lion to break into the lair of a nimble doe and crush her unweaned fawns, to seize them in his powerful jaws and rob them of their tender life. Even if the doe is close at hand, she cannot help them. She is terrified herself; and off she flies, crashing through the forest undergrowth and sweating in her haste to save herself from the claws of the formidable beast. So with these two. There was not a Trojan there to save them from destruction. Indeed, the Trojans were in rout before the Argives.

Agamemnon next attacked Peisander and stalwart Hippolochus, who were the sons of Antimachus. This astute nobleman had had his eye on Paris's gold and in the hope of lavish bribes had been more eloquent than any in defeating all proposals to give back Helen to red-haired Menelaus. And now it was his two sons that were captured by King Agamemnon. They were in one chariot and both had been trying to control their spirited horses. But these were in confusion, for the polished reins had slipped from the drivers' hands. Atreides sprang at them like a lion; and without even dismounting they begged him for mercy: 'Take us alive, Lord Agamemnon, and you shall have an ample ransom. Antimachus, our father, is rich and has plenty of treasure in his house, bronze and gold and wrought iron. He would pay you a princely ransom if he heard that we had been taken alive to the Achaean ships.'

Such was their tearful appeal to the King. Their tone was ingratiating: the answer was not. 'If you two,' said Agamemnon, 'are sons of Antimachus, the man who had the hardihood to argue in the Trojan Assembly that Menelaus, who had come there on an embassy with King Odysseus, should be killed on the spot and not allowed to return to Achaea, you shall pay now for your father's infamy.'

He had no sooner said this than he struck Peisander on the breast with his spear, flung him out of the chariot and brought him to earth, flat on his back. Hippolochus leapt down; and him he killed on the ground. He slashed off his arms and head with his sword, and sent his body rolling like a rounded boulder through the crowd.

Agamemnon left the two there and dashed in where the fighting was hottest, backed by the rest of the bronze-clad Achaeans. Infantry fell on infantry and cut them up as they fled before them; and the charioteers with their bronze made havoc of the charioteers, while from the ground below them there rose a cloud of dust, kicked up by the thundering hooves of their horses. And all the while King Agamemnon, shouting to his Argives, followed up and killed. Like a virgin forest when a raging fire blown hither and thither by the swirling wind attacks the trees, and thickets topple headlong before the onslaught of the flames, the routed Trojans were mown down by the onslaught of Agamemnon son of Atreus. Many a pair of horses tossed their heads and rattled their empty chariots down the corridors of battle, missing the master hand of their charioteers, while these lay sprawling on the ground, a more enticing spectacle to the vultures than to their wives.

From the flying missiles, from the dust, from the slaughter, the blood and the turmoil, Hector was withdrawn by the hand of Zeus, and Atreides was left to sweep on. To such effect did he inspire his men that by noon the fleeing Trojans, in their eagerness to reach the city, were past the barrow made in olden days for Ilus son of Dardanus, past the wild fig-tree, and half-way over the plain. And still they were chased by Atreides with his terrible war-cry, still bespattering his invincible hands with gore. But when they reached the Scaean Gate and the oak, they came to a halt and gave their slower friends a chance to catch them up. For some were still flying in panic over the open plain, pursued by Atreides, who swept them on like cattle, killing the hindmost, as a lion does when he stampedes a herd at dusk, and sudden death comes to a solitary heifer, whose neck he pounces on and breaks with his powerful jaws before he settles down to devour her blood and entrails. Thus King Agamemnon dealt with them, and many a charioteer was cast down by him from his car on back or face, so all-devouring was the vehemence of his spear.

They had almost reached the shelter of the city and its frowning walls, when the Father of men and gods descended from Heaven with a thunderbolt in his hands, sat down on the heights of Ida of the many springs, and sent out Iris of the Golden Wings as his ambassador. 'Off with you, Iris, fast as you can,' he said. 'Give Hector this message from me. As long as he sees King Agamemnon storming in the front line and mowing down the Trojan ranks, let him give ground, though ordering his men to keep the enemy closely engaged. But directly the King is hit by a spear or an arrow and takes to his chariot, I will give Hector strength to kill, until he reaches the well-found ships and the sun sets and the blessed darkness intervenes.'

Fleet Iris of the Whirlwind Feet made no ado, but sped down from the peaks of Ida to sacred Ilium, where she found Prince Hector, son of the wise Priam, standing among the horses and the wooden chariots. She went up and saluted him by his name and princely titles. 'Father Zeus,' she said, 'has sent me down to deliver his word to you. As long as you see King Agamemnon storming in the front line and mowing down the Trojan ranks, refrain from fighting, but order your men to keep the enemy closely engaged. Directly the King is hit by a spear or an arrow and takes to his chariot, Zeus will give you strength to kill, until you reach the well-found ships and the sun sets and the blessed darkness intervenes.'

Her message delivered, Iris of the Nimble Feet withdrew. Hector jumped down from his chariot at once in all his armour, and swinging a pair of sharp spears in his hand went everywhere among his men, exhorting them to make a stand and rousing their martial spirit. As a result, the Trojans turned in their tracks and confronted the Achaeans. But these on their side reinforced their ranks. Thus the battle was set, the two armies faced each other, and Agamemnon, eager to be the foremost of them all, led off by charging at the foe.

Tell me now, you Muses that have your home in Olympus, who was the first man to face King Agamemnon? Was he a Trojan, or was he one of their renowned allies?

He was the tall and handsome Iphidamas, a son of Antenor. This man had been brought up in rich-soiled Thrace the mother of sheep. Cisses, his mother's father and father of Theano of the lovely cheeks, had reared him from infancy in his own palace, and when Iphidamas had reached the heyday of his youth, had done his best to keep him at home by offering him his daughter's hand. But Iphidamas had no sooner married her than he was enticed from the arms of his bride by news of the Achaean expedition. He sailed with a squadron of twelve beaked ships, left the trim vessels in harbour at Percote, and himself reached Ilium on foot. This was the man who now confronted Agamemnon son of Atreus.

When they had come to close quarters, Atreides started the fight, but with a miss: his spear went astray. Iphidamas, in his turn, stabbed Agamemnon on the belt under his cuirass. But though he followed up the blow with his own full weight, keeping his grip on the spear, he failed to pierce the glittering belt – failed utterly, for when his spear-point met the silver it was bent like a bit of lead. Imperial Agamemnon got his hand on the shaft, and pulling it towards him with the fury of a lion, dragged it out of the man's grasp. Then, with his sword, he hit him on the neck and brought him to earth. Thus Iphidamas fell, and as he fell, sank into the sleep that is not broken. Unlucky man! He was fighting for his country, far from the wife he had just married but had no joy of, though he had given so much to win her. He had paid a hundred head of cattle at the time, with the promise of a thousand animals to follow, mixed sheep and goats from his unnumbered flocks. And now Agamemnon son of Atreus stripped his corpse and went off with his splendid armour into the Achaean ranks.

When the admirable Coön, Antenor's eldest son, saw what

had happened, his eyes were dimmed in anguish for his fallen brother, and he came in on the off side with his spear and caught the noble Agamemnon unawares. He struck him below the elbow in the middle of the forearm, and the gleaming spear-point passed right through. Agamemnon King of Men shuddered; but far from giving up the fight and withdrawing, he charged at Coön, brandishing his wind-devouring spear. Coön had got hold of Iphidamas' foot and was hastily dragging his brother into the crowd and calling on all his best men to help him with his father's son. As he did so, Agamemnon struck him with a bronze-headed spear under his bossed shield, and brought him to earth. Then he ran up and cut off his head, over the body of Iphidamas. Thus at the hands of royal Atreides these sons of Antenor fulfilled their destiny and went down into the House of Hades.

As long as blood was still running warm from his wound, Agamemnon continued to harry the enemy ranks with spear and sword and boulder. But when the blood stanched and the wound began to dry, he felt a stabbing pain, sharp as the pangs which seize a woman in childbirth, the bitter pangs that are sent by the Eileithyiae, the travail-makers, who are Daughters of Here and dispense the pains of labour. Atreides, overcome by agony, leapt into his chariot, told his charioteer to drive to the hollow ships, and in his sore distress called aloud to the Danaans: 'Friends, Captains and Counsellors of the Argives; it is for you now to save our seagoing ships from the fury of war, since Zeus in his wisdom will not let me fight against the Trojans all day long.'

Agamemnon said no more, and his driver whipped his long-maned horses and started them towards the hollow ships. The pair flew off with a will, and their breasts were flecked with foam, their bellies grey with dust, as they carried off the wounded King from the battlefield.

When Hector saw Agamemnon withdraw, he called to the Trojans and Lycians in a loud voice: 'Trojans and Lycians and you Dardanians that revel in a fight; be men, my friends, and recall your martial valour. The best man they have is gone, and Zeus the Son of Cronos has given me a great victory. Drive your good horses straight at these mighty Danaans and win a greater victory yet.'

Thus he roused them and put fresh heart into each. As a hunter sets on his snarling hounds against a savage wild-boar or a lion, Hector son of Priam, forceful as the murderous Wargod, spurred the proud Trojans on against the Achaeans. He took his own place in the forefront with high thoughts in his heart and flung himself into the battle like a squall that swoops down from the heights and lashes the blue waters of the sea.

And who were the first and last that fell to Hector son of Priam, now that Zeus vouchsafed him victory? Asaeus first, and Autonous and Opites; Dolops son of Clytius, Opheltius and Agelaus; Aesymnus, Orus and the staunch Hipponous. These were the Danaan leaders whom he killed. Then he fell on the rabble, like a full gale when it strikes from the West and scatters the white clouds that the South Wind has marshalled; when the great billows start their march and the foam flies high on the wings of the travelling wind. So and in such numbers did the enemy fall before the onslaught of Hector.

Irreparable disaster now threatened the Achaeans, who in their flight would soon have reached the ships and fallen there, had not Odysseus called out to Diomedes son of Tydeus: 'Tydeides, what is the matter with us? Where is our resolution gone? For God's sake, my good friend, come here and make a stand beside me. Think of the infamy if Hector of the flashing helmet captures the ships.'

'Indeed I will stand and take what comes,' the mighty Diomedes answered. 'But our friends will not benefit by that for long. Zeus the Cloud-gatherer has decided he would rather see the Trojans win than us.'

With this he flung his spear at Thymbraeus, hit him on the left breast and brought him down from his chariot, while Odysseus, for his part, dealt with Molion, the prince's noble squire. Leaving these where they fell – and for them there was no more fighting – the pair dashed into the crowd and ran riot like a couple of wild-boars who turn in high fury and charge the hounds that have chased them. Thus they rounded on the Trojans and destroyed their attackers, giving the Achaeans a welcome pause for breath in their flight from illustrious Hector.

A chariot and two chieftains fell to them instantly. They were sons of Merops of Percote, the ablest prophet of his day. He had forbidden his sons to go off to the war and throw away their lives. But these two, beckoned by the black hand of Death, had disobeyed him. And now the famous spearman Diomedes son of Tydeus took their life and spoiled them of their glorious arms, while Odysseus killed and stripped Hippodamus and Hypeirochus.

The Son of Cronos, looking down from Ida, stabilized the battle now, and for a time the slaughter was mutual. Tydeides struck Agastrophus the noble son of Paeon on the hip-joint with a javelin. This man had been unable to escape him, as his chariot was nowhere near. He had made the fatal mistake of leaving it behind in charge of his squire and dashing up into the front line on foot. This cost him his life. But now Hector, glancing through the ranks and seeing where the weakness lay, made for Diomedes and Odysseus with a great shout, which brought the Trojan companies after him. Even Diomedes of the loud war-cry was shaken when he saw him. He turned at once to Odysseus, who was close at hand, and said: 'We two are in for trouble. Here comes the formidable Hector. Don't let us move. We will stand and drive him off.'

With that he swung up his long-shadowed spear and hurled it. He had aimed at Hector's head and did not miss: he struck him on the crest of the helmet. But his bronze was turned by Hector's, and never reached the flesh: it was stopped by the helmet with its triple plates and vizor, which Phoebus Apollo had given him. Hector promptly ran a long way back and took cover with his men. Sinking to his knees he supported himself with one great hand on the ground, and the world went black as night before his eyes. Meanwhile Tydeides was following up his spear-cast, right across the front lines to the spot where he had seen the weapon fall. So Hector had time to come to. And when he did so, he leapt once more into his chariot and drove off into the crowd. He had escaped destruction. But the great Diomedes, rushing up with his spear, had something yet to say to him. 'You cur,' he cried, 'once more you have saved your skin – but only just. Phoebus Apollo took care of you again: no doubt you say your prayers to him before you venture within earshot of the spears. But we shall meet once more, and then I'll finish you, if I too can find a god to help me. For the moment I shall try my luck against the rest.'

Diomedes then resumed the stripping of Agastrophus, the spearman he had killed. But now Paris, the husband of Helen of the lovely hair, drew a bow on Tydeides the great captain, leaning for cover against the column on the mound which men of a bygone age had made for their chieftain, Ilus son of Dardanus. As Diomedes was engaged in pulling the burnished cuirass from the stalwart Agastrophus' breast, the shield from his shoulder, and the heavy helmet from his head, Paris drew the centre of his bow, and shot. The arrow did not leave his hand for nothing. Hitting Tydeides on the flat of his right foot, it went right through and stuck in the earth. Paris, with a happy laugh, leapt out from his ambush and gloated over Diomedes. 'You are hit,' he cried; 'I did not shoot for nothing. I only wish I had hit you in the belly and shot you dead. Then the Trojans, who quake before you like bleating goats before a lion, would have had some respite from this blight.'

Unperturbed, the mighty Diomedes answered him: 'Bowman and braggart, with your pretty lovelocks and your glad eye for the girls; if you faced me man to man with real weapons, you would find your bow and quiverful a poor defence. As it is, you flatter yourself. All you have done is to scratch the sole of my foot. And for that I care no more than if a woman or a naughty boy had hit me. A shot from a coward and milksop does no harm. But *my* weapons have a better edge. One touch from them, and a man is dead, his wife has lacerated cheeks, and his children have no father; the earth turns red with his blood, and there he rots, with fewer girls than vultures at his side.'

As Diomedes spoke, the renowned spearman Odysseus came up and covered him. Diomedes sat down behind his friend and withdrew the sharp arrow from his foot. Pain stabbed his flesh, and in great distress he got into his car and told his charioteer to drive back to the hollow ships.

Left to himself without a single Argive to support him, now that all were panic-stricken, even the renowned Odysseus was perturbed and took counsel with his indomitable soul. 'What,' he asked himself with a groan, 'is coming to me next? It would be infamy to take to my heels, scared by the odds against me; but even more unpleasant to be caught alone, now that Zeus has set all the rest of the Danaans on the run. But why do I discuss the point? Do I not know that cowards leave their post, whereas the man who claims to lead is in duty bound to stand unflinching and to kill or die?'

While Odysseus was engaged in this inward debate, shield-bearing Trojan companies bore down upon him and surrounded him. They had caught a tartar in their net. It was like the moment when the strong young huntsmen with their hounds are baiting a wild-boar. Whetting his white tusks in his crooked jaws, he comes out from the depths of his lair. They rush at him from every side. There is a noise of snapping jaws. But formidable as he is, they hold their ground against him. Thus the encircling Trojans harried King Odysseus. But he started well. Leaping at the noble Deïopites with his sharp spear, he wounded him in the shoulder from above. Next he killed Thoön and Ennomus; and then Chersidamas, who had jumped down from his chariot. He struck him with his spear in the navel, under his bossed shield; and Chersidamas fell in the dust and clutched at the earth. Leaving them where they fell, Odysseus with his spear stabbed Charops, son of Hippasus. He was a brother of the wealthy Socus, a gallant noble-man who now hastened to his help and confronted Odysseus. 'Illustrious Odysseus,' Socus said to him, 'arch-schemer, arch-adventurer; to-day you shall either triumph over two sons of

Hippasus and boast about the splendid pair you have killed and stripped, or be felled by my spear and die yourself.'

With that he cast and struck the round shield of Odysseus. His weighty spear passed through the glittering shield, pressed on through the ornate cuirass and ripped the flesh clean off Odysseus' flank, though Pallas Athene did not allow it to penetrate his bowels. Odysseus, knowing that it had not touched a vital spot, drew back and said to Socus: 'Now, my unhappy friend, your doom is sealed. You may have stopped me from fighting the Trojans, but I tell you that here and now you are going to meet your fate and die. Conquered by my spear, you shall yield your life to Hades of the Fabled Horse, and the glory to me.'

Socus turned and started to run, but he had no sooner wheeled about than Odysseus caught him with his spear in the back, midway between the shoulders, and drove it through his chest. He came down with a thud, and the great Odysseus triumphed over him: 'Ah, Socus, son of Hippasus the doughty charioteer! So after all Death was too quick for you and you did not escape. *Your* eyes, poor wretch, will not be closed for you by your father and your lady mother, but the carrion birds will gather round you with their flapping wings and tear your corpse to pieces. *I*, if I die, shall have funeral honours from my noble countrymen.'

As he spoke he pulled out the heavy spear of the doughty Socus from his own wound and bossed shield. Blood gushed up as the point came out, and Odysseus was in sore distress. When the gallant Trojans saw his blood, they called to each other across the mêlée and attacked him in a body. Odysseus gave ground, shouting to his friends for help. He called three times at the top of his voice, and the gallant Menelaus, hearing his three cries, turned quickly to Aias, who happened to be near, and said: 'My lord Aias, royal son of Telamon, I hear the dauntless Odysseus crying out. It sounds as though the Trojans had cut him off in the heat of the fight and were over-powering him. You and I had better dash in to the rescue. I am afraid he will come to grief if we leave him alone with the enemy. And what a loss to the Danaans if so fine a soldier fell!'

As he spoke, he led the way and the godlike Aias went with him. They soon found King Odysseus, beset on either side by Trojans; and there followed such a scene as is enacted in the hills when an antlered stag is beset by tawny jackals. The stag, who has been wounded by an arrow from a huntsman's bow, is fast enough to leave the man behind as long as the blood flows warm and his legs will carry him. But when the arrow-wound has sapped his strength, the mountain jackals catch him in the twilight of the woods, and are tearing him to pieces with their carrion jaws, when suddenly a hungry lion enters on the scene. The jackals scatter: it is the lion's turn to use his jaws. Thus, while the Trojan chivalry were storming round the wise Odysseus of the many wiles, and that gallant man by lunging with his spear was keeping death at bay, Aias with his towerlike shield came up and covered him. The Trojans scattered in all directions, and Menelaus favourite of Ares took Odysseus by the arm and supported him through the crowd, till they reached his own chariot, which his squire drove up.

Aias flung himself on the Trojans and killed Doryclus, a bastard son of Priam's; then he wounded Pandocus and Lysander, and Pyrasus and Pylartes. As a river swollen by the winter rains comes rushing down in spate from the mountains to the plain, sweeps up dead oaks and pines, and carries tons of silt into the sea, illustrious Aias stormed the plain and fell on the enemy, destroying horse and man.

Hector knew nothing of all this. He was engaged on the far left, by the banks of Scamander, where the slaughter was heaviest and a desperate fight had flared up round the great Nestor and the fierce Idomeneus. Hector was busy here. He was doing marvels with chariot and javelin, and mowing down the Achaean youth. Yet even so the brave Achaeans would not have given ground to him, if Paris, Lady Helen's husband, had not disposed of Machaon the great captain, who was bearing the brunt of the attack, by striking him with a three-barbed arrow in the right shoulder. The Achaeans, who had been fighting gamely, were filled with anxiety for their chief. They thought he might be captured as the battle swayed, and Idomeneus at once called out to the noble Nestor: 'Quick, my lord Nestor, flower of Achaean chivalry! Into your chariot, pick up Machaon, and drive with all speed to the ships. A surgeon who can cut out an arrow and heal the wound with his ointments is worth a regiment.'

The Gerenian horseman Nestor did not hesitate. He promptly mounted his chariot, and Machaon, son of Asclepius the peerless physician, got in beside him. Nestor touched the horses with his whip, and the willing pair flew off towards the hollow ships. They had wished for nothing better.

Cebriones, who was serving as Hector's driver, saw that the Trojans on the other wing had been put to flight, and drew Hector's attention to the fact. 'Here are we,' he said, 'engaged with the Danaans on the very fringe of the battle, while our troops on the other wing are being routed pell-mell, horse and foot. Telamonian Aias is sweeping them before him: I recognize him easily by the broad shield on his shoulders. Let us drive over there and join in where the charioteers and infantry are putting up the stiffest fight, where men are killing men and the roar of battle never stops.'

Cebriones touched his long-maned horses with his whistling lash, and they no sooner heard the stroke than they swept the fast chariot off at a gallop towards the battling Trojans and Achaeans, trampling on corpses and shields, so that the axle-tree under the car, and the rails that ran round it, were sprayed with the blood thrown up by their hooves and by the tyres. Hector was eager to get in among the throng of fighting men, to leap in and break through. But though his coming brought confusion to the Danaans and he spared his javelin not at all, he avoided battle with Aias son of Telamon, and attacked elsewhere with spear and sword and boulder.

In the end it was Father Zeus himself on his high throne who caused Aias to turn tail. Aias lost his nerve and came to a halt. Then with an anxious glance at the numbers round him, he swung his sevenfold shield across his back, turned in retreat, and step by step gave ground, as wild beasts do, with many a backward look. He was like a tawny lion driven from a cattle-yard by the dogs and farm hands who have stayed awake all night to save the fattest of their heifers from his maw. Hungry for meat, the lion charges; but he does no good by that. Showers of darts and blazing faggots hurled at him by strong hands scare him for all his eagerness, and at dawn he slinks off disappointed. Thus and in such discontent, Aias withdrew before the Trojans, much against his will and acutely conscious of the danger to the Achaean ships. Even so, he was as stubborn as a donkey who gets the better of the boys in charge of him, turns into a field they are passing, and helps himself to the standing crop. So many sticks have been broken on his back that their feeble cudgelling leaves him unconcerned, till at last they drive him out with much ado, but not before he has eaten all he wants. Thus the proud Trojans and their far-famed allies hung on the heels of the great Telamonian Aias, pricking the centre of his shield with their spears. At times, in a fit of renewed fury, Aias would wheel and hold the ranks of the horse-taming Trojans at bay; and then once more he would turn and resume his retreat. Thus he managed to fend off the whole force that was threatening the ships, standing and laying about him single-handed as he was, midway between the Trojans and Achaeans. Launched by brawny arms, many a spear that had a hankering to go farther still was held up by his ample shield, and many another without tasting his white flesh fell short and stuck in the earth, balked of the feast it craved.

When Eurypylus, Euaemon's highborn son, saw Aias labouring under this discharge of missiles, he ran up to support him, let fly his glittering javelin and struck the chieftain Apisaon son of Phausius in the liver under the midriff, bringing him forthwith to the ground. Then, dashing up, he began to take his armour from his shoulders. But as he stripped his man, he was observed by Prince Paris, who quickly bent his bow at him and hit him with an arrow in the right thigh.

Eurypylus, his leg hampered by the broken shaft, saved himself from certain death by taking cover with the men of his own company. But he gave a great shout to the Danaans: 'My friends, Captains and Counsellors of the Argives; turn in your tracks and make a stand to save Aias from destruction. Shot at as he is, I cannot see how he can disengage himself. A rally, then, round the great Aias son of Telamon!'

The wounded Eurypylus had done his part, and they closed in and rallied round him, crouching behind sloped shields, with their spears at the ready. Aias came up to them, and once he had reached their friendly line, he faced about once more and stood.

So the fight went on, like an inextinguishable fire. Meanwhile the mares of Neleus' breed, sweating as they ran, were bearing Nestor from the field, and with him Machaon shepherd of the people. And it so happened that the great Achilles of the nimble feet, who had been watching the crisis of the battle and the lamentable rout from the stern of his capacious ship, saw him and took note. He called at once to his friend Patroclus, shouting for him from the ship. Hearing his call in the hut, Patroclus came out, looking like the god of war; and that was the beginning of his end. Before Achilles could explain himself, he said: 'Why did you call, Achilles? What do you want me for?' And Achilles the great runner said: 'My dear prince and my heart's delight, at last I see the Achaeans gathering at my knees to abase themselves, for they are in desperate straits. But what I wish you to do now, my lord Patroclus, is to go and ask Nestor who is the wounded man he is taking from the field. Seen from behind, he looks exactly like Machaon son of Asclepius, but the horses passed by me in such a hurry that I did not see his face.' Patroclus obeyed his friend at once and set off at a run along the Achaeans' huts and ships.

When Nestor and Machaon reached Nestor's hut they stepped down from the car to the bountiful earth, while the horses were unyoked by Eurymedon, the old king's squire. Then they stood in the breeze by the sea-shore to dry the

sweat from their tunics, and after that went into the hut and
sat down on easy-chairs. A pottage was prepared for them by
the lady Hecamede, whom the old man had had from Tenedos
when Achilles sacked the place. She was a daughter of the
great-hearted Arsinous, and had been picked out for him by
the Achaeans as a tribute to their ablest counsellor. She began
by moving up to them a handsome polished table with enamel-
led legs. On this she put a bronze dish with an onion to flavour
the drink, some yellow honey, and sacred barley-meal; and
beside these a magnificent beaker adorned with golden studs,
which the old man had brought from home. It had four
handles. Each was supported by two legs; and on top of each,
facing one another, a pair of golden doves were feeding. Any-
one else would have found it difficult to shift the beaker from
the table when it was full, but Nestor, old as he was, could
lift it without trouble. In this cup, their comely attendant
mixed them the pottage with Pramnian wine, and after
making it ready by grating into it some goat's milk cheese
with a bronze grater and sprinkling white barley on top, she
invited them to drink, which they did.

They had quenched their parching thirst and were engaged
in friendly conversation, when Patroclus suddenly appeared
in the doorway, like a god. The old man looked up, rose from
his polished chair, drew him forward by the hand, and begged
him to be seated. But Patroclus was reluctant to come farther
in and made his excuses: 'I have no time to sit down, my
venerable lord; you will not persuade me. I have too much
respect and reverence for the master who sent me on my
errand, which was to ask you who the man is whom you
brought in wounded. But as I see for myself that it is my lord
Machaon, I will go back at once and report to Achilles. For
you know well enough, my venerable lord, what a difficult
man he is, quite capable of finding fault without a reason.'

'I cannot understand,' replied Nestor the Gerenian horse-
man, 'why Achilles is so much concerned about a casualty here
or there, while ignoring the disaster that the whole army has
suffered. Our very best men are lying by the ships wounded

by arrows or spears. The mighty Diomedes son of Tydeus
has been hit; Odysseus the great spearman has been wounded;
so has Agamemnon; Eurypylus too has had an arrow in his
thigh; and here is another whom I have just brought off the
field hit by an arrow from a bow. Yet Achilles, though he is a
fighter too, has no concern or pity for the Danaans. Is he
waiting till in spite of all we can do our gallant ships go up in
flames beside the sea and our army is destroyed piecemeal? I
cannot take his place: my limbs are not so supple now and my
old strength is gone. Ah, if only I were still as young and
vigorous as I was when we and the Eleans came to blows
about the lifting of some cattle, and I killed Itymoneus the
gallant son of Hypeirochus, who lived in Elis. I was raiding
his herds by way of reprisal, and when he took the lead in
their defence, he was brought down by a javelin from my
hand. His rustic levies scattered in panic; and what a haul of
booty we rounded up from the field – fifty herds of cattle, as
many flocks of sheep, as many droves of pigs, and as many
scattered herds of goats, as well as a hundred and fifty chestnut
horses, all of them mares and many with foals beside them.
In the night we drove them in to Neleus' city of Pylos, and
Neleus was delighted that an unfledged warrior like myself
should have had such luck. At dawn our town-criers sum-
moned all who had debts owed to them in Elis to attend, and
the leading men in Pylos held a meeting and divided the
spoils, which came in very handy, as the Epeans were in
debt to a number of our people. Indeed, we in Pylos were in a
bad way then, the few of us that were left after the mighty
Heracles had come and done his worst to us in previous
years and all our best men had been killed. The excellent
Neleus had had twelve sons, of whom I alone survived – all
the rest had perished. As a result the Epean soldiery had be-
come insupportable: they treated us with contempt and op-
pressed us shamefully. But now the old king Neleus got a
herd of cattle and a great flock of sheep out of our spoils – he
chose three hundred for himself together with their shepherds
– all by way of recouping a heavy loss he had sustained in the

good land of Elis. For when he sent four race-horses there with a chariot to run in the games and compete for the tripod, King Augeas kept them and sent back their driver, a horseless and a sorry man, with an insulting message. Neleus resented the wording of this as much as the King's high-handed action. So now he helped himself liberally to the booty, leaving the remainder to the people to divide in such a way that no one should go short of his proper share.

'We had just despatched the last details of this business and were sacrificing to the gods at various points in the town, when, on the third day, the whole strength of Elis, horse and foot, bore down on us in hot haste, and with them marched the two Moliones, who were still lads at the time with no experience of war.

'There is an outlying stronghold called Thryoessa, perched on a steep hill overlooking the Alpheus, on the borders of sandy Pylos. Their aim was to destroy this place; so they invested it and also overran the surrounding plain. But in the night Athene came speeding down from Olympus and warned us to get under arms. She found us not unwilling. In fact the whole force she raised in Pylos was spoiling for a fight. But Neleus did not wish me to join in. He felt I knew too little about serious fighting, and he hid my horses from me. All the same, and though I went on foot, Athene so arranged the affair that I managed to outshine even our own charioteers.

'There is a river called Minyeius, which falls into the sea near Arene. Here the Pylian horse halted till dawn, while the infantry battalions came rolling up. From that point a rapid march in battle order brought us by noon to the sacred River Alpheus. We sacrificed there to almighty Zeus and also offered a bull to the River-god, a bull to Poseidon and a heifer of the herd to Athene of the Flashing Eyes. Then we ate our supper in our several messes and settled down for the night on the banks of the stream, every man with his armour on.

'The Epeans meanwhile were beleaguering the citadel, full of confidence and determined on its downfall. They had no idea of the trouncing they were going to get instead. No sooner had the Sun shown his face above the horizon than we gave battle, with a prayer to Zeus and Athene; and when the two armies came to grips the first man fell to me and I possessed myself of his excellent horses. He was a spearman called Mulius, a son-in-law of Augeas, married to his eldest daughter, auburn-haired Agamede, who knew every magic herb that grows in the wide world. As he came at me, I struck him with my bronze-headed spear and he fell headlong in the dust. I leapt into his chariot; I took my place in the front rank; and the proud Epeans broke and ran in all directions, when they saw the captain of their horse, their best fighter, brought to earth. But I was after them like a black squall. I captured fifty chariots; and by each of them a couple of men, felled by my spear, bit the dust. In fact I would have killed the twin Moliones of the House of Actor too, had not their Father, Poseidon the Imperial Earthshaker, hidden them in a thick mist and rescued them from the field. Yes, Zeus gave us a great victory there. We chased them across open country, killing the men and gathering up their splendid arms, till our chariots were rolling through the cornlands of Buprasion and we reached the Olenian Rock and the place called Alision Hill. At that point Athene saw fit to turn our forces back, and there I killed and left my last man. Our charioteers withdrew from Buprasion and drove back to Pylos, all of them giving glory to Zeus among the gods and to Nestor among men.

'Thus I acquitted myself among the men of my day, as surely as I live. Now look at Achilles. He is a brave man. Yet who but he will profit by that bravery? And mark my words, he too will shed tears when the army is destroyed – tears of remorse. My friend, do you remember what your father Menoetius told you, that day he sent you from Phthia to join Agamemnon? I and King Odysseus were in the house and heard it all. We were on a recruiting tour through the fertile land of Achaea, when we came to Peleus' splendid house, where we found the lord Menoetius and yourself, and Achilles with you. Peleus the old charioteer was burning fat from an ox's

thigh in honour of Zeus the Thunderer in his stable-yard.
He had a golden chalice in his hand and was accompany-
ing the burnt offering by a libation of sparkling wine,
while you two were preparing the meat. At that moment,
Odysseus and I appeared at the gate. Achilles leapt up in
astonishment, took us by the hand and brought us in. He gave
us chairs and with all the usual hospitality offered us refresh-
ment. When we had satisfied our hunger and thirst, I dis-
closed the object of our visit and invited you and Achilles to
enlist. You were more than willing, and your fathers both
gave you their blessing. While the old man Peleus exhorted
his boy Achilles always to strive for the foremost place and
outdo his peers, Menoetius son of Actor was giving you his
own advice. I remember his words. "My son," he said,
"Achilles is of nobler birth than you, and he is also by far the
stronger man. But you are older than he is. It is for you to
give him sound advice, to set him an example and to take the
lead, which he will follow to his own advantage." Those were
your old father's precepts – which you have forgotten. But
even so it is not too late for you to talk in this strain to
Achilles. He might well have sense enough to listen. Who
knows? A friend's advice is often most effective, and with a
little luck you may yet coax him into action. But if he is
secretly deterred by some prophecy, some word from Zeus
that his lady Mother has disclosed to him, let him at least
allow *you* to take the field with the Myrmidon force at your
back, and so perhaps bring salvation to the Danaans. Let him
give you his own glorious armour to fight in, so that the Tro-
jans may take you for him and break off the battle. That
would give our weary forces time to recuperate; and even a
short breathing-space makes all the difference in war. The
Trojans themselves have fought to the point of exhaustion,
and you, being fresh, might well drive them back to the city
from the ships and huts.'
Patroclus was profoundly moved by Nestor's words and
set off at the double along the line of ships to rejoin his royal
master. He was still running when he reached the ships of

King Odysseus, the place where they held their assemblies and their legal sessions and had put up their altars to the gods. There he was met by Euaemon's highborn son Eurypylus, limping back from the battle with a wound from an arrow in his thigh. Sweat was pouring from his head and shoulders, and the blood ran dark from his painful wound, but his mind was not affected. The gallant Patroclus was moved to compassion at the sight, and in his distress for Eurypylus he pictured all the Danaan Captains and Counsellors, far from their dear ones and the land of their fathers, filling the nimble dogs of Troy with their white flesh. He appealed to Eurypylus. 'My noble lord,' he asked, 'is there any hope of holding the monstrous Hector in check, or will the Achaeans fall to his spear and be destroyed to-day?'

'My lord Patroclus,' replied the wounded Eurypylus, 'there is no salvation for the Achaeans now; they will fall by their own black ships. All our former champions are lying there already, wounded by Trojan spears or arrows, and all the time the enemy grow stronger. But at least you can rescue me, and see me safe to my black ship. I want you to cut out this arrow from my thigh, wash off the blood with warm water and spread soothing ointment on the wound. They say you have some excellent prescriptions that you learnt from Achilles, who was taught by Cheiron, the civilized Centaur. I cannot appeal to our surgeons Podaleirius and Machaon, for I hear that one of them is lying wounded in camp, in need of a good physician himself, while the other is still hotly engaged with the Trojans in the field.'

'This is intolerable!' Menoetius' gallant son exclaimed. 'What are we to do, my lord Eurypylus? I am on my way to Achilles, my wise master, with a message from Gerenian Nestor, the Warden of Achaea. All the same, I am not going to leave you in the lurch, exhausted as you are.'

As he spoke, he put his arm round the great captain's waist and supported him to his hut. When he saw him, Eurypylus' squire spread some hides on the floor, and there Patroclus laid him down, cut the sharp point of the arrow out of his

XII

HECTOR STORMS THE WALL

WHILE the gallant Patroclus was attending to Eurypylus' wound in the hut, the Argives and Trojans fought on, throwing in all their men. It did not look as though the Danaans' trench and the thick wall behind it would hold out much longer. When they built this wall for the ships, with the trench alongside, they had failed to make ritual offerings to the gods and so to provide themselves with a safe enclosure for their fleet and the vast spoils they had taken. The wall was built without the goodwill of Heaven, and it did not last for long. While Hector was alive and Achilles sulked, in fact as long as King Priam's city remained unsacked, the great Achaean wall survived. But later, when all the best of the Trojans were dead and many of the Argives too, though some were left; when Priam's city had been sacked in the tenth year of the siege, and the Argive expedition had sailed home, Poseidon and Apollo decided to destroy the wall by turning against it the united waters of all the rivers that run down from the range of Ida to the sea. Rhesus, Heptaporus, Caresus and Rhodius; Granicus and Aesepus; lovely Scamander and Simoïs, on whose banks many a shield and helmet and many a warrior of that heroic generation had fallen in the dust – all these rivers Phoebus Apollo brought together at one mouth, and for nine days he flung their waters at the wall, while Zeus rained without ceasing, to submerge it the quicker. Trident in hand, the Earthshaker himself directed the torrent, washed out to sea all the wooden and stone foundations that the Achaeans had laid down with such labour, and levelled the shore of the fast-flowing Hellespont. When the wall had disappeared, he covered the wide beach once more with sand, and turned the rivers back into the channels down which their limpid streams had run before.

All this remained to be done by Poseidon and Apollo. At the moment, the wall stood unimpaired and was the scene of a tumultuous battle, the woodwork of its towers resounding to the enemy's missiles. For the Argives, cowed by the lash of Zeus, were penned in and held beside the hollow ships in fear of Hector, the mighty panic-maker, who was raging as ever with the fury of a gale. He was like a wild-boar or a lion when he turns this way and that among the hounds and huntsmen to defy them in his strength. They close their ranks, confront him like a wall, and pelt him with showers of darts. But there is no fear nor any thought of flight in his dauntless heart – his very courage kills him. Time and again he turns and tries some new point in the ring of men; and wherever he charges, the ring gives way.

Thus Hector darted to and fro among his men, goading the charioteers to cross the trench. But when it came to the point, his own fast horses jibbed. They were frightened by its width and halted at the brink, neighing shrilly. Indeed the dyke was by no means easy to take at a bound or to cross at all. Both banks were overhanging all along, and on top there was a row of pointed stakes, close-set and strong, which the Achaean troops had planted there to keep out their enemies. So this was not a place where horses could break in with a chariot trundling after them. However, the infantry were eager to attempt the passage; and with this in view Polydamas went up to the lion-hearted Hector and made a suggestion to him and the other Trojan and allied commanders. 'It would be folly,' he said, 'to cross the trench in our chariots. The palisade on top makes it well-nigh impossible; and close behind comes the Achaean wall, leaving the charioteers no room whatever to dismount and fight – in fact, so narrow a strip that I am certain they would come to grief. If Zeus the Thunderer is really on our side and means the Danaans to be utterly destroyed, then well and good – there is nothing I want more than to see them perish far from Argos, here and now, and be forgotten. But what if they round on us? If we are driven back from the ships by a rally on their part and get entangled in the trench, I do not think a single man would escape to bring the news to Troy. I have a better plan, and I hope you will adopt it. Let our squires hold our horses at the trench, while we, on foot and in our full equipment, follow Hector in a body. The Achaeans won't stand up to us if their doom is really sealed.'

This advice from Polydamas seemed excellent to Hector. He jumped down at once from his chariot in his full armour, and all the other Trojans abandoned chariot formation when they saw Prince Hector dismount. Leaping out, they told their drivers to keep their horses drawn up in proper order by the trench. Then they stood clear, sorted themselves out, and fell in behind their own captains in five companies.

Of these, the best and biggest was that which Hector and the peerless Polydamas commanded. None showed greater eagerness to breach the wall and fight by the hollow ships. Cebriones, in whose stead Hector had left a less valuable man with his chariot, was third in command. The second company was led by Paris, Alcathous, and Agenor; and the third by two of Priam's sons, Helenus and the godlike Deiphobus, and, as third in command, the noble Asius son of Hyrtacus, whom his big and glossy horses had brought from Arisbe and the River Selleïs. Aeneas, the handsome son of Anchises, led the fourth company, supported by two sons of Antenor, Archelochus and Acamas, men with experience in every kind of fighting. Sarpedon commanded the glorious allies, and had appointed under him Glaucus and the warlike Asteropaeus, whom he considered beyond question the best men among the allies next to himself, he being the finest soldier of them all. Thus they drew up, shield touching oxhide shield, and resolutely advanced on the Danaans, in the confidence that nothing could stop them now from swooping down on the black ships.

Of the Trojans and their famous allies, all except Asius son of Hyrtacus adopted the tactics suggested by the admirable Polydamas. But Asius, who was a ruling prince, objected to

leaving his chariot behind with his squire in charge, and
decided instead to drive right up to the good ships with his
whole equipage. He was a fool. He was not destined to evade
his evil fate and drive back his chariot and pair in triumph
from the ships to windy Ilium. In the spear of the sublime Ido-
meneus, Deucalion's son, abominable doom was waiting to
engulf him. For he did drive, aiming at the left flank of the
ships, where the Achaeans had a causeway that they used
themselves when returning from the plain. Here Asius drove
his chariot and horses over, and coming to the gateway found
that the doors had not been closed nor the long bar put in
place. The defenders were holding them open to give strag-
glers flying from the field a chance to reach the ships. So
Asius in his chariot made straight for the gate, backed by his
company, uttering their piercing war-cry. These foolish
people thought the Achaeans could not stop them now from
sweeping down on the black ships. But at the gate they met
two champions, both of them proud scions of the warlike
Lapith race. One was the stalwart Polypoetes son of Peirithous,
and the other, Leonteus, a peer of the murderous War-god.
This pair had planted themselves in front of the high gate,
like lofty mountain oaks that resist the wind and rain for ever,
supported by their long and sturdy roots. Thus the two, rely-
ing on their brawny arms, awaited the onslaught of the great
Asius and stood firm. The Trojans, massing themselves around
King Asius, Iamenus, Orestes, Adamas son of Asius, Thoön
and Oenomaus, held up their leather shields and with a
mighty shout made straight for the wall.

For a while the two Lapithae encouraged the Danaan men-
at-arms inside the ramparts to fight there for the ships. But
when they saw the Trojans storming at the wall and heard
sounds of disorder and panic among the Danaans behind
them, they came right out and fought in front of the gate,
like a pair of wild-boars in the mountains, facing a noisy mob
of men and dogs, charging to either flank, and crushing and
rooting up the undergrowth around them to the sound of
clattering tusks, till at last they are hit by someone's javelin

and killed. Thus the shining bronze on the breasts of the Lapi-
thae rang out as it met the enemy's blows. For they put up a
superb defence, trusting in their own strength and in their
friends on the wall above, who were battling for their lives
and for their camp and gallant ships by flinging stones down
from the well-built ramparts. The Trojans too hurled stones;
and showers of rock from the hands of either side came pelting
to the ground like the flakes in a blizzard, when the dark
clouds fly before the wind and the bountiful earth is blanketed
with snow. Helmets and bossed shields rang harshly out as the
great boulders hit them.

Asius son of Hyrtacus was in despair. He groaned, he slap-
ped his thighs, and he cried out: 'Ah, Father Zeus, I did not
know that you too were such a lover of the lie. I never
thought these bold Achaeans could withstand our fury: I
fancied we were irresistible. But look at them now, ready, the
pair of them, to kill or be killed before they give way from
the gate, like supple-waisted wasps or bees that have built in a
hollow by a rocky path and won't be driven from their home,
but stay and fight it out with the huntsmen for their children's
sake!'

This outburst from Asius had no effect on Zeus, who had
made up his mind to let Hector have the glory. Meanwhile
other Trojan companies had carried the fighting to other
gates. But how can I picture it all? It would take a god to
tell the tale. All along the stone wall, fierce fires had broken
out, and the hard-pressed Argives were compelled to fight
for their very ships. All the gods who had taken sides with
them were broken-hearted.

But here it was the two Lapithae who now attacked.
Peirithous' son, the stalwart Polypoetes, cast his spear and hit
Damasus on his bronze-sided helmet. The metal of the helmet
failed to check the metal of the spear. The point went through
it, pierced the bone and spattered the inside of the helmet with
the man's brains. That was the end of Damasus and his part in
the assault. Next, Polypoetes killed Pylon and Ormenus.
Meanwhile, Leonteus, offshoot of Ares, had flung his spear at

Hippomachus son of Antimachus and caught him on the belt. Then he drew his sharp sword from its sheath and dashed into the throng, where the first man he encountered was Antiphates. Closing, he struck him with his sword and brought him crashing to the ground, flat on his back. Then, in swift succession, he brought Menon, Iamenus and Orestes all nearer than they had been to the kindly soil.

While the Lapithae were stripping the resplendent armour from these men, the young warriors under Polydamas and Hector, who formed the best and biggest of the companies and had shown the greatest eagerness to breach the wall and set the ships on fire, were standing at the trench, still hesitating to advance. Just as they were going to cross, a portent had appeared to them, an eagle flying high along their front on the left, with a blood-red snake in his talons. The monster was alive and still gasping. And he showed signs of fight. Writhing back, he bit his captor on the breast beside the neck; whereupon the eagle in his pain released his hold, let the snake drop among the troops, and with a loud cry sailed away down the wind.

The Trojans were appalled when they saw the snake lie shimmering in their midst, to indicate the will of aegis-bearing Zeus. Polydamas went straight up to the dauntless Hector. 'Hector,' he said, 'as a rule you object when I offer sound advice at our Assemblies. You consider it impertinent for a commoner to disagree with you either in the council-chamber or in the field – your authority must always be upheld. But once again I am going to speak my mind and say what I think best. We ought not to advance and dispute the ships with the enemy. I know exactly what will happen – if the portent does not lie. Just as we were ready to cross, the eagle appeared to us out of the sky, flying on the left along our front, with a monstrous blood-red snake in his talons. The snake was alive, and the bird had to drop it before he reached his nest – he failed to get it home and give it to his young. In the same way, even if by a great effort we succeed in breaking down the Achaean gate and wall, and the enemy give way, our retirement from the ships over the same ground will prove disastrous. The Achaeans will be fighting for their ships. They will kill numbers of our men; and we shall have to leave them all behind. That is how a soothsayer who really understood such omens and had the army's confidence would interpret this portent.'

Hector of the flashing helmet gave him a black look. 'Polydamas,' he said, 'I do resent this interference on your part. Surely you could have done better than that. If you really mean what you say, the gods themselves must have addled your brains. Zeus the Thunderer in his own person and with all solemnity made me certain promises. These you tell me to forget; and instead you would have me base my actions on the flight of birds, winged creatures who do not interest me at all – in fact I do not care whether they fly to the right towards the morning sun or to the left into the western gloom. Let us pin our faith to the mandate of almighty Zeus, who governs all mankind and the gods as well. Fight for your country – that is the best and only omen. But why should you, of all men, shrink from battle? Even if the rest of us are slaughtered wholesale by the Argive ships, you need have no fear for your own safety – you are not the man to stand and fight it out. None the less, if you do shirk, or dissuade any of the others from fighting, I shall not hesitate to strike you with this spear and take your life.'

Thereupon Hector gave the signal to advance, and with a mighty roar his men went after him. From the Mountains of Ida, Zeus who delights in thunder unleashed a gusty wind, which raised the dust and blew it straight at the ships, thus bewildering the Achaeans and giving the advantage to Hector and the Trojans. Trusting in this token of the god's goodwill and in their strength, they now made determined efforts to breach the great Achaean wall, tearing at the parapets of the towers, pulling down the battlements, and levering up the projecting buttresses that the Achaeans had let into the ground outside to support the towers, in the hope that by undermining these they might bring down the wall itself. Yet for

all that the Danaans would not yield them entrance. They
closed up the embrasures with oxhide screens and from the
battlements pelted the enemy as they came up beneath the
wall.

The two Aiantes ranged everywhere along the top, direct-
ing the defence and exhorting the Achaeans. Some they dis-
posed of with a mild rebuke, but to others, who had aban-
doned all resistance, they used harsher terms. Knowing too
that it takes all kinds to make an army, they appealed not only
to their picked men but to those of average ability and to the
inferior troops. 'Friends, Argives,' they said; 'to-day there is
work for every man of you. You know this well enough your-
selves. Let no one listen to the Trojans' threats and turn his face
to the ships. Forward instead, straight at the enemy, cheering
each other on and trusting that Olympian Zeus, Lord of the
Lightning, will let us counter this attack and chase them back
to their town.' Thus the two Aiantes by their exhortations
held the Achaean front together.

By now the stones were falling thick as snowflakes on a
winter day when Zeus the Thinker has begun to snow and let
men see the javelins of his armament; when he has put the
winds to sleep and snows without ceasing, till he has covered
the high hill-tops and the bold headlands of the coast and the
clover meadows and the farmers' fields; till even the shores and
inlets of the grey sea are under snow, and only the breakers
fend it off as they come rolling in – everything else is blanketed
by the overwhelming fall from Zeus's hand. Such were the
showers of stones that flew in both directions, as the Achaeans
pelted the Trojans, and the Trojans the Achaeans, till the
whole length of the wall was thundering to the volleys they
exchanged.

But even now illustrious Hector and his Trojans would
not have broken down the gate in the wall and the long bar, if
Zeus the Counsellor had not inspired his son Sarpedon to fall
on the Argives as a lion falls on cattle. Sarpedon swung his
round shield to the front – his splendid shield of beaten
bronze, hammered out by the smith and backed with hide

after hide, stitched together with gold wire that ran right round the circle. With this in front of him, and brandishing two spears, he set out like a mountain lion who has long been short of meat and has the hardihood to assault the very walls of a homestead and explore the pens. Even if he finds herdsmen on the spot guarding the sheep with dogs and spears, he has no mind to be chased away without a venture in the fold, and either leaps in and pounces on a sheep, or is himself struck down on meeting the defence by a javelin from a quick hand. Thus did the godlike Sarpedon feel impelled to assault the wall and break through the battlements. He turned to Glaucus, Hippolochus' son. 'Glaucus,' he said, 'why do the Lycians at home distinguish you and me with marks of honour, the best seats at the banquet, the first cut off the joint, and never-empty cups? Why do they all look up to us as gods? And why were we made the lords of that great estate of ours on the banks of Xanthus, with its lovely orchards and its splendid fields of wheat? Does not all this oblige us now to take our places in the Lycian van and fling ourselves into the flames of battle? Only so can we make our Lycian men-at-arms say this about us when they discuss their Kings: "They live on the fat of the land they rule, they drink the mellow vintage wine, but they pay for it in their glory. They are mighty men of war, and where Lycians fight you will see them in the van."

'Ah, my friend, if after living through this war we could be sure of ageless immortality, I should neither take my place in the front line nor send you out to win honour in the field. But things are not like that. Death has a thousand pitfalls for our feet; and nobody can save himself and cheat him. So in we go, whether we yield the glory to some other man or win it for ourselves.'

Glaucus did not turn a deaf ear to Sarpedon's call, and the two went forward, with the great Lycian force at their heels. When he saw them coming, Menestheus son of Peteos shuddered, for it was against his sector of the Achaean ramparts that the menace was directed. Looking along the wall for some commander who could save his company from disaster, he saw the two Aiantes, those gluttons for battle, standing quite near, with Teucer, who had just come from his hut. But shouting was no good. The noise was so great that he could not make them hear. The very sky was assaulted by the din of smitten shields and crested helmets, let alone the pounding at the gates, for these were all closed by now, and the Trojans had come up and were trying to break them down and force their way in. Quickly deciding what to do, Menestheus sent the herald Thoötes with a message to Telamonian Aias. 'An errand for you,' he said, 'my good Thoötes. Run and call Aias: or rather both of them. That would be best of all; for we shall soon be wiped out here. The Lycian captains are making straight at us; and we know what savages these Lycians can be when they come to grips. But if the two of them over there are as hard-pressed as ourselves, let us at least have the brave Telamonian Aias, and tell him to bring Teucer the great bowman with him.'

The herald set out promptly on his errand, ran along the Achaean wall, and when he reached the Aiantes accosted them at once. 'My lords and commanders,' he said, 'Menestheus, my noble master, begs you to come over, if only for a little while, and lend him a hand in his difficulties, preferably both of you – that is what he would like best of all. For we shall soon be wiped out over there. The Lycian captains are making straight at our sector; and we all know what savages these Lycians can be when they come to grips. But if you are equally hard-pressed here, he hoped that you at least, my gallant lord, the son of Telamon, would join him and bring Teucer the great bowman with you.'

The mighty Telamonian Aias did not refuse his help. Turning to Oïleus' son, he instructed him carefully. 'Aias,' he said, 'I want you and our stalwart Lycomedes to stay here and see that our people keep the enemy engaged, while I go and counter the attack over there. I shall soon be back – directly I have saved our friends.'

With that, Telamonian Aias set off, and his brother Teucer, his own father's son, went with him attended by Pandion carrying his crooked bow. Since they were making for a spot where the pressure was intense, they went along inside the wall, and so reached the sector commanded by the great-hearted Menestheus. Here they found the redoubtable vanguard and captains of the Lycians storming at the battlements like a tempest in the dark. They hurled themselves at the enemy and the tumult was intensified.

Telamonian Aias was the first to kill his man, a comrade of Sarpedon's, the generous Epicles. He hit him with a jagged lump of rock that he picked up inside the battlements from the top of a heap beside an embrasure. This great chunk, which the sturdiest youngster of our generation would have found difficult to lift with both his hands, Aias heaved above his head and flung, crushing the helmet with its quadruple ridge and smashing the man's skull to pieces. Epicles dropped from the high tower like a diver and the spirit left his bones. Meanwhile Glaucus the stalwart son of Hippolochus was accounted for by Teucer. As he charged, Teucer saw his arm exposed and struck it with an arrow shot down from the rampart, spoiling the fight for Glaucus, who drew back hastily and unobtrusively from the wall so that the Achaeans might not see that he was wounded and gloat over him. Sarpedon suffered keenly when he realized that Glaucus was gone. Yet for all that his ardour was not quenched. He thrust up with a spear at Thestor's son Alcmaon, struck him, and tried to drag the weapon out. The man came with it, falling headlong from the wall, and his ornate bronze equipment rang upon him. Then Sarpedon got his mighty hands on the battlement. He gave a pull, and a whole length of the breastwork came away, exposing the top of the wall. He had made a breach big enough for a company.

But he still had to reckon at one and the same time with Aias and Teucer. An arrow from Teucer hit the bright baldric that ran across his breast and supported his man-covering shield. And though Zeus saved him from destruction (not wishing that his son should meet his doom by the sterns of the ships), Aias now came charging down on him and struck his shield. Again, the weapon failed to penetrate, but it staggered him in his onset and he had to withdraw a little from the battlements. Even so Sarpedon did not go right back. He was still filled with hopes of glory, and wheeling round he shouted to his godlike Lycians: 'Lycians, why have you let your resolution seep away like this? Strong as I am, I can hardly breach the wall alone and make a pathway to the ships. After me, then! And the more the better.'

The Lycians took the King's rebuke to heart and on either side of their royal leader attacked with greater vehemence than ever. But the Argives for their part reinforced the companies behind the wall, and the struggle that ensued was desperate for both sides. Neither could the stalwart Lycians break down the Danaan wall and establish a road to the ships, nor were the Danaan spearmen able to thrust back the Lycians, once they had gained a footing on the wall. Divided by the battlements between them, they were like two men quarrelling across a fence in the common field with yardsticks in their hands, each of them fighting for his fair share in a narrow strip. Over the breastwork, they hacked at each other's leather shields – the great round bucklers or the light targets that they held across their chests. The cruel bronze bit into many a warrior's flesh, and that not only when a man swung round and bared his back – it often went home clean through the shields themselves. All along, the towers and battlements were drenched with mingled Trojan and Achaean blood. And yet the Trojans were unable to set their enemies on the run. The Achaeans held on, and the battle was as nicely balanced as the scales in which an honest working-woman balances the wool against the weights to make sure of the meagre pittance she is earning for her children. The struggle was as equal as that, till the moment when Zeus gave the mastery to Hector son of Priam, who was the first to leap inside the Achaean wall.

He used his voice and sent it ringing through the Trojan ranks. 'On with you, Trojan charioteers!' he cried. 'Down with the Argive wall, and let us see the ships go up in flames.'

There was no Trojan ear that did not catch his stirring call. Massing together, they charged at the rampart and began to scale the parapet with sharp spears in their hands. But Hector seized and brought along a rock that was lying in front of the gate. Broad at the base though running to a point, it would have taxed the strength of the two best men in any city of these latter days to lever it up from the ground onto a cart. But Hector handled it alone without an effort – Zeus in his wisdom made it light for him. As easily as a shepherd picking up a ram's fleece in one hand carries it off and scarcely feels the weight, he lifted up the rock and brought it to bear on the panels that filled in the morticed framework of the high double doors, which were held on the inner side by two sliding bars locked by a single bolt. He went right up and taking a firm stance with his legs well apart to make sure of a powerful throw, he cast, hit the doors full in the middle, and broke the hinges off on either side. Its own momentum carried the rock within, and there was a great roar from the gate, as the panels were smashed to splinters by the impact of the stone and the bars gave way. Glorious Hector leapt inside, with a look like nightfall on his face. He held two spears in his hand and the bronze on his body shone with a baleful light. None but a god could have met and held him as he sprang through the gate. And now, with fire flashing from his eyes, he turned to the crowd behind him and called on the Trojans to surmount the wall. His men responded promptly. Some swarmed over the wall; others poured in through the gate itself. The panic-stricken Danaans fled among the hollow ships, and hell was let loose.

XIII

THE BATTLE AT THE SHIPS

WHEN Zeus had brought Hector and the Trojans up to the ships, he left them there with their enemies to the toil and agony of the unending struggle, and turned his shining eyes away into the distance, where he surveyed the lands of the horse-breeding Thracians, the Mysians who fight hand to hand, the lordly Hippemolgi who drink mares' milk, and the Abii, the most law-abiding folk on earth. Not another glance of his bright eyes did he give to Troy. It never occurred to him that any of the immortals would now come down to help either the Trojan or the Danaan arms.

But the Lord Poseidon at his own post kept a sharper look-out. He too had sat down, high on the topmost peak of wooded Samothrace, and was watching the battle spellbound. He had risen from the sea and sought out this spot because from here the whole of Ida as well as Priam's city and the ships of the Achaeans could be seen. He pitied the Achaeans in their hour of defeat and was enraged with Zeus.

Now he got up and came swinging down the rocky slope. The high hills and the forest lands trembled under the death-less feet of the descending god. He made three strides and with the fourth reached Aegae, his goal, where his famous palace built of gleaming gold stands deep in the lagoon and will stand for ever. There he harnessed to his chariot his two swift horses, who had brazen hooves and flowing golden manes. He clothed himself in gold, picked up his well-made golden whip, mounted his chariot and drove out across the waves. The monsters of the sea did not fail to recognize their King. On every side they issued from their caves and gambolled at his coming. The sea itself made way for him in its delight, so that his bounding horses flew along, and the bronze axle of his chariot remained dry below as they carried him towards the Achaean fleet.

Midway between Tenedos and rugged Imbros there is a large cavern, down in a deep sea-pool. Here Poseidon the Earthshaker unyoked and left his horses, after throwing down some ambrosial fodder beside them and tying their legs with golden hobbles they could neither break nor shake off, to make sure of their staying there till their Master's return. Then he made his way to the Achaean camp.

Here, like a high wind or a conflagration, the massed Trojans were sweeping on in the wake of Hector son of Priam with indomitable fury, and wasting no breath on their usual war-cry, so hopeful were they now of capturing the ships and killing all the best of the Achaeans beside them. But at this moment Poseidon the Earthshaker and Girdler of the World emerged from the depths of the sea to put fresh heart into the Argives. Borrowing the form and tireless voice of Calchas, he first accosted the two Aiantes, whom he found in little need of exhortation. 'My lords,' he said, 'you two can save the Achaean army if you keep your courage high and entertain no craven thought of panic. The Trojans have climbed the great wall in force, but irresistible as they seem, I am not concerned for the rest of the front, where the bronze-clad Achaeans will hold them all in check. It is here that I dread disaster, where that madman Hector, who pretends that his father was almighty Zeus, is storming in their van like a raging fire. If some god could only make you see that this is the place for you two to stand fast and rally the rest, you might yet fend him off from the gallant ships, for all his fury and the encouragement he gets from the Olympian himself.'

Thereupon the Earthshaker and Girdler of the World, touching them with his staff, filled them both with dauntless resolution and made new men of them. Then, with the speed of a striking hawk who leaves his post high up on a rocky precipice, poises, and swoops to chase some other bird across the plain, Poseidon the Earthshaker disappeared from their ken. Of the two Aiantes, it was Oïleus' son, the Runner, who first knew him for a god. Turning at once to the son of Telamon he said: 'Aias, it was one of the gods that live on Olympus who urged us just now to fight by the ships. He took the prophet's form, but he was not Calchas, our seer and diviner. His heels and the backs of his knees as he left us were proof enough for me – it is not hard to recognize a god. Not only that, but I feel a change in my own heart. I am twice as eager as I was for the fight. My feet and hands are itching to be at them.'

'I feel the same,' said Telamonian Aias. 'My mighty hands are itching on my spear; my spirit is roused; and my feet are dancing to be off. Single-handed I should be happy to meet Hector son of Priam in his fury.'

While the two Aiantes were talking to one another and savouring the joy of battle which the god had put into their hearts, the Girdler of the World was stirring up the Achaeans in the rear, who were trying to recover their spirits beside the gallant ships. They were not only unmanned by sheer exhaustion but demoralized by the sight of the Trojans who had swarmed across the great wall in such numbers. When they looked at them their eyes filled with tears and they saw no hope of salvation. But now, with the ease of a god, the Earthshaker went in among the ranks and hounded them on. Teucer was the first he visited and roused, with Leitus, the lord Peneleos, Thoas, Deipyrus, and Meriones and Antilochus, the turmoil-makers. With stinging words he put fresh heart into them: 'Argives, shame on you! Are you raw recruits? You are the very men on whose gallantry I had relied to save our ships. If *you* give up because the fight is so severe, the day for our conquest by the Trojans has indeed arrived. Ah, what a portent for my eyes, a fearful thing I never dreamt of seeing, the Trojans at our very ships! In the old days they were like the cowardly does that trot through the woods in their weak and aimless way, fodder for jackals, panthers and wolves, with no fight in them. That is how the Trojans used to behave, taking care never for a moment to stand up to us and meet us hand to hand. Now, they have left their city far behind them and are fighting by the hollow ships, all through the incompetence of our Commander-in-Chief and the slackness of the troops, who are so disgusted with their leader that they would rather die beside their fast ships than defend them. Yet even if the whole blame does rest with our overlord Agamemnon son of Atreus, who insulted the great runner Achilles, we have no excuse whatever for giving up the struggle. But brave men can recover: let us be quick to repair our faults. For instance, it is not a pretty sight to see you, sirs, who are numbered among the best men in the forces, slacking off like this. I could forgive some feeble wretch for throwing up the game. But you are different, and with you I quarrel heartily. My friends, this inactivity of yours is half-way to a far worse thing. Does it not occur to each of you to think of the shame and obloquy his conduct may bring on him, in a crisis like this, when the great Hector has broken down the gate and the long bar, and his war-cry is sounding by the very ships?'

With these stirring words the Girdler of the World rallied the Argives so effectively that they formed up on the two Aiantes, and in such strength as would have given pause to the War-god himself or Athene Marshaller of the Host. There stood the very pick of their best men awaiting Prince Hector and the Trojans, an impenetrable hedge of spears and sloping shields, buckler to buckler, helmet to helmet, man to man. So close were the ranks that when they moved their heads the glittering peaks of their plumed helmets met and the spears overlapped as they swung them forward in their sturdy hands. They looked steadily to their front and were eager for the clash.

The Trojans came on in a mass, with Hector in the van sweeping forward like a boulder bounding down a rocky slope, when a river swollen by winter rain has washed its supports away and thrust the misbegotten thing over the brow of the hill. Leaping high in the air it hurtles down through echoing woods and then runs on unchecked till it reaches level ground, where it stops rolling, much against its will. Thus Hector threatened for a while to reach the sea with ease through the Achaean huts and ships, killing as he went. But when he ran into that solid block of men, he stopped short, hard against them; and the Achaeans facing him lunged at him with their swords and double-pointed spears, and thrust him off. Hector was shaken and fell back, but in a loud voice he called upon his men: 'Stand by me, Trojans and Lycians, and you Dardanians who like your fighting to be hand to hand. The Achaeans will not hold me up for long, packed together though they are, like the stones in a wall. They will give before my spear, if it is true that I was brought here by the best of all gods, the Thunderer and Lord of Here.'

His rousing call inspired every man in the company, and his brother Deiphobus strode out among them with a high heart, swinging his rounded shield to the front. As he stepped airily forward, advancing under its cover, Meriones let fly at him with a glittering lance. And he did not miss his man: he struck his rounded oxhide shield. But the long shaft, far from passing through, broke off at the socket – Deiphobus had held the leather shield at arm's length, having good reason to fear a lance from the doughty Meriones. So that nobleman now took cover once more with the friends behind him. He was enraged both at the loss of his broken lance and at missing a victory, and he went off at once to the Achaean camp and ships to fetch a long spear that he had left in his hut.

But the rest fought on and the tumult of battle filled the air. Teucer son of Telamon was the first to kill his man, the spear-man Imbrius, son of the horse-fancier Mentor. He had lived at Pedaeum before the Achaean expedition came, and was married to Medesicaste, an illegitimate daughter of Priam's. But when the Danaans arrived in their rolling ships, he returned to Ilium and won a place of honour for himself among the Trojans, living with Priam, who treated him like one of his children. Teucer hit this man below the ear with a long lance, which he then pulled out. Imbrius fell like an ash that has stood as a landmark on a high hill-top till an axe brings it down and it sweeps the ground with its delicate leaves. Thus Imbrius fell, and his ornate bronze equipment rang upon him.

Teucer ran up, eager to get his armour off, and as he did so, Hector let fly at him with a glittering spear. But Teucer was looking out and managed by a hair's breadth to avoid the weapon, which struck Amphimachus son of Cteatus of the House of Actor in the breast as he rushed into the fray. He fell with a thud and his armour rang about him. As Hector dashed in to tear the close-fitting helmet from the temples of the gallant Amphimachus, Aias aimed at him with a shining spear. But no part of his body was exposed; he was completely hidden by a grim sheath of bronze; and all Aias hit was the boss of his shield. Yet the force of the blow was so great that Hector had to give ground and leave the two dead men to be removed by the Achaeans. Amphimachus was conveyed into their lines by Stichius and Prince Menestheus, the Athenian captains, while the two Aiantes, disdaining all hazards, possessed themselves of Imbrius' corpse. Like a couple of lions who have snatched a goat away from under the noses of the goatherd's snarling dogs and lift it clear of the ground as they carry it off in their jaws through the undergrowth, the helmeted Aiantes held Imbrius aloft and stripped him of his arms. And in his fury at Amphimachus' death, the son of Oïleus severed Imbrius' head from his soft neck and with a swing sent it whirling like a ball through the crowd to drop in the dust at Hector's feet.

When Poseidon saw his grandson Amphimachus killed in this encounter, he was bitterly grieved and went along by the huts and ships of the Achaeans to stir them up and brew trouble for the Trojans. He met Idomeneus the famous spearman. Idomeneus had been with a member of his own company who had just come out of the fight with a spear-wound in the ham. This man had been carried in by his comrades, and Idomeneus, after instructing the surgeons, was going to his own hut, with every intention of returning to the fight, when the Royal Earthshaker accosted him, imitating the voice of Thoas, Andraemon's son, who was King of all Pleuron and

mountainous Calydon and was worshipped by the Aetolians
he ruled. 'Idomeneus,' he said, 'Commander of the Cretans,
what has become of all the threats that we Achaeans used to
make against the Trojans?'

'Thoas,' said Idomeneus, the Cretan King, 'as far as I can
see, no individuals are to blame. We are all veterans. Nobody
is unmanned by fear or has run away from this horrible battle
in panic. I can only think that it must be the pleasure of the
mighty Son of Cronos that the Achaeans should come to an
inglorious end in this remote spot far away from Argos. But
you, Thoas, have always been a steady man and are good at
heartening others when you see them breaking down. Do not
slacken now. Put the men on their mettle.'

'Idomeneus,' replied Poseidon the Earthshaker, 'may the
man who does not fight his best to-day never come home
from Troy but stay here to delight the dogs! Come, take your
arms and follow me. We must put our backs into this business
together, if the pair of us are going to be of any use. Even the
poorest fighters turn into brave men when they stand side by
side; and you and I have always taken our place in battle by
the very best.'

With that, the god went back again into the turmoil, and
Idomeneus made his way to his well-built hut, put on his
splendid armour, seized a couple of spears and came out
looking like the lightning that the Son of Cronos takes in his
hand, when he has a message for mankind, and discharges from
the glittering summit of Olympus to flash into the distant sky.
Thus the bronze flashed on the breast of Idomeneus as he ran.

He had hardly left his hut when he was met by Meriones,
his noble squire, who had come to fetch himself a bronze
spear. 'My dearest comrade-in-arms, my brother's son, Meri-
ones of the nimble feet!' the great Idomeneus exclaimed.
'Why have you left the battlefield to come down here?
Are you wounded? Worn out, perhaps, by the pain from an
arrow-head? Or have you come with some message for me?
I assure you that I have no desire to sit in my hut, but am
eager for the fight.'

'My lord and commander,' replied Meriones, who under-
stood him well, 'I have come for a spear, hoping to find one
left in your hut. I broke the one I had, when I hit the shield of
the insolent Deiphobus.'

'If it is a spear you want,' said Idomeneus the Cretan chief,
'you will find not one but twenty leaning against the bur-
nished wall by the entrance of my hut. They are Trojan
spears: I take them from the men I kill. I do not believe in
fighting the enemy at a distance. Hence my collection of
spears and bossed shields, helmets and glittering cuirasses.'

'I too,' Meriones was quick to reply, 'have plenty of Trojan
weapons in my hut and my black ship, but not where I can
pick them up at once. Moreover, I do not consider myself to
have failed in my duty any more than you. In the field of
honour, I take my place in the front line whenever battle is
joined. I should have expected any other of the bronze-clad
Achaeans to be blind to my prowess rather than you, who have
seen it for yourself.'

'There is no need for you to dwell on that,' said Idomeneus
the Cretan King. 'I know your mettle, and how it would be
proved if all we noblemen were being detailed by the ships
for an ambuscade. For there is nothing like an ambush for
bringing a man's worth to light and picking out the cowards
from the brave. A coward changes colour all the time; he
cannot sit still for nervousness, but squats down, first on one
heel, then on the other; his heart thumps in his breast as he
thinks of death in all its forms, and one can hear the chattering
of his teeth. But the brave man never changes colour at all
and is not unduly perturbed, from the moment when he
takes his seat in ambush with the rest. All he prays for is to
come to grips with the enemy as quickly as may be. Nobody
on such an occasion would think lightly of your daring and
your strength. Even if you were hit in the action by an arrow
or spear, it would not be behind on your neck or back that the
weapon would fall; it would strike you in the chest or belly,
as you rushed forward to keep your tryst with the others in
the front line. But we must not stay here and chatter like

little boys, or people may be scandalized. Go into my hut and get yourself a heavy spear.'

Meriones, bold as the god of battles, snatched up a bronze spear from inside the hut and went after Idomeneus with a high heart bent on war. The two were like Ares the Killer and his son, the fierce and indomitable Panic-maker before whom the staunchest warrior turns tail, when they set out for the wars, marching from Thrace to join the Ephyri or the haughty Phlegyans and to bring victory to one side and turn a deaf ear to the others' prayers. Thus Meriones and Idomeneus, leaders of men, set out for the battle in their resplendent bronze.

'My lord,' said Meriones to his companion, 'at what point do you propose to enter the fight? On our right wing, in the centre, or on the left? It is there I imagine that the Achaean defence is most likely to break down.' To which Idomeneus the Cretan commander replied: 'There are others to look after the ships in the centre. The two Aiantes are there, and so is Teucer, the best bowman we have and a good man in a scrimmage too. They will give my lord Hector his bellyful of fighting, formidable though he is. Indeed he will not find it easy, for all his rage, to break the spirit of those men and wear down their indomitable strength, as he must before he sets the good ships on fire, unless the Son of Cronos helps and throws a burning brand among them. The great Telamonian Aias will never yield to a mortal man who eats the bread of Mother Earth and can be cut by bronze or brought down by a rock. Aias would not give way even to Achilles, the breaker of the battle-line, at all events not in a standing fight, though neither he nor anyone else can run like Achilles. So let us make for the left wing here; and we shall soon find out whether we are going to win glory from some other man or he from us.'

Eager as the War-god, Meriones led off in the direction indicated by his chief, and they reached the front. When the Trojans saw Idomeneus come up, fierce as a flame, and his squire with him, both in their decorated arms, they called to each other across the ranks and attacked him in a body. The fighting became general by the sterns of the ships, and their battalions were rolled up together, as the dust, when it lies thick in the roadways on a stormy day, is caught up by the blustering wind and rolled into a great and solid cloud. In that chaotic mass it was the one aim of every man to stab his neighbour. The field of death bristled with the long flesh-cutting spears they wielded, and the eye was dazzled by the glint of bronze from the assemblage of so many shimmering helmets, burnished cuirasses and resplendent shields. None but the most insensible of men would have enjoyed the spectacle and not been moved.

Thus the two mighty Sons of Cronos, taking different sides, brought tribulation to the gallant men-at-arms. Zeus had in mind a victory for the Trojans and Hector, with a view to exalting Achilles of the nimble feet. But he did not mean the Achaean army to be utterly destroyed in front of Ilium: he was humouring Thetis and her strong-willed son. Poseidon, on the other hand, had come stealthily up out of the grey surf to join the Argives and inspire them. It distressed him to see them beaten by the Trojans, and he was furious with Zeus. Yet the two gods' descent and parentage were the same, though Zeus was the older and the wiser. For which reason, Poseidon was careful not to help the Argives openly. He took the form of a man and in that disguise kept moving to and fro, stirring up the troops. Thus the gods saw to it that the rope they had knotted for this desperate and even tug-of-war was tautened either way. The rope was unbreakable and no one could undo the knot; but it undid many a man.

Idomeneus, though he was no longer a young man, flung himself into the fight with a shout to his troops. He struck panic into the Trojans by killing Othryoneus, an ally who had joined them from Cabesus. Drawn by news of the war, this man was a newcomer to Troy, who had asked Priam for the hand of Cassandra, the most beautiful of his daughters. Instead of paying him for his bride, he had promised to do marvels for Priam and drive the Achaeans from his shores. The old king, accepting the offer, had pledged him his

daughter's hand; and it was on this understanding that Othry-
oneus took part in the fighting. But now Idomeneus let fly at
him with a glittering spear and caught him as he swaggered
along. The bronze cuirass that he was wearing served him ill:
the spear-point landed in the middle of his belly, and he fell
to earth with a crash. Idomeneus mocked him. 'Othryoneus,'
he cried, 'I congratulate you on your bethrothal to King
Priam's daughter – subject, of course, to your part of the con-
tract being duly fulfilled. Could not *we* do business with you
on the same lines? If you will help us to sack the great citadel
of Ilium, we will send over to Argos for the loveliest of
Atreides' daughters and make her your bride. Step this way
with me to our seagoing ships, where we can come to terms
about your marriage. You will find that our price for brides is
not exorbitant.'

Taunting him thus, the lord Idomeneus seized him by the
foot and began to drag him through the crowd. But now Asius
came to the rescue. He was on foot in front of his chariot,
which the driver kept so close to him that his shoulders were
fanned all the time by the horses' breath. Asius did his utmost
to despatch Idomeneus. But Idomeneus was too quick for
him. He hit him with a spear on the throat, under the chin,
and the point went right through. Asius fell like an oak or a
poplar or a towering pine that woodmen cut down in the
mountains with whetted axes to make timbers for a ship. So
Asius lay stretched in front of his chariot and horses, groaning
and clutching at the bloodstained dust. His charioteer, losing
such wits as he possessed, had not even the presence of mind to
turn his horses round and slip out of the enemy's hands, but
was caught by a spear from the cool-headed Antilochus,
which struck him in the middle. The bronze corslet he was
wearing was of no avail: the spear-point went home in the
centre of his belly. With a gasp he fell headlong from the
well-built chariot, and Antilochus, son of the noble-hearted
Nestor, drove his horses out of the Trojan into the Achaean
lines.

Deiphobus, distressed at Asius' death, came up close to Ido-

meneus and let fly a shining lance. But Idomeneus was look-
ing out and avoided the bronze spear by sheltering behind the
rounded shield he always carried. It was built of concentric
rings of oxhide and of glittering bronze, and was fitted with a
couple of crossbars. He crouched under cover of this, and the
bronze spear flew over him, drawing a deep note from the
shield as it grazed its edge. But the spear had not flown for
nothing from Deiphobus' sturdy arm. It struck a chieftain,
Hypsenor son of Hippasus, in the liver under the midriff, and
forthwith brought him down. Deiphobus was elated by his
triumph and cried aloud: 'So Asius does not lie unavenged!
Even on his way to Hades, the mighty Warden of the Gate, I
feel that he will travel with a light heart now that I have given
him an escort.'

The Argives listened to his jubilation in disgust, and none
with such resentment as the doughty Antilochus, who in his
sorrow did not forget his comrade, but ran to bestride him
and covered him with his shield. Then two of their trusty
men, Mecisteus son of Echius and the worthy Alastor, lifted
him from the ground and, groaning heavily, carried him off
to the hollow ships.

But there was no pausing for Idomeneus in the high fury
that possessed him. His one desire was to bring down black
night on a Trojan's eyes, or himself to fall in saving the
Achaeans from destruction. His next victim was the noble
Alcathous, son of royal Aesyetes, and son-in-law to Anchises,
whose eldest daughter, Hippodameia, was his wife. This
lady, as a girl at home, had been the darling of her father and
her gentle mother. Indeed, there was no other woman of her
age with such beauty, skill and brains. Small wonder that the
best man in the broad realm of Troy had married her – the
man who now fell to Idomeneus, with Poseidon's help. For
the god cast a spell on Alcathous' bright eyes and so encum-
bered his legs that he could neither escape to the rear nor leap
aside, and was standing as still as a monument or a tall tree
crowned with leaves when the spear of the lord Idomeneus
hit him. It struck him full in the chest and pierced the coat of

bronze which he was wearing – the coat that hitherto had
saved his flesh from harm, but now rang sharply out as the
spear rent it. Alcathous fell with a crash. The spear was fixed
in his heart, which had not yet stopped beating and shook it
to the very butt till at last the god of battle stilled it with his
heavy hand.

Idomeneus in his triumph called out in a loud voice: 'Dei-
phobus, three killed for the one you bragged about so much!
I think we may cry quits. But why not tackle me yourself,
my friend, and learn the quality of one of Zeus's stock who is
visiting your land. For it was Zeus who established our line.
He made his son Minos King of Crete; the peerless Deucalion
was Minos' son; and I am Deucalion's. I succeeded him as
King of a great people in our spacious isle; and now my ships
have brought me here to be a curse to you and your father and
everyone in Troy.'

Idomeneus' challenge left Deiphobus in two minds, whether
to fall back and call on one of his gallant compatriots for sup-
port, or to see what he could do alone. Deciding that he had
better look for help, he went after Aeneas and found him
standing idle at the back of the crowd – Aeneas always bore
King Priam a grudge because he made so little of him though
he was as good a man as any. Deiphobus went up and appealed
to him as one of the leading men in Troy. 'Aeneas,' he said,
'you are badly needed, for the rescue of Alcathous, your
brother-in-law. If you care about your family at all, come and
help me save your sister's husband, who lived in your house
and looked after you as a child. He has just fallen to the great
Idomeneus' spear.'

Aeneas' heart was stirred and he made for Idomeneus in an
ugly mood. But Idomeneus was not to be scared off like a
little boy. He waited for him with the self-reliance of a moun-
tain boar when he is caught by a crowd of huntsmen in some
lonely spot and faces the hue and cry with bristling back and
eyes aflame, whetting his tusks in his eagerness to take on all
comers, hound or man. Thus the renowned spearman Ido-
meneus awaited the onslaught of Aeneas and gave no ground

at all. But he did call for support, looking especially to Asca-
laphus, Aphareus and Deipyrus, as well as to Meriones and
Antilochus. To these tried men he made an urgent appeal.
'My friends,' he cried, 'come to my help. I am alone and
dreading an attack by the swift Aeneas, who is making for me
now. I know him for a mighty killer in a fight; and he has the
great advantage of youth. If our ages were matched as our
mood is now, there would soon be a triumph for Aeneas or
myself.'

With one accord they all closed in and rallied round Ido-
meneus, crouching behind sloped shields. But Aeneas, on his
side, also called upon his friends, looking for help to Dei-
phobus and Paris and the excellent Agenor, his fellow com-
manders in the Trojan army. The troops, moreover, backed
him too, like sheep following a bellwether from the pasture to
drink at a stream; and Aeneas was as happy to see the main
body behind him as the shepherd is when he sees his sheep.

Volleys of long spears were exchanged over the body of
Alcathous at close range, and the bronze rang grimly on their
breasts as they cast at each other across the throng. But there
were two warriors, Aeneas and Idomeneus, peers of Ares,
who surpassed all the rest in their eagerness to tear each other's
flesh with the remorseless bronze. Aeneas cast at Idomeneus
first. But Idomeneus was looking out and dodged his bronze
spear, which flew by and quivered in the ground. It had leapt
from his strong hand for nothing. Then Idomeneus cast. He
struck Oenomaus full in the belly, breaking the plate of his
corslet, through which the spear-point let his bowels out.
Oenomaus fell down in the dust and clutched at the ground.
Idomeneus dragged his long-shadowed spear out of the body,
but overwhelmed as he was by missiles, he was unable to strip
the man's splendid arms and armour from his shoulders. He
was no longer nimble enough to make a spurt in following up
his own cast or avoiding someone else's; and being too slow
on his feet to save his life by running, he made it a practice to
fight where he stood and so keep death at bay. Now, as he
moved slowly off, Deiphobus, who was still nettled by his

taunts, let fly a shining spear at him. For the second time he missed Idomeneus; but the spear hit Ascalaphus, a son of the War-god. The heavy weapon went right through his shoulder, and he fell in the dust and clutched at the ground. But it was only later that his mighty Father, Ares of the Brazen Voice, heard that his son had fallen in action. At the moment he was sitting high up on Olympus under the golden clouds, where he was detained by order of Zeus, together with the rest of the immortal gods, for whom the war was out of bounds.

It was now over Ascalaphus that they fought hand to hand. Deiphobus had just torn the glittering helmet from his head, when Meriones, swift as the War-god, leapt in and struck his arm near the shoulder with a spear. The helmet with its heavy vizor dropped from his hand and rang on the ground; and like a vulture Meriones swooped in again, withdrew the weighty spear from his arm, and then took cover with his friends once more. Polites, Deiphobus' brother, putting his arm round his waist, supported him out of the turmoil and brought him to his fast horses, who were waiting for him in a quiet spot behind the fighting with their driver and his painted chariot. They carried him off to the city, groaning heavily and worn with pain, for the blood was pouring from the fresh wound in his arm.

But the rest fought on and the tumult was intensified. Aeneas now charged in and with his sharp spear struck Aphareus son of Caletor on the throat, which happened to be turned towards him. The man's head lolled on one side; he crumpled up under his shield and helmet; and soul-devouring Death engulfed him. Meanwhile Antilochus, seizing a moment when Thoön's back was turned his way, leapt in and struck. He cut clean through the vein that runs right up the back to the neck. Thoön dropped backwards in the dust, stretching his hands out to his comrades-in-arms. Antilochus fell upon him and began to strip him of his armour; but with a wary eye, for Trojans were coming up on every side. They pricked his broad and glittering shield, but they could not get behind it or so much as scratch the smooth skin of Antilochus' neck with their cruel bronze. For this son of Nestor's was protected by Poseidon the Earthshaker even in such a hail of darts as this. Unable to shake off his enemies, he faced them, now on this side, now on that. His spear was never still for a moment, but followed his thoughts, swinging round in his hand as he menaced a distant foe or threatened to lunge at a near one.

He was just preparing to cast into the crowd, when Adamas son of Asius, who had watched for the chance, leapt in and struck the centre of his shield with his sharp spear. But Poseidon of the Sable Locks grudged it the life of Antilochus and caused it to miscarry, with the result that half of it stuck in the shield like a charred stake while the other half fell on the ground. Adamas tried to save himself by retiring among his men. But Meriones followed him as he withdrew and caught him with his lance half-way between the navel and the privy parts, the most painful spot in which a wretched soldier can be struck. There the weapon went home, and Adamas collapsing writhed round it, as a bull twists about when the herdsmen have caught and roped him in the hills and bring him in against his will. Thus the stricken warrior writhed, but not for long – only till the lord Meriones came up and pulled the spear out of his flesh. Then night descended on his eyes.

Helenus closed with Deipyrus and struck him on the temple with his big Thracian sword, shearing his helmet off. The dislodged helmet fell to the ground and was picked up by an Achaean as it rolled among the fighters' feet. The unlovely night of Death descended on Deipyrus' eyes.

The son of Atreus, Menelaus of the loud war-cry, was grieved when he saw this and made for Prince Helenus with a menacing shout, brandishing a sharp spear. Helenus replied by bending his bow. So the two were ready to let fly at the same moment, one with a sharp spear and the other with an arrow from his string. Helenus son of Priam hit Menelaus on the breast with his keen dart, striking the plate of his corslet. But the dart rebounded. As the black beans or chickpeas on a

broad threshing-floor leap from the flat shovel, with the
whistling wind and the winnower's force behind them, the
deadly arrow bounced from the corslet of the illustrious Mene-
laus and sped into the distance. But the son of Atreus, Mene-
laus of the loud war-cry, did better. He struck Helenus on the
hand in which he was holding his polished bow, and the
bronze spear went clean through his hand into the bow.
Helenus in fear for his life fell back among his friends, with
his hand hanging down at his side and dragging the ashen
spear along. The spear was withdrawn from his wound by the
noble Agenor, who bound up the hand with a bandage of
fine-spun wool. It was really a sling, which the lord Agenor's
squire was able to lend him.

Peisander now made straight for the illustrious Menelaus.
It was an evil Fate that led him on this path, with death at the
end of it, death, Menelaus, in battle with you. The two men
closed, and Atreides began with a miss – his spear went
wandering. Peisander did better: he struck the shield of the
illustrious Menelaus, but without sufficient force to drive the
point right through. The broad shield held it up, and the spear
snapped at the socket. Yet Peisander was well pleased and
confident of victory. But now Atreides drew his silver-
studded sword and charged him. Peisander, from under his
shield, brought out a fine bronze axe with a long smooth haft
of olive-wood. They met; and Peisander struck the cone of
the other's helmet, on top, just below the horsehair plume.
But Menelaus caught Peisander, as he came at him, on the
forehead above the base of the nose. The bones cracked, and
his eyes, all bloody, dropped in the dust at his feet. He reeled
and fell. Menelaus put his foot on his chest and as he stripped
him of his arms, he triumphed over him. 'That,' he said, 'is
the nearest you shall come to the ships of the horse-loving
Danaans, you insolent Trojans, who are always spoiling for
blood. Not that there are not other forms of infamy and other
vices that you dabble in. Witness the shame you put me to,
you curs, when you broke the laws of hospitality and defied
the wrath of Zeus the Thunderer, who made them, and who is

going before long to bring your city tumbling down. You stole my wife, when she was your hostess, and you gaily sailed away with her and half my wealth. And now you won't be satisfied till you have made our travelled ships go up in flames, and slaughtered us. Nevertheless, for all your fury, you shall be stopped. Ah, Father Zeus, they say you are wiser than any man or god – and all this is your doing! Why are you so indulgent to these Trojan bullies in whom destruction is a passion, and who enjoy the din of a pitched battle so much that they wish it to go on for ever? People tire of everything, even of sleep and love, sweet music and the perfect dance, things that take far longer than a battle to make a man cry out "Enough!" But these Trojans are not normal men; they are gluttons for war.'

As he spoke, the peerless Menelaus stripped the blood-stained armour from the corpse and handed it to his men. Then he went off and took his place once more in the front line. No sooner was he there than he was attacked by Har-palion, son of King Pylaemenes, who had come with his father to the Trojan war, never to return to his own country again. Closing with Atreides, Harpalion struck the centre of his shield with a spear; but having failed to drive the weapon through it, he thought he would save himself by slinking back into his own company, keeping a lookout on every side for any missile that might come his way. As he withdrew, Meriones shot at him with a bronze-headed arrow and hit him on the right buttock. The arrow went clean through his bladder and came out under the bone. Harpalion collapsed forthwith, gasped out his life in the arms of his friends, and lay stretched on the ground like a worm, while the dark blood poured out of him and soaked the earth. Gathering round, the valiant Paphlagonians lifted him into a chariot, and with heavy hearts drove him to holy Ilium. His weeping father went with them, leaving his son's death unavenged.

But the slaughter of Harpalion roused Paris to fury, for this Paphlagonian had been his guest, and he shot an arrow to avenge his friend. There was an Achaean called Euchenor, son of the seer Polyidus, a man of substance and good birth who lived in Corinth. When he embarked for Troy, he knew well enough the melancholy end that awaited him, for his old father, the good Polyidus, had often told him he must either die in his bed of a painful disease or sail with the Achaeans and be killed at Troy. So he went, saving his wealth from the heavy fine they would have made him pay, and himself from a loathsome malady and the pain he did not wish to bear. Now, Paris with his arrow struck him under the jaw and ear. So he did not have a lingering death. He was engulfed by the unlovely dark.

Here then, the fight went on like an inextinguishable fire. But Prince Hector, who had not been kept informed, had no idea that on the left of the ships the enemy were doing such execution among his men – indeed, the Argives very nearly got the upper hand, to such effect did the Earthshaker and Girdler of the World inspire them, besides exerting his own strength in their support. So Hector was still on the offensive in that part of the front where he had broken the shield-bearing Danaan companies and stormed the gate and wall, and where the ships of Aias and Protesilaus were drawn up on the shore of the grey sea. There, the protecting wall had been lower than anywhere else and the Danaan infantry and chariots were putting up the fiercest defence.

The troops at this point, the Boeotians, the Ionians with their long tunics, the Locrians, Phthians and splendid Epeans, had the utmost difficulty in holding Prince Hector's attack on the ships and were quite unable to thrust him back: he came at them like fire. Picked men from Athens were fighting here, led by Menestheus son of Peteos, supported by Pheides, Stichius and the brave Bias; while the Epeans were commanded by Meges son of Phyleus, Amphion and Dracius; and the Phthians by Medon and the staunch Podarces. One of these, Medon, was a bastard son of King Oïleus and so a brother of Aias. But he had been exiled for homicide and lived in Phylace, having killed a kinsman of his step-mother Eriopis, the wife of Oïleus. Podarces, the other, was a son of

Iphiclus the son of Phylacus. These two in their full armour were fighting to defend the ships in the van of the great-hearted Phthians and side by side with the Boeotians. Aias himself, the Runner and son of Oïleus, was never separated even for a moment from Aias the son of Telamon. They made one think of a couple of dun oxen straining at the ploughshare in fallow ground, each as hard as the other. With the sweat pouring out at the base of their horns, and separated only by the polished yoke, they press on down the furrow till they are brought up by the ridge at the end of the field. Thus these two stuck to one another and stood cheek by jowl. But there was this difference between them. The son of Telamon was backed by a strong and well-trained body of retainers, who were always ready to relieve him of his shield when he was over-come by heat or fatigue; whereas the gallant son of Oïleus was not accompanied by his Locrian troops, who had no stomach for hand-to-hand fighting, unprovided as they were with the usual arms, a plumed helmet of bronze, a rounded shield and ashen spears. They believed in the bow and the sling of fine-spun wool. It was with these weapons that they had followed their chief to Ilium; and there were indeed occasions when a Trojan company was cut to pieces by their volleys. So now, while the heavy-armed troops in front en-gaged the Trojans and bronze-clad Hector, the Locrians kept shooting at them from a safe distance in the rear, till the Tro-jans, thrown into confusion by the arrows, began to lose their relish for the fight.

In fact they might have had to leave the ships and huts and go back discomfited to windy Ilium, but for Polydamas, who went up to the formidable Hector once more and said: 'Hector, you are an obstinate man when it comes to taking advice. Just because Heaven has made you a magnificent fighter, you like to think that you know better than anyone else how to plan a battle too. But you cannot possibly take everything on yourself. People differ in their gifts. One man can fight, another dance, or play the lute and sing; and yet another is endowed by all-seeing Zeus with a good brain, to the frequent advantage of his friends, whom it saves from disaster time and again, as *he* knows even better than they do. However, I will speak my mind and say what I think best. The fighting has spread all round you in a ring. Our gallant men certainly stormed the wall, but having done so they are either standing idle under arms, or are scattered among the ships and fighting against odds. I suggest that you should break away and call in all your best men. We could then consult and settle the whole question, whether to fall on the well-found ships in the hope of a decisive victory, or failing that to withdraw from them intact. I, for one, am afraid that the Achaeans may be going to pay us out for what we gave them yesterday. They have a man lying idle at the ships who is a glutton for battle; and I cannot believe that he will keep out of the fighting altogether.'

Hector had no fault to find with this advice and replied without hesitation: 'Stay here, Polydamas, and keep all the best men round you, while I go and face the situation yonder. I shall soon be back, when I have set our people there to rights.'

With that he sped away, glittering like a snow-capped peak, and as he passed swiftly through the Trojan ranks and those of their allies he shouted to his men. They all ran up when they heard Hector's voice and massed themselves round Panthous' son, the amiable Polydamas. But Hector went questing down the front line to see if he could find Deiphobus anywhere, and the stalwart Prince Helenus, Adamas son of Asius, and Asius himself, the son of Hyrtacus. He was soon to discover that by now not one of these was both alive and unhurt. Two had fallen to the Argives and lay dead by the sterns of the ships, while the others were back within the city wall, wounded at long or short range. He did find one man quickly enough, on the left flank, where the Trojans had suffered so grievously, and that was the noble Paris, the husband of Helen of the lovely hair. Paris was encouraging his men and driving them into battle, when Hector came up to him and abused him roundly. 'Paris,' he said, 'you pretty boy, you woman-struck seducer; where, I ask you, are Deiphobus and the great Prince Helenus, Adamas son of Asius, and Asius son of Hyrtacus? And what have you done with Othryoneus? This is indeed the end of Ilium: its topmost towers are down. There is nothing for you now but death.'

'Hector,' retorted Paris, 'you are blaming an innocent man in your rage. If I have ever shrunk from fighting, I have not done so to-day. I too can claim that I was not born to be an utter coward; and from the moment when you told your men to attack by the ships, we have held our ground here and kept the Danaans engaged relentlessly. The friends you ask about are killed, except Deiphobus and the great Prince Helenus, who have withdrawn. Each was wounded by a long spear in the arm, but had the luck to come away alive. Lead us now wherever you wish. We shall follow you with a will and, I may say, with no lack of courage either, so far as in us lies. What a man cannot do, however keen, is to fight beyond his powers.'

So Paris pacified his brother, and they went off together into the very heart of the battle, which was raging now round Cebriones and the admirable Polydamas, Phalces, Orthaeus, the godlike Polyphetes, Palmys, and the sons of Hippotion, Ascanius and Morys, who had arrived from deep-soiled Ascania as reliefs in the morning of the previous day and now felt impelled to join in the fight. The Trojans came on like an angry squall that swoops down from a thunder-laden sky to strike salt water, bringing indescribable turmoil to the moaning sea, where the great waves hiss and arch their foaming backs in a never-ending procession. Thus the Trojans came on behind their officers, rank after serried rank glittering with bronze, and with Hector son of Priam like the murderous War-god in their van. In front of him he held his rounded shield, with its close layers of hide and its ample sheath of beaten bronze; and his burnished helmet swayed upon his temples.

Time and again Hector dashed up and probed the enemy line at various points in the hope that it would break before him as he charged under cover of his shield. But he did not shake the Achaeans' resolution. And one of them, Aias, stepped out into the open with great strides and challenged him. 'You there,' he called to Hector, 'come closer, and give up these futile efforts to make Argives run away. We do know something about war, and if we took a thrashing, it was Zeus with his wicked scourge that gave it us. I suppose you imagine that you are going to destroy our ships? But we too have hands, which are ready to fight for them, and likely, long before you get the ships, to capture your fine town and sack it. As for you, I say the time is drawing near when, in your haste to save yourself, you will pray to Father Zeus and the other gods to make your long-maned horses faster than falcons as they gallop home with you to Troy in clouds of dust.'

A lucky omen, in the form of an eagle flying high on the right, signalized these words of Aias. The Achaean troops were heartened by the sight and shouted for joy. But the illustrious Hector was not to be silenced. 'Aias,' he said, 'arrant nonsense is what one expects from a clodhopper; but you surpass yourself. Of one thing I am sure – sure as I am that I should love to spend my days as the son of aegis-bearing Zeus and the Lady Here with the honours of Athene and Apollo – and *that* is that this day will be disastrous for the whole Argive force, and that you will die with the rest of them, if you dare to stand up to my long spear, which is going to tear your lily-white skin. Yes, you shall fall by your own ships, and your flesh and fat shall glut the Trojan dogs and birds of prey.'

With that, Hector led a charge, and his men came after him with a deafening roar, while the whole force behind them took up the cry. The Argives answered with their own war-cry, and summoning up their courage, awaited the onslaught of the Trojans' best. The clamour from the two armies reached the upper air and assaulted the lamp of day.

XIV

ZEUS OUTMANOEUVRED

THE din was so great that it reached the ears of Nestor, who was drinking in his hut. He turned in alarm to the son of Asclepius and said: 'My lord Machaon, we must consider what to do. The sounds of battle are growing louder by the ships. Sit here for the time being and drink your sparkling wine, while the lady Hecamede heats some water and washes the clotted blood from your wound. I will go quickly to some place where I can get a view and discover how things are.'

As he spoke, Nestor picked up a well-made shield of gleaming bronze that was lying in the hut and belonged to his son, Thrasymedes tamer of horses, who was using his father's. He took a strong spear too with a sharp point of bronze, and had no sooner stepped outside his hut than he saw a lamentable sight. His friends were in full rout, with the insolent Trojans close on their heels. The Achaean wall had fallen.

There are times when the great sea is darkened by a soundless swell. It has come to its knowledge that a gale is on its way; but that is all it knows, and the waves cannot begin their march, this way or that, till the wind sets in steadily from one side or the other. Thus the old man faltered between two courses, unable to make up his mind whether to join the horse-loving Danaans in the fight or to seek out Agamemnon son of Atreus, his Commander-in-Chief. In the end he decided that the best thing was to go to Agamemnon. Meanwhile the fighting and slaughter continued, and the hard bronze rang out upon men's bodies as it met the thrust of sword or double-pointed spear.

On his way, Nestor fell in with the royal lords who had been wounded, Diomedes, Odysseus and Agamemnon son of

Atreus. They were coming up from their ships, which were stationed on the shore of the grey sea a long way from the present fighting, being the first row that was drawn up on land, whereas the wall was built along those farthest from the sea. For the beach itself, wide as it was, had proved unable to hold all the ships, and the Achaeans, cramped for room, had drawn them up in tiers, covering the whole seaboard of the long bay from headland to headland. So in order to get a view of the battle, the kings were making their way inland together, using their spears as staves, and in a sorry frame of mind. When they met the old man Nestor, their hearts sank, and King Agamemnon questioned him at once: 'Nestor son of Neleus, flower of Achaean chivalry; why have you turned your back on the carnage that is going on and come down here? I am afraid the redoubtable Hector is going to do to us what he said he would, one day when he was speaking to his men and swore he would never fall back from the ships to Ilium before he had sent them up in flames and slaughtered us as well. That was the promise he made them; and now everything he said is coming true. I have the unhappy feeling that the whole army must be disloyal to me like Achilles, if they refuse to make a stand at the outer line of ships.'

'Some such calamity is certainly upon us,' said Nestor the Gerenian Knight; 'and Zeus the Thunderer himself could not avert it. We thought the wall was an impregnable defence for the fleet and for ourselves. That has now fallen, and our men are committed to a long and desperate fight beside the gallant ships. Look as hard as you will, you cannot tell whether the Achaeans are being chased and harried from the front or from the rear, so confused is the slaughter, so overwhelming the din. We must put our heads together and consider what is best – if thinking can do any good. The one thing I do not suggest is that we should throw ourselves into the battle. No wounded man can fight.'

'Nestor,' said Agamemnon King of Men, 'since the fighting has reached the outer line of ships, and neither the strong wall nor the trench that cost us so much toil has been of any use, though we looked on them as an impregnable defence for the fleet and for ourselves, I must conclude that it is the pleasure of almighty Zeus that the Achaeans should perish here, far from Argos, and be obliterated. I felt this when he was helping the Danaans with all his heart, and I realize it now, when he is exalting the Trojans to the level of the happy gods and has reduced us to impotence. There is nothing for it – you must all do as I say. Let us drag down the ships that were drawn up next to the sea, launch them on the good salt water, and moor them well out, till the friendly night allows us to drag down all the rest – unless the Trojans go on fighting even then. There is nothing to be ashamed of in running from disaster, even by night. It is better to save one's skin by running than to be caught.'

'My lord,' said Odysseus of the nimble wits, scowling at Agamemnon, 'this is preposterous. What fatal leadership! You should have had a set of cowards to command, instead of leading people like ourselves, whose lot it is from youth to age to see wars through to their bitter end, till one by one we drop. So this is how you propose to bid farewell to Troy of the broad streets, for which we have undergone so many hardships! You had better hold your tongue, or the men may get wind of this idea of yours, which nobody with any sense in his head would ever have put into words, least of all a king with a huge army like yours at his command. You can have no brains at all to have made such a suggestion – to expect us, in the middle of a pitched battle, to drag our ships into the sea, and put the Trojans, who have beaten us already, in an even better position to do exactly as they like with us and wipe out the whole expedition. Do you imagine that our men are going to keep a steady front while their ships are being dragged down into the sea? They will do nothing but look behind them, and lose all heart for the fight. That will be the disastrous effect of your tactics, my Commander-in-Chief.'

'A harsh rebuke, Odysseus!' said Agamemnon King of Men. 'But I acknowledge its force. Very well, I will not order the men to drag their ships into the sea against their better judgment. But now one of *you* must come forward with a sounder scheme than mine. Seniority does not matter – I shall be pleased to hear him.'

This emboldened Diomedes of the loud war-cry to speak. 'The man we need,' he said, 'is close at hand. We shall not have far to seek, if you will be persuaded by me and not resent the fact that I am the youngest man among you. After all, I too can boast of noble birth. My father was Tydeus, whose bones lie buried under a mound in Thebes. And he was descended from Portheus, who had three excellent sons, living in Pleuron and rugged Calydon – Agrius, Melas and lastly Oeneus the charioteer, my father's father, who was the bravest of them all. Oeneus did not move from his old home, but Zeus and the other gods must have planned a different life for my father Tydeus, who migrated to Argos, where he married one of Adrestus' daughters and settled down in luxury, with a house, some good cornland, many private orchards and plenty of livestock. And there was no Achaean to compare with him in spearmanship. But you must have heard all this, and know that it is true. So you cannot take exception to any proposal I put forward (if it is a good one) on the grounds that I am a baseborn commoner. What I now suggest is that we visit the battlefield – indeed we must, wounded as we are. When we are there, let us ourselves refrain from fighting and keep out of range, or one of us may get a second wound. But what we *can* do is to press others into the fight, those, I mean, who have had a grievance to nurse and have kept out of it.'

The other chieftains had no fault to find with Diomedes' suggestion and accepted it. Agamemnon King of Men led off, and they all set out.

None of this had escaped the vigilant eye of the great Earthshaker. Disguising himself as an old man, he went after them, and taking hold of King Agamemnon's right hand, spoke to him as one who knew. 'My lord,' he said, 'no doubt Achilles is rejoicing in his evil heart as he sees the Achaeans put to flight and slaughtered, fool that he is, without a grain of sense. Well, let us hope that his folly will destroy him, and that Heaven will cast him down. And you, my lord – you must not think that the happy gods feel nothing but ill will towards you. On the contrary, the day is still coming when the Trojan captains and commanders will fill the wide plain with dust, and you, with your own eyes, will see them fleeing to their city from your ships and huts.'

When Poseidon had spoken, he sped off across the plain with a great shout, as loud as the war-cry of nine thousand or ten thousand warriors joined in battle. Such was the cry that came from the throat of the Royal Earthshaker and greatly heartened every Achaean in the field to withstand the enemy and carry on the fight.

Now Here of the Golden Throne, looking out from where she stood on the summit of Olympus, was quick to observe two things. She saw how Poseidon, who was both her Brother and her Brother-in-law, was bustling about on the field of battle, and she rejoiced. But she also saw Zeus sitting on the topmost peak of Ida of the many springs; and this sight filled the ox-eyed Lady Here with disgust. She began to wonder how she could bemuse the wits of aegis-bearing Zeus; and she decided that the best way to go about the business was this. She would deck herself out to full advantage and visit him on the mountain. If he succumbed to her beauty, as well might be, and wished to fold her in his arms, she would benumb his busy brain and close his eyes in a soothing and forgetful sleep. Accordingly, she made her way to the bedroom that had been built for her by her own Son Hephaestus, who had fitted the stout doors, when he hung them on their posts, with a secret lock which no other god could open. Here went in and closed the polished doors behind her. She began by removing every stain from her comely body with ambrosia, and anointing herself with the delicious and imperishable olive-oil she uses. It was perfumed and had only to be stirred in the Palace of the Bronze Floor for its scent to spread through heaven and earth. With this she rubbed her lovely skin; then she combed her hair, and with her own hands plaited her shining locks and let them fall in their divine beauty from her immortal head. Next she put on a fragrant robe of delicate material that Athene with her skilful hands had made for her and lavishly embroidered. She fastened it over her breast with golden clasps and, at her waist, with a girdle from which a hundred tassels hung. In the pierced lobes of her ears she fixed two earrings, each a thing of lambent beauty with its cluster of three drops. She covered her head with a beautiful new headdress, which was as bright as the sun; and last of all, the Lady goddess bound a fine pair of sandals on her shimmering feet.

Her toilet perfected, she left her room, beckoned Aphrodite away from the other gods and had a word with her in private. 'I wonder, dear child,' she said, 'whether you will do me a favour, or will refuse because you are annoyed with me for helping the Danaans while you are on the Trojans' side.' To this, Aphrodite, Daughter of Zeus, replied: 'Here, Queen of Heaven and Daughter of mighty Cronos; tell me what is in your mind, and I shall gladly do what you ask of me, if I can and if it is not impossible.'

Queen Here's answer was calculated to deceive. 'Give me Love and Desire,' she said, 'the powers by which you yourself subdue mankind and gods alike. I am going to the ends of the fruitful earth to visit Ocean, the forbear of the gods, and Mother Tethys, who treated me kindly and brought me up in their home after taking me from Rhea, when all-seeing Zeus made Cronos a prisoner under the earth and barren sea. I am going to see them and bring their interminable quarrels to an end. They have been estranged for a long time now and in the bitterness of their hearts have ceased to sleep with one another. If by talking the matter over I could bring them round and induce them once more to sleep in each other's loving arms, I should win their affection and esteem for ever.'

'To refuse a request from you that sleep in the arms of the King of Heaven, would be both wrong and impossible,' replied laughter-loving Aphrodite, and took from her bosom the curiously embroidered girdle in which all her magic resides, Love and Desire and the sweet bewitching words that turn a wise man into a fool. 'There,' she said, handing it to Here; 'take this girdle and keep it in your bosom.' And as she pointed out the curious stitches, she added: 'All my power resides in this, and I have no fear that you will come back from your mission unsuccessful.'

The ox-eyed Lady Here smiled, and as she tucked the girdle into her bosom she smiled again. Aphrodite Daughter of Zeus went home, and Here sped down from the summit of Olympus. First she dropped to the Pierian range and to lovely Emathia; then passed swiftly over the snowy mountains of the horse-breeding Thracians, sweeping the highest peaks but never setting foot on the ground. From Athos she travelled over the foaming sea, and so came to Lemnos, the city of King Thoas, where she found the god of Sleep, the brother of Death. She took him by the hand and told him her need. 'Sleep,' she said, 'Master of all the gods and all mankind; if ever you listened to me in the past, do what I ask of you now, and I shall be grateful to you for ever. Seal the bright eyes of Zeus for me in sleep, directly I have lain in his loving arms, and in return I will give you a beautiful chair of imperishable gold, which the lame god Hephaestus, my own Son, will make for you with his cunning hands, with a footstool underneath it, on which you can rest your comely feet as you dine.'

To this, Sweet Sleep replied: 'Here, Queen of Heaven and Daughter of mighty Cronos; I should think it a small matter to put any of the other eternal gods to sleep, even Ocean Stream himself, who is the forbear of them all; but I dare not go near to Zeus the Son of Cronos or send him to sleep unless he asks me to do so himself. I have learnt my lesson from the task you set me once before, when Heracles, that arrogant son of his, set sail from Ilium after sacking the Trojans' town, and you made up your mind to do him a mischief. With my gentle ministrations I lulled aegis-bearing Zeus to sleep, while you raised a tempest on the sea and carried Heracles off to the peopled isle of Cos, away from all his friends. Zeus was enraged when he awoke. He hurled the gods about in his palace and looked for me everywhere as the chief offender. I

should have been cast from heaven into the sea and never
heard of again, if Night, who dictates to gods and men alike,
had not rescued me. I found sanctuary with her, and Zeus, for
all his fury, had to stop and think twice before doing some-
thing that the swift Night would take amiss. And now you
come to me once more with another impossible request!'

'Sleep,' said the ox-eyed Lady Here, 'why do you harp on
the danger of the task? Can you suppose that all-seeing Zeus
will exert himself as much in the matter of help for the
Trojans as he did when it was the abduction of his own son
Heracles that had enraged him? Come, do as I wish, and I
will give you one of the young Graces in marriage. She shall
be called the wife of Sleep.'

'Very well,' said Sleep, who was attracted by her offer.
'Swear to me now by the inviolable waters of Styx, grasping
the bountiful earth with one hand and the shimmering sea
with the other, so that all the gods that are below with
Cronos may be our witnesses; and promise that you will give
me one of the young Graces, Pasitheë, whom I have been in
love with all my life.'

The white-armed goddess Here agreed and gave him her
oath in the way he had prescribed, naming all the gods under
Tartarus, who are called Titans. When she had duly sworn, the
two wrapped themselves in mist and set out, leaving the cities
of Lemnos and Imbros behind them, and travelling fast. They
reached Ida of the many springs, the mother of wild beasts,
by way of Lecton, where they left the sea and passed over the
dry land, causing the tree-tops to sway beneath their feet.
But now, to avoid the eye of Zeus, Sleep came to a halt and
climbed up into a tall pine-tree, the tallest on Ida, which had
pierced the lower air and shot up into the sky. There he
perched, hidden by the branches, in the form of a songbird
of the mountains which is called bronze-throat by the gods
and nightjar by men.

Meanwhile Here rapidly drew near to Gargarus, the highest
crest of lofty Ida. Zeus the Cloud-compeller saw her, and at
the first look his heart was captured by desire, as in the days

when they had first enjoyed each other's love and gone to
bed together without their parents' knowledge. He rose to
meet her and said: 'Here, what business brings you here from
Olympus? And why no horses and no chariot to drive in?'

The Lady Here gave him a crooked answer. 'I am on my
way,' she said, 'to the ends of the fruitful earth, to visit Ocean,
the forbear of the gods, and Mother Tethys, who treated me
kindly and brought me up in their home. I am going to see
them and bring their interminable quarrels to an end. They
have been estranged for a long time now and in the bitter-
ness of their hearts have ceased to sleep with one another. My
horses are waiting at the foot of Ida of the many springs, ready
to carry me over the water and the solid land. But at the
moment I have come here from Olympus to see *you*, fearing
that you might be angry with me afterwards if I paid a visit to
the deep stream of Ocean without letting you know.'

'Here,' said the Cloud-gatherer Zeus, 'that is a journey you
may well postpone. To-day, let us enjoy the delights of love.
Never has such desire, for goddess or woman, flooded and
overwhelmed my heart; not even when I loved Ixion's wife,
who bore Peirithous to rival the gods in wisdom; or Danaë of
the slim ankles, the daughter of Acrisius, who gave birth to
Perseus, the greatest hero of his time; or the far-famed
daughter of Phoenix, who bore me Minos and the godlike
Rhadamanthus; or Semele, or Alcmene in Thebes, whose son
was the lion-hearted Heracles, while Semele bore Dionysus to
give pleasure to mankind; or Demeter Queen of the Lovely
Locks, or the incomparable Leto; or when I fell in love with
you yourself – never have I felt such love, such sweet desire,
as fills me now for you.'

'Dread Son of Cronos, you amaze me,' said the Lady Here,
still dissembling. 'Suppose we do as you wish and lie down in
each other's arms on the heights of Ida where there is no
privacy whatever, what will happen if one of the eternal gods
sees us asleep together and runs off to tell the rest? I certainly
do not relish the idea of rising from such a bed and going
back to your palace. Think of the scandal there would be.

No, if it is really your pleasure to do this thing, you have a bedroom that your own Son Hephaestus built for you, and the doors he made for it are solid. Let us go and lie down there, if that is what you wish to do.'

'Here,' said Zeus the Cloud-compeller, 'you need not be afraid that any god or man will see us. I shall hide you in a golden cloud too thick for that. Even the Sun, whose rays provide him with the keenest sight in all the world, will not see us through the mist.'

As he spoke, the Son of Cronos took his Wife in his arms; and the gracious earth sent up fresh grass beneath them, dewy lotus and crocuses, and a soft and crowded bed of hyacinths, to lift them off the ground. In this they lay, covered by a beautiful golden cloud, from which a rain of glistening dew-drops fell.

While the Father lay peacefully on top of Gargarus with his arms round his Wife, conquered by sleep and love, the gentle god of Sleep flew off to the Achaean ships to tell the Earthshaker the news. He went up to the Girdler of the World and unburdened himself of his secret. 'Poseidon,' he said, 'you may help the Danaans now with all your heart and give them the upper hand, if only for a short time, till Zeus wakes up. I sent him into a deep and gentle sleep after Here had tricked him into lying in her arms.'

Sleep then went off to ply his business with the famous nations of mankind, leaving Poseidon more zealous than ever in his championship of the Danaans. He sprang out beyond the front rank to give them his commands. 'Argives,' he cried, 'are we going once more to leave the victory to Hector son of Priam, to let him take the fleet and reap the glory? He says he will; but his only pretext for such boastful talk is the fact that Achilles sits in dudgeon by his hollow ships. Yet Achilles won't be missed so very much, if the rest of us can only rouse ourselves to stand by one another. Listen, all of you, to my plan and carry it out. We must equip ourselves with the best and biggest shields in the camp, put dazzling helmets on our heads, and go into the fight with the longest spears we can lay our hands on. I myself will take command, and I do not think Prince Hector will stand up to us long, for all his fury. Let every soldier who has proved his worth in battle, but carries a small buckler, hand it over to a weaker man and equip himself with a larger shield.'

They gladly took Poseidon at his word. Wounded as they were, the kings themselves, Tydeides, Odysseus and Agamemnon son of Atreus, prepared their men for the struggle, visiting the ranks and interchanging their arms, so that the best soldiers were now the best equipped, parting with their inferior weapons to inferior troops. When all had donned their gleaming bronze, they set out, with the Earthshaker Poseidon at their head, carrying his long and formidable sword in his great hand. This sword is like a lightning flash. It is sacrilege to touch it in battle, and men shrink from it in terror.

On the other side illustrious Hector brought the Trojans into battle order. And now the most appalling fight of all was staged by Poseidon of the Sable Locks and glorious Hector, one battling for the Argives, the other leading the Trojans on. As they met, with a deafening clamour, the sea washed up to the Argives' huts and ships. But neither the thunder of breakers on the beach, driven in from the deep by a northerly gale; nor the roar of the flames when fire attacks the forest in a mountain ravine; nor the wind's moan in the high foliage of the oaks when it rises to a scream in its wrath, is so loud as the terrible war-cry that the Trojans and Achaeans raised as they fell upon each other.

Illustrious Hector began by hurling a spear at Aias as he faced him full. He did not miss, but he hit Aias where the two baldrics, one for his shield and one for his silver-studded sword, were stretched across his breast, and they saved his tender flesh. Hector was angry at having made a powerful spear-cast to no purpose, and sought cover once more with his men in fear for his own life. As he withdrew, the great Telamonian Aias picked up one of the many boulders that had been used to prop the ships and had rolled among the feet of the combatants, and with this struck Hector on the chest just below the neck, over the rim of his shield, making him spin and travel round like a top. Thus Hector in his gallantry was brought down in the dust by as sudden a stroke as that of Father Zeus when he uproots an oak, unnerving all who happen to be near, by the violence of his bolt and the appalling reek of sulphur it gives off. Hector's second spear fell from his hand; he crumpled up under his shield and helmet, and the bronze trappings of his armour rang upon him.

The Achaean men-at-arms rushed towards him with triumphant cries, hoping to drag him off, and discharging a volley of javelins. But no one had a chance, with either spear or dart, of touching the Commander-in-Chief: he was surrounded too quickly by his gallant lieutenants, Polydamas, Aeneas and the noble Agenor, Sarpedon the King of the Lycians, and the admirable Glaucus. And of the rest there was not one that neglected his commander. They all held their rounded shields in front of him. Then, putting their arms underneath him, his comrades lifted him up and carried him out of the fray to his fast horses, who had waited for him in a quiet spot behind the fighting with their driver and his painted chariot, and who now bore him off, groaning heavily, towards the town. But when they reached the ford of eddying Xanthus, the noble River whose Father is immortal Zeus, Hector's men lifted him from the chariot, laid him on the ground and poured water over him. Hector came to and opened his eyes. He sat up on his heels and vomited dark blood. Then he sank back once more on the ground and the world went black as night before his eyes. He had not yet recovered from the blow.

When the Argives saw Hector withdraw, they fell on the Trojans with a better will and recaptured their zest. The first of them to draw blood was Aias son of Oïleus, the famous spearman and runner. He charged with his sharp-pointed spear and struck Satnius, whom a flawless Nymph had borne to his father, Enops, when he was tending his herds on the banks of Satnioïs. Aias leapt in and wounded him in the flank. Satnius collapsed; and a fierce tussle ensued around him. The spearman Polydamas son of Panthous, coming to the rescue, struck Prothoenor son of Areilycus on the right shoulder. The heavy spear pursued its course through his shoulder, and he fell in the dust and clawed the earth. Polydamas uttered a great yell of triumph over him. 'That,' he cried, 'was another spear from the strong arm of Panthous' proud son that did not go astray, but found its home in an Argive's flesh. He can use it as a staff as he goes down to Hades' Hall.'

The Argives heard his jubilation with disgust, and none resented it more than the other Aias, the doughty son of Telamon, who had been nearest to the spot where Prothoenor fell. He made a swift cast with a glittering spear at Polydamas as he withdrew. Polydamas himself avoided certain death by leaping to one side. It was Antenor's son, Archelochus, who received the spear. The gods meant him to die, and he was struck where the head meets the neck, on the last segment of the spine. Both the sinews were severed, and as he fell, his forehead, mouth and nose hit the ground before his shins and knees. It was Aias' turn to raise a shout. He called across to the peerless Polydamas: 'Think it over, Polydamas, and tell me frankly whether this man's death does not make up for Prothoenor's. To judge by his looks, he was certainly no craven, nor basely born – more like a brother or maybe a son of my lord Antenor's. The family likeness is striking.'

Aias, when he said this, knew well enough whom he had killed; and the hearts of the Trojans sank. But Acamas bestrode Archelochus, who was his brother; and when a Boeotian called Promachus tried to drag off the body from between his legs, he brought him down with his spear. Then in insolent triumph over his victim he shouted aloud: 'You Argives, who are so brave with your bows and free with your threats; don't think that troubles and disasters are reserved for us alone. We have had our losses: yours are coming. Look at your man Promachus, put to sleep by my spear, in prompt repayment for my brother's death. That is what a wise man prays for – a kinsman to survive him and avenge his fall.'

The Argives were revolted by this boastful talk. The

doughty Peneleos, in particular, was stung by it into action. He made for Acamas, but Acamas did not stand up to his attack, and it was Ilioneus who fell to King Peneleos. He was a son of the sheep-owner Phorbas, a favourite in Troy of the god Hermes, who had made him a rich man. But Ilioneus' mother had given Phorbas no other child, and now this only son of hers was struck by Peneleos under the eyebrow in the socket of the eye. The spear dislodged his eyeball, pierced the socket and came out at the nape of his neck. He sank down and stretched out both his hands. But Peneleos, drawing his sharp sword, hit him full on the neck and brought head and helmet tumbling to the ground. The heavy spear was still stuck in the eye as Peneleos raised it aloft, like a poppy-head, for the Trojans to see, and exulted over his enemy. 'Trojans,' he cried, 'be so good as to instruct the father and mother of my lord Ilioneus to start lamenting him at home. That is only fair; for the wife of Promachus son of Alegenor will never have the happiness of seeing *him* again, when we Achaeans sail from Troy.' This made the knees of all the Trojans quake, and each man peered around to find some sanctuary from sudden death.

Tell me now, you Muses that live on Olympus, who was the first of the Achaeans to take a bloodstained set of armour from the foe, now that the glorious Earthshaker had swayed the battle in their favour? It was Telamonian Aias, who began by striking Hyrtius son of Gyrtias, a leader of the lion-hearted Mysians. Next, Antilochus killed Phalces and Mermerus; Meriones slew Morys and Hippotion; and Teucer slew Prothoon and Periphetes. Then Atreides smote the great captain Hyperenor in the flank. Tearing its way in, the bronze let out his entrails; his soul incontinently fled through the gaping wound; and darkness came down on his eyes. But it was to Aias, fleet son of Oïleus, that the greatest number fell; for when a panic had set in, there was nobody like Aias for chasing the routed enemy on foot.

XV

THE ACHAEANS AT BAY

THE fleeing Trojans recrossed the palisade and trench, suffering severely at the hands of the Achaeans, and did not stop till they had reached their chariots. As they paused there, shattered and pale with terror, Zeus, who was still lying on the heights of Ida beside Here of the Golden Throne, awoke and leaping to his feet took stock of the battle. And this is what he saw: the Trojans thrown back and the Danaans in hot pursuit; the Lord Poseidon helping in the chase; and Hector lying on the ground with his comrades sitting round him.

Hector was breathing with difficulty and spitting blood. He was not yet fully conscious; and small wonder, for the man who had hit him was by no means the feeblest in the Achaean ranks. The Father of men and gods was filled with compassion at the sight of him. He turned on Here with a black look and his voice was terrible as he called her to account. 'Here,' he said, 'you are incorrigible: I am sure this is your doing. It is through your wicked wiles that Prince Hector has been stopped from fighting and his people have been routed. I have half a mind to strike you with my bolt and let you be the first to reap the fruits of your unconscionable tricks. Have you forgotten the time when I strung you aloft with a couple of anvils hanging from your feet and your hands lashed together with a golden chain you could not break? There you dangled, up in the air and in among the clouds; and the gods on high Olympus, though they rallied round you in their indignation, found it impossible to set you free. For I seized anyone I caught in the attempt; I hurled him from my threshold, and when he reached the ground he was too weak to stir. But even that did not relieve the heartache I still felt for the godlike Heracles, whom you, after suborning the Winds to abet you

in your evil schemes, had sent scudding over the barren sea
before a northerly gale. You swept him off in the end to the
peopled Isle of Cos; but I rescued him from Cos and brought
him back to Argos where the horses graze, safe after all he
had been through. I am reminding you of this to put a stop
to your intrigues and teach you how little you can rely on the
loving embraces you enjoyed when you came here from
Olympus and cajoled me into your arms.'

The ox-eyed Lady Here shuddered as she listened to this,
and hastened to reassure him: 'Now let my witnesses be
Earth, and the wide Heavens above, and the falling waters of
Styx (the greatest and most solemn oath the blessed gods can
take), and your sacred head, and our own bridal couch, by
which I would never dare to forswear myself – that it is due
to no prompting of mine that Poseidon the Earthshaker is
doing Hector and the Trojans harm, and helping the other
side. I can only suppose that he was sorry for the Achaeans
when he saw them hard-pressed beside the ships, and acted of
his own free will. Indeed, I am quite ready to remonstrate
with him and pack him off. You have only to say where he
shall go, Lord of the Black Cloud.'

This drew a smile from the Father of men and gods, and he
replied more mildly: 'Here, my ox-eyed Queen, if from now
on I could count on you to support me in the Council of the
gods, Poseidon would soon come round and see eye to eye
with you and me, however much he might be otherwise in-
clined. However, if you have been honest and told me the
truth, go back now to the gods and order Iris and Apollo the
Archer to come here. I wish Iris to visit the bronze-clad
Achaeans and tell my Lord Poseidon to stop fighting and go
home; and Phoebus Apollo to bring Hector back into the
battle after putting fresh heart in him and making him forget
the pain that is unnerving him. Phoebus must then strike
panic into the Achaeans and make them take to their heels.
They will fall back on the well-found ships of Achilles son of
Peleus, who will send his friend Patroclus into the fight.
Patroclus, after killing a number of his stalwart enemies in-

cluding my own noble son Sarpedon, will fall to the spear of the illustrious Hector in front of Ilium; and Prince Achilles, infuriated at his death, will kill Hector himself. From that moment I shall cause the tide of battle to ebb from the ships and steadily recede, till the day when the Achaeans capture the high fortress of Ilium through the machinations of Athene. But in the meantime I remain hostile to the Danaans, and I will not permit any other of the immortals to come down to their assistance before the wishes of Achilles are fulfilled, in accordance with the promise I gave him (and confirmed with a nod of my head) that day when the divine Thetis put her arms round my knees and implored me to vindicate her son, the sacker of cities.'

Zeus had spoken, and the white-armed goddess Here did not disobey, but set out from Mount Ida for high Olympus, flying in her haste with the speed of thought, just as a man who has travelled widely and has fond memories of many places has only to retire within himself and say, 'I wish I were in that spot or in that', and he is there.

On reaching the peak of Olympus, the Lady Here presented herself to the immortal gods, who were assembled in the Palace of Zeus. When they saw her they all leapt to their feet and pledged her with their cups. Ignoring the rest, Here accepted a cup from Themis of the Lovely Cheeks, who was the first to come running up to her, with questions pouring from her lips. 'Here!' she said. 'What brings you here looking like one distraught? The Son of Cronos seems to have scared you thoroughly, though he *is* your Husband.' 'Lady Themis, no questions about that, I pray,' replied the white-armed goddess Here. 'You know yourself how harsh and unbending he is liable to be. But if you will give the other gods a lead by taking your place at table in the hall, you and the rest shall hear all about the mischief Zeus is contemplating. And in case there are any who still think all is well with the world as they sit down to their dinner, I can assure them that the news will not please everybody on Olympus or on earth.'

With this, the Queen of Heaven took her seat, and up and

down the hall of Zeus the gods were filled with consternation, for though there was a smile on Here's lips, her forehead and her dark brows belied it. Indeed, it was an angry goddess that addressed the company. 'What fools we were!' she exclaimed. 'What lunatics, to quarrel with Zeus! Yet here we are, still itching to get at him and to stop him, if not by talking, then by force; and all the while he sits there by himself, quite un-perturbed, snapping his fingers at us. And well he may, since he knows that for brute strength he is beyond question first among the gods – an excellent excuse for all of you to take whatever troubles he may send you lying down! And that reminds me. Ares, if I am not mistaken, has already had his punishment dealt out to him. A son and favourite of his, Ascalaphus, has fallen in action. My lord the god of War does claim to be his Father, does he not?'

Ares flew into a passion when he heard this news, and slap-ped his sturdy thighs with the flat of his hands. 'Gods of Olympus,' he cried, 'you cannot blame me now if I go down to the Achaean ships and avenge the slaughter of my son, even though it be my fate to be struck down by Zeus's bolt and lie among the corpses in the blood and dust.' And he called to Terror and Panic to harness his horses, while he himself put on his glittering arms.

And now another quarrel, even bitterer and more disastrous than the last, would have broken out between Zeus and the immortals, if Athene in her terror for the whole community had not leapt from her chair and dashed out after Ares through the porch. She snatched the helmet from his head, the shield from his shoulder, and the bronze spear from his sturdy hand; then, as she put the spear away, she gave the impetuous War-god a piece of her mind. 'Blockhead! Maniac!' she cried. 'You will be wiped out. Have you no ears to hear with? Have you no sense and no restraint? Did you not hear what we were told by the white-armed goddess Here, who has come straight from Olympian Zeus? Or do you wish to get a thrashing for yourself and to be chased back to Olympus with your tail between your legs, while the rest of us reap the whirlwind you have sown? For I tell you, Zeus will leave the gallant Trojans and Achaeans without a moment's pause and come straight here to overwhelm us in Olympus, seizing us each in turn, innocent and guilty alike. Take my advice then, and set aside all thoughts of avenging your son. Many a finer and stronger man than he has been killed before now and will be killed hereafter. We can hardly be expected to keep our eyes on the pedigree of every man on earth.'

With this, Athene led the impetuous War-god back to his chair. Here then asked Apollo, and Iris who served the immortal gods as go-between, to accompany her out of doors, and there she faithfully delivered her message. 'Zeus,' she said to them, 'requires you two to go with all speed to Ida. When you have reached the place and appeared before him, you will carry out whatever orders he may give you.'

The Lady Here then went in again and sat down on her throne, while the pair flew off on their errand. When they reached Mount Ida of the many springs, the mother of sheep, they found the all-seeing Son of Cronos sitting on the summit of Gargarus, enveloped in a perfumed mist. They presented themselves to Zeus the Cloud-compeller and awaited his pleasure. Zeus noted their arrival, and having no fault to find with their despatch in carrying out his Consort's orders, began by giving Iris her instructions. 'Off with you, Iris, fast as you can,' he said. 'Convey my words in full to my Lord Poseidon, and see that you make no mistakes. Tell him to stop fighting, to retire from the field, and to rejoin the other gods' or withdraw into his own sacred sea. If he chooses to ignore my explicit commands, let him take counsel with himself and consider whether, powerful as he is, he would dare to stand up to an attack from me, who claim to be by far the stronger god and his senior by birth. Not that he hesitates on that account to behave as the equal of Zeus, of whom the other gods all stand in dread.'

Wind-swift Iris of the Fleet Foot obeyed these orders promptly and set out from Mount Ida for sacred Ilium, dropping in her eager haste like the snow or chilling hail that falls from the clouds when a squall comes down from the bitter North. She went straight up to the great Earthshaker and said: 'Girdler of the World, god of the Sable Locks, I have come here with a message for you from aegis-bearing Zeus. He commands you to stop fighting, to retire from the field, and to rejoin the other gods or withdraw into your own sacred sea. If you disregard his explicit commands, he threatens that he too will come here in person to take the field against you. And he warns you not to come to grips with him, maintaining that he is by far the stronger god as well as your senior by birth. Not that that appears to deter you (he says) from claiming equality with him, of whom the other gods all stand in dread.'

The great Earthshaker was infuriated. 'This is outrageous!' he cried. 'Zeus may be powerful, but it is sheer bluster on his part to talk of forcing me, who enjoy the same prestige as he does, to bend my will to his. There are three of us Brothers, all Sons of Cronos and Rhea: Zeus, myself, and Hades the King of the Dead. Each of us was given his own domain when the world was divided into three parts. We cast lots, and I received the grey sea as my inalienable realm. Hades drew the nether dark, while Zeus was allotted the broad sky and a home among the clouds in the upper air. But the earth was left common to all of us, and high Olympus too. So I am not going to let Zeus have his way with me. Powerful as he is, let him stay quietly in his own third of the world. And do not let him try to scare me with threats of violence, as though I were an arrant coward. He would do better to give his own Sons and Daughters a piece of his mind. He is their Father, and they will have to listen when he orders them about.'

'Girdler of the World, god of the Sable Locks,' said windswift Iris of the Fleet Foot, 'do you really wish me to convey to Zeus this contumacious and peremptory reply? Will you not change your mind? It is a mark of excellence to relent. And you know how the Avenging Furies always support an elder brother.'

'Lady Iris,' said Poseidon the Earthshaker, 'you are right in what you say. How excellent it also is for an ambassador to show discretion! But it galls me, it cuts me to the quick, to be bullied and scolded by a god with whom Fate has decreed that I should share the world on equal terms. However, I will give in now, though not without resentment. But let me add a word of warning about my own feelings. If Zeus, against my wishes and those of the Warrior Athene, of Here, of Hermes and of my Lord Hephaestus, spares the citadel of Ilium and will not have it sacked, giving the Argives a resounding victory, let him know that there will be an irreparable breach between us two.'

With that the Earthshaker left the Achaean army, much to the regret of those gallant men, and withdrew into the sea.

Zeus the Cloud-gatherer instructed Apollo next. 'I wish you now, dear Phoebus, to seek out Hector of the bronze arms. The Earthshaker and Girdler of the World has by now retired into the sacred sea to avoid the severity of my displeasure. Indeed, if we had come to blows, everyone would have heard of it, even the gods who live with Cronos in the world below. But it was a far better thing for both of us that, angry as he was, he should have yielded to me without feeling my strength – there would certainly have been much sweat before we reached a settlement. Now take my tasselled aegis in your hands and strike panic into the Achaean chieftains by shaking it fiercely. And make illustrious Hector your special concern, my Archer Lord. Fill him with desperate courage until such time as the Achaeans shall reach the ships and Hellespont in rout. At that point I myself will decide what must be said and done to give them respite from their punishment.'

Zeus had spoken, and Apollo turned no deaf ear to his Father's words, but swooped down from the mountains of Ida with the speed of a dove-destroying hawk, which is the fastest thing on wings. Prince Hector, son of the wise Priam, was no longer prostrate when he found him, but was sitting up. He had just regained consciousness and could recognize the friends about him, having ceased to pant and sweat from the moment when aegis-bearing Zeus had willed his recovery.

The Archer Apollo came up to him and said: 'Prince Hector, why are you sitting here, away from your troops and in such a sorry state? Have you been hurt?'

'What god are you, my lord, and why do you come to me for news?' said Hector of the bright helmet in a feeble voice. 'Do you not know that Aias of the loud war-cry, as I was killing his men by the outer line of ships, struck me on the breast with a piece of rock? There was no fight left in me. Indeed I thought that this very day I was going to breathe my last and go down among the dead in Hades' Halls.'

'Courage!' said the Archer-King Apollo. 'Trust the confederate whom the Son of Cronos sends you from Ida to take his place beside you and protect you – myself, Phoebus Apollo of the Golden Sword, who in days gone by have saved not only you but your high citadel as well. Up, now! Command your many charioteers to drive at the gallop right up to the hollow ships, and I will go ahead of them making the whole way smooth for their horses' feet and putting the Achaean lords to flight.'

Apollo, as he spoke, breathed power into the Trojan commander, who now ran off on nimble feet with lightened limbs. He was like a stallion who breaks his halter at the manger where they keep and fatten him, and gallops off across the fields in triumph to his usual bathing-place in the delightful river. He tosses up his head; his mane flies back along his shoulders; he knows how beautiful he is; and away he goes, skimming the ground with his feet, to the haunts and pastures of the mares. Thus Hector sped away, when he had heard the god speak, to lead his charioteers to battle.

Up to this moment the Danaans had been advancing steadily in mass formation, using their swords and double-pointed spears to good effect. But now they behaved like a set of rustics with a pack of hounds who have been hunting an antlered stag or wild goat unsuccessfully and have lost him in a dark wood or some rocky fastness, when suddenly a bearded lion, roused by their cries, makes his appearance in their path and sends the whole party scuttling back, with no more stomach for the chase. Thus the Danaans, when they saw Hector once more marshalling his men, were filled with consternation, and their hearts sank into their heels.

At this juncture it was left to Thoas, Andraemon's son, to give a lead to the Danaans. He was by far the finest of the Aetolians, skilled with the javelin, and a good man too in a hand-to-hand fight. Moreover, there were few Achaeans who could defeat him when the younger orators were vying in debate. Now, he came forward and did his best for his friends. 'A miracle!' he cried. 'And a most unwelcome one for us! Hector has risen from the dead. Just when we were all thinking that Telamonian Aias had disposed of him, some god has taken him in hand and brought him back to life, as though he had not killed enough of us already. And there is more of that to come. Hector would not be back in the front line threatening us like this, if Zeus the Thunderer had not put him there. Well now, this is what I think we should do, and I hope you will agree. Let the main body retire on the ships, while we that claim to be the best men in the force make a stand, with our spears at the ready, in the hope of holding Hector's first attack. He will certainly do his best to press it home, but I have an idea that he will think twice before he meddles with the main body.'

These tactics were at once adopted. They gathered in their best men to face Hector and his Trojans, massing them on Aias and King Idomeneus, Teucer, Meriones and that compeer of the War-god, Meges. Behind them, the main force retired on the Achaean ships.

The Trojans came on in close formation with Hector striding in their van. And in front even of him, with a mist round his shoulders, went Phoebus Apollo, holding the invincible aegis, grimly resplendent with its tasselled fringe, the very aegis that the Master-smith Hephaestus had given to Zeus to strike panic into men. With this in his hand, Apollo led the Trojan host.

But the Argives kept together and awaited them. A deafening roar went up from either side; and now the arrows leapt from the string, and launched by brawny arms many a spear found its home in a young warrior's body, and many another without tasting the white flesh fell short and stuck in the earth, balked of the feast it craved.

As long as Phoebus Apollo kept the aegis steady in his hands, volley and counter-volley found their mark, and men kept falling. But the moment came when, looking the horse-loving Danaans full in the face, he shook it at them and gave a great shout. Then their hearts were turned to water and their courage ebbed away. Like a herd of cows or some great flock of sheep suddenly attacked at dusk, when the herdsman is not there, and stampeded by a couple of wild beasts, the Achaeans quailed and fled. It was Apollo himself who turned them into cowards and gave Hector and his Trojans victory.

Having broken their ranks, the Trojans began to pick off the Achaeans singly. Hector killed Arcesilaus and Stichius, one a leader of the bronze-clad Boeotians, and the other a loyal follower of the great-hearted Menestheus. Meanwhile Aeneas slew Medon and Iasus. Medon was an illegitimate son of King Oïleus and so a brother of Aias; but he had been exiled for homicide and lived in Phylace, having killed a kinsman of his step-mother Eriopis, Oïleus' wife. Iasus was one of the Athenian officers, and his father was Sphelus son of Bucolus. Polydamas killed Mecisteus; Echius fell to Polites in the first clash; and the noble Agenor slew Clonius. Deiochus, as he joined the other leaders in their flight, was struck from behind at the base of the shoulder by Paris, whose bronze passed clean through him.

While the victors were stripping the dead men of their arms, the Achaeans, flung back on the trench and palisade and thrown by these into complete disorder, had perforce to take refuge behind the wall. Seeing this, Hector called to the Trojans in a loud voice to leave the bloodstained arms and press on to the ships. 'Any straggler that I see,' he added, 'anyone who does not follow me there, I will put to death on the spot. What is more, he shall get no funeral from his kinsmen and his womenfolk. The dogs shall rend him outside Troy.'

With that, swinging his arm right back, he whipped his horses and sent a great cry down the Trojan ranks. His charioteers gave an answering shout, and all drove off with a mighty roar, horses and chariots in line with his. In their van Phoebus Apollo, with the ease of a god, kicked down the banks of the deep trench and piled them in the middle, making a broad and ample causeway, wide as the space that a man covers with a spear-cast when he is testing his strength. Here they poured across, squadron by squadron, led by Apollo with his glorious aegis. Then, with equal ease, the god knocked down the Achaean wall, like a boy at the seaside playing childish games with the sand, building a castle to amuse himself and then with his hands and feet destroying the whole work for fun. That is how you, Lord Apollo, spoilt the Argives' work and started a panic in the men who had toiled at it so painfully.

The Achaeans once more reached the ships and came to a halt beside them. There they called to each other and every man lifted his hands up and poured out prayers to all the gods – none more fervently than Gerenian Nestor, the Warden of the race, who stretched out his arms to the sky that holds the stars and cried: 'Father Zeus, if ever any of us, over in the wheatlands of Argos, burnt you the fat thigh of an ox or sheep as he prayed for a safe return, and you promised it to him with a nod of your head, remember now, Olympian; save him from this fatal day; and do not let the Trojans overwhelm us so completely.' Thus Nestor prayed, and Zeus the Thinker thundered loudly when he heard the prayer of the aged son of Neleus.

But when the Trojans heard the thunderclap from aegis-bearing Zeus, their zest was renewed and they fell on the Argives more fiercely than ever. With a roar they swept across the wall, like a billow on the high seas rolling before the wind, the great wave-maker, and tumbling over the bulwarks of a ship. They drove their horses in as well; and in a moment they were fighting hand to hand at the ships, the Trojans from their chariots with double-pointed spears, and the Achaeans from high up on the black sterns where they had climbed, with the great poles built up of many lengths and tipped with bronze which they kept on board for fights at sea.

Now Patroclus, so long as the Achaeans and Trojans were disputing the wall and were some way from the ships, sat with the amiable Eurypylus in his hut, and while entertaining him with his talk, applied ointment to his severe wound to deaden the sharpness of the pain. But when he saw the Trojans swarming across the wall and heard the Danaans yelling as they fled, he gave a groan and slapped his thighs with the flat of his hands. 'Eurypylus,' he cried in distress, 'I cannot stay here with you any longer, however much you need me. The crisis is upon us. Your squire must see to your comfort while I hurry back to Achilles and do my best to make him fight. Who knows? A friend's opinion can do good, and with a little luck I may yet coax him into action.' Before he had finished speaking, his feet were on the move.

Meanwhile the Achaeans resolutely blocked the way for the oncoming Trojans, but though they outnumbered them they had not the strength to fling them back from the ships. Nor for their part were the Trojans ever able to break the Danaan lines and penetrate among the ships and huts. The fight was balanced to a nicety and the front swayed no more than the line that is stretched along a ship's timber to test its truth by a skilful carpenter who has mastered his trade in the school of Athene.

While parties of his men attacked at other ships, Hector made straight for the illustrious Aias, and a tussle ensued between them for a single ship. Hector strove in vain to drive Aias off the ship and set it on fire, but Aias was equally unable to get rid of Hector once the god had brought him to the spot. However, illustrious Aias did succeed in killing Caletor son of Clytius. He struck him in the breast with a spear as he was carrying fire to the ship. Caletor fell with a thud and the brand dropped from his grip. Hector, seeing his cousin fall in the dust in front of the black ship, called to the Trojans and

Lycians in a loud voice: 'Trojans and Lycians and you Dardanians that enjoy close fighting, don't yield an inch in this tight corner we are in. Rescue Caletor, or the Achaeans will have his armour off him as he lies among the ships.'

With that, he flung a shining lance at Aias, but missing him, struck Lycophron son of Mastor, a Cytherian squire of Aias, who had come to live with him after killing a man in sacred Cythera. He was standing by Aias when Hector's sharp bronze struck him on the head above the ear. He tumbled backwards from the ship's stern to the ground, and gave up his life in the dust. Aias shuddered and called to his brother: 'We have lost a faithful friend, my dear Teucer – Lycophron son of Mastor, who came from Cythera to live with us, and whom we thought as much of as we did of our own parents. The great Hector has just killed him. Where are your deadly arrows and the bow you had from Phoebus Apollo?'

Teucer understood him, and hastening to his side with his incurved bow and a full quiver, began at once to shoot arrows at the Trojans. The first man he struck was Cleitus, the noble son of Peisenor and squire to the proud Polydamas son of Panthous. Teucer caught him with the reins in his hands. He was in trouble with his horses, having driven into the thick of the infantry, who were themselves in some disorder, with the idea of doing Hector and the Trojans a good turn. His punishment was swift, and one from which no zealous friend could save him, for the arrow with its load of grief struck him in the back of the neck and brought him crashing down from his chariot. His horses shied and ran away with the empty car rattling behind them, till their master, Polydamas, who had been the first to notice the affair and make a move, planted himself in their path. He handed them over to Astynous son of Protiaon, and was careful to impress it on the man that he must watch his movements and keep them close at hand. Then he went back to his place in the front line.

Teucer aimed his next arrow at Hector in his arms of bronze. He would have put an end to the battle by the Achaean ships, had he struck and killed Hector in the hour of his glory. But

Zeus, who is too wary to be caught, was looking after Hector and had kept an eye on Telamonian Teucer. He robbed him of his triumph by breaking the twisted cord of his strong bow as he was taking aim at his man. The arrow with its load of bronze went wandering off, and the bow fell from his hand. Teucer shuddered and turned to his brother with an oath. 'Some evil Power,' he exclaimed, 'is spoiling everything we try to-day! He has knocked the bow out of my hand and broken a fresh string that I bound on this morning to carry the many arrows that I meant to shoot.'

'Well, my friend,' said the great Telamonian Aias, 'you might as well put down your bow and all those arrows, now that some god who is annoyed with us has made them of no use. Lay your hand on a long spear instead, sling a shield on your shoulder, and so meet the enemy and give a lead to our men. The Trojans may have beaten us, but we can at least show them once more how we can fight, and make them pay dearly for the well-found ships.'

When Teucer heard this he laid his bow down in his hut, slung a shield of fourfold leather on his shoulder, and put a stout helmet on his sturdy head. It had a horsehair crest and the plume nodded grimly from on top. Then, picking up a powerful spear with a sharp point of bronze, he set out at a run and in a moment was at Aias' side.

Hector, when he saw that something was amiss with Teucer's archery, cried out to his Trojan and Lycian troops: 'Trojans and Lycians, and you Dardanians that like fighting hand to hand; be men, my friends, and show your prowess here by the hollow ships. I saw with my own eyes how one of their best men was stopped by Zeus from shooting any more. There is no mistaking help from Zeus. He makes it plain, both to the side for whom he is planning victory and to those whom he is leaving in the lurch. See how he is breaking down the Argives' resistance and supporting us. Stick together, then, and attack at the ships. If any of you meets his fate and stops an arrow or a spear, well, let him die. He will have fallen for his country, and that is no dishonourable death. He will leave his wife and children safe, and his house and bit of land secure for ever, once these Achaeans have sailed home.'

Thus Hector encouraged his men and put fresh heart in each, while Aias on his side did the same. He called out to his followers: 'Argives, remember your duty! To-day we have no choice but to perish here or save the ships and live. Or do you think you will all get home on foot if Hector of the shining helmet takes the ships? He is itching to set them on fire – cannot you hear him driving his whole army on? And believe me, he is not inviting them to join in a dance; he is leading them into battle. We must make up our minds that there is nothing for it but to meet them man to man and hand to hand. Whether we live or die, it is better to settle the matter once and for all than in this feeble way to let a weaker enemy squeeze us to death in a long struggle by the ships.'

Aias' exhortation put new life into all his men. And now Hector killed Schedius son of Perimedes, a Phocian chieftain; Aias killed Laodamas the noble son of Antenor, an infantry commander; and Polydamas slew Cyllenian Otus, a leader of the proud Epeans and a friend of Meges son of Phyleus. Meges, when he saw this, leapt at Polydamas, but Polydamas avoided his attack by stooping – Apollo was not going to let the son of Panthous fall in the front line – and Meges, missing him, caught Croesmus full in the chest with his spear. Croesmus fell with a thud, and Meges began to strip the armour from his shoulders. But as he did so, he was assaulted by Dolops, who was an expert with the lance. This man was a son of Lampus son of Laomedon, the best son he had and a practised fighter. Attacking at close range, he pierced the centre of Meges' shield with his spear. But Meges was well served by the stout corslet he was wearing, with its metal plates. His father, Phyleus, had brought this corslet from Ephyre and the River Selleïs, where his host, King Euphetes, had made him a present of it, to wear when he went to war and protect him from his enemies. Now it did further service: it saved his son from destruction.

Meges replied with a thrust of his sharp-pointed spear

which struck the plumed crown of Dolops' brazen helmet and sheared the horsehair crest clean off the top. The whole ornament, resplendent in its fresh purple dye, fell down in the dust. But Dolops did not despair of winning; he stood his ground and still showed fight. What he did not notice was that the formidable Menelaus, spear in hand, had come to Meges' help and crept up on his flank. Menelaus struck him in the shoulder from behind with such violence that the eager spear-point forced its way through and came out at his breast. Dolops fell headlong, and Menelaus and Meges rushed in to strip the bronze equipment from his shoulders.

Hector called on his kinsmen to rally. He appealed to all of them, but he singled out the stalwart Melanippus son of Hicetaon for reprimand. This man, before the invasion, had lived at Percote, where he grazed his shambling cattle; but when the Danaans arrived in their rolling ships, he returned to Ilium and won an honourable place among the Trojans, living with Priam, who treated him like one of his own children. 'Melanippus,' Hector shouted at him angrily, 'are we to take things lying down like this? Is it nothing to you that they have killed your cousin, Dolops? Or don't you see them helping themselves to his armour? Follow me now. We cannot hold off any longer. We must grapple with these Argives till we have destroyed them or they bring Ilium tumbling down and slaughter all its men.' With this, Hector led off, and Melanippus followed him, like the gallant man he was.

Meanwhile the great Telamonian Aias was stirring up the Argives. 'My friends,' he cried, 'be men, and think of your honour. Fear nothing in the field but dishonour in each other's eyes. When soldiers fear disgrace, then more are saved than killed. Neither honour nor salvation is to be found in flight.' Though they had scarcely needed this incitement to defend themselves, the Argives took his words to heart and ringed their ships with a fence of bronze. But Zeus still spurred the Trojans to attack.

Menelaus of the loud war-cry chose this moment to suggest a deed of daring to Antilochus. 'We have nobody younger than you, Antilochus,' he said, 'and no one quicker on his feet, or bolder in a fight. Why not sally out and see if you can bring a Trojan down?' Menelaus promptly withdrew, but he had said enough to put Antilochus on his mettle. He leapt out from the front line, took a quick look round, and let fly with his glittering lance. The Trojans sprang back from his spear-cast. But he had not thrown for nothing. He caught Melanippus, the proud son of Hicetaon, beside the nipple on his breast, as he was coming up into the fight. Melanippus fell with a crash and night descended on his eyes. Antilochus pounced on him like a hound leaping on a stricken fawn that a huntsman has killed with a lucky shot as it started from its lair. Thus, Melanippus, did the dauntless Antilochus leap at you to strip you of your arms. But noble Hector, who had seen what he had done, came running up through the mêlée to confront him; and Antilochus, for all his gallantry, did not await his coming. He turned tail like a wild beast that has committed the enormity of killing a dog or the man in charge of the cattle, and takes to his heels before a crowd collects to chase him. Thus the son of Nestor fled, pursued by deafening cries and a hail of deadly missiles from the Trojans and Hector. But directly he reached his own company, he faced about and stood.

The Trojans now stormed at the ships like flesh-eating lions, doing the duty assigned to them by Zeus, who kept heightening their fury, and dashing the spirits of the Argives by denying them all success and emboldening their enemies. He was scheming to give Prince Hector the upper hand so that he could set the beaked ships thoroughly ablaze. This, thought Zeus the Plan-maker, would enable him to satisfy in full the extravagant demands of Thetis. So he was waiting till he saw the blaze of a ship on fire. From that moment he intended the Trojans to be thrust back from the ships and the Danaans to be victorious. All this was in his mind as he spurred on Hector son of Priam to attack the hollow ships. Not that Hector lacked the necessary zeal. He raged like the War-god spear in hand, or like a fire on the mountains, working destruction in the deep recesses of the woods. There was foam on his mouth; his eyes flashed under lowering brows; there was menace even in the swaying of the helmet on his temples as he fought. Zeus himself was serving as his ally in the sky, and had selected him from that great crowd of men for signal honour, since he had but a short time to live. Pallas Athene was already speeding up the fatal day when he should fall to the mighty son of Peleus.

Hector's aim was to break the enemy line, and wherever he saw the greatest numbers and the best-armed men he made the attempt. But he failed to break through, for all the ferocity of his assault. They stood as firm and close as the stones in a wall, moving no more than a great beetling cliff that faces the grey sea unshaken by the onslaught of the howling winds and the towering waves that roar at its foot. So resolutely did the Danaans stand up to the Trojans and dismiss all thoughts of flight.

At last Hector, aflame from head to foot, burst into their midst. Picture a wave raised by a gale and sweeping forward under the scudding clouds. It breaks on a gallant ship. She is smothered in foam; the angry wind booms in her sail; and the crew, saved from destruction by a hair's breadth, are left trembling and aghast. That is how Hector fell upon the Achaeans, striking panic into their hearts.

And they stampeded, as cattle do when a savage lion finds them grazing in their hundreds in some great water-meadow under a herdsman who has not learnt the art of dealing with a cattle-killing beast, but keeps level with the front or rear, leaving the lion to strike at the centre of the herd and devour his kill. Thus the whole force was put to flight by Hector and by Father Zeus – which was a miracle, for Hector killed a single Danaan only.

His victim was a Mycenean, Periphetes son of Copreus. Copreus had been the go-between employed to carry King Eurystheus' orders to the mighty Heracles. But Periphetes was a great improvement on his worthless father; he was ex- cellent in all respects, a fast runner, a good soldier and one of the ablest men in Mycenae. The value of the man enhanced the glory of his conqueror. He had just turned to fly when he tripped against the rim of the shield which he carried to keep missiles off and which came down to his feet. Thrown off his balance, he fell backwards, and as he reached the ground his helmet rang out loudly on his temples, at once attracting Hector's notice. Hector ran up to him and drove a spear into his chest, killing him in the very presence of his friends, who could do nothing to help their comrade, for all their horror at his death, since the noble Hector had terrified them all.

Very soon the Argives were in among the ships and protected by the upper works of the first row. But the Trojans poured in too, and the Argives were forced to fall back from the first line to the adjoining huts. There they came to a halt, not scattering all over the camp, but kept together by a sense of shame and fear, and by the mutual recriminations they exchanged. Nobody did more by way of exhorting them than Gerenian Nestor, the Warden of the race, who appealed to each and every man in his parents' name. 'Be men, my friends,' he said. 'Think of your reputation in the world. Remember your children too, and your wives, your property and your parents, whether they are alive or dead. For the sake of your absent dear ones I beseech you to stand firm and not to turn and fly.'

Nestor's appeal put fresh heart into every man; and Athene cleared away from their eyes the unnatural mist that had befogged them. There was daylight now in both directions, behind them, where the rest of the ships lay, and in front, where the battle was still undecided. Hector of the loud war-cry and his men were visible to all, including those who were standing idle in the rear as well as those that were engaged beside the gallant ships.

The idea of joining the Achaeans who had detached themselves from the fighting did not commend itself to the proud heart of Aias. Instead, he kept moving up and down the decks of the ships with great strides, swinging a huge pole twenty-two cubits long, which was made of pieces spliced together

and was designed for sea-battles. He was like a trick-rider
with a team of four picked horses which he gallops in from
the country to a big city down a busy road, where there are
plenty of men and women to admire the skill with which he
keeps jumping on and off his several mounts as they fly along.
Thus Aias kept moving from one ship's deck to another with
enormous strides; and his voice went up into the sky, as he
exhorted the Danaans with terrific shouts to defend their
ships and huts.

Hector was equally unwilling to linger with the crowd and
stay among his Trojan men-at-arms. As a tawny eagle swoops
on a flock of birds – geese, cranes or long-necked swans – that
are feeding by a river, Hector dashed to the front and made
straight for a blue-prowed ship. Zeus pushed him from behind
with his tremendous hand and spurred his men to follow him.

So once again the struggle by the ships was fierce. You
would have thought they had gone into the tussle fresh and
unfatigued, so eagerly did they come to grips. But in their
temper as they fought there was this difference. The Achaeans
felt that they were in for a disaster: they saw themselves de-
stroyed. But every Trojan there was filled with the hope of
burning up the ships and killing the Achaean lords. Such were
their feelings as they closed.

Hector at last got his hands on the stern of a seagoing ship.
It was the fast salt-water craft that had brought Protesilaus to
Troy, though it never carried him home again to his own
country. Round this the Achaeans and Trojans fought each
other hand to hand. For the Achaeans, it was not a matter
now of holding off and standing up to a volley of arrows or
of javelins. United in their resolution they stood man to man
and there they fought, with sharp axes and hatchets, with
long swords and double-pointed spears. Many a fine black-
hilted sword fell to the ground from warriors' hands, and
many another was ripped from their shoulders as they fought.
The earth ran black with blood.

Hector, once he had laid hold of the ship, never let go, but
kept his hands on the mascot at the stern and shouted to the

Trojans: 'Bring fire; and raise the war-cry, all of you to-
gether. Zeus is repaying us for everything to-day: the ships
are ours. They came here against the will of the gods, and they
started all these troubles for us. But that was through the
cowardice of our Elders. When I wished to carry the fighting
up to the ships, they stopped me and withheld the troops.
But as surely as all-seeing Zeus blinded us then, he is backing
us to-day and sweeping us on.'

This made them fall on the Argives with even greater
ferocity. Aias himself, overwhelmed by missiles, could no
longer keep his post, but in fear of death gave way a little and
retired from the afterdeck of the trim ship to the seven-foot
bridge amidships. There he stood, on the alert; and when any
Trojan came up with a blazing torch, he fended him off from
the ships with his pole. And all the time, in that terrible voice
of his, he was calling to the Danaans to fight on. 'Friends,
gallant Danaans, servants of Ares,' he cried, 'be men and re-
call your former prowess. Do you imagine we have allies in
the rear, or a stronger wall which might keep disaster off?
There is no walled city hereabouts with reinforcements that
would save the day. We are in the Trojan plain; all Troy is
up in arms; the sea is at our backs; and our country is a long
way off. That means that we must fight, and not too gently
either, if we are going to save our skins.'

As he spoke, he kept thrusting furiously with his pointed
pole. Whenever a Trojan came near the hollow ships with a
burning brand (in the hope of gratifying Hector, who was
hounding them on), Aias was ready and struck him with his
enormous spear. He wounded twelve men in front of the
ships without parting from his weapon.

XVI

PATROCLUS FIGHTS AND DIES

WHILE this battle was raging round the well-found ship, Patroclus reached his sovran lord, Achilles. Hot tears were running down his face like water trickling from a spring in dark streaks down a precipice. Highborn Achilles of the nimble feet was distressed when he saw his friend's condition and at once enquired what ailed him. 'Patroclus, why are you in tears,' he asked, 'like a little girl trotting at her mother's side and begging to be carried, plucking her skirt to make her stop and looking up at her with streaming eyes till at last she takes her in her arms? That, Patroclus, is how you look, with the tear-drops rolling down your cheeks. Have you something to tell the Myrmidons or myself? Some news from Phthia that has reached you privately? If either of our fathers were dead we should indeed have cause for grief, but I understand that yours, Menoetius son of Actor, is still in the land of the living, and Peleus son of Aeacus is certainly alive among his Myrmidons. Perhaps you are weeping for the Argives who are being slaughtered by the hollow ships in payment for their own iniquities? Out with it now! Don't keep the secret to yourself, but share it with me.'

What did the knight Patroclus say to this? He gave a great sigh and replied: 'My lord Achilles, noblest of the Achaeans; do not grudge me these tears. The army is indeed in terrible distress. All our former champions are lying by their ships, wounded by arrows or spears. The mighty Diomedes son of Tydeus has been hit; Odysseus the great spearman has been wounded; so has Agamemnon; and Eurypylus too has had an arrow in his thigh. Surgeons are attending them with all the remedies at their command, and while they try to heal their wounds, you, Achilles, remain intractable. Heaven pre-

serve me from the vindictive feelings you cherish, warping a
noble nature to ignoble ends. What will future generations
have to thank you for, if you will not help the Argives in
their direst need? Pitiless man, you are no son of Thetis and
the gallant Peleus. Only the grey sea and its frowning crags
could have produced a monster so hard-hearted. Is it possible
that you are secretly deterred by some prophecy, some word
from Zeus that your lady Mother has disclosed to you?
Then at least allow *me* to take the field at once with the
Myrmidon force at my back – I might yet bring salvation to
the Danaans. And lend me your own armour to put on my
shoulders so that the Trojans may take me for you and break
off the battle, which would give our weary troops time to re-
cuperate. Even a short breathing-space makes all the difference
in war. The Trojans themselves have fought to the point of
exhaustion, and we, being fresh, might well drive them back
to the city from the ships and huts.'

So Patroclus made his appeal. But how simple he was! Had
he but known it, he was praying for his own doom and an
evil death.

Meanwhile he had certainly roused Achilles the great
runner, who began by crying out at him: 'Prophecies, my
lord Patroclus? What are you talking about? If I do know of
any, it does not affect my conduct. Nor is it true that I have
privately had word from Zeus through my lady Mother.
What has cut me to the quick is that a fellow no better than
myself should want to plunder me and take away the prize I
won, just because he has more power. After all I have gone
through in the war, it is more than I can bear. That girl – the
army made a special point of giving her to me; I had sacked a
walled town; I had won her with my own spear. And now
she is snatched from my arms by King Agamemnon son of
Atreus, and I am served like some disreputable tramp.

'But what is done cannot be undone. I was wrong in sup-
posing that a man could nurse a grudge for ever, though I
did think of keeping up the feud till the tumult and the
fighting reached my own ships. Dress yourself, then, in my

glorious armour and lead my battle-loving Myrmidons into the field, now that the conquering Trojans are swirling round the ships like a black cloud, and the Argives hanging on to a narrow strip of ground with the beach at their backs. The whole town of Troy seems to have taken heart and turned out against us. And no wonder, when they do not see the vizor of *my* helmet flashing in the foreground. They would soon take to their heels and fill the gullies with their dead, if King Agamemnon would treat me as a friend. As it is, they are fighting round the very camp. The spear of Diomedes son of Tydeus is no longer storming in his hands to save the Danaans from destruction; and I have not even heard the hateful voice of Agamemnon. It is the murderous Hector's shouts that ring in my ears, as he hounds on his yelling Trojans, who have covered the plain and are trouncing the Achaeans. Nevertheless, Patroclus, you must save the ships. Attack with all your force before they send them up in flames and cut us off from home. But listen while I tell you exactly how far to go, in order to induce the whole Danaan army to value and respect me as they should and to send the lovely lady back to me, with ample compensation too. Return to me, directly you have swept the Trojans from the ships. Even if Zeus the Thunderer offers you the chance of winning glory for yourself, you must not seize it. You must not fight without *me* against these warlike Trojans – you would only make me cheaper. So do not lead on your men to Ilium in the flush of victory, killing Trojans as you go, or one of the eternal gods from Olympus may cross your path – the Archer-King Apollo loves the Trojans dearly. Turn back when you have saved the situation at the ships, and leave the rest to do the fighting on the plain. Ah, Father Zeus, Athene and Apollo, how happy I should be if not a Trojan got away alive, not one, and not an Argive either, and if we two survived the massacre to pull down Troy's holy diadem of towers single-handed!'

While Achilles and Patroclus were talking to one another, the moment came when Aias could no longer keep his post. He was conquered by the will of Zeus and overwhelmed with missiles from the hands of the triumphant Trojans. His shining helmet, their constant mark, rang terribly upon his temples, as dart after dart impinged on the stout plates on either side. His left shoulder was exhausted by the prolonged effort of swinging his shield, though even so the impact of their volleys failed to bring it crashing in upon him. He was panting hard, and the sweat streamed from all his limbs. He had not an instant to relax. Whichever way he looked, each moment added to his troubles.

Tell me now, you Muses that live on Olympus, how the Achaean ships were first set on fire. Hector went right up to Aias, struck his ashen spear with his great sword below the socket of the point and sheared the head clean off, leaving the truncated shaft to dangle foolishly in Telamonian Aias' hand, while the bronze head sped away from him and fell to the ground with a clang. Deep in his noble heart, Aias realized with a shudder that the gods were taking a hand in the affair and that Zeus the Thunderer, intent on a Trojan victory, was rendering all his struggles futile. So he fell back out of range; the Trojans threw blazing brands into the gallant ship; and in a moment she was wrapt in inextinguishable flames.

As the fire swirled round her stern, Achilles slapped his thighs and turned to Patroclus. 'Up,' he cried, 'my royal lord Patroclus, Commander of the Horse! I see a blaze at the ships: they are going up in flames. If only they don't capture them and cut off our retreat! Quick, get your armour on, while I assemble the men.'

Patroclus put on the shimmering bronze. He began by tying round his legs the splendid greaves, which were fitted with silver clips for the ankles. Next he put on his breast Achilles' beautiful cuirass, scintillating like the stars. Over his shoulders he slung the bronze sword, with its silver-studded hilt, and then the great thick shield. On his sturdy head he set the well-made helmet. It had a horsehair crest, and the plume nodded grimly from on top. Last, he picked up two powerful spears which suited his grip. The only weapon of the peerless Achilles that he did not take was his heavy, long and formidable spear. No Achaean could wield this but Achilles, who knew the way to handle it. It was made from an ash on the top of Mount Pelion and had been given by Cheiron to his father, Peleus, to bring death to his noble foes.

To drive the horses, Patroclus chose Automedon, and told him to harness them quickly. He thought more highly of this man than of anyone but Achilles, the breaker of the battle-line, having found that in action he was the most reliable of drivers, keeping always within call. So Automedon yoked for him Achilles' horses, Xanthus and Balius, the wind-swift pair whom Podarge, the Storm-Filly, had foaled for their sire, the Western Gale, when she was grazing in the meadows beside Ocean Stream; and he put in as an outrigger the thoroughbred Pedasus, whom Achilles had brought away with him when he captured Eëtion's city. Pedasus was only an ordinary horse but he kept up with the immortal pair.

Meanwhile Achilles had gone the round of the huts and got all his Myrmidons under arms. They fell in like flesh-eating wolves in all their natural savagery, wolves that have killed a great antlered stag in the mountains and rend him till their jowls are red with blood, then go off in a pack to lap the dark water from the surface of a deep spring with their slender tongues, belching gore, and still indomitably fierce though their bellies are distended. Thus the captains and commanders of the Myrmidons rushed to their posts round the gallant squire of the swift son of Peleus. And there was Achilles himself, like the War-god, marshalling the charioteers and the shield-bearing infantry.

Each of the fifty fast ships that Prince Achilles brought to Troy had a crew of fifty on its benches. He himself was in supreme command, but he appointed five lieutenants under him. The first company was led by Menesthius of the flashing cuirass, a son of the divine River Spercheus and the beautiful Polydora, a daughter of Peleus. He was thus the love-child of a woman and a god, Spercheus of the Tireless Stream. But a man called Borus son of Perieres had come forward with a handsome dowry and married his mother; so he was known as the son of Borus.

The second was commanded by the warlike Eudorus. His mother too, Polymele daughter of Phylas, was an unmarried girl. She was a beautiful dancer, and the great god Hermes the Giant-killer had fallen in love with her when she caught his eye as she was playing her part in the choir of Artemis of the Golden Distaff, the goddess of the chase. The gracious Hermes took her straight up to her bedroom unobserved, lay in her arms, and made her the mother of a splendid child destined, as Eudorus, to be a great runner and man of war. When in due course the baby had been brought into the world by Eileithyia, the goddess of travail, and had opened his eyes to the sun, a powerful chieftain, Echecles son of Actor, married the mother, for whom he paid an ample dowry, and took her home with him, while Eudorus was carefully looked after and brought up by his old grandfather, Phylas, who could have shown him no greater devotion had he been his own son.

The third company was commanded by the gallant Peisander son of Maemalus, who of all the Myrmidons was the best spearman next to Patroclus, the squire of Achilles. The old charioteer Phoenix led the fourth; and the fifth was commanded by Alcimedon, Laerces' noble son.

When Achilles had drawn them all up, officers and men, in their proper places, he made them a forceful speech. 'Myrmidons,' he said, 'let none of you forget what you have been threatening to do to the Trojans all the time I kept you here beside your ships while I indulged my anger. There is not one of you who did not abuse your prince. You called me a brute for keeping my men idle here against their will. I was a sort of monster, brought up on bile instead of mother's milk. "Achilles," you said, "is in such an evil mood that we might as well take to the ships and sail home again." I know you often met and discussed me in this style.

'Well now, a bit of real work has come your way, just such a fight as you have longed for. Go to it then, and fall on the Trojans like brave men.'

His words filled every one of them with daring, and the ranks dressed closer when they heard their prince. Their helmets and their bossed shields were as tightly packed as the blocks of stone that a mason fits together when he is building the wall of a high house and wishes to make sure of keeping out the wind. They stood so close together, shield to shield, helmet to helmet, man to man, that when they moved their heads the glittering peaks of their plumed helmets met. And in front of them all, Patroclus and Automedon took their battle post, two men with one desire between them, to fight in the Myrmidons' van.

But Achilles went off to his hut. There he lifted the lid of a beautiful inlaid chest which Thetis of the Silver Feet had packed with tunics, wind-proof cloaks and thick rugs, and put on board for him to take on his journey. In this he kept a lovely cup from which no other man was allowed to drink the sparkling wine, and which he himself used for libations to no other god but Father Zeus. He took it from the chest, and after fumigating it with sulphur, rinsed it in a rill of fresh water, washed his hands and drew some sparkling wine. Then he went to the middle of the forecourt to pray and looked up into the sky as he poured out the wine, watched all the time by thunder-loving Zeus. 'Lord Zeus,' he began; 'Dodonean, Pelasgian Zeus; you that live far away and rule over wintry Dodona, surrounded by your prophets the Helli, who leave their feet unwashed and sleep on the ground; you listened when I prayed to you before, and you showed your regard for me by striking a mighty blow at the Achaean army. Grant me another wish. I myself am going to stay among the ships; but I am sending my comrade with many of the Myrmidons into the field. Bless him with victory, all-seeing Zeus, and fill his heart with daring, so that Hector himself may find out whether my squire can fight on his own, or whether his hands are invincible only when *I* throw myself into the fray. And directly he has swept the tumult and the fighting from the ships, let him come back to me, here at my own ships, safe and sound with all his armour and his men-at-arms.'

Zeus the Counsellor heard Achilles' prayer and granted him half of it but not the rest. The Father agreed that Patroclus should chase the Trojans from the ships, but not that he should come back safely from the battle. When Achilles had made his libation and prayer to Father Zeus, he went back into his hut and put the cup away in the chest. Then he came out and stood in front of the hut, for his interest was by no means exhausted and he wished to see the clash between the Trojans and Achaeans.

Meanwhile the armed companies entrusted to the heroic Patroclus marched on, till in their fury they could fall upon the Trojans.

Picture a horde of wasps pouring out from the side of a road. They are used to being teased by boys, for the young fools provoke them every time they pass their wayside nest. The result is a public menace. No sooner does a traveller come by and unwittingly disturb them than they are up in arms and one and all fly out to fight for their little ones. That was the spirit in which the Myrmidons poured out from behind the ships, with an indescribable din, through which the loud voice of Patroclus could be heard exhorting his troops. 'Myrmidons,' he cried, 'soldiers of Prince Achilles, be men, my friends, display your old audacity, and win glory for the son of Peleus, the best man in the Argive camp, with the best companies in his command. Teach his imperial majesty King Agamemnon what a fool he was when he trifled with the best Achaean of them all.'

Patroclus had put every man on his mettle. They fell on the Trojans in a body, and the Achaean war-cry was re-echoed grimly by the ships all round.

But when the Trojans saw the stalwart son of Menoetius and his squire Automedon beside him, in all the brilliance of their bronze equipment, their hearts sank and the lines began to waver, for they thought Achilles of the nimble feet must have given up the feud that had kept him by his ships and reconciled himself with Agamemnon. Every man looked anxiously around to find some sanctuary from sudden death.

Patroclus was the first to cast a glittering lance. He hurled it straight into the mass of men who were swarming round the stern of the great Protesilaus' ship, and he struck Pyraechmes, who had brought his Paeonians in their plumed helmets from Amydon and the banks of the broad River Axius. He hit him in the right shoulder. With a groan, Pyraechmes fell on his back in the dust, and his Paeonian troops, panic-stricken one and all when they saw their captain and best fighter killed, took to their heels. Patroclus, having swept them from the ships, extinguished the fire that was blazing in Protesilaus' vessel, leaving it half-burnt. Meanwhile the Trojans themselves had taken fright. They fell back in utter confusion; and with a deafening roar the Danaans poured out upon them through the gaps between the hollow ships.

Thus the Danaans saved their fleet from going up in flames and for a while could breathe more freely. It was like the moment when the Lightning-maker Zeus shifts a dense cloud from the summit of a lofty mountain, and every peak and headland and ravine starts into sight, as the infinite depths of the sky are torn open to the very firmament. But the gallant Achaeans had not done with fighting. The Trojans had been forced back from the black ships, but not as yet in headlong rout. They still confronted them.

Now that the mêlée had been broken up, the Achaeans started picking off the Trojan leaders singly. The valiant Patroclus began by striking Areilycus with a sharp spear in the thigh, just as he had turned. The bronze point drove through and broke the bone; the man fell headlong to the ground. Meanwhile Menelaus favourite of Ares struck Thoas in the breast, which he had exposed above his shield, bringing him down. Amphiclus charged at Meges, but Meges had his eye on him and got in first, with a spear-thrust on the root of the thigh, where a man's thickest muscle is found. The spear-point tore through the sinews and darkness descended on the eyes of Amphiclus. Then one of Nestor's sons, Antilochus, struck Atymnius with his sharp spear and drove the bronze head through his flank. Atymnius fell with a crash before him. But

Maris, infuriated by his brother's death, charged at Antilochus, spear in hand, and planted himself in front of the body. However, before he could do any damage, another son of Nestor, the godlike Thrasymedes, made a swift lunge at him and caught him on the shoulder, just where he had aimed. The point of his spear, striking the base of the arm, severed the ligaments and wrenched the bone right out. Maris fell with a thud, and darkness came down on his eyes. Thus these two men were conquered by two brothers and went down to Erebus. They had done good service as spearmen in Sarpedon's company and were the sons of Amisodarus, who had kept the Chimaera, the monster that brought so many men to grief.

Aias son of Oïleus dashed in among the rabble, where Cleobulus was in difficulties, and took him alive. But he gave him his quietus soon enough, with a stroke on the neck from his hilted sword – the blood made the whole blade warm. Fate set her seal on him and purple Death descended on his eyes.

Next, Peneleos and Lycon came to grips. Each had made a bad cast with his spear and missed the other. So now they ran at one another with their swords. Lycon struck the cone of the other's plumed helmet and his sword broke off at the hilt. But Peneleos hit Lycon on the neck behind the ear and his sword-blade went right through. Nothing held but a piece of skin, and from that the head was hanging down as Lycon sank to the ground.

Meriones, running hard, caught up Acamas and wounded him in the right shoulder as he mounted his chariot. Acamas tumbled out of the chariot and a mist descended on his eyes. Meanwhile, Idomeneus struck Erymas on the mouth with his relentless bronze. The metal point of the spear passed right through the lower part of his skull, under the brain, and smashed the white bones. His teeth were shattered; both his eyes were filled with blood; and he spurted blood through his nostrils and his gaping mouth. Then the black cloud of Death descended on him.

So each of these Danaan chieftains killed his man. They harried the Trojans like predatory wolves harrying lambs or

kids and snatching them from under their dams when they
are lost on the mountains through the shepherd's carelessness
and the wolves seize their chance to pick off the timid crea-
tures. The Trojans had no stomach left for the fight, and fell
into disorderly retreat.

It was now the one desire of the great Telamonian Aias to
have a cast at bronze-clad Hector. But Hector was no in-
experienced fighter. He protected his broad shoulders with
his bull's hide shield, and had his ear cocked for whistling
arrows and for hurtling spears. He was well aware that the
enemy's reinforcements had won them the day, yet even so he
kept the field and tried to save his gallant men.

But by now the Trojan withdrawal from the ships had
turned into a noisy rout, wild as the onrush through the sky of
a storm-cloud from Olympus and the clear heavens above it,
when a tempest is unleashed by Zeus. They fled across the
Achaean works with their tails between their legs; and as for
Hector, he was carried off at a gallop, arms and all, abandon-
ing to their fate such of his men as were perforce detained by
the hazards of the trench. For many a pair of fast war-horses
snapped off the end of their shaft in the trench and left their
master's car behind.

Patroclus chased them with slaughter in his heart, hounding
on the Danaans relentlessly, while the Trojans, whose forma-
tions had been broken up by now, filled every roadway with
the noise of rout. The dust went rolling up to the clouds as
their strong horses made at full speed for the town, leaving
the ships and huts behind them. Wherever Patroclus saw the
greatest numbers flying before him, he gave a wild halloo and
followed up. Men tumbled headlong from their cars beneath
his axle-trees, and their chariots overturned with a crash. But
he himself was driving an immortal pair, the splendid present
that the gods had given Peleus, and they pressed on without a
check and cleared the trench at a single bound in their
eagerness to bring him within range of Hector. For it was
Hector that he yearned to kill. But Hector had fast horses too,
and they carried him away.

There are days in autumn when the whole countryside lies darkened and oppressed under a stormy sky and Zeus sends down torrential rain as a punishment to men. His anger is roused because regardless of the jealous eye of Heaven they have misused their powers, delivered crooked judgments in a public session and driven justice out. In consequence their streams all run in spate, hillsides are scarred by torrents, and the rivers, wrecking the farmlands in their way, rush down headlong from the mountains with a great roar into the turbid sea. Such was the din that went up from the Trojan horse as they fled.

Patroclus had by now cut up the nearest companies and was heading them off in their own tracks towards the ships. He defeated all their efforts to take refuge in the city, and there, between the ships, the river and the high wall, he kept charging in and killing men, in compensation for the Achaean dead. Pronous was his first victim. With a shining spear he hit him on the breast, which he had exposed above his shield, and brought him down with a crash. Next he attacked Thestor son of Enops, who was sitting hunched up in his polished chariot. This man had lost his head completely and the reins had slipped from his hands. Patroclus came up beside him and struck him on the right side of the jaw, driving his spear between the teeth. Then, using the spear as a lever, he hoisted him over the chariot-rail as a fisherman sitting on a jutting rock pulls a monster fish out of the sea with his line and burnished hook. Thus with his bright spear Patroclus hauled his gaping catch out of the car and dropped him on his face, to die as he fell. Next, as Erylaus rushed at him, he hit him with a rock full on the head. Inside the heavy helmet the man's skull was split in two; he fell face downward on the ground, and soul-devouring Death engulfed him. Then, in swift succession, Patroclus dealt with Erymas, Amphoterus and Epaltes; Tlepolemus son of Damastor, Echius and Pyris; Ipheus, Euippus and Polymelus son of Argeas, bringing them all nearer than they had been to the kindly soil.

When Sarpedon saw how his beltless Lycians were falling

to Patroclus son of Menoetius, he told his gallant soldiers what he thought of them. 'For shame, Lycians!' he cried. 'Where are you off to – with such admirable speed? Wait till I meet that fellow over there. I mean to find out who it is that is carrying all before him and has done the Trojans so much harm already, bringing so many of our best men down.'

As he spoke he leapt down from his chariot with all his arms, and on the other side Patroclus, when he saw him, did the same. Then the two men, uttering defiant cries, made for each other like a couple of vultures with their crooked claws and curved beaks fighting on a rocky height and screaming as they fight.

The Son of Cronos of the Crooked Ways saw what was happening and was distressed. He sighed, and said to Here, his Sister and his Wife: 'Fate is unkind to me – Sarpedon, whom I dearly love, is destined to be killed by Patroclus son of Menoetius. I wonder now – I am in two minds. Shall I snatch him up and set him down alive in the rich land of Lycia, far from the war and all its tears? Or shall I let him fall to the son of Menoetius this very day?'

'Dread Son of Cronos, you amaze me!' replied the ox-eyed Queen of Heaven. 'Are you proposing to reprieve a mortal man, whose doom has long been settled, from the pains of death? Do as you please; but do not expect the rest of the immortals to applaud. There is this point too that you should bear in mind. If you send Sarpedon home alive, what is to prevent some other god from trying to rescue his own son from the fight? A number of the combatants at Troy are sons of gods, who would resent your action bitterly. No; if you love and pity Sarpedon, let him fall in mortal combat with Patroclus, and when the breath has left his lips send Death and the sweet god of Sleep to take him up and bring him to the broad realm of Lycia, where his kinsmen and retainers will give him burial, with the barrow and monument that are a dead man's rights.'

The Father of men and gods made no demur. But he did send down a shower of bloody raindrops to the earth, as a

tribute to his beloved son, whom Patroclus was about to kill
in the deep-soiled land of Troy, far from his own country.

When the two had come within range of one another,
Patroclus cast. He struck the celebrated Thrasymelus, King
Sarpedon's noble squire, in the lower part of the belly, and
brought him down. Sarpedon, casting second with his shining
spear, missed Patroclus, but struck his horse Pedasus on the
right shoulder. The horse whinnied in the throes of death,
then fell down in the dust and with a great sigh gave up his
life. The other two horses sprang apart; the yoke creaked; and
their reins became entangled with those of their companion
on the ground. But the great spearman Automedon soon
found the remedy for this. He drew his long sword from his
sturdy thigh, jumped down and deftly cut the trace-horse
clear. The pair righted themselves and tugged at their harness
once more, while the two men resumed their deadly duel.

Sarpedon cast a glittering lance, but missed his mark; the
point passed harmlessly over Patroclus' left shoulder. Patro-
clus took the second cast; and his weapon did not leave his
hand for nothing. It struck where the diaphragm comes up
against the busy heart; and like an oak or a poplar or a tower-
ing pine felled in the hills by men with whetted axes to make
timbers for a ship, Sarpedon came to earth. Groaning and
clutching at the dust his blood had stained, the captain of the
Lycian men-at-arms lay stretched in front of his chariot and
horses. But even as he yielded up his life to Patroclus he
breathed defiance, like some proud tawny bull who is brought
down among the shambling cows by a lion that has attacked
the herd, and bellows as the lion's jaws destroy him.

'Glaucus!' cried Sarpedon, naming his dearest friend.
'Dear Glaucus, man among men! Now is the time for you to
show your spearmanship and daring. Now is the time for
you to fall in love with evil war, if there is any prowess in
you. Run to our captains everywhere and whip them in to
rally round Sarpedon. And then fight over me with your own
bronze. Every day of your life the thought of me will make
you hang your head for shame, if you let the Achaeans spoil

me of my arms, here where I fell, beside their ships. Hold out
then, with all your strength, and throw every man we have
into the fight.'

Sarpedon said no more, for Death had descended on his
eyes and cut short his breath. Patroclus put his foot on his
chest and withdrew the spear from his flesh. The midriff came
with it: he had drawn out the spear-point and the man's soul
together. Close by, the Myrmidons held Sarpedon's panting
horses, who were showing signs of panic now that their
chariot was bereft of its masters.

Glaucus was distraught when he heard Sarpedon's call. His
impotence to help him wrung his heart; and he gripped his
damaged arm with his other hand, tormented as he was by
the arrow-wound that Teucer, fighting for his comrades'
lives, had given him when he charged at the Achaean wall.
Then he prayed to the Archer-god Apollo: 'Listen to me,
Lord, whether you are in the rich land of Lycia or in Troy;
for you can hear him anywhere when a man is in distress, as I
am now. Look at the grievous wound I have. My arm is
racked with pain; the blood refuses to dry up; my shoulder is
paralysed; I cannot hold my spear steady nor go out and fight
the foe. And now our best man has been killed, Sarpedon son
of Zeus. But Zeus will not lift a finger, even for his son; and
it is you, Lord Apollo, whom I ask to heal this cruel wound
and lull the pain, giving me strength to rally my companions
and to fight over the body of our dead King myself.'

Phoebus Apollo heard his prayer and at once relieved his
pain, dried up the dark blood from his cruel wound, and
filled his heart with strength. Glaucus was conscious of his
help and rejoiced that the great god had lent so ready an ear
to his prayer. He went at once to all the Lycian captains and
exhorted them to rally round Sarpedon. Then he went
striding off to find some Trojans also, and approached Poly-
damas son of Panthous and the noble Agenor. He sought
Aeneas too, and Hector in his arms of bronze. He went up
to them and begged their help. 'Hector,' he said, 'you have
completely forgotten your allies, who are giving their lives

for you far from their dear ones and their native land. At any rate you show no eagerness to help them. Sarpedon, leader of the Lycian men-at-arms, lies dead. He was the just and strong defender of the Lycian realm, and now the brazen War-god has cut him down with Patroclus' spear. Make a stand by him, my friends. Think of the shame of it, if the Myrmidons, in revenge for the many Danaans who fell to our spears beside the gallant ships, should take Sarpedon's arms and desecrate his corpse.'

The Trojans were heart-broken at the news: it was intolerable. Sarpedon, though a foreigner, had been a buttress of their city and the finest soldier in the great army he had brought them. Their sorrow knew no bounds. Eager to avenge him, they made straight for the Danaans, with Hector in their van, infuriated by Sarpedon's death.

Meanwhile the Achaeans were spurred on by Menoetius' son Patroclus of the shaggy breast. He began with the Aiantes, a pair who stood in little need of exhortation. 'My lords,' he said, 'let this news whet your appetite for battle and make you two the men you used to be, or even better. Sarpedon lies dead. He was the first man to storm the Achaean wall. Let us see if we can capture and besmirch his corpse, strip the armour from his back, and at the same time cut to pieces some of the friends who will protect him.'

Even before Patroclus spoke, they had been spoiling for the fight. And now, when the two forces had strengthened their ranks, Trojans and Lycians on the one side and Myrmidons and Achaeans on the other, they joined battle over the fallen Sarpedon with a terrific roar. The armour on men's bodies rang aloud, and Zeus eclipsed the field in dreadful night, to make the struggle over his beloved son all the more terrible.

At first the Trojans were able to repel the Achaeans of the flashing eyes, who lost one of the best men in the Myrmidon force, the noble Epeigeus, son of the great-hearted Agacles. He had at one time been ruler of the fine town of Budeion, but having killed a highborn kinsman, he took sanctuary with Peleus and Thetis of the Silver Feet, who sent him off to

Ilium the land of noble horses, with Achilles, breaker of men, to fight against the Trojans. This man had just laid his hands on the corpse when illustrious Hector struck him on the head with a rock. Inside the heavy helmet his skull was split in two; he fell face down across the corpse, and soul-devouring Death enveloped him. Patroclus, grieved at his comrade's loss, sped through the front line swift as a falcon when he scatters the jackdaws and the starlings. That was how Patroclus, Master of the Horse, flew at the Lycians and Trojans in his fury at the death of his man. He hit Sthenelaus son of Ithaemenes on the neck with a boulder, and broke his sinews. The Trojan front line and glorious Hector himself fell back before his onslaught.

But they withdrew, under pressure from the Achaeans, only as far as a man can throw a long javelin when he is doing his best in a match, or even in a battle, with the enemy thirsting for his blood. Glaucus, captain of the shield-bearing Lycians, was the first to halt. Facing about, he killed the gallant Bathycles, the son of Chalcon, who had a house in Hellas and was one of the most prosperous of the Myrmidons. Bathycles was just about to catch him up, when Glaucus suddenly turned on his pursuer and struck him with his spear in the middle of the chest, bringing him down with a crash. The loss of this fine man was a heavy blow to the Achaeans; but the Trojans were delighted and rallied round his corpse.

However, the Achaeans' impetus was not exhausted and they still bore down in strength upon the enemy. It was now the turn of Meriones to kill a Trojan man-at-arms, Laogonus, the valiant son of Onetor, who was priest of Idaean Zeus and was worshipped by the people. Meriones struck him under the jaw and ear. And he had no lingering death: he was engulfed by the unlovely dark. Aeneas retaliated with a spear-cast at Meriones, hoping to catch him as he strode forward under cover of his shield. But Meriones was on his guard and avoided the bronze spear by ducking. The long shaft came to ground behind him and stuck there with the butt-end quivering till the War-god stilled it with his heavy hand. Aeneas was enraged and shouted at Meriones: 'You may be a fine dancer, but my spear would have stopped you for good and all, if only I had hit you.' To which the famous spearman Meriones replied: 'Aeneas, powerful as you are, you can hardly expect to put everyone who meets you out of action. You are made of mortal stuff like the rest of us, and I too might say that if I caught you in the belly with a sharp spear, you would soon yield your life to Hades of the Fabled Horse and the glory to me, for all your strength and your belief in brawn.'

The great Patroclus overheard this and reproved him. 'Meriones,' he said, 'you are too fine a soldier for such silly talk. Believe me, friend, the Trojans are not going to be pushed back from Sarpedon's body by a few rude remarks. There will be some dead men on the ground before they go. Battles are won by deeds; the council-chamber is the place for words. So let us have some fighting now, and no more speeches.' With that he led the way and Meriones went with him, looking like a god.

From their bronze and leather gear and their tough shields as they met the thrust of sword or double-pointed spear, the trodden earth sent up a din like the clatter that is heard on distant hills when the woodcutters are working in a glade. The sharpest eye would now have failed to recognize the admirable Sarpedon, completely covered as he was from head to foot with weapons, blood and dust. They swarmed round the corpse as flies in a cattle-yard buzz round the brimming pails on a day in spring when the vessels overflow with milk. And all the time, while they were swarming thus round the body of Sarpedon, Zeus never shifted his bright eyes from the scene, but kept them fixed on the struggling mass of men and took counsel with himself about the killing of Patroclus. For a long time he was in two minds, whether to let him fall to Prince Hector's spear over the godlike Sarpedon in this very fight and let Hector strip the armour from his shoulders, or whether to allow Patroclus to bring still more of his enemies to grief. In the end Zeus decided that the gallant squire of highborn Achilles should drive the Trojans and bronze-clad

Hector back towards the city, taking many lives. So he began with Hector and made a coward of him.

Hector leapt into his chariot and wheeled it round for flight, shouting to the other Trojans to take to their heels – he knew that Zeus had tipped the Sacred Scales against him. Then, not even the valiant Lycians stood; they fled one and all. Had they not seen their own King stricken in the heart and lying where the dead were heaped? For in that battle-royal that the Son of Cronos staged, many a man had fallen dead upon Sarpedon.

Thus the Achaeans were enabled to strip the gleaming bronze from Sarpedon's shoulders. The stalwart son of Menoetius handed it to his men and told them to take it to the hollow ships. But the Cloud-gatherer Zeus had not yet done. Turning to Apollo he said: 'Quick, my dear Phoebus; go and take Sarpedon out of range, and when you have wiped the dark blood off, carry him to some distant spot where you will wash him in running water, anoint him with ambrosia, and wrap him up in an imperishable robe. Then, for his swift conveyance, put him in the hands of Sleep and his twin-brother Death, who will make all speed to set him down in the broad and fertile Lycian realm. There his kinsmen and retainers will give him burial, with a barrow and a monument, the proper tribute to the dead.'

Apollo did not turn a deaf ear to his Father's words, but descended from the Idaean Mountains into the turmoil of the fight. He at once picked up the noble Sarpedon from among the fallen darts and carried him to a distant spot, where he washed him in running water, anointed him with ambrosia and wrapped him up in an imperishable robe. Then he entrusted him to Sleep and his twin-brother Death for swift removal, and they quickly set him down in the broad and fertile realm of Lycia.

Meanwhile Patroclus, with a shout to Automedon and his horses, went in pursuit of the Trojans and Lycians. He was a fool and made a fatal error. Had he kept to his orders from Achilles, he would have saved himself from doom and the black night of Death. But the thoughts of Zeus outstrip the thoughts of men. In a moment, the god can make a brave man run away and lose a battle; and the next day he will spur him on to fight. And now he made Patroclus overbold.

Who was the first man, who the last, to fall to you, Patroclus, as the gods beckoned you to your death? Adrestus first, and Autonous and Echeclus; Perimus son of Megas, Epistor and Melanippus; and then Elasus and Mulius and Pylartes. All these Patroclus killed, though the rest of them had the sense to fly. So all-devouring was the vehemence of his spear that Troy of the High Gates would now have fallen to Patroclus and the Achaean arms, if Phoebus Apollo had not taken his stand on the well-built wall in his eagerness to help the Trojans and bring his exploits to an evil end. Three times Patroclus scaled an angle of the lofty wall, and thrice Apollo hurled him off, thrusting his bright shield with his immortal hands. But when he came on like a demon for the fourth time, the god checked him with a terrible shout. 'Back,' he cried, 'my lord Patroclus! The city of the lordly Trojans is not destined to be captured by your spear, nor even by Achilles, who is a far better man than you.' When he heard this, Patroclus fell a good way back to avoid the wrath of the Archergod Apollo.

Hector had pulled up his galloping horses at the Scaean Gate. There he debated whether to drive into the rout once more and fight, or to order all his men to withdraw into the town. He was still in two minds when Phoebus Apollo appeared beside him, borrowing the stalwart and upstanding form of Asius, an uncle of horse-taming Hector's – he was a brother of Hecabe, and a son of Dymas, who lived in Phrygia on the banks of the Sangarius. In this disguise, Apollo son of Zeus addressed him. 'Hector,' he asked, 'why have you stopped fighting and neglected your duty? I wish I were as much your better as you are mine! I would soon teach you to your sorrow that it does not pay to shirk a battle. Off with you now; and chase Patroclus with your splendid pair. You may catch him yet, with the goodwill of Apollo.'

The god went back into the battling crowd when he had spoken, and illustrious Hector told the doughty Cebriones to lash his horses into the fight. Apollo, merging with the throng, cast the Argives into confusion and gave the upper hand to Hector and the Trojans. But Hector left the rest of the Danaans alone, and killing none of them, drove his powerful horses straight at Patroclus. On his side, Patroclus leapt from his chariot to the ground with his spear in his left hand. With the other he picked up a jagged, sparkling stone – his hand just covered it – and standing in no awe of Hector threw it with all his force. He did not make an idle cast, for the sharp stone caught Hector's driver Cebriones, King Priam's bastard son, on the forehead, with the horses' reins in his hands. It shattered both his eyebrows, crushing in the bone; and his eyes fell out and rolled in the dust at his feet. He dropped from the well-built chariot like a diver and yielded up his life.

The knight Patroclus jeered at him: 'Ha! Quite an acrobat, I see, judging by that graceful dive! The man who takes so neat a header from a chariot on land could dive for oysters from a ship at sea in any weather and fetch up plenty for a feast. I did not know that the Trojans had such divers.' And he hurled himself at the noble Cebriones with the fury of a lion who has been wounded in the breast while assaulting the pens and falls a victim to his own audacity. Thus, Patroclus, did you fling yourself at Cebriones.

Hector had jumped down from the chariot on the other side, and the two fought for Cebriones like a couple of lions on the mountain heights, each as hungry and high-mettled as the other, disputing the dead body of a stag. Thus, with Cebriones between them, these two artificers of war, Patroclus and illustrious Hector, strove with the cruel bronze to tear each other's flesh.

Hector got hold of Cebriones' head, and never once let go; Patroclus, at his end, clung to a foot; and the rest of the Trojans and Danaans rushed in and made a scrimmage of it. There followed such a tussle as the East and South winds have with one another in a mountain glen, when they tumble the high woods, causing the long boughs of beech and ash and smooth-barked cornel-tree to jostle each other with a wild tattoo and the noise of snapping branches. Thus the Trojans and Achaeans leapt at one another and destroyed. There was no thought of craven flight on either side. The ground by Cebriones bristled with sharp spears and feathered arrows that had leapt from the bowstring; many a huge rock crashed on the shields of those that fought about him; and there he lay, in a whirl of dust, great even in his fall, thinking no more of a charioteer's delights.

So long as the Sun was still high in the sky, volley and counter-volley found their mark and men kept falling. But when he began to drop, towards the time when the plough-man unyokes his ox, the Achaeans cheated Fate and proved themselves the better men. They dragged the noble Cebriones from among the weapons and the yelling Trojans, and they stripped the armour from his back.

But Patroclus wished to do more execution yet and rushed among the enemy. Three times he charged with a terrific cry, like the wild god of War, and every time he killed nine men. But when he leapt in like a demon for the fourth time – alas Patroclus! – the end came into sight. In the heart of the battle Phoebus encountered him, Phoebus most terrible. Patroclus had not seen him coming through the rout: the god had wrapped himself in a thick mist for this unfriendly meeting. But Phoebus Apollo stood behind him now, and striking his broad shoulders and back with the flat of his hand, he made the eyes start from Patroclus' head and knocked off his vizored helmet. It rolled away with a clatter under the horses' hooves and its plume was smeared with blood and dust. The crested helmet that no man had ever been allowed to tumble in the dust when it protected the head and comely face of the divine Achilles fell into Hector's hands, and Zeus let him wear it for a little while, since his end was very near.

Not only that, but the long-shadowed spear, huge, thick and heavy with its head of bronze, was shattered in Patroclus' hands; the tasselled shield with its baldric fell from his shoulder to the ground; and King Apollo Son of Zeus undid the corslet on his breast. Patroclus was stunned; his shapely legs refused to carry him; and as he stood there in a daze, a Dardanian called Euphorbus came close behind and struck him with a sharp spear midway between the shoulders. This Euphorbus, one of Panthous' sons, was the best spearman, runner and horseman of his years, and in this very battle (the first he had fought in as a charioteer learning the art of war) he had brought twenty men from their chariots to the ground. He was the first, then, to let fly at the knight Patroclus. But he did not despatch him; and after pulling out the ashen spear from his flesh he ran back again and mingled with the crowd – he was not going to stay and fight Patroclus, naked though he was. And now, unmanned by the god's blow and Euphorbus' spear, Patroclus tried to escape his fate by slinking back among the friendly Myrmidons.

When Hector saw the great Patroclus creeping wounded from the field, he made his way towards him through the ranks, and coming up, he struck him with a spear in the lower part of the belly, driving the bronze clean through. Patroclus fell with a thud; and the whole Achaean army was appalled. It was like the conquest of an indomitable wild-boar by a lion, after a battle fought in high fury up in the mountains over a little stream at which both wish to drink. The lion's strength prevails and his panting enemy is overcome. So, after killing many men himself, Menoetius' valiant son fell to a short spear-cast from Hector son of Priam, who now addressed him as his conqueror. 'Patroclus,' he said, 'you thought you would sack my town, make Trojan women slaves, and ship them off to your own country. You were a fool. In their defence, Hector's fast horses were hasting into battle; and so was Hector himself, I, Hector, finest spearman of the war-loving Trojans, who stand between them and the day of slavery. So now the vultures here are going to eat you up. Poor wretch; even the strong arm of Achilles did not save you. I can imagine all he told you when he sent you out – and stayed behind. "Patroclus, Master of the Horse, don't let me see you back at the hollow ships, till you have torn the tunic on man-killing Hector's breast and soaked it with his blood." That is what he must have said; and like a lunatic you took him at his word.'

And what did the knight Patroclus say to this? 'Hector,' he replied in a failing voice, 'boast while you may. The victory is yours – a gift from Zeus the Son of Cronos and Apollo. *They* conquered me. It was an easy task: they took the armour from my back. If twenty Hectors had confronted me, they would all have fallen to my spear. No; it was hateful Destiny and Leto's Son that killed me. Then came a man, Euphorbus; you were only the third. But listen to this and ponder it well. You too, I swear it, have not long to live. Already sovran Destiny and Death are very close to you, death at the hands of Achilles the peerless son of Peleus.'

Death cut Patroclus short and his disembodied soul took wing for the House of Hades, bewailing its lot and the youth and manhood that it left. But illustrious Hector spoke to him again, dead though he was. 'Patroclus,' he said, 'why be so sure of an early end for me? Who knows? Achilles, son of Thetis of the Lovely Locks, may yet forestall me by ending *his* life with a blow from my spear.'

Hector put his foot on Patroclus to withdraw his bronze spear from the wound, and thrust at the corpse till it came off the spear and fell face upwards on the ground. Then with the same spear and without a pause, he went after Automedon, the noble squire of the swift son of Peleus. He was eager to catch him. But Automedon was carried out of harm's way by his swift immortal horses, the splendid gift that Peleus had received from Heaven.

XVII

THE STRUGGLE OVER PATROCLUS

MENELAUS son of Atreus, favourite of Ares, was quick to note that Patroclus had been vanquished by the Trojans. Resplendent in his bronze equipment he hastened through the front ranks and bestrode his body like a fretful mother-cow standing over the first calf she has brought into the world. Thus red-haired Menelaus stood over Patroclus and covered him with his spear and round buckler, ready to kill all comers. But Panthous' son, Euphorbus of the ashen spear, was interested also in the body of the peerless Patroclus. Coming close up to it, he said to the warlike Menelaus: 'My lord, King Menelaus son of Atreus; retire, and leave this dead man and his bloodstained arms. I was the first among the Trojans and their famous allies to hit Patroclus with a spear in this battle. Let me enjoy the credit for my victory in Troy, or I will cast at you and take your precious life.'

Red-haired Menelaus was furious with the man. 'Father Zeus,' he cried, 'have you ever seen such arrogance? We know the courage of the panther and the lion, and the fierce wild-boar, the most high-spirited and self-reliant beast of all; but that, it seems, is nothing to the prowess of these sons of Panthous with their famous ashen spears! Yet Hyperenor tamer of horses did not long survive to savour the delights of youth, when he had insulted and stood up to me. He said I was the most contemptible of the Danaan men-at-arms. But I seem to remember that it was not on his own feet that he went home to delight his loving wife and his fond parents. And I'll cut *your* coxcomb for you as I did for him, if you come up against me. Get back now, join the rabble, and don't stand up to me, or you will come to grief. It is the height of folly to be wise too late.'

But Euphorbus was not cowed. 'This very day, King Mene-
laus,' he retorted, 'you are going to pay the price for my
brother, whom you killed and boast about, and whose wife
you left a widow forlorn in her new bridal chamber. You
caused his parents untold tears and misery; yet I could still
console the unhappy pair if I brought back your head and
armour and put them in the hands of Panthous and the lady
Phrontis. But our business will not take long to settle. A quick
fight will decide the issue between life and death.'

With that, he struck Menelaus on his round shield. But the
bronze did not break through: the point was bent back by the
stout shield. Then Menelaus son of Atreus brought his spear
into play, with a prayer to Father Zeus. As Euphorbus fell
back, he struck him in the base of the throat, following up the
thrust with his own full weight and keeping his grip on the
spear. The point went clean through the soft flesh of the man's
neck. He came down with a thud, and his armour rang upon
him. His hair had been as lovely as the Graces' locks – he used
to bind the little curls with gold and silver twine. Now, all
was drenched with blood, and he lay there like a fallen
sapling. A gardener takes an olive shoot and plants it in a
place of its own where it can suck up plenty of moisture. It
grows into a fine young tree swayed by every breeze, and
bursts into white blossom. But a gusty wind blows up one
day, uproots it from its trench and stretches it on the earth.
Thus Panthous' son, Euphorbus of the ashen spear, lay pro-
strate, as his killer, Menelaus son of Atreus, stripped him of his
arms.

Not a single Trojan had the daring to come near the illus-
trious Menelaus. He was like a mountain lion who believes
in his own strength and pounces on the finest heifer in a
grazing herd. He breaks her neck with his powerful jaws, and
then he tears her to pieces and devours her blood and entrails,
while all round him the herdsmen and their dogs create a din
but keep their distance – they are heartily scared of him and
nothing would induce them to close in. So Atreides would
have found it easy to despoil Euphorbus, if Phoebus Apollo

had not grudged him the splendid arms and sent Hector to attack him like the rabid god of War. Apollo went to Hector in the disguise of a man called Mentes, a leader of the Cicones, and said: 'Hector, why have you set your heart on catching the horses of Achilles, which are so hard to master and difficult to drive, at any rate for a mere man or anyone but Peleus' son, whose Mother is a goddess? While you are chasing this will-o'-the-wisp, the redoubtable Menelaus is standing over Patroclus' body and has killed the best man in Troy. Euphorbus son of Panthous will never fight again.'

With that the god went back into the heart of the battle, and Hector's very soul was wrung by grief. But presently he peered across the ranks and sure enough he saw the pair of them, Menelaus removing the splendid arms, and Euphorbus lying on the ground with the blood pouring from his gaping wound. With a loud cry Hector set off down the front line, resplendent in his gleaming bronze, like the inextinguishable flames in the furnace of the Master-smith. Menelaus did not fail to recognize his war-cry. He was dismayed and took counsel with his indomitable soul. 'What shall I do?' he asked himself in his distress. 'If I abandon these fine arms and the body of Patroclus, who fell here fighting to exact repayment for my wrongs, I shall be an object of contempt to any Danaan who sees me. But if for honour's sake I fight with Hector and the Trojans single-handed, I am likely to be cut off and overwhelmed, for Hector of the bright helmet has all the Trojans at his heels. But why debate the point? When a man decides, without the goodwill of the gods, to fight another who enjoys their favour, he has disaster coming to him. Surely then, no Danaan will take it amiss when he sees me giving way to Hector, who fights with the gods at his back. And if only I knew where the great Aias could be found, the pair of us might go and make another stand, even with Heaven against us, and try to save the body for my lord Achilles, which would at all events be something gained.'

While he was still engaged in this inward debate, the Trojan

companies bore down upon him with Hector in their van.
Abandoning the corpse, Menelaus turned and retreated, but
with many a backward look, like a bearded lion who feels
the chill of fear in his stout heart when he is chased from the
fold with spears and shouts by the shepherds and their dogs,
and much against his will abandons the farmyard. Thus red-
haired Menelaus withdrew from Patroclus' body. But when
he reached his own company, he faced about and stood,
looking everywhere for the great Telamonian Aias. He saw
him presently, out on the left flank, exhorting and hounding
on his men, whom Phoebus Apollo had filled with super-
natural fears. Menelaus set off at a run and was soon at his side.
'Aias, my friend,' he said, 'come with me over there and let
us strike a blow for the dead Patroclus. We might at least
save the body for Achilles, naked though it is. But not the
armour – Hector has taken that.' The valiant Aias was stirred
by his appeal, and he and red-haired Menelaus set off together
through the front lines.

Hector was tugging at the body of Patroclus. He had
stripped him of his noble armour and now he wanted to
behead him with his sharp sword, drag off the trunk, and give
it to the dogs of Troy. But when Aias came up with his
tower-like shield, Hector slunk off, rejoined his company, and
leapt into his chariot. He gave the beautiful armour to some
Trojans to take into the city, where he hoped that the trophy
would redound to his honour. Meanwhile Aias covered Pat-
roclus with his broad shield and stood at bay, like a lion who is
confronted by huntsmen as he leads his cubs through the
forest, and plants himself in front of the helpless creatures,
breathing defiance and lowering his brows to veil his eyes.
Thus Aias planted himself by the lord Patroclus. On the other
side of him, Menelaus son of Atreus, favourite of Ares, took
his stand. And every moment added to his grief.

Glaucus son of Hippolochus, the leader of the Lycian
forces, was displeased with Hector. He gave him a black look
and took him to task. 'Hector,' he said, 'you make a fine show
on parade, but in battle you are useless. Your splendid reputa-

tion hides a coward after all. Ask yourself how you are going
to save the town and citadel with nobody to help you but the
native Trojans; for none of the Lycians will be going out to
fight the Danaans for Troy, now they have learnt that they
get no credit for struggling with the enemy day in, day out.
What hope has a man in the ranks of being rescued by you
in a tight corner, when you have callously left Sarpedon,
your guest and comrade-in-arms, like carrion in the Argives'
hands? You and your city owed much to him while he was
alive; yet you have not even had the pluck to save him from
the dogs. So now, if I have any influence with the Lycians, we
go home. And that will mean the end of Troy. Why, if the
Trojans had any real courage, the dauntless spirit that enters
into men who are defending their country and makes them
fight their enemies tooth and nail, we should soon drag Patro-
clus into Ilium. And if that man's body could be brought in
from the field and lodged in the great city of King Priam, the
Argives would at once return Sarpedon's splendid armour,
and we could bring *his* body into Ilium. It is a question of the
dead man's rank: Patroclus was squire to the greatest soldier
in the Argive camp, with the best companies in his command.
But you have failed us. You did not dare, with the enemy
war-cry ringing in your ears, to face the lion-hearted Aias, to
look him in the eye, and fight it out with him – because he is
the better man.'

Hector of the glittering helmet gave him an ugly look.
'Glaucus,' he said, 'I am amazed at such effrontery in a man
like you. I always took you for the wisest man in the whole of
deep-soiled Lycia; but you have destroyed my faith in your
judgment by talking like this and suggesting that I dared not
stand up to the gigantic Aias. Believe me, fighting and the
noise of chariots do not frighten me. But we are all puppets in
the hands of aegis-bearing Zeus. In a moment, Zeus can make
a brave man run away and lose a battle; and the next day the
same god will spur him on to fight. But bear with me now,
my friend; stand by my side and see what I can do; see
whether you are right and I shall prove a coward all day long,

or whether I can stop some of these Danaans, ferocious as they are, from fighting any longer for Patroclus' body.'

Then in a loud voice he gave an order to his troops. 'Trojans,' he cried, 'Lycians, and you Dardanians that fight hand to hand; be men, my friends, and put forth all your strength, while I equip myself in the armour of the peerless Achilles, the splendid armour that I took from the great Patroclus when I killed him.'

With that, Hector of the burnished helmet left the battle-field and ran after his men who were carrying the famous armour of the son of Peleus to the town. He soon caught them up, for they had not gone far, and he ran fast. Then he changed his equipment in a spot which the lamentable fighting had not reached, telling his war-loving Trojans to take his own arms to sacred Ilium, and putting on the imperishable armour of Achilles, which the gods of Heaven had given to Peleus, his father. Peleus, when he grew old, had passed it on to his son. But the son was not destined to grow old in his father's armour.

When Zeus the Cloud-compeller saw Hector from afar equipping himself in the arms of the divine Achilles, he shook his head and said to himself: 'Unhappy man! Little knowing how close you are to death, you are putting on the imperishable armour of a mighty man of war, before whom all others quail. And it was you that killed his comrade, the brave and lovable Patroclus, and stripped the armour from his head and shoulders with irreverent hands. Well, for the moment great power shall be yours. But you must pay for it. There will be no home-coming for you from the battle, and Andromache will never take the glorious armour of Achilles from your hands.' The Son of Cronos bowed his sable brows in confirmation of his thoughts, and caused the armour to sit easily on Hector.

The savage spirit of the dread War-god now entered into Hector's heart, and power and fresh vigour filled his limbs. Uttering his piercing war-cry he went in search of his renowned allies, and presented himself to all of them resplend-

ent in the armour of the lion-hearted Achilles. To rouse their
spirit he went up and spoke to each of them in turn: to
Mesthles and Glaucus; to Medon and Thersilochus; to Astero-
paeus, Deisenor and Hippothous; to Phorcys and Chromius
and Ennomus the augur. And he made a speech to incite them.
He said: 'Attend to me in your multitudes, my allies and
neighbours. I neither sought nor wanted numbers when I
summoned each of you here from your own cities. What I
needed was men who would fight the fierce Achaeans with a
good grace in defence of the women and little children of
Troy. It is for that end that I impoverish my own people,
who supply you all with free provisions, and so keep your
courage high. Straight then at the enemy, every one of you –
to live or die! That is the soldier's tryst. To the man who
forces Aias back and brings Patroclus, dead though he is, into
the Trojan lines, I will give half the spoils, keeping half for
myself, so that he will share the glory equally with me.'

In response to this, they lifted their spears and charged at
the Danaans with all their weight, filled with high hopes of
retrieving the body from Telamonian Aias. They were ill
advised: Aias was going to take many a life over Patroclus'
corpse. But for the moment he turned to Menelaus of the
loud war-cry and said: 'My friend, Menelaus nursling of
Zeus; I am beginning to think that you and I will never get
home safely from this fight, let alone the corpse. In fact I am
not so much concerned for Patroclus' body, which will soon
be glutting the Trojan dogs and birds, as I am about the
danger to myself and you, with Hector ready to engulf us
like a black cloud. Death is staring us in the face. Quick! Try a
call to the Danaan chieftains. Somebody might hear.'

Menelaus of the loud war-cry complied and gave the
Danaans a piercing call. 'Friends,' he cried, 'Captains and
Counsellors of the Argives; who drink your wine at the
public cost by the side of the Atreidae, Agamemnon and
Menelaus; who share in the high command and derive your
titles and your majesty from Zeus; it is impossible for me in
the wild confusion of this fight to pick out every chief. Come

forward, each of you, without being named. And think it infamy that the dogs of Ilium should have Patroclus for a toy.'

Aias the Runner, son of Oïleus, heard every word of this and was the first to come running up to Menelaus through the mêlée. He was followed by Idomeneus and Idomeneus' squire Meriones, that peer of the man-killing War-god. As for the rest that came behind to reinforce the Achaean line, where is the man who could remember all their names?

Led by Hector, the Trojans came on in a mass, with a roar like that of a great wave when it meets the current at the mouth of a heaven-fed river and the headlands on either side throw back the thunder of the invading sea. But united in their resolution the Achaeans faced them, making a fence of their bronze shields around Patroclus. Moreover, the Son of Cronos spread a thick mist about their burnished helmets. He had had no quarrel with Patroclus while he was alive and squire to Achilles, and he loathed the thought of his becoming carrion for the dogs of hostile Troy. So now he emboldened his comrades-in-arms to fight in his defence.

At first the Trojans flung back the bright-eyed Achaeans, who abandoned the corpse and gave ground before them. Even so, the haughty Trojans did not succeed in killing any of them with their spears, for all the pains they took. But the Trojans did start dragging off the corpse. However, the Achaeans were not going to leave it in their hands for long. They were soon rallied by Aias, who next to the peerless son of Peleus was the finest Danaan of all in looks and the noblest in action. He dashed through the front line, fierce as a wild-boar who turns at bay in the mountains and with one charge sends the hounds and stalwart huntsmen flying down the glades. Thus the proud Telamon's son, illustrious Aias, charged into the Trojan ranks, and scattered the party that had gathered round Patroclus and made up their minds that *they* were going to win the glory and drag his body into Troy.

Hippothous, the noble son of Pelasgian Lethus, had tied his baldric round the tendons of Patroclus' ankle and was hauling him by the foot through the battling throng. He hoped to do Hector and the Trojans a good turn. But he did himself a bad one, for he soon ran into trouble, and not all the goodwill of his friends could save him. Telamon's son rushed up to him through the crowd and struck him through his bronze-cheeked helmet. The plumed helmet, hit by the heavy spear and the great hand behind it, was rent open by the point, and the man's blood and brains came gushing through the vizor from his wound. Hippothous collapsed. He let the foot of the great Patroclus drop from his hand to the ground, and following it up, came down face forward on the corpse. He was a long way from deep-soiled Larissa when the spear of Aias cut him off. His life had been too short, and now he could never repay his parents for their care.

At this point Hector took a turn and hurled a glittering lance at Aias. But Aias was looking out and just avoided the bronze spear, which hit a man called Schedius, son of the valiant Iphitus and best of the Phocians, a powerful prince whose home was in the famous town of Panopeus. Hector struck him under the middle of the collar bone. The bronze spear-point went through and stuck out below his shoulder. He fell with a thud and his armour rang upon him. In his turn, Aias struck Phorcys, the doughty son of Phaenops, full in the belly, as he bestrode Hippothous, and broke the plate of his corslet. The spear-point let his bowels out, and falling in the dust he clutched at the ground. The Trojan front and glorious Hector himself fell back, while the Argives with triumphant cries dragged away the bodies of Phorcys and Hippothous and removed the armour from their shoulders.

Defeated and disheartened, the Trojans might now have been driven back into Ilium by the conquering Achaeans, who would thus, by their own valour and exertions, have won an even greater victory than Zeus had planned, if Apollo had not roused Aeneas. The god took the form of a herald, Periphas son of Epytus, who was kindly disposed to Aeneas, having served his old father as a herald till he himself was old. In this disguise, Apollo son of Zeus accosted him and said:

'Aeneas, if Heaven were indeed against you, how could you hope to save the citadel of Ilium? I have known men who saved their country notwithstanding Zeus, by relying on their own strong arms, their bravery and their numbers. But Zeus is on our side! He wishes us to beat the Danaans. And yet you are scared out of your senses and refuse to fight.'

Aeneas looked him in the face and knew him for the Archer-King Apollo. He gave Hector a great shout. 'Hector,' he cried, 'and all you Trojan and allied commanders; it is a shameful thing to let the conquering Argives drive us like cowards into Ilium. Besides, one of the gods came up to me just now and told me that Zeus the Supreme Counsellor is still our ally in this war. So let us go straight for the Danaans and see that they do not find it too easy to bring the dead Patroclus to their ships.'

With that he sallied out and took his stand well in front of the foremost fighters. As a result the Trojans turned about and faced the Achaeans. Then Aeneas cast his spear and struck Leiocritus son of Arisbas. This man was a gallant follower of Lycomedes, and the valiant Lycomedes was distressed to see him fall. He ran up, stood beside him, and let fly with his shining lance, which struck a chieftain, Apisaon son of Hippasus, in the liver under the midriff, bringing him forthwith to the ground. Apisaon was one of those that had come from fertile Paeonia. In fact he was their best soldier, next to Asteropaeus, peer of the War-god; and Asteropaeus, distressed at his fall, now made a fierce charge at the Danaans himself. But he was too late to accomplish any good. They had surrounded Patroclus with a fence of shields and levelled spears. The gigantic Aias had gone round and given strict orders to them all. No one was to back from the corpse, and no one to break away and fight in front. They were all to stick close to Patroclus and each other.

As a result of these tactics of Aias, the earth was empurpled with blood, and men fell in heaps, the Trojans and their haughty allies mingling their corpses with the Danaan dead. For the Danaans did not fight a bloodless battle either. And yet they lost far fewer men. They remembered their duty to each other, and in the hurly-burly friend saved friend from death.

So the battle raged like a fire, and you would not have thought that the sun and moon were still in commission, for a fog had spread over that part of the field where the pick of the men were disputing the body of Patroclus. Elsewhere, however, the Trojans and the Achaean men-at-arms were battling in comfort under a clear sky. There was brilliant sunshine over all, and not a cloud in sight above the plain or on the hills. The fighting was desultory; they kept their distance and avoided trouble from each other's spears. It was only in the centre that, what with the fog and the enemy and the crushing burden of their bronze armour, the best of the Achaeans were suffering distress. And there were two of them, the famous pair Thrasymedes and Antilochus, who did not even know that the peerless Patroclus had been killed. They thought he was still alive and fighting Trojans where the two lines met. So they stayed in their own part of the field, looking out for casualties or signs of panic in their own company, as Nestor had told them to do when he saw them off from the black ships to the battle.

But the grim struggle that had begun over the noble squire of swift Achilles continued unabated all day long, and all the while the knees, the shins, the feet, the very hands and eyes of the contending forces streamed with the sweat of their exertions. Tugging the body to and fro between them in that restricted space, they were like the men to whom a tanner gives the job of stretching a great bull's hide soaked in fat. They take the hide, stand round in a ring, and tug at it with many hands till it is taut in every part and the moisture comes out while the fat sinks in. Each party had high hopes, the Trojans of dragging Patroclus into Ilium, and the Achaeans of bringing him back to the hollow ships. The result was such a scrimmage over the corpse as would not have displeased even the warmonger Ares, or Athene, in their most pugnacious mood. Such was the toil and agony that Zeus dispensed that day to man and horse alike over the body of Patroclus.

Highborn Achilles had as yet no inkling of Patroclus' death. They were fighting a long way from the gallant ships, under the walls of Troy, and it never entered his head that Patroclus had been killed. He thought of him as pressing on to the very gates, but then returning safe and sound. For he certainly never expected him to sack the town without him, or with him either. He had often been told that this was not to be, by his own Mother, who used to give him private information of almighty Zeus's plans. Not that she told him now of the terrible thing that had happened and the loss of his dearest friend.

Over the dead man, meanwhile, those others with their pointed spears were locked in an unending struggle and killing one another. The bronze-clad Achaeans felt that it would be a disgrace to their name to fall back on the hollow ships. 'Friends,' they said among themselves, 'if we let the horse-taming Trojans drag this body off in triumph to their town, the best thing that could happen would be that the black earth should swallow us, here where we stand.' And on their side the gallant Trojans felt the same. 'Comrades,' said one of them, 'even if all of us are destined to be killed beside this corpse, let none retire.' That is how they felt and encouraged one another. So the fight continued, and the metallic din went up through the waste spaces of the air and struck the copper sky.

Far from the conflict, the horses of Achilles had been weeping ever since they learnt that their charioteer had been brought down in the dust by the murderous Hector. Auto-medon, Diores' stalwart son, did all he could with them: he lashed them repeatedly with his whistling whip, he coaxed them, and he cursed them freely; but the pair refused either to go back to the ships and the broad Hellespont or into the battle after the Achaeans. Firm as a gravestone planted on the barrow of a dead man or woman, they stood motionless in front of their beautiful chariot with their heads bowed to the earth. Hot tears ran from their eyes to the ground as they mourned for their lost driver, and their luxuriant manes were soiled as they came tumbling down from the yoke-pad on either side of the yoke. The Son of Cronos when he saw their grief was sorry for them. He shook his head and said to himself: 'Poor beasts! Why did we give you, who are ageless and immortal, to King Peleus, who is doomed to die? Did we mean you to share the sorrows of unhappy men? For of all creatures that breathe and creep about on Mother Earth there is none so miserable as man. One thing I *will* not have: Prince Hector shall not drive you and your splendid chariot. Are the arms and the brief exultation they have brought him not enough? No; I will fill your legs with vigour and your hearts with courage, so that you may at least save Automedon and bring him back from the battle to the hollow ships. For I mean the Trojans to recover and to smite the Argives till they reach the well-found ships and the sun sets and the blessed darkness intervenes.'

With that, Zeus breathed fresh power into the horses. They shook the dust from their manes and galloped off with their fast chariot to join the Trojans and Achaeans. Behind them, Automedon took the fighter's place, though he missed his comrade sorely, and swept into the battle with his chariot like a vulture after geese. His horses' speed made it easy for him to avoid entanglements in the fray, and as easy to dash into it and pursue an enemy through the crowd. But he could not kill the men he chased. Alone as he was in the sacred chariot, he found it impossible to control the fast horses and at the same time bring a spear into play. At last, however, a friend in his own company, Alcimedon son of Laerces and grandson of Haemon, saw the difficulties he was in, and coming up behind the chariot said to him: 'Automedon, which of the gods has robbed you of your wits and put this silly notion in your head? What sense is there in taking on the front-line Trojans single-handed? Do you not know that your fighter has been killed and that Hector himself is swaggering about in the armour of Achilles?'

'Alcimedon,' replied Automedon son of Diores, 'there was nobody like you at taming and managing these immortal horses, except Patroclus, while he lived; and he had learnt the master-touch from Heaven. But now he is dead and gone. So take the whip and the polished reins yourself, while I get down and fight.' With that, Automedon dismounted, while Alcimedon leapt into the fast war-chariot and seized the whip and reins.

They were observed by illustrious Hector. He turned to Aeneas, who happened to be near, and said: 'Aeneas, Counsellor of the bronze-clad Trojans, I see the horses of my lord Achilles coming into battle with a feeble pair of charioteers. I think we could capture them, if you would care to join me. Those two would never stand and fight if you and I attacked them.'

The brave son of Anchises was not unwilling; so the two men went forward, protecting their shoulders with their shields of tanned and toughened oxhide overlaid with bronze. Chromius and the godlike Aretus both went with them, and they had high hopes of killing the men and driving off their high-necked horses. They deluded themselves: they were not going to disengage from Automedon without the shedding of some blood.

Meanwhile Automedon had prayed to Father Zeus, and there was no room for weakness or fear in his impassioned heart. He swung round to Alcimedon, his trusted friend, and said: 'Alcimedon, keep near me with the horses; let me feel their breath on my back. I am afraid that, if he is not killed in the front line himself, there won't be any holding Hector in his fury till he has killed us both, jumped up behind the long-maned horses of Achilles and put the Argive ranks to flight.'

Then he called to the Aiantes and Menelaus: 'You two Aiantes, Commanders of the Argives, and you, Menelaus; come to our help and leave the best men you can find to bestride the corpse and hold the enemy. We are alive and in mortal peril, here in the thick of this appalling fight, with Hector and Aeneas, the best of the Trojans, bearing down on us full tilt. Meanwhile, and since one never knows one's luck, I am going to try a cast myself and leave the rest to Zeus.'

As he spoke, he swung up his long-shadowed spear and hurled it. The bronze point struck the round shield of Aretus, which failed to stop it. Piercing the shield, it pressed on through the belt into his abdomen, and he sprang forward and fell down on his back, as a farmyard ox leaps up and then collapses when a strong man with a keen axe strikes it behind the horns and cuts through the sinews. The sharp spear quivered in his guts and he was dead.

Hector then cast at Automedon with his glittering lance. But Automedon was looking out and avoided the bronze weapon by leaning forward. The long shaft came to earth behind him and stuck there with the butt-end trembling till the War-god stilled it with his heavy hand. And now they would have been at one another's throats with their swords, if the two Aiantes, who had come up through the press in answer to their comrade's call, had not parted them in their fury. Frightened of such a pair, Hector, Aeneas and the noble Chromius drew back, leaving the stricken Aretus to lie where he fell. Automedon, leaping in like Ares, stripped him of his arms, and gave vent to his satisfaction. 'That,' he said, 'consoles me somewhat for my lord Patroclus' death, though he was a better man than the one I have killed.' Then he lifted the bloodstained armour into his chariot and mounted it himself, with bloody feet and hands, like a lion that has eaten a bull.

Once more the struggle raged around Patroclus, and this time it was fierce and grim indeed, for it was sponsored by Athene. She came down from heaven to rouse the Danaans at the instance of all-seeing Zeus, who had changed his mind. Wrapping herself in a lurid mist, like a sombre rainbow hung in the sky by Zeus to warn mankind of war or the coming of a cold squall that stops work in the fields and brings discomfort to the sheep, she dropped among the Achaean soldiery and put fresh heart in one and all. The stalwart Menelaus son of Atreus, who happened to be nearest, was the first man that Athene accosted and exhorted. Borrowing the shape and tireless voice of Phoenix, she said: 'It is you, Menelaus, who will bear the blame and the disgrace, if nimble dogs are allowed to maul the friend of proud Achilles under the walls of Troy. Hold on then, relentlessly, and make all your people fight.'

'Phoenix, my venerable lord and ancient friend,' said Menelaus of the loud war-cry, 'I only wish Athene would give me strength and keep the missiles off. Then I should gladly take a hand and fight for Patroclus, whose death has touched my very heart. But Hector's fury burns like a flame, and his bronze is all-destroying. Zeus wishes him to win.'

Athene of the Flashing Eyes was delighted to note that Menelaus had prayed to her before all other gods. She strengthened his shoulders and his knees and implanted in his breast the daring of a fly, which is so fond of human blood that it returns to the attack however often a man may brush it from his face. Filled by the goddess to the very core with such dauntlessness as that, he took his stand beside the body of Patroclus and cast his glittering spear.

There was a Trojan called Podes son of Eëtion. He was a man of wealth and breeding, and Hector's favourite among the Trojan people – they had become friends over the wine-cups. This man was struck on the belt by red-haired Menelaus' spear as he started to run away. The spear went right through him; he fell with a crash; and Menelaus son of Atreus dragged his body from among the Trojans and gave it to his men.

But now Apollo brought Hector into the affair. He went up to him disguised as Phaenops son of Asius, who came from Abydus and was Hector's favourite among his foreign guests. 'Hector,' he said to him, 'what Achaean will ever fear you again, if you let yourself be scared by Menelaus, who has never been much of a fighter, though he did come into our lines just now and drag a dead man out alone. It was your good friend Podes son of Eëtion, one of our best men, that he killed.'

The news was like a mortal wound to Hector, but none the less he set off through the front line resplendent in his arms of bronze. And at this moment the Son of Cronos, who had hidden Ida under clouds, discharged a lightning flash with a great clap of thunder, and taking up his glittering tasselled aegis, shook it out, gave victory to the Trojans and filled the Achaeans with panic.

Peneleos the Boeotian was the first of them to turn tail. He had been steadily facing the enemy, when a spear from Polydamas, who had come up and cast at short range, struck him on the top of the shoulder. It was a glancing blow, but the spear-point grazed the bone. Then Hector, also at close quarters, wounded Leitus son of the great-hearted Alectryon in the wrist and put him out of action. Leitus, knowing that he could no longer handle a spear against the enemy, gave one look round and took to his heels. As Hector went in chase of him, Idomeneus son of Deucalion hit him on the cuirass by the nipple on his breast. But the long spear broke at the socket, and the Trojans gave a yell. Hector retaliated with a cast at Idomeneus, who by now had mounted a chariot. He missed him by a little, but he struck Coeranus, the squire and driver of Meriones, who had come with him to the war from the city of Lyctus. As Idomeneus had set out that day from the trim ships on foot, he would have presented the enemy with a triumph if this man Coeranus had not galloped to the rescue with his fast horses. He was a godsend to Idomeneus and saved his life; but he lost his own to Hector killer of men, whose spear-head, striking him under the jaw and ear, knocked all his teeth out and cut his tongue in half. Coeranus tumbled out of the chariot, dropping the reins on the earth. Meriones stooped down, picked them up from the ground with his own hands, and said to Idomeneus: 'Lay on now, till you reach the ships. You don't need me to tell you we have lost the day.' Idomeneus lashed the long-maned horses and drove off to the hollow ships. He was a frightened man.

Menelaus and the lion-hearted Aias were also well aware that Zeus had thrown in his powers to make a Trojan victory. The great Telamonian Aias turned with an exclamation of disgust to Menelaus. 'Any fool,' he said, 'can see that Father Zeus himself is helping the Trojans. Every spear they cast goes home. Whether it comes from a bungler's or a marksman's hand, Zeus sees it to its target, while ours fall gently to the ground and do no harm at all. Well, we must contrive without him, and see how we can manage both to bring the corpse away and please our friends behind by getting safely back to them ourselves. They must be watching us in some anxiety and wondering whether anything can stop the invincible Hector in his murderous rage from swooping down on our black ships. If only one of our men could run with a message to Achilles – I don't believe he has even heard the dreadful news of his friend's death. But I cannot see the man for the task: men and horses are all lost in fog. Ah Father Zeus, save us from this fog and give us a clear sky, so that we can use our eyes. Kill us in daylight, if you must.'

Moved by this tearful protest, the Father quickly cleared away the darkness and dispersed the fog. The sun shone out on them, bringing the whole field into view; and Aias said to Menelaus of the loud war-cry: 'Now look, King Menelaus, and see whether you can find Antilochus, my lord Nestor's son. If he is still alive, tell him to run quickly to the great Achilles with the news that his best friend is dead.'

Menelaus of the loud war-cry did not refuse, but he went unwillingly. He was like a lion retreating from a farmyard when he is tired of pitting himself against the dogs and men, who have stayed awake all night to save the fattest of their heifers from his maw. In his hunger for meat, he has charged them, but without success. Showers of darts and burning faggots hurled by strong hands have scared him away, for all his eagerness; and at dawn he slinks off disappointed. Thus Menelaus of the loud war-cry retired from the body of Patroclus. He did not wish to go at all, for he was much afraid that the Achaeans in an access of panic might make the enemy a gift of it. However, he did his best to put the men he left behind him on their mettle. 'You two Aiantes, Commanders of the Argives, and you, Meriones,' he said; 'now is the time to remember how lovable a man Patroclus was. To every one of us he was the soul of kindness while he·lived. Now, Death and Destiny have claimed him.'

With that, red-haired Menelaus went off, peering all round him like an eagle, who is said to have the sharpest sight of any bird in the air, and who is not deceived, high though he is, by the swift hare crouching under a leafy bush, but swoops down, seizes him, and takes his life. So, royal Menelaus, did your brilliant eyes range everywhere among your many men, to see whether Nestor's son Antilochus was still alive.

Red-haired Menelaus quickly spied his man, on the far left of the battle, encouraging his troops and driving them to fight. He went near and called him. 'Prince Antilochus,' he cried, 'come here and let me tell you of a terrible thing, which I wish to God had never happened. You must have seen for yourself that Heaven has sent disaster to the Danaan arms, and success to the Trojans. And now Patroclus, our best man, has been killed – a blow that every Danaan will feel. Will you run at once to the ships, tell Achilles, and ask him to make haste to bring the body safely to his ship? There is nothing left upon it. Hector of the bright helmet has the arms.'

Antilochus was horrified when he heard this. For a while he was unable to speak; his eyes filled with tears; the words stuck in his throat. But he took note, none the less, of Menelaus' commands, and set off at a run, after handing his armour to his worthy squire, Laodocus, who had been driving his horses to and fro beside him. And as he left the field hotfoot with the evil news for Achilles son of Peleus, Antilochus wept.

For his part, King Menelaus was not disposed to stay and help the weary Pylians whom Antilochus had left, though they missed their leader sorely. Instead, he put the noble Thrasymedes in command, and himself returned to his post beside the lord Patroclus. Rejoining the two Aiantes at a run, he reported immediately: 'I have sent our man to the good ships with a message for Achilles. But I dare not hope that he will come at once, however angry he may be with Hector – he could not fight the Trojans naked. We must do our best without him and see how we can manage both to bring the corpse away and save our own lives from these yelling Trojans.'

To this the great Telamonian Aias replied: 'You are quite right, my noble lord Menelaus. Will you and Meriones put your arms under the body and carry it out of this turmoil as fast as you can, while the pair of us stay and keep Prince Hector and the Trojans engaged? Aias and I have the same name and the same spirit. This is not the first time we have fought in a tight corner side by side.'

The two men raised Patroclus from the ground and with a powerful effort hoisted him above their heads. The pursuing Trojans gave a shout when they saw the Achaeans carrying off the corpse, and charged like the hounds that launch themselves at a wounded boar in front of the young huntsmen, and race along for a while as if they meant to tear him to bits, only to recoil and bolt in all directions when the boar takes the offensive and runs amuck within the pack. Thus for a time the Trojans followed up in a mass, smiting with their swords and double-pointed spears. But when the two Aiantes turned about and planted themselves in the way, their colour changed and none of them had the heart to dash in and dispute the corpse.

So Menelaus and Meriones laboured to retrieve Patroclus' body from the field and bring it to the hollow ships, with the battle raging round them, fierce as a fire that in a moment blazes up, falls on a town and consumes the houses in a mighty conflagration. As the roaring wind beats on the flames, so did the ceaseless din from fighting men and horses beat upon them as they went. They struggled along with their burden like mules who put out all their strength to drag a log or some huge timber for a ship down from the mountains by a rocky track, tugging away till they nearly break their hearts, what with the labour and the sweat. Behind them, the two Aiantes held the enemy, as a wooded ridge that stretches out across the countryside holds back the floods, and even when the big rivers come down in spate, confronts their torrents unimpaired and diverts the deluge onto lower ground. Thus all

the time the two Aiantes fended off the Trojans who attacked
the rear. But they were hard beset, and by two men in par-
ticular, Aeneas son of Anchises and the illustrious Hector. As
a flock of starlings or jackdaws take wing and cry out in alarm
when they see that a falcon, who is death to little birds, is after
them, the Achaean warriors with cries of terror fled before
Aeneas and Hector, losing all stomach for the fight; and many
a fine weapon was dropped at the trench and round about it
by the fleeing Danaans, who were given no respite from
attack.

XVIII

ARMOUR FOR ACHILLES

So the fight went on, like an inextinguishable fire. Meanwhile Antilochus ran hotfoot to Achilles with his news and found him in front of his beaked ships. Achilles had had a presentiment of what had happened, and was communing, in his anguish, with that great heart of his. 'Why,' he asked himself with a groan, 'are the long-haired Achaeans bolting once more across the plain and flocking to the ships? Heaven forfend that I should have to suffer what my heart forebodes – my Mother's prophecy. She told me once that while I was still alive the best of the Myrmidons would fall to the Trojans and leave the light of day. And now I am sure that Menoetius' gallant son is dead. Foolhardy man! Did I not order him to come back here when he had saved the ships from fire, and not to fight it out with Hector?'

While these thoughts were chasing through his mind, King Nestor's son halted before him with the hot tears pouring down his cheeks and gave him the lamentable news: 'Alas, my royal lord Achilles! I have a dreadful thing to tell you – I would to God it were not true. Patroclus has been killed. They are fighting round his naked corpse and Hector of the flashing helmet has your arms.'

When Achilles heard this he sank into the black depths of despair. He picked up the dark dust in both his hands and poured it on his head. He soiled his comely face with it, and filthy ashes settled on his scented tunic. He cast himself down on the earth and lay there like a fallen giant, fouling his hair and tearing it out with his own hands. The maidservants whom he and Patroclus had captured caught the alarm and all ran screaming out of doors. They beat their breasts with their hands and sank to the ground beside their royal master.

On the other side, Antilochus shedding tears of misery held the hands of Achilles as he sobbed out his noble heart, for fear that he might take a knife and cut his throat.

Suddenly Achilles gave a loud and dreadful cry, and his lady Mother heard him where she sat in the depths of the sea beside her ancient Father. Then she herself took up the cry of grief, and there gathered round her every goddess, every Nereid that was in the deep salt sea. Glauce was there and Thaleia and Cymodoce; Nesaea, Speio, Thoe and ox-eyed Halie; Cymothoe, Actaee, and Limnoreia; Melite, Iaera, Amphithoe and Agaue; Doto, Proto, Pherusa and Dynamene; Dexamene, Amphinome and Callianeira; Doris, Panope and far-sung Galatea; Nemertes, Apseudes and Callianassa. Clymene came too, with Ianeira, Ianassa, Maera, Oreithuia, Amatheia of the Lovely Locks, and other Nereids of the salt sea depths. The silvery cave was full of nymphs. With one accord they beat their breasts, and Thetis led them in their lamentations: 'Attend to me, my sister Nereids: I wish every one of you to know all the sorrows of my heart. Ah misery me, the unhappy mother of the best of men! I brought into the world a flawless child to be a mighty hero and eclipse his peers. I nursed him as one tends a little plant in a garden bed, and he shot up like a sapling. I sent him to Ilium with his beaked ships to fight against the Trojans; and never again now shall I welcome him to Peleus' house. And yet he has to suffer, every day he lives and sees the sun; and I can do no good by going to his side. But I *will* go, none the less, to see my darling child and hear what grief has come to him, although he has abstained from fighting.'

With that she left the cave. The rest went with her, weeping, and on either side of them the surging sea fell back. When they reached the deep-soiled land of Troy, they came up one by one onto the beach, where the Myrmidon ships were clustered round the swift Achilles. His lady Mother went up to him as he lay groaning there, and with a piercing cry took her son's head in her hands and spoke to him in her compassion. 'My child,' she asked him, 'why these tears? What is

it that has grieved you? Tell me and do not keep your sorrow
to yourself. Some part, at any rate, of what you prayed for
when you lifted up your hands to Zeus has been fulfilled by
him. The Achaeans have been penned in at the ships for want
of you, and have suffered horribly.'

Achilles of the nimble feet gave a great sigh. 'Mother,' he
said, 'it is true that the Olympian has done that much in my
behalf. But what satisfaction can I get from that, now that my
dearest friend is dead, Patroclus, who was more to me than
any other of my men, whom I loved as much as my own life?
I have lost Patroclus. And Hector, who killed him, has strip-
ped him of my splendid armour, the huge and wonderful
arms that the gods gave Peleus as a wedding-present on the
day when they married you off to a mortal man. Ah, how I
wish that you had stayed there with the deathless salt-sea
Nymphs and that Peleus had taken home a mortal wife! But
you became my mother; and now, to multiply *your* sorrows
too, you are going to lose your son and never welcome him
at home again. For I have no wish to live and linger in the
world of men, unless, before all else, Hector is felled by my
spear and dies, paying the price for slaughtering Menoetius'
son.'

Thetis wept. She said: 'If that is so, my child, you surely
have not long to live; for after Hector's death you are doomed
forthwith to die.'

'Then *let* me die forthwith,' Achilles said with passion,
'since I have failed to save my friend from death. He has
fallen, far from his motherland, wanting my help in his ex-
tremity. So now, since I shall never see my home again, since
I have proved a broken reed to Patroclus and all my other
comrades whom Prince Hector killed, and have sat here by
my ships, an idle burden on the earth, I, the best man in all
the Achaean force, the best in battle, defeated only in the war
of words ... Ah, how I wish that discord could be banished
from the world of gods and men, and with it anger, insidious
as trickling honey, anger that makes the wisest man flare up
and spreads like smoke through his whole being, anger such

as King Agamemnon roused in me that day! However, what
is done is better left alone, though we resent it still, and we
must curb our hearts perforce. I will go now and seek out
Hector, the destroyer of my dearest friend. As for my death,
when Zeus and the other deathless gods appoint it, let it come.
Even the mighty Heracles did not escape his doom, dear as he
was to Zeus the Royal Son of Cronos, but was laid low by
Fate and Here's bitter enmity. And I too shall lie low when I
am dead, if the same lot awaits me. But for the moment,
glory is my aim. I will make these Trojan women and deep-
bosomed daughters of Dardanus wipe the tears from their
tender cheeks with both their hands as they raise the dirge, to
teach them just how long I have been absent from the war.
And you, Mother, as you love me, do not try to keep me from
the field. You will never hold me now.'

   'Indeed, my child,' said Thetis of the Silver Feet, 'it could
not be an evil thing for you to rescue your exhausted comrades
from destruction. But your beautiful burnished armour is in
Trojan hands. Hector of the flashing helmet is swaggering
about in it himself – not that he will enjoy it long, for he is
very near to death. So do not think of throwing yourself into
the fight before you see me here again. I will come back at
sunrise to-morrow with a splendid set of armour from the
Lord Hephaestus.'

   With that, she turned away from her son and spoke to her
sister Nereids. She told them to withdraw into the broad
bosom of the deep and make their way to the Old Man of the
Sea, returning to her Father's house. 'Tell him everything,'
she said. 'I myself am going to high Olympus to ask the
Master-smith Hephaestus whether he would like to give my
son a splendid set of glittering arms.'

   The Nymphs now disappeared from view into the heaving
waters of the sea, and the divine Thetis of the Silver Feet set
out for Olympus to procure a glorious set of armour for her
son.

   While she was on her journey to Olympus, the Achaean
men-at-arms, fleeing with cries of terror from man-killing

Hector, reached the ships and the Hellespont. It was more
than they could do to drag the body of Achilles' squire
Patroclus out of range. Once more it was overtaken by the
Trojan infantry and horse, and Hector son of Priam, raging
like a fire. Three times illustrious Hector, coming up behind
and shouting for his men's support, seized its feet and tried to
drag it back; and thrice the two Aiantes flung him from the
corpse, fighting like men possessed. But Hector's resolution
was unshaken. When he was not hurling himself into the
press, he stood his ground, calling aloud to his men, and he
never once fell back. The bronze-clad Aiantes could no more
scare Prince Hector from the corpse than the shepherds in the
fields can chase a famished lion off his kill. In fact Hector would
have hauled it away and covered himself with glory, if Iris
of the Whirlwind Feet had not come down in hot haste from
Olympus to tell Achilles to prepare for battle. (She was sent
by Here; Zeus and the other gods were not consulted.) Pre-
senting herself to Achilles she delivered her message. 'Up,
my lord Achilles, most redoubtable of men. Rise and defend
Patroclus, for whom they are fighting tooth and nail and men
are killing men beside the ships, the Achaeans in their efforts
to protect his corpse, and the Trojans in the hope of hauling it
away to windy Ilium. Prince Hector above all has set his heart
on dragging off Patroclus. He wants to cut his head off from
his tender neck and stick it on the palisade. So up with you,
and lie no longer idle. The very thought that Patroclus may
become a plaything for the dogs of Ilium should appal you.
It is you who will be put to shame if the body comes into your
hands defiled.'

The admirable swift Achilles replied with a question.
'Lady Iris, may I ask what god it was that sent you to me with
this message?'

'It was Here, worshipful Consort of Zeus, that sent me,' said
fleet Iris of the Whirlwind Feet. 'The Sublime Son of Cronos
was not told, nor was any other of the gods that live on
snowy Olympus.'

'But how can I go into action?' said the great runner

Achilles. 'My armour is in enemy hands, and my own Mother forbade me to dress for battle till I should see her here once more – she undertook to bring me a splendid set from Hephaestus. I know of no one else whose armour I could wear – except maybe the shield of Telamonian Aias. And he, I expect, is in his place in the front line, battling with his spear for the dead Patroclus.'

'We gods,' said wind-swift Iris, 'are well aware that your glorious armour has been taken. Nevertheless, go to the trench as you are and present yourself to the Trojans. They may be scared of you and break off the battle, giving the tired Achaeans time to breathe. Every little respite is valuable in war.'

Fleet-foot Iris took her leave, and Achilles favourite of Zeus leapt up. Athene cast her tasselled aegis round his sturdy shoulders; and the great goddess also shed a golden mist around his head and caused his body to emit a blaze of light. Thus, from some far-away beleaguered island, where all day long the men have fought a desperate battle from their city walls, the smoke goes up to heaven; but no sooner has the sun gone down than the light from the line of beacons blazes up and shoots into the sky to warn the neighbouring islanders and bring them to the rescue in their ships. Such was the blaze that made its way to heaven from Achilles' head.

He went beyond the wall and took his stand by the trench; but remembering his Mother's strict injunction, he did not join the Achaean soldiery. There he stood and cried aloud, while in the distance Pallas Athene raised the war-cry too. The Trojans were utterly confounded. Achilles' cry was as piercing as the trumpet call that rings out when a city is beset by murderous enemies; and their hearts all turned to water when they heard that brazen voice. Even the long-maned horses felt something evil in the wind and began to pull their chariots round. And their charioteers were dumbfounded as they saw the fire, fed by Athene of the Bright Eyes, blaze with a fierce and steady glare from the head of the lion-hearted son of Peleus. Thrice the great Achilles sent his voice ringing over the trench, and thrice the Trojans and their famous allies were thrown into chaos. A dozen of their best men perished there and then, by their own chariots, on Trojan spears.

Meanwhile, with thankful hearts, the Achaeans drew Patroclus out of range. They laid him on a stretcher and his own men gathered round him in a weeping throng. Achilles the great runner joined them, and the hot tears ran down his cheeks when he saw his faithful friend lying on the stretcher mangled by the cruel bronze. He had sent him into battle with his chariot and horses, never again to welcome his return.

Here, the ox-eyed Queen of Heaven, now told the tireless Sun to sink into the Stream of Ocean. The Sun had been disposed to linger, but at last he set, and the brave Achaeans enjoyed a respite from the grim struggle and the give-and-take of war. The Trojans, on their side, withdrew from contact with the enemy, unyoked the horses from their chariots, and before thinking of supper, gathered together for debate. Nobody dared sit down and they held the meeting on their feet, since all of them had been appalled by Achilles' reappearance after his long absence from the front. The discussion was begun by the wise Polydamas son of Panthous, the only man among them who could look into the future as into the past. He was a comrade of Hector's – they were born on the same night – and as brilliant in debate as Hector in a battle. He was much concerned for the safety of his fellow-countrymen, and this is what he said: 'Think carefully, my friends. It is my opinion that, at this distance from the walls, we ought to withdraw into the city now and not wait for daylight here in the open by the ships. So long as Achilles was at loggerheads with King Agamemnon, the Achaeans were easier to deal with, and I myself enjoyed the night we spent beside the fleet and the hopes we entertained of capturing their rolling ships. But now I am terrified of the man. That fiery spirit will never be content to stay in the plain, where we and the Achaeans used to meet each other halfway out on equal terms, but will make our town itself and our womenfolk his target. So let me persuade you to retire on Troy. Otherwise, I know what will happen. For the moment, the blessed night has checked the swift Achilles. But if to-morrow he should sally out with all his arms and catch us here, well, you will not find him hard to recognize. The man who gets away from him and reaches sacred Ilium may thank his stars; for the dogs and vultures will have their fill – of *Trojan* flesh I say; Heaven falsify my words! But if you follow my advice, distasteful as it is, we will husband our strength by bivouacking in the market-place, while the city will be safely guarded by its walls and lofty gates, sealed by the high wooden doors that we have hung upon them. At daybreak, fully armed, we will take our posts along the battlements; and if Achilles likes to sally from the ships and meet us at the walls, so much the worse for him. When he has tired his horses out by trotting to and fro below the walls, he will have to drive them home again. He will not have the nerve to force his way inside. He will never sack the town. Before that can happen, he will be eaten by the nimble dogs.'

But these ideas were frowned upon by Hector of the glittering helmet. 'Polydamas,' he said, 'the man who tells us to retire and shut ourselves up in the town sees eye to eye with me no longer. Are you not sick of being caged inside those walls? I know there was a time when the opulence, the gold and bronze, of Priam's city was the talk of all the world. But that has passed. Our houses have been emptied of their works of art; most of our treasures have been sold to Phrygia and to lovely Maeonia – we had incurred the wrath of Zeus. Yet at the very moment when that mighty god has let me have a victory at the ships and drive the Achaeans back against the sea, you, like a fool, advise us to defend the town. I forbid you to put such notions in the people's heads. Not that a single Trojan will follow your lead – I should not let him.

'Listen, all of you, to me instead. Let the whole army have supper now in its several messes, not forgetting to mount guard and the need for every man to keep alert. Meanwhile I advise any Trojan who is worried overmuch about his property to collect it and hand it over to the state for public use –

it would be better for the people to enjoy it than the Achaeans. Then, at peep of dawn, we will arm, and attack them fiercely at the hollow ships. And what if the great Achilles *has* decided to bestir himself and leave his camp? As you have said, so much the worse for him, if that is what he does. *I* am not going to shirk a fight and run away from him. I will meet him face to face and we shall see who wins the victory. The War-god has no favourites: he has been known to kill the man who thought that *he* was going to do the killing.'

Hector finished his speech and the Trojans in their folly shouted approval. Pallas Athene had destroyed their judgment. Polydamas, whose strategy was sound, had not received a single vote; but they applauded Hector and his bad advice. And now the whole army settled down for supper.

All night long the Achaeans wept and wailed for Patroclus. The son of Peleus was their leader in the melancholy dirge. He laid his man-killing hands on his comrade's breast and uttered piteous groans, like a bearded lion when a huntsman has stolen his cubs from a thicket and he comes back too late, discovers his loss and follows the man's trail through glade after glade, hoping in his misery to track him down. Thus Achilles groaned among his Myrmidons. He thought with a pang of the idle words he had let fall one day at home in his attempts to reassure Patroclus' noble father. 'I told Menoetius,' he said, 'that I would bring him back his son to Opus from the sack of Ilium, covered with glory and laden with his share of plunder. But Zeus makes havoc of the schemes of men; and now the pair of us are doomed to redden with our blood one patch of earth, here in the land of Troy. For I shall never see my home again, nor be welcomed there by Peleus the old charioteer and my Mother Thetis, but shall be swallowed by the earth I stand on. So then, Patroclus, since I too am going below, but after you, I shall not hold your funeral till I have brought back here the armour and the head of Hector, who slaughtered you, my noble-hearted friend. And at your pyre I will cut the throats of a dozen of the highborn youths of Troy, to vent my wrath on them for killing you. Till then, you shall lie as you are by my beaked ships, wailed and wept for day and night by the Trojan women and the deep-bosomed daughters of Dardanus whom we captured after much toil, with our own hands and our long spears, when we sacked rich cities full of men.'

Prince Achilles then told his followers to put a big three-legged cauldron on the fire and make haste to wash the clotted gore from Patroclus' body. They put a large cauldron on the glowing fire, filled it with water, and brought faggots, which they kindled beneath it. The flames began to lick the belly of the cauldron and the water grew warm. When it came to the boil in the burnished copper, they washed the corpse, anointed it with olive oil and filled the wounds with an unguent nine years old. Then they laid it on a bier and covered it from head to foot with a soft sheet, over which they spread a white cloak. And for the rest of the night the Myrmidons with the great runner Achilles wept and wailed for Patroclus.

Zeus, watching with his Wife and Sister Here, turned to her and said: 'So you have had your way once more, my ox-eyed Queen, and roused the swift Achilles. Anyone might think that the long-haired Achaeans were children of your own.' To which Here the ox-eyed Queen replied: 'Dread Son of Cronos, how have I offended? Even a man, a mortal not equipped with such wisdom as ours, takes action for his friends. How then could I, who claim to be the Queen of Heaven, both by right of birth and because I am your acknowledged Consort and you are King of all the gods – how could I possibly refrain from making trouble for my enemies in Troy?'

While these two were talking to each other, Thetis of the Silver Feet made her way to the palace of Hephaestus, which the god of the Crooked Foot had built, with his own hands, of imperishable bronze. It shines like a star and stands out among the houses of the gods. She found Hephaestus hard at work and sweating as he bustled about at the bellows in his forge. He was making a set of twenty three-legged tables to stand round the walls of his well-built hall. He had fitted

golden wheels to all their legs so that they could run by them-
selves to a meeting of the gods and amaze the company by
running home again. They were not quite finished. He had
still to put on the ornamental handles, and was fitting these
and cutting the rivets.

Hephaestus was engaged upon this task, which called for
all his skill, when Thetis, goddess of the Silver Feet, arrived.
Charis, the illustrious lame god's wife, beautiful in her shim-
mering headdress, came out of the house and saw her. She
took her hand in hers and said: 'Thetis of the Long Robe!
What brings you to our house? You are an honoured and a
welcome guest, though in the past your visits have been few.
But follow me indoors and let me offer you refreshment.'

With that, the gracious goddess led her in and seated her in
a beautiful chair with silver decorations and a footstool under-
neath. Then she called to the Master-smith: 'Hephaestus!
Come in here. Thetis wants to ask a favour of you.' 'Thetis
here?' the illustrious lame god exclaimed. 'The very goddess
whom I honour and revere for saving me in my hour of
agony, after my great fall, when my wicked Mother had tried
to do away with me because I was a cripple! Ah how I
should have suffered, if Thetis had not taken me to her bosom,
Thetis and Eurynome, Daughter of Ocean of the Circling
Stream. I stayed nine years with them, making bronze orna-
ments, buckles and spiral bracelets, rosettes and necklaces,
there in their vaulted cave lapped by the never-ending Stream
of Ocean, seething with foam. No one on earth or in heaven
knew the secret but Eurynome and Thetis who had rescued
me. And here is Thetis in our house, Thetis of the Lovely
Locks. I must certainly repay my benefactress. Entertain her
well, while I put away my bellows and my tools.'

Hephaestus raised his monstrous bulk from the anvil. He
limped, but he was nimble enough on his slender legs. He
removed the bellows from the fire, collected all the tools he
used, and put them in a silver chest. Then he sponged his face
and hands, his sturdy neck and hairy breast, put on his tunic,
picked up a thick staff and came limping from the forge.

Golden maidservants hastened to help their Master. They looked like real girls and could not only speak and use their limbs but were endowed with intelligence and trained in handwork by the immortal gods. Supported by his toiling escort, the Lord Hephaestus made his clumsy approach to the spot where Thetis was seated, and himself sat down on a polished chair, took her hand in his and greeted her. 'Thetis of the Long Robe!' he said. 'What brings you to our house? You are an honoured and a welcome guest, though in the past your visits have been few. But tell me what you wish of me. I shall be glad to serve you if I can and if the task is not impossible.'

Thetis burst into tears. 'Hephaestus,' she said, 'of all the goddesses in Olympus, is there a single one who has had such persecution to endure as I have suffered from the Son of Cronos? I, to begin with, was the Sea-Nymph whom he picked out from the rest to give in marriage to a man, to Peleus son of Aeacus; and much against my will I had to put up with a mortal husband, who lies at home now weighed down by the burden of his years. But there was more to follow. Zeus let me bring into the world and nurse a child who was destined to outshine his peers. I nursed him as one tends a little plant in a garden bed; and he shot up like a sapling. I sent him to Ilium with his beaked ships to fight against the Trojans; but now I shall never welcome him again to Peleus' house. And yet he has to suffer, every day he lives and sees the sun; and I can do no good by going to his side. Now, King Agamemnon has taken from his arms the girl whom the Achaean army gave him as a prize of honour. He missed her sorely and was distraught by his grief. In consequence the Trojans have been able to drive the Achaeans back among their ships, from which they will not let them move. Argive ambassadors were sent to plead with Achilles and made him a magnificent offer. But he refused it: he was not going to save them from disaster by any exertions of his own. However, he lent his armour to Patroclus and sent him into battle with a strong force behind him. They fought all day by the Scaean Gate, and would have taken Troy by storm before night fell, if Apollo had not given Hector the upper hand by killing the brave Patroclus in the front line after he had made havoc of the Trojan ranks. So I have come to throw myself at your knees and ask you to give my son, who is so soon to die, a shield and helmet, a pair of fine greaves fitted with ankle-clasps, and a cuirass. His former set of armour was lost when his good friend was overwhelmed by the Trojans; and Achilles is lying on the ground in misery.'

'Distress yourself no more,' replied the illustrious lame god. 'You can leave everything to me. In fact I only wish it were as easy for me to save him from the pains of death when his hour of doom arrives, as to provide him with a splendid set of armour which will be the wonder of all beholders.'

With that, Hephaestus left her and went back to his forge, where he turned the bellows on the fire and bade them get to work. The bellows – there were twenty of them – blew on the crucibles and gave a satisfactory blast of varying force, which increased at critical moments and subsided at others, according to Hephaestus' requirements and the stage that the work had reached. He cast imperishable bronze on the fire, and some tin and precious gold and silver. Then he put a great anvil on the stand and gripped a strong hammer in one hand and a pair of tongs in the other.

He began by making a large and powerful shield, adorned all over, finished with a bright triple rim of gleaming metal, and fitted with a silver baldric. The shield consisted of five layers, and he decorated the face of it with a number of designs, executed with consummate skill and representing, first of all, Earth, Sky and Sea, the indefatigable Sun, the Moon at the full, and all the Constellations with which the heavens are crowned, the Pleiads, the Hyads, the great Orion, and the Bear, nicknamed the Wain, the only constellation which never bathes in Ocean Stream, but always wheels round in the same place and looks across at Orion the Hunter with a wary eye.

Next he showed two beautiful cities full of people. In one

of them weddings and banquets were afoot. They were bring-
ing the brides through the streets from their homes, to the loud
music of the wedding-hymn and the light of blazing torches.
Youths accompanied by flute and lyre were whirling in the
dance, and the women had come to the doors of their houses
to enjoy the show. But the men had flocked to the meeting-
place, where a case had come up between two litigants, about
the payment of compensation for a man who had been killed.
The defendant claimed the right to pay in full and was an-
nouncing his intention to the people; but the other contested
his claim and refused all compensation. Both parties insisted
that the issue should be settled by a referee; and both were
cheered by their supporters in the crowd, whom the heralds
were attempting to silence. The Elders sat on the sacred bench,
a semicircle of polished stone; and each, as he received the
speaker's rod from the clear-voiced heralds, came forward in
his turn to give his judgment staff in hand. Two talents of gold
were displayed in the centre: they were the fee for the Elder
whose exposition of the law should prove the best.

The other city was beleaguered by two armies, which were
shown in their glittering equipment. The besiegers were un-
able to agree whether to sack the place outright – it was a
lovely town – or to divide all the movable property it con-
tained between themselves and the inhabitants. But these had
not yet capitulated: they were secretly preparing for an
ambush. Leaving the walls defended by their wives and little
children, together with the older men, they sallied forth under
the leadership of Ares and Pallas Athene, who were both
shown in gold. Fully armed and dressed in golden clothes,
they were big and beautiful as gods should be, and stood out
above their troops, who were of smaller build. When they
had found a likely place for an ambush, in a river-bed where
all the cattle came to drink, they sat down there in their
shining bronze, after posting two scouts in the distance to
watch for the coming of the sheep and the cattle with their
crooked horns. These soon appeared, in charge of two herds-
men, who were playing on their pipes, suspecting no evil.

The ambushed men caught sight of them, dashed out and promptly headed off the herds of oxen and the fine flocks of white sheep, killing the shepherds. But when the besiegers, who were sitting in debate, heard the commotion raised by this affair among the herds, they mounted at once behind their high-stepping horses and made for the scene of action, which they quickly reached. A pitched battle ensued on the banks of the river, and volleys of bronze spears were exchanged. Strife and Panic were shown at their work, and there was the dreadful Spirit of Death laying her hands on a freshly wounded man who was still alive and another not yet wounded, and dragging a corpse by its foot through the crowd. The cloak on her shoulders was red with human blood; and the soldiers met and fought and dragged away each other's dead like real men.

Next he depicted a large field of soft, rich fallow, which was being ploughed for the third time. A number of ploughmen were driving their teams across it to and fro. When they reached the ridge at the end of the field and had to wheel, a man would come up and hand them a cup of mellow wine. Then they turned back down the furrows and toiled along through the deep fallow soil to reach the other end. The field, though it was made of gold, grew black behind them, as a field does when it is being ploughed. The artist had achieved a miracle.

He also showed a king's estate, where hired reapers were at work with sharp sickles in their hands. Armfuls of corn fell down in rows along the furrow, while others were tied up with straw by the sheaf-binders. Three of these were standing by, and the boys who were gleaning behind came running up to them with bundles in their arms and kept them constantly supplied. And there among them was the King himself, staff in hand, standing by the swathe in quiet satisfaction. Under an oak in the background his attendants were preparing a feast. They were cooking a great ox that they had slaughtered, and the women were sprinkling the meat for the labourers' supper with handfuls of white barley.

The next scene was a vineyard laden with grapes. It was beautifully wrought in gold, but the bunches themselves were black and the supporting poles showed up throughout in silver. All round it he ran a ditch of blue enamel and outside that a fence of tin. The vineyard was approached by a single pathway for the pickers' use at vintage time; and the delicious fruit was being carried off in baskets by merry lads and girls, with whom there was a boy singing the lovely song of Linus in a treble voice to the sweet music of his tuneful lyre. They all kept time with him and followed the music and the words with dancing feet.

He also showed a herd of straight-horned cattle, making the cows of gold and tin. They were mooing as they hurried from the byre to feed where the rushes swayed beside a murmuring stream. Four golden herdsmen accompanied the cattle, and there were nine dogs trotting along with them. But at the head of the herd a pair of savage lions had seized a bellowing bull, who roared aloud as they dragged him off. The young men and dogs ran up to the rescue. But the lions had rent the great bull's hide and were lapping up his dark blood and entrails. It was in vain that the shepherds incited and egged on their fast dogs, who had no intention of biting the lions. They were careful to avoid them, though they stood and barked as close as they dared.

To this picture the illustrious lame god added a big grazing ground for white-fleeced sheep, in a beautiful valley, complete with its farm buildings, pens and well-roofed huts.

Next the god depicted a dancing-floor like the one that Daedalus designed in the spacious town of Cnossus for Ariadne of the lovely locks. Youths and marriageable maidens were dancing on it with their hands on one another's wrists, the girls in fine linen with lovely garlands on their heads, and the men in closely woven tunics showing the faint gleam of oil, and with daggers of gold hanging from their silver belts. Here they ran lightly round, circling as smoothly on their accomplished feet as the wheel of a potter when he sits and works it with his hands to see if it will spin; and there they ran in lines to meet each other. A large crowd stood round enjoying the delightful dance, with a minstrel among them singing divinely to the lyre, while a couple of acrobats, keeping time with his music, threw cart-wheels in and out among the people.

Finally, round the very rim of the wonderful shield he put the mighty Stream of Ocean.

When the shield was finished, in all its size and strength, he made Achilles a cuirass brighter than blazing fire. Then he made a massive helmet to fit on his temples. It was beautifully chased, and he put a golden crest on the top. He also made him greaves of pliant tin.

When the renowned lame god had finished every piece, he gathered them up and laid them before Achilles' Mother. She took the glittering armour from Hephaestus and swooped down with it like a falcon from snow-clad Olympus.

XIX

THE FEUD IS ENDED

As Dawn in her saffron mantle rose from the River of Ocean
to bring daylight to the immortals and to men, Thetis reached
the ships with the god's gifts in her hands. She found her son
Achilles prostrate with his arms round Patroclus. He was
weeping bitterly, and many of his men stood round him
wailing. The gracious goddess went up to them and taking
her son's hand in her own she said to him: 'My child, the
man who lies here was struck down by the will of Heaven.
No grief of ours can alter that. So let him be now, and receive
this splendid armour I have brought you from Hephaestus,
armour more beautiful than any man has ever worn.'

With this, the goddess laid the arms before him in their
elaborate loveliness. They rang aloud and all the Myrmidons
were struck with awe. They did not dare to look at them, and
backed away. But the more Achilles looked, the more his
passion rose, and from underneath their lids his eyes flashed
fiercely out like points of flame. He picked up the god's
splendid gifts and fondled them with delight. And when he
had taken in all their beauty, he turned to Thetis and said:
'Mother, this armour of the god's – this is indeed the work-
manship we might expect from Heaven. No mortal could
have made it. I will go to battle in it now. But I am terribly
afraid meanwhile that flies may defile the corpse of my lord
Patroclus by settling on the open wounds and breeding worms
in them. Life has gone out of him, and all his flesh would rot.'

'My child,' said the divine Thetis of the Silver Feet, 'have
no anxiety whatever on that score. I will arrange to keep
away the flies and save him from those pests that devour the
bodies of men killed in battle. He could lie here through all
the seasons of a year and still his flesh would be preserved; in-

deed it might be fresher than now. So go and summon the Achaean troops to Assembly, reconcile yourself with Agamemnon the Commander-in-Chief, and then arm for battle quickly and prepare to put out all your strength.'

With that, she breathed indomitable valour into her son; and to save Patroclus from decay, she treated his body with ambrosia and red nectar, which she instilled through his nostrils. Meanwhile Prince Achilles went along the beach shouting at the top of his voice to call out the Achaean troops. As a result, even the men who used to hang about the ships (the helmsmen in charge of the steering-oars, who were left on board to serve as stewards and deal out provisions) came to the Assembly, now that Achilles had reappeared after his long abstention from the toil of war. Those two servants of Ares, the steadfast Tydeides and the excellent Odysseus, came limping in, still troubled by their wounds and using spears for staves. They sat down in the front row; and last of all came Agamemnon King of Men. He too was suffering, from the wound that Coön son of Antenor had given him with his bronze-headed spear in the thick of the fray.

When all the Achaeans were gathered together, Achilles the great runner rose to speak. 'My lord Atreides,' he began, 'we have been at daggers drawn. But has it proved a good thing, either for you or me, to keep up this desperate feud about a girl? I only wish that Artemis had killed her with an arrow on board ship that day I chose her for myself when I had sacked Lyrnessus. Fewer Achaeans would then have bitten the dust of this wide world, slaughtered by the enemy while I sat aloof in my anger. It was Hector and the Trojans who profited by our quarrel; the Achaeans will have cause to remember it for many a long day. But we must let bygones be bygones, for all our resentment, and curb our hearts perforce – far be it from me to persist in my rancour. And now, as far as I am concerned, our feud is at an end, and I suggest that you immediately summon the long-haired Achaeans to battle, so that if the enemy decide to bivouac by the ships I may pit myself against their strength once more. I warrant that any Trojan who dodges my spear and comes out of this battle alive will think himself a lucky man when he can rest his legs.'

The Achaean men-at-arms shouted for joy when they heard the noble-hearted son of Peleus thus renounce his feud. But it remained for Agamemnon King of Men to have his say. He rose from his seat, but instead of moving to the centre, he spoke from where he stood.

'Friends, Danaan men-at-arms, servants of Ares,' he began; 'when a man stands up to speak, it is only courteous to give him a hearing and not interrupt. The best of orators could hardly cope with such disorder. How can one talk or hear when everyone is making enough din to drown the loudest voice? I am addressing myself to my lord Achilles, but I wish all the rest of you to hear, and to take in what I say.

'The Achaeans have often cried out against me, making the very point with which you, sir, began your speech. But I was not to blame. It was Zeus and Fate and the Fury who walks in the dark that blinded my judgment, that day at the meeting, when on my own authority I confiscated Achilles' prize. What could I do? At such moments there is a Power that takes complete command, Ate, the eldest Daughter of Zeus, who blinds us all, accursed spirit that she is, never touching the ground with those insubstantial feet of hers, but flitting through men's heads, corrupting them, and bringing this one or the other down. Why, even Zeus was blinded by her once, and he is known to stand above all men and gods. He was tricked by Here and her feminine wiles, on the day when Alcmene was going to give birth to the mighty Heracles in Thebes of the Great Walls. He made a solemn pronouncement to the assembled gods. "Listen to me, all you gods and goddesses," he said. "I wish you to know that this day Eileithyia, the goddess of travail, will bring into the world a human child, born of a stock with my blood in their veins, who shall have dominion over all his neighbours." The Lady Here took this up and set a trap for Zeus. "That is a lie," she said, "as time will show – a prophecy that you will not fulfil.

Come now, Olympian, give me your solemn word that the child who is to issue from a woman's womb to-day and to come of a stock with your blood in their veins shall have dominion over all his neighbours." Zeus saw no harm in this and took his solemn oath; he was completely blinded. But Here sped down from the summit of Olympus and hastened to Achaean Argos, where, as she knew, the noble wife of Sthenelus son of Perseus also had a baby on its way, but only seven months gone. Here brought this child into the light of day before his proper time, and postponed Alcmene's delivery by forbidding the goddesses of travail to attend her. Then she went to Zeus the Son of Cronos and gave him the news herself. "Father Zeus," she said, "Lord of the Lightning Flash; I hasten to inform you that to-day there has been born a noble child who is to be King of the Argives. They have called him Eurystheus, and his father is Sthenelus son of Perseus. So he comes of your stock, and it is quite a proper thing that he should have dominion over the Argives." Zeus was deeply mortified. In his rage he seized Ate by her glossy hair, and swearing a mighty oath that this arch-destroyer of the mind should never set foot in Olympus and the starry sky again, he whirled her round his head and cast her down from heaven and its stars. Ate soon found herself in the world of men. But Zeus could not think of her without a groan, when he saw Heracles, his own beloved son, toiling at the sordid tasks that were set him by Eurystheus. It was the same with me. When the great Hector of the flashing helmet was once more slaughtering Argives at the sterns of the ships, I could not forget the Ate who had blinded me that day. But since I *was* blinded and Zeus robbed me of my wits, I am willing to make amends and pay you ample compensation. So gird yourself for battle and lead the whole army out. As for the gifts, here am I, ready to produce all that my lord Odysseus promised when he went to you yesterday in your hut. If you like, you can wait before fighting, though I know how eager you are, and my servants shall fetch the presents for you from my ship, so that you may assure yourself of their excellence.'

Achilles of the nimble feet replied: 'Your majesty, Atreides, Agamemnon King of Men; the gifts can wait. Produce them, if you like, at your convenience; or keep them with you. But now let us turn our thoughts to battle without further pause. With a great task before us, we ought not to stay here arguing and wasting time. Once more Achilles must be seen in the front line destroying Trojan companies with his bronze spear. Think of him, each of you, as you come to grips with your man.'

This brought a remonstrance from the wise Odysseus. 'Most worshipful Achilles,' he said, 'the men have not break-fasted, and gallant as you are yourself, you must not order them to march on Troy and fling them like this at the enemy. The battle will not soon be over, once the two forces are en-gaged and their fighting spirit has been roused. Urge the men rather to take some food and wine by the ships – their courage and strength depend on nourishment. It is impossible for a man to stand up to the enemy all day long till sunset without food. His heart may be set on fighting, but exhaustion takes him unawares, he is attacked by thirst and hunger, and his legs give under him. But when a man has had his fill of wine and food before an all-day battle, he can carry on with a high heart and unflagging strength till the fight is broken off. I ask you, then, to dismiss the troops and tell them to prepare a meal. As for the gifts, let King Agamemnon have them laid before the Assembly so that all the men may see them for themselves and you be satisfied. Further, let him stand up before the whole army and give you his solemn oath that he has never been in the girl's bed and slept with her. In return, you too must show a forgiving spirit. Then, as a peace-offering, let him give you a rich banquet in his hut and so complete your vindication. And may I recommend *you*, my lord Atreides, to be more scrupulous in your future dealings? It is no disgrace for a king, when he has given offence, to come forward and repair the breach.'

'My lord Odysseus,' said King Agamemnon, 'to me, your intervention has been very welcome. Nothing was missing:

you dealt faithfully with every point. I am not only ready but anxious to take the oath you prescribe – I shall not be forswearing myself. But meanwhile let Achilles wait here, though I know he is eager for action, and let all the rest of you remain in your places, till the gifts are brought from my hut and we can make a formal pact. You yourself, Odysseus, are the man I entrust with this task. Pick out some young men, the best you can find in the whole force, go to my ship and fetch all the presents that we promised Achilles yesterday, not forgetting the women. And let Talthybius make haste to prepare me a boar for sacrifice to Zeus and the Sun in the presence of this vast Achaean army.'

But Achilles the great runner rose once more to his feet. 'Your majesty, Atreides, Agamemnon King of Men,' he said; 'you are taking the right steps, but you would do better still to take them at some other time, when a lull comes in the fighting and my blood is not up, as it is now. Our friends who fell to Hector in his hour of triumph are lying mangled on the plain – and you and Odysseus choose this moment to announce a meal! My way is different. I should make the men fight now, fasting and hungry, and give them a square meal at sunset, when we have wiped out our shame. Till that is done, I myself shall not let sup or crumb pass through my lips, with my friend lying dead in my hut, mangled by the sharp bronze, his feet towards the door and his comrades weeping round him. With that in mind, I cannot interest myself in your programme, or in anything but blood and slaughter and the groans of dying men.'

'Achilles, son of Peleus, flower of Achaean chivalry,' Odysseus of the nimble wits replied, 'you are a stronger man than I, and not a little better with the spear, but in view of my greater age and experience I may well claim to have more judgment than you; and that being so, you must constrain yourself to accept my ruling. Nothing exhausts a man so quickly as a pitched battle, where the sword is like a sickle that strews the field with straw for very little grain, when the reaping is done and Zeus, the arbiter of battles, has inclined his scales. You wish the troops to express their grief for a man's death by starving. That is impossible. Day after day men fall in their hundreds – there would never be an end to such austerity. No; we must steel our hearts, bury our dead, and let one day's tears suffice them. All, moreover, who survive the carnage must pay attention to their food and drink, if we are to continue under arms and carry on the struggle to the bitter end. So let none of you hold back and wait for any second call to action. This *is* your summons. It will go hard with anyone who is left behind at the ships. We are going to rope in every man and fling our whole force at these horse-taming Trojans.'

With no more said, Odysseus picked his men for the duty assigned him – King Nestor's sons, Meges son of Phyleus, Thoas, Meriones, Lycomedes son of Creon, and Melanippus – and they set out for King Agamemnon's hut. Once there, a few sharp orders and the work was done. They fetched out from the hut the seven tripods he had promised Achilles, the twenty cauldrons of gleaming copper and the twelve horses; and immediately after, they brought out the skilled workwomen, seven of them, or rather eight with Briseis of the lovely cheeks. Then Odysseus, who had weighed out a sum of ten talents in gold, led the way back, followed by the young Achaean noblemen carrying the gifts. They laid them down in the middle of the Assembly and Agamemnon rose to his feet. Beside the King stood Talthybius of the godlike voice, holding a boar between his hands. Atreides drew the knife that he always carried beside the great scabbard of his sword, and began the ritual by cutting a little hair from the boar's head and lifting up his hands in prayer to Zeus, while the Argives all sat quietly in their places, as custom prescribed, and listened to their King. He looked up into the broad sky and prayed in these words: 'I call first on Zeus, the highest and best of the gods, and then on the Earth and the Sun and the Furies who make men pay for perjury in the world below, to be my witnesses that I have never laid hands on the girl Briseis either by way of bringing her to my bed or for any other purpose whatsoever. She was untouched during her whole stay in my huts. If a word of this is false, may the gods deal out to me all the penalties that they impose on those who take their names in vain.'

When he had finished, he cut the boar's throat with his relentless bronze. Talthybius took the carcass and with a swing flung it out into the bosom of the grey sea for the fish to eat. Then Achilles rose to address the Argive warriors. 'How utterly,' he said, 'a man can be blinded by Father Zeus! I cannot think that my lord Agamemnon would have stirred me to such lasting bitterness or been so unconscionable as forcibly to take my girl, if Zeus had not been planning an Achaean massacre. But go now, take your meal, and then to battle!'

The troops were quick to accept this dismissal and scattered to their several ships, while the haughty Myrmidons took charge of the gifts and carried them off to Prince Achilles' quarters, where they laid them down, and left the women in his hut. The horses were driven in among his own herd by his noble squires.

So Briseis came back, beautiful as golden Aphrodite. But when she saw Patroclus lying there, mangled by the sharp bronze, she gave a piercing scream, threw herself on his body and tore her breast and tender neck and her fair cheeks with her hands. Lovely as a goddess in her grief, she cried: 'Alas, Patroclus, my heart's delight! Alas for me! I left you in this hut alive when I went away; and now I have come back, my prince, to find you dead. Such is my life, an endless chain of misery. I saw the husband to whom my father and my lady mother gave me lie mangled in front of his city by the cruel bronze; and I saw my three brothers, my dear brothers, borne by the same mother as myself, all meet their doom. But you, when the swift Achilles killed my man and sacked King Mynes' city – you would not even let me weep; you said you would make me Prince Achilles' lawful wife and take me in your ships to Phthia and give me a wedding-feast among the Myrmidons. You were so gentle with me always. How can I ever cease to mourn you?'

Thus Briseïs wept, and the other women took up the lament, ostensibly for Patroclus, but each at heart for her own unhappy lot. As for Achilles, the Achaean chieftains gathered round and pressed him to take food. But he refused with a groan. 'Kind friends,' he said, 'if you have any regard for my wishes, I beseech you not to ask me in my terrible distress to satisfy my thirst and hunger now. I intend to hold out at all costs till sunset.'

This proved enough to rid him of the rest, but the two Atreidae stayed, and so did the admirable Odysseus, with Nestor, Idomeneus and Phoenix the old charioteer. They tried to comfort him in his anguish. But no comfort could reach his heart till he had flung himself into the bloody jaws of battle. Memories came to his mind and he broke out afresh: 'How often you yourself, my most unhappy and beloved friend, have laid a dainty meal before me in this hut, in your quick and ready way, when all was set for an attack on the horse-taming Trojans! And now you lie mangled here and I go fasting. There is still plenty in the hut, but I cannot bear the thought of it, so much do I miss you. Indeed I could have suffered no crueller blow than this, not even the news of my father's death, who is shedding big tears in Phthia at this moment, I dare say, for me, the dear son he has lost, while I am fighting Trojans in a foreign land for wretched Helen's sake; nor even if they told me that my son, who is growing up in Scyros, the noble Neoptolemus, was dead. Perhaps he is. And yet I liked to think that I alone should perish, here in Troyland, far from Argos where the horses graze, and that you would get home to Phthia and be able to fetch my son from Scyros in a fast black ship, and show him everything, all my possessions and my servants and my big house with its high roof. For I suspect that Peleus, if he is not dead and gone by now, is only half alive, crushed by the burden of old age and in daily expectation of the dreadful news that I myself am dead.'

Achilles wept as he spoke, and the chieftains murmured in sympathy, each of them thinking of all that he had left at

home. The Son of Cronos, observing their distress, was sorry
for them. He turned at once to Athene and said: 'My child,
have you deserted your favourite? Is there no longer any room
in your heart for Achilles, who is sitting there in front of his
high-beaked ships mourning for his best friend, and fasting,
without taste of sup or crumb, while all the rest have gone to
eat? Run and distil some nectar and sweet ambrosia into his
breast to save him from starvation.'

With this encouragement from Zeus, Athene, who had
scarcely needed it, swooped down from heaven through the
upper air, like a shrieking, long-winged bird of prey. While
the Achaeans were arming themselves throughout the camp,
she distilled nectar and sweet ambrosia into Achilles' breast to
preserve him from the pangs of hunger. This done, she made
her way back to her almighty Father's palace, as the troops
poured out from among the gallant ships.

Thick and fast as the cold flakes that come scudding down
from the clouds before a northerly gale, resplendent helmets,
bossed shields, plated cuirasses and ashen spears came pouring
from the ships. The glory of their arms lit up the sky; the
glitter of bronze rippled like laughter over the plain, and the
earth resounded to the feet of marching men.

Among all these the admirable Achilles donned his arms.
In the intolerable fury that possessed him, he gnashed his
teeth, and his eyes blazed like fire as he put on the divine gifts
that Hephaestus had made for him, with a heart full of evil
for the Trojans. He began by tying round his legs the splendid
greaves with their silver ankle-clips. Next he put the cuirass on
his breast, and over his shoulder slung the bronze sword with
its silver-studded hilt. Then he took up the great thick shield,
which flashed into the distance like the moon, or like the
gleam that sailors catch at sea from a fire on a lonely upland
farm, when they are driven away from home down the high-
ways of the fish by adverse winds. Such was the sheen that
went up into the sky from Achilles' ornamented shield. Next
he picked up the massive helmet and placed it on his head.
It scintillated like a star, and above it danced the golden

plumes that Hephaestus had lavished on the crest. Prince
Achilles tried himself in the armour to see if it fitted and
allowed his splendid limbs free movement. It felt as light as a
pair of wings and lifted him up. Finally he took his father's
spear from its case, the heavy, long and formidable spear that
no Achaean could wield but he, who knew the way to handle
it. It was made from an ash on Mount Pelion and had been
given by Cheiron to his father, Peleus, to bring death to his
noble foes.

Meanwhile Automedon and Alcimus saw to the yoking of
the horses. They settled the breast-straps on their chests, put
the bits in their mouths and drew the reins back into the well-
built chariot. Then Automedon picked up the shining whip by
its handle and leapt in behind the pair. Achilles, girt for battle,
followed him in, resplendent in his armour like the dazzling
Sun, and reproved his father's horses in a terrible voice:
'Xanthus and Balius, Podarge's celebrated foals, try this time
to do better and bring your charioteer back to his friends alive,
when the fighting is done, instead of leaving him dead on the
field as you left Patroclus.'

From under the yoke he was answered by one of the horses,
Xanthus of the glancing feet, whom the white-armed god-
dess Here had endowed with human speech. Xanthus had
lowered his head, so that his mane came tumbling from the
yoke-pad by the yoke and swept the ground. He said: 'In-
deed, my dreaded master, we will once more bring you safely
home to-day. Yet the hour of your death is drawing near; and
it is not we who will be the cause of it, but a great god and the
strong hand of Destiny. Nor was it by our indolence or lack of
speed that the Trojans were enabled to strip the armour from
Patroclus' shoulders. It was the best of the gods, the Son of
Leto of the Lovely Tresses, that killed him in the front line
and let Hector have the glory. Run though we may with the
West Wind's speed – and there is nothing faster known on
earth – you too are doomed to fall in battle to a god and a
man.'

He had got so far when the Furies struck him dumb.

Achilles of the nimble feet was angry with him and replied: 'Xanthus, you waste your breath by prophesying my destruction. I know well enough that I am doomed to perish here, far from my dear father and Mother. Nevertheless, I am not going to stop till I have given the Trojans their bellyful of war.'

With that, he raised the battle-cry and drove his powerful horses to the front.

XX

THE GODS GO TO WAR

THUS by the beaked ships the Achaeans drew up for battle round the indefatigable son of Peleus, and on the other side the Trojans too fell in, on the high ground of the plain. At the same time Zeus ordered Themis, from the summit of rugged Olympus, to call the gods to Assembly, and she went the rounds and summoned them to his Palace. Excepting Ocean not a single River stayed away, nor did any of the Nymphs that haunt delightful woods, the sources of streams, and the grassy water-meadows. They all came to the Cloud-compeller's house and sat down in the marble gallery that Hephaestus the great Architect had made for Father Zeus.

When all had foregathered in the Palace, the Earthshaker Poseidon (who had not ignored the goddess's call, but had come up out of the sea to join them and had sat down in their midst) enquired what purpose Zeus might have in mind. 'Lord of the Lightning Flash,' he said, 'why have you ordered the gods to assemble? Are you concerned for the Trojans and Achaeans, who at this moment are about to come to grips once more?'

'Lord of the Earthquake,' replied Zeus the Cloud-compeller, 'you have read my mind aright and know why I have summoned this gathering. They do concern me, even in their destruction. Nevertheless I propose to stay here and seat myself in some Olympian glen from which I can enjoy the spectacle. The rest of you have my permission to join the Trojans and Achaeans, and to give your help to either side as your sympathies dictate. For if Achilles is allowed to fight the Trojans without interference, they will not for a moment hold that fiery spirit. Even before, they used to tremble and run at the sight of him; and now that he has been embittered by the loss of his friend, I am afraid he may cheat Destiny and storm the walls of Troy.'

These words from the Son of Cronos unleashed the dogs of war. The immortals at once set out for the scene of action in two hostile groups. Here and Pallas Athene made their way to the Achaean fleet. So did Poseidon the Girdler of the World, and Hermes the Bringer of Luck and the cleverest wonder-worker of them all. Hephaestus followed them, exulting in his enormous strength, for though he limped he was active enough on his slender legs. To the Trojan side went Ares in his flashing helmet, Phoebus of the Flowing Hair, Artemis the Archeress, Leto, the River Xanthus, and laughter-loving Aphrodite.

Up to the moment when the gods came down among the men, the Achaeans carried all before them. Achilles had re-appeared after his long absence from the front, and the knees of all the Trojans quaked beneath them in their terror at the sight of the fleet son of Peleus, resplendent in his arms and deadly as the War-god. But the scene changed when the Olympians reached the field and Strife the great Battle-maker rose in all her strength. For though Athene raised the war-cry, now standing by the trench beyond the wall and now sending her voice down the echoing shore, she was answered on the other side by Ares, who raged like a black squall and incited the Trojans by the piercing cries he gave, at one moment from the heights of the citadel, and at the next from the banks of Simoïs, as he ran along the slopes of Callicolone.

Thus the blessed gods threw the two forces at each other's throats and at the same time opened a grievous breach in their own ranks. Up on high the Father of men and gods thundered ominously, and down below, Poseidon caused the wide world and the lofty mountain-tops to quake. Every spur and crest of Ida of the many springs was shaken. The Trojan city and the ships of the Achaeans trembled; and in the underworld Hades, King of the Dead, took fright and leapt with a cry from his throne. He was afraid that Poseidon and his earthquakes might split open the ground above his head and expose to mortal and immortal eyes the hateful Chambers of Decay that fill the gods themselves with horror.

Such was the turmoil as the battle of the gods began. And little wonder, when the Lord Poseidon was faced by Phoebus Apollo with his winged arrows, and Athene of the Flashing Eyes by Ares; when Here was confronted by Apollo's Sister, Artemis of the Golden Distaff, the Archeress and goddess of the chase; Leto by the formidable Hermes, Bringer of Luck; and Hephaestus by the mighty swirling River who is called Xanthus by the gods and Scamander by mankind.

Thus they went to war, god against god. As for Achilles, he wished for nothing better than to meet Hector son of Priam in the throng. Hector's was the blood with which he yearned to glut the stubborn god of War. But Apollo, Marshaller of the Host, intervened at once and moved Aeneas, after filling him with daring, to confront the son of Peleus. Disguising himself and mimicking the voice of Lycaon, one of Priam's sons, the great god said to him: 'Aeneas, Counsellor of the Trojans, what has become of all your boastful threats? Did you not tell the Trojan princes over the wine-cups that you would face Achilles son of Peleus man to man?'

'Lycaon,' replied Aeneas, 'why do you press me to pit myself against the haughty son of Peleus? I hate the thought of it, for this will not be the first time I have been confronted by the swift Achilles. Once before, he chased me with his spear from Ida, when he raided our cattle and sacked Lyrnessus and Pedasus. On that occasion I was saved by Zeus, who gave me strength and speed of foot, or I should have fallen to Achilles and Athene. For Athene went ahead of him to make things safe, and egged him on to slaughter Leleges and Trojans with his spear. Which makes me feel that it is impossible for any man to fight Achilles. He always has a god with him to save his skin. And quite apart from that, his spear has a way of flying straight and never stopping till it lands in human flesh. However, if the gods decide to see fair play between us, he will not have an easy victory, even though he likes to think that he is made of bronze.'

'My lord,' said King Apollo Son of Zeus, 'why not invoke the deathless gods yourself? Are you not known to be the son of Aphrodite Daughter of Zeus, whereas Achilles' Mother, though a goddess, is of humbler rank, with the Old Man of the Sea for Father as compared with Zeus? Straight at him, then, with the hard bronze! And do not let his threats and insults put you off.'

With that, Apollo breathed courage into the heart of Prince Aeneas, who now came forward through the front lines, resplendent in his bronze equipment. But the white-armed goddess Here was not taken unawares, and when she saw the son of Anchises advancing through the press to attack the son of Peleus, she beckoned her friends to her side and said: 'Poseidon and Athene, I look to you to handle this affair. Here comes Aeneas to attack Achilles, resplendent in his arms of bronze and backed by Phoebus Apollo. Come, let us send him forthwith to the right about. Or to take the cue from our opponents, one of *us* might stand by Achilles and enhance his powers. His spirit must not be allowed to fail him. He must be made to feel that the best of the immortals love him, and that those who up till now have saved the Trojans from defeat are of no account whatever. We all came down from Olympus to join in this battle so that Achilles should not suffer any harm at Trojan hands to-day, though later on he must endure what Destiny spun for him with the first thread of life when he came from his mother's womb. But if all this is not conveyed to him in a message from Heaven itself, he will be terrified when he finds himself confronted by a god. The gods are difficult for any man to deal with when they face him openly.'

But Poseidon the Earthshaker restrained her. 'Here,' he said, 'you must control yourself and not be so outrageously aggressive. I, for one, am not anxious to set the gods at each other's throats, and I suggest that we should move out of the way and leave the men to do the fighting while we sit down and watch from a convenient place. Of course, if Ares or Apollo starts the fight, or if they lay hands on Achilles to keep him out of action, then we ourselves will be immediately embroiled. But not for long, I think. Our enemies will soon have to break the battle off and go back to the other gods on Olympus, overwhelmed by our sheer strength.'

With no more said, the god of the Sable Locks took his companions away with him to the lofty earthwork that the Trojans and Pallas Athene had made for the heroic Heracles, as a place of refuge from the great sea-beast when it came up from the beach to attack him on dry land. There Poseidon and the other gods sat down and spread impenetrable mist round their shoulders. Their divine opponents sat down also, on the brow of Callicolone, round the Lord Phoebus and Ares, Sacker of Towns. Thus both the parties settled down in their respective camps for further thought. Each of them shrank from plunging first into the horrors of war, and Zeus from his seat on high still kept control.

Meanwhile the plain was filled by human combatants and sparkled with the bronze of infantry and horse. The earth shook beneath their feet as the two forces rushed towards each other. And now, in the intervening space, their two great champions, Aeneas son of Anchises and the godlike Achilles, came together bent on single combat. Aeneas was the first to step forward, with a gesture of defiance. His massive helmet nodded on his head; he held his gallant shield in front of him, and he brandished his bronze spear. From the other side, the son of Peleus sprang to meet him. He was like a lion whose ravages have caused a villageful of men to turn out and destroy him. At first the lion goes his way and treats them with contempt, but when one of the bolder young men has hit him with a spear, he gathers himself up with a snarl, the froth collects on his jaws, he growls to himself in noble indignation, he lashes his ribs and flanks with his tail to work himself up into a fighting fury, and then with eyes aflame he charges, determined in his passion to kill or perish at the first encounter. Thus Achilles was impelled by his fury and his pride to attack the magnificent Aeneas. When they had come within range, it was the great runner Achilles who spoke first. 'Aeneas,' he said, 'what has induced you to desert the ranks and venture out so far to meet me? Do you propose to fight me in the hope of stepping into Priam's shoes and being King of the horse-taming Trojans? Your killing me will not make Priam abdicate for you. He has sons of his own; his health is sound; and he is not half-witted either. Perhaps the Trojans have offered you a piece of their best land with plenty of vineyards and cornfields for your private use, if you succeed in killing me? Well, I think you will find it difficult. I seem to recollect that once before you fled from my spear. Or have you forgotten that time I caught you alone, cut you off from your cattle, and sent you scuttling down the slopes of Ida? You ran so fast on that occasion that you had not even time to look behind, and you escaped me. You took refuge in Lyrnessus. I followed up, and I sacked the place with the help of Athene and Father Zeus, carrying off into slavery the women I captured, though you yourself eluded me with the aid of Zeus and the other gods. But this time I do not think he is going to protect you, as you fondly hope. In fact I recommend you to get back now, join the rabble, and not stand up to me, or you will come to grief. It is the height of folly to be wise too late.'

'My lord Achilles,' Aeneas answered him, 'you need not imagine that you are going to scare me with words as though I were a child, for if it comes to insults and abuse I am well prepared to give you equal measure. You and I know each other's pedigree, and we know each other's parents, for though you have never set eyes on mine nor I on yours, their names are familiar to our ears as household words. It is common knowledge that you are a son of the admirable Peleus and of Thetis of the Lovely Locks, the Child of the Brine, while I can claim the magnificent Anchises as my father and Aphrodite as my Mother. Of those two couples, one or the other is going to mourn the loss of a son to-day, for I am sure that you and I will not settle our affair and leave the field with no more than a little small-talk such as this. But if you would care to hear the whole story of my house, well-known as it is, here is the tale, starting with Dardanus, who was a son of Zeus the Lord of the Clouds. Dardanus founded Dardania at a time when the sacred city of Ilium had not yet been built to shelter people on the plain and they still inhabited the watered slopes of Ida. Dardanus had a son, King Erichthonius, who was the richest man on earth. He had three thousand mares feeding in the marshlands and rejoicing in their little foals. One day as they were grazing there, the North Wind himself, overcome by their beauty, took the form of a black stallion to make love to them, and in due course they produced twelve foals. These in their frolics on land could run across a field of corn, brushing the highest ears, and do no harm to it; and when they made the rolling sea their playground, they skimmed the white foam on the crests of the waves. Erichthonius had a son called Tros, who was King of the Trojans; and Tros himself had three excellent sons, Ilus, Assaracus, and the godlike Ganymedes, who grew up to be the most beautiful youth in the world and because of his good looks was kidnapped by the gods to be cupbearer to Zeus and foregather with the immortals. Ilus was father to the noble Laomedon, whose sons were Tithonus, Priam, Lampus, Clytius and Hicetaon offshoot of Ares. But Assaracus was the father of Capys, whose son Anchises is my father, whereas Prince Hector is the son of Priam. That, sir, is my pedigree; such is the blood I claim as mine.

'As for prowess in war, that is a gift from almighty Zeus, who endows a man with it in greater measure or in less as he thinks fit. But come, do not let us stand here in the heart of a battle talking like silly boys. We could sling plenty of insults at each other – enough in fact to sink a merchantman. The tongue is glib. With a wide range of words at its command, it can express our thoughts in any style; and as a rule one gets the kind of answer one has asked for. But what call is there for you and me to stand and blackguard one another like a couple of nagging women who have lost their tempers and come out into the middle of the street to pelt each other with abuse, not caring in their fury what is true or false? In any case I want to fight, and no words of yours shall put me off till we have stood and had it out with spears. Enough now! Let us taste each other's bronze.'

With that, Aeneas hurled his heavy spear at the other's formidable shield. The point of the weapon rang loud on the unearthly shield, which Achilles in alarm thrust forward with his mighty hand, thinking that the long-shadowed spear of the magnanimous Aeneas was bound to pierce it. His fears were foolish: he had forgotten that the splendid gifts of the gods are not liable to fail and crumple up when human hands assault them. And now they served him well – even the heavy spear of the doughty Aeneas did not break through the shield, but was stopped by the gold that Hephaestus had put into his gift. It did succeed in passing through two layers, but there were three to come, for the Lord of the Crooked Foot had put on five of them, two of bronze, two on the inner side of tin, and one of gold. It was in this layer that the ashen spear was held.

Achilles now took his turn and cast a long-shadowed spear. He struck Aeneas's rounded shield on the very edge, where the bronze and the oxhide backing were thinnest. The ashen shaft from Pelion burst right through with a resounding crack. Aeneas ducked, thrusting his man-covering shield above himself in terror; and the spear, stripping the leather from the bronze, passed over his back and ended its career by sticking in the ground. The long shaft had not touched Aeneas, but he was so appalled by the closeness of the shot that he stood there with unseeing eyes and utterly discomfited. But Achilles, drawing his sharp sword, came charging at him with a terrific shout. Aeneas then picked up a lump of rock. Even to lift it was a feat beyond the strength of any two men bred to-day; but he handled it alone without an effort. And as Achilles came on, Aeneas might well have struck him with the boulder on the helmet or the shield (which had already saved Achilles' life), and Achilles would have closed and killed Aeneas with his sword, had it not been for the quick eye of Poseidon. The Earthshaker was watching, and at this point he turned to the gods beside him with a cry of concern.

'I cannot help being sorry,' he said, 'for the magnanimous Aeneas. In a moment he will fall to Achilles and go down to Hades' Halls, because like a fool he took Apollo at his word – as though the Archer-King would save his life! Why should this innocent man, who has always been liberal with his offerings to the gods of the broad sky, suffer for no reason at all except that he is involved in other people's troubles? Let us take action and rescue him from death. Even the Son of Cronos might be angry if Achilles killed Aeneas, who after all is destined to survive and to save the House of Dardanus from extinction – a house whose founder Zeus loved more than any other child he had by a mortal mother. Priam's line has fallen out of favour with the Son of Cronos, and now the great Aeneas shall be King of Troy and shall be followed by his children's children in the time to come.'

'Shaker of Earth,' said Here the ox-eyed Queen, 'you must decide for yourself whether to rescue Aeneas or to leave him alone. Pallas Athene and I have repeatedly sworn in the presence of all the gods never to save the Trojans from their doom, not even on the day when their whole city is consumed by the devastating fires that will be lit there by the warrior sons of Achaea.'

Poseidon the Earthshaker heard her out and then plunged through the mêlée and the rain of spears, making for the spot where Aeneas and the famous son of Peleus were engaged. Once there, his first step was to spread a mist before Achilles' eyes. Then he withdrew the ashen spear entangled in the noble Aeneas' shield, laid it at Achilles' feet, and swept Aeneas off the ground high into the air. Aeneas was propelled with such force by the god's hand that he vaulted over all the intervening lines of infantry and horse and came down on the very edge of the battlefield, where the Caucones were preparing to enter the fight. Poseidon the Earthshaker caught up with him there and took him to task. 'Aeneas,' he said, 'what is the meaning of this recklessness? Which of the gods told you to fight with the proud Achilles, who is not only a better soldier than you but a greater favourite with the immortals?

If ever you come up against that man, withdraw at once, or you will find yourself in Hades' Halls before your time. But when he is dead and gone, you can boldly play your part in the front line, for no one else on the Achaean side is going to kill you.'

Poseidon, with so much in explanation, left Aeneas there, and returning quickly to Achilles removed the mist from his eyes. It had baffled Achilles, who now stared with all his might and decided for himself that he had witnessed a miracle, since his spear was lying there on the ground and the man he had meant to kill with it was nowhere to be seen. He gave an exclamation of disgust. 'The immortal gods,' he thought, 'must be very fond of Aeneas too, though I did feel that there was little truth in all the boastful things he said. Well, let him go. He will be so thankful to have saved his skin this time that he won't be anxious for another fight with me. Now I will put the Danaans on their mettle and see what I can do against the other Trojans.'

Achilles hurried down the ranks with a word of exhortation for every man. 'Noble Achaeans,' he said, 'do not stand there waiting for the Trojans, but each pick out your man and put your heart into the fight. I may be strong, but I can scarcely deal alone with such a force and fight them all. Even immortal gods like Ares or Athene could do little damage if they threw themselves at such a mass of men. Not that I propose to take it easy – not at all. Whatever a swift foot and a strong arm can do shall be done. I am going straight through their lines, and I do not envy any Trojan who comes near my spear.'

Thus Achilles inspired his men. But on the other side illustrious Hector was hounding on the Trojans. He even talked of attacking Achilles. 'Gallant Trojans,' he cried, 'do not be frightened by the son of Peleus. I too could fight the gods themselves with words, though with a spear it would be harder – they are too strong for us. Achilles won't do all he says. He may succeed up to a point, but there he will stop short. And I am going to meet him, though his hands are like fire, yes, though his hands are like fire and his heart like burnished steel.'

With this encouragement from Hector, the Trojans brought their spears to the ready, the two forces fell upon each other, and the battle-cry went up. But Phoebus Apollo went to Hector and told him on no account to seek a meeting with Achilles. 'Stay with the rest,' he said, 'and let him find you in the crowd. Otherwise, he will fell you with a spear-cast, or close and strike you with his sword.' This warning sent Hector back into the ranks: his heart misgave him when he heard the god's voice.

But there was no room for fear in Achilles' heart and he sprang at the Trojans with his terrible war-cry. The first man he killed was Iphition, the gallant son of Otrynteus and the leader of a large contingent. His mother was a Naiad who had borne him to Otrynteus sacker of towns below the snowy heights of Tmolus in the rich land of Hyde. The great Achilles, as this man came on against him, caught him with a spear full on the head, splitting his skull in two. He came down with a crash and Achilles made a mock of him: 'You have fallen low, son of Otrynteus, most redoubtable of men. *This* is where you die, born though you were at the Gygaean Lake, on your father's estate by the swirling streams of Hermus and Hyllus where the fishes breed.'

As Achilles triumphed over him, the night of death descended on Iphition's eyes. He left him where the front lines met, to be torn to pieces by the tyres of Achaean chariots, and went on to kill Demoleon, one of Antenor's sons, a staunch and veteran fighter. He hit him on the temple through his bronze-sided helmet. The metal of the helmet failed to check the eager spear. The point went through, pierced the bone and spattered the inside of the helmet with his brains. Demoleon's zeal was quenched. Hippodamas was the next. He had leapt from his chariot and was flying before him when Achilles struck him with a spear in the back. He yielded his life with a bellow like that of a bull when he is dragged round the altar of the Lord of Helicon by the young men in whose ministrations the Earthshaker delights. Such was the roar that came from Hippodamas as his proud spirit left his bones. But Achilles was already after Polydorus with his spear. This prince was one of Priam's sons, the fastest runner of them all. His father had forbidden him to fight, because he was his favourite and youngest child. But the foolish boy had seized the occasion to display his speed; and he dashed about among the front-line men until he met his death. For Achilles too was quick on his feet, and as the young man darted by, he caught him with a javelin full in the back, where the golden buckles of his belt were fastened and the corslet overlapped. The point transfixed him and came out by his navel. He fell on his knees with a groan; the world went black before his eyes, and as he sank he clasped his bowels to him with his hands.

When Hector saw his brother Polydorus sink to the ground clutching his entrails, his eyes were dimmed with tears. He felt he could no longer bear to stay aloof, and he made at Achilles like a raging fire, brandishing his sharp spear. Directly Achilles saw him, he leapt to meet him, saying to himself in exultation: 'Here is the man who struck me the cruellest blow of all when he killed my dearest friend. We have done now with dodging one another down the corridors of battle.' And greeting Prince Hector with a black look, he said to him: 'Come quickly on, and meet your fated end the sooner.'

'My lord Achilles,' Hector of the bright helmet answered unperturbed, 'do not imagine that you can frighten me with words as though I were a child, for if it comes to insults and abuse I am well prepared to give you tit for tat. I know that you are a good man, better by far than myself. But matters like this lie on the knees of the gods, and though I am not so strong as you, they may yet decide to let me kill you with a cast of my spear, which before now has proved as sharp as any.'

With that he poised and hurled his spear. But Athene, by a miracle that cost her but a little breath, blew the spear away from the illustrious Achilles, so that it flew back to Hector and fell at his feet. Achilles, in his eagerness to kill, charged with a terrific cry. But Apollo hid Prince Hector in a dense mist and snatched him away – an easy feat for a god. Three times the noble swift Achilles dashed in with his bronze spear, and thrice he lunged at empty mist. Charging like a demon for the fourth time, he railed at Hector in a terrible voice. 'You cur!' he cried. 'Once more you have saved your skin – but only just. Phoebus Apollo took care of you again: no doubt you say your prayers to him before you venture within earshot of the spears. But we shall meet once more, and then I'll finish you, if I too can find a god to help me. For the moment I shall try my luck against the rest.'

Even as he spoke, he struck Dryops full in the neck with his spear. Dryops came down with a crash at his feet. Achilles left him there, and cast at Demuchus, the tall and handsome son of Philetor. He hit him on the knee and brought him down; then took his life with his long sword. Next he attacked Laogonus and Dardanus, sons of Bias, and hurled them both from their chariot to the ground, one with a spear-cast, and the other at close quarters with a stroke of his sword. Tros son of Alastor was the next. This man came up to clasp Achilles' knees in the hope that he would shrink from killing one of his own age and merely take him prisoner and let him off alive. The young fool might have known that his prayers were doomed to fail. Achilles was not kind or tender-hearted, but a man of fierce passions; and when Tros in his eagerness to plead for mercy put his hands on his knees, he struck him in the liver with his sword. The liver came out and drenched his lap with dark blood. He swooned, and night descended on his eyes. Achilles then went up to Mulius and struck him on the ear with his javelin, so hard that the bronze point came out at the other ear. The next was Echeclus son of Agenor. Achilles caught him full on the head with a stroke of his hilted sword – the blood made the whole blade warm. Fate set her seal on Echeclus, and the shadow of Death descended on his eyes. Deucalion next. Achilles pierced his forearm with the bronze point of his spear, just where the sinews of the elbow are attached. Deucalion, waiting for him with his arm weighed down by the spear, looked Death in the face. Achilles struck the man's neck with his sword and sent head and helmet flying off together. The marrow welled up from the vertebrae, and the corpse lay stretched on the ground. The next quarry of Achilles was Rhigmus, the noble son of Peiros, who had come from the deep-soiled land of Thrace. He cast at him and caught him full. The bronze javelin came to rest in his lung and he tumbled from his chariot. Then Achilles with his sharp spear struck Areïthous, the squire of Rhygmus, in the back. Areïthous was turning the horses round, and when he too was swept from the chariot, they bolted.

Thus Achilles ran amuck with his spear, like a driving wind that whirls the flames this way and that when a conflagration rages in the gullies on a sun-baked mountain-side and the high forest is consumed. He chased his victims with the fury of a fiend, and the earth was dark with blood. At their imperious master's will the horses of Achilles with their massive hooves trampled dead men and shields alike with no more ado than when a farmer has yoked a pair of broad-browed cattle to trample the white barley on a threshing-floor and his lowing bulls tread out the grain. The axle-tree under his chariot, and the rails that ran round it, were sprayed with the blood thrown up by the horses' hooves and by the tyres. And the son of Peleus pressed on in search of glory, bespattering his unconquerable hands with gore.

XXI

ACHILLES FIGHTS THE RIVER

WHEN they reached the ford of eddying Xanthus, the noble River whose Father is immortal Zeus, Achilles cut the Trojan force in two. One party he drove citywards across the fields, where the Achaeans had been hurled back in panic on the previous day when illustrious Hector ran amuck. These spread across the plain in wild disorder; and to hamper their escape, Here confronted them with a dense fog.

The rest were chased into a bend of the river, where Xanthus of the Silver Pools ran deep. They fell into the water with resounding splashes that were echoed by the very river-bed, and as they swam about, whirled round in the eddies, the banks on either side threw back their cries. It was as though a swarm of locusts, driven to the river by the sudden outbreak of a raging fire, had huddled in the water to escape from the flames. But here Achilles was the force that drove, cluttering the torrent with a medley of men and horses, and making Xanthus roar again.

The prince, leaving his spear propped against a tamarisk on the bank and taking nothing but his sword, leapt in like a demon, with murder in his heart, and laid about him right and left. Hideous groans went up from the men who met his sword and the water was reddened with blood. Like the small fry that flee in terror before a huge dolphin and crowd into the corners of a sheltered cove, knowing that to be caught is to be eaten up, the Trojans cowered under the overhanging banks of that terrible river. Achilles, when the work of slaughtering them had tired his arms, selected twelve young men and took them alive from the river to pay the price for the lord Patroclus' death. He drove them, dazed like fawns, onto the bank, and tied their hands behind them with the stout leather straps with which their own knitted tunics were equipped. Then he left them for his followers to take down to the hollow ships, and in his eagerness for slaughter threw himself at the enemy again.

His first encounter was with Lycaon, one of Dardanian Priam's sons, who was making his escape from the river. He had met this man before, in a night sortie, and taken him captive from his father's vineyard, where Lycaon was trimming the young shoots of a fig-tree with a sharp knife to make chariot rails when the great Achilles descended on him like a bolt from the blue. On that occasion Achilles had put him on board ship and sold him in the city of Lemnos – it was Jason's son who bought him. From Lemnos he was ransomed at a heavy price by a man he had befriended, Eëtion of Imbros, who sent him to sacred Arisbe; but he slipped away from his protectors there and managed to come home to Troy. However, he enjoyed the company of his friends for no more than eleven days after his return from Lemnos, for on the twelfth Fate cast him once more into the hands of Achilles, who was going this time to send him willy-nilly on a journey to the Halls of Hades. The swift and excellent Achilles recognized him easily, since he was quite unarmed, with neither helmet, shield, nor spear, having thrown his equipment on the ground, limp and exhausted as he was by the sweat and struggle of his escape from the river. Achilles gave a cry of anger and surprise. 'Marvels will never cease!' he said to himself. 'I shall have every Trojan I have killed rising up against me out of the western gloom, if they take their cue from this fellow here, this runaway slave, who was sold in sacred Lemnos and now turns up again, treating the high seas as though they were no barrier at all to would-be travellers. Well, I will do more for him this time: he shall taste the point of my spear. I want to satisfy myself and see whether he will come back as easily as before from his new destination, or whether the fruitful Earth, who has so many strong men in her lap, will hold him down.'

As Achilles stood there wondering, Lycaon approached him

and tried to reach his knees, stupefied by fear and possessed by one desire, to avoid his fate and escape a dreadful death. The great Achilles raised his long spear and aimed a cast at him; but Lycaon ducked, ran in, and grasped his knees, while the spear passed over his back and planted itself in the ground, still hungering for human flesh. Laying one hand on Achilles' knees and with the other gripping the spear and never letting go, Lycaon made his supplication. 'Achilles,' he said, 'I cast myself at your knees: be merciful and spare me. I have some claim on your regard, my prince, for you were the first Achaean whose bread I broke when you captured me in our lovely vineyard, carried me off from my father and my friends and sold me in sacred Lemnos. I fetched you a good price; but I was ransomed for three times as much, and after many hardships I reached Ilium twelve days ago. And now some evil chance has brought me into your hands again – how Father Zeus must hate me to have made me twice your prisoner! I am the son of Laothoe (short-lived, it seems), and she is a daughter of old Altes, King of the warlike Leleges, who lives in the high fortress of Pedasus on the banks of Satnioïs. Priam made this daughter of Altes one of his many wives, and she had two sons, both of whom you will have butchered, since the noble Polydorus fell to you and your sharp spear in the front line, and an evil end awaits me here. For I have little hope of escaping, now that God has delivered me into your hands. But there *is* another reason why you should spare my life, and I beg you not to overlook it. I was not borne by the same mother as Hector, who killed your brave and gentle friend.'

Thus the highborn son of Priam pleaded for mercy with Achilles. But there was no mercy in the voice that answered him. 'You fool,' he heard Achilles say, 'do not talk to me of ransom: I wish to hear no speeches. Before Patroclus met his end, I was not disinclined to spare the Trojans; I took many alive and sold them abroad. But now not a single man whom God brings into my hands in front of Ilium is going to live; and that holds good for every Trojan there may be, for sons of

Priam above all. Yes, my friend, you too must die. Why make such a song about it? Even Patroclus died, who was a better man than you by far. And look at me. Am I not big and beautiful, the son of a great man, with a goddess for my Mother? Yet Death and sovran Destiny are waiting for me too. A morning is coming, or maybe an evening or a noon, when somebody is going to kill me too in battle with a cast of his spear or an arrow from his bow.'

When he heard this, Lycaon's spirit failed him and he collapsed. Letting go the spear, he sat with both his hands held out. But Achilles drew his sharp sword and struck him on the collar bone beside the neck. The two-edged blade was buried in his flesh; sinking forward he lay stretched on the ground, and the dark blood ran out of him and drenched the earth. Achilles took him by the foot and hurled him into the river with a few taunting words by way of farewell. 'Lie there among the fish,' he said, 'where they can lick the blood from your wound in comfort. Your mother will not lay you on a bier and mourn for you, but swirling Scamander will roll you out into the broad bosom of the sea, where many a fish will dart through the water to the dark ripples on the top to eat the white flesh of Lycaon. Perdition to you all, till we reach the citadel of sacred Ilium, you in rout, I killing from behind. Nothing shall save you, not even fair Scamander of the Silver Eddies, to whom for years you have been sacrificing bulls and into whose pools you throw living horses. One by one, for all that, you shall come to an evil end, till you have paid for the killing of Patroclus and for the beaten Achaeans whom you slaughtered by their gallant ships when I was away.'

The River, displeased already, was exasperated by this reference to himself and began to ponder ways and means of bringing Prince Achilles' exploits to an end and saving the Trojans from disaster. Meanwhile the son of Peleus, bent on slaughter, hurled himself with his long-shadowed spear at Asteropaeus. This man was the son of Pelegon, himself a love-child of Periboea, the eldest daughter of Acessamenus,

and the broad River Axius of the Swirling Stream. When
Achilles attacked him, Asteropaeus had just emerged from the
water and stood facing him with two spears in his hands, em-
boldened by Xanthus, who resented the slaughter of the
youths whom Achilles was butchering mercilessly up and
down his stream. As he came up to Asteropaeus, the swift and
excellent Achilles challenged him. 'And who on earth are
you,' he asked, 'that dare to face Achilles? Who are your
people? The fathers of men who meet me in my fury are
liable to weep.'

'Royal son of Peleus,' said the noble Asteropaeus, 'why do
you ask for my pedigree? It is a far cry to the deep-soiled land
of Paeonia from which I came to Ilium eleven days ago at the
head of my long-speared Paeonian troops. I am descended
from Axius of the Broad Stream. Axius was the father of the
famous spearman Pelegon, and I, they say, am Pelegon's son.
But enough now! Let us fight, my lord Achilles.'

He spoke defiantly, and Prince Achilles raised the ashen
spear of Pelion. But the brave Asteropaeus, who was ambi-
dextrous, cast both his spears at once. With one he hit Achilles'
shield, but failed to pierce it, for the point was stopped by the
gold that the god had put into his gift. With the other he
grazed the right elbow of Achilles, causing the dark blood to
flow; but the spear passed over him and stuck in the ground,
still hungering for flesh. It was now Achilles' turn, and he
hurled his straight-grained ashen shaft at Asteropaeus with
deadly intent, but missed his man and struck the high river-
bank instead, with such force that he buried half the length of
his ashen spear in the earth. Drawing his sharp sword from his
side, the son of Peleus charged at Asteropaeus, who was now
trying in vain to drag the ashen pole out of the bank with his
great hand. Three times, in his efforts to retrieve the spear, he
shifted it a little, but every time he had to give up the struggle.
He tried again, this time to bend and break the ashen shaft of
Peleus, but before he could do so, Achilles was upon him and
killed him with his sword. He hit him in the belly by the
navel, and all his entrails poured out on the ground. He lay

there gasping, and night descended on his eyes. Achilles, trampling on his chest, removed his armour and triumphed over him. 'Lie there,' he said, 'and learn how difficult it is, even for children of a River-god, to fight the scions of almighty Zeus. You said you were descended from a noble River, but I can trace my pedigree to Zeus himself. Peleus son of Aeacus, the King of many Myrmidons, is my father; Aeacus was a son of Zeus; and a descendant of Zeus is greater than the scion of a River by as much as Zeus himself is greater than all Rivers that run murmuring to the sea. Look at the River that is flowing past you now. He is a mighty one and would help you if he could. But there is no fighting against Zeus the Son of Cronos. Even Achelous, King of Rivers, is not a match for Zeus. Nor is the deep and potent Stream of Ocean, the source of all rivers, every sea, and all the springs and deep wells that there are. Even he is afraid of almighty Zeus's bolt and his terrible thunder when it peals from heaven.'

Achilles pulled his bronze spear out of the bank and left the man whom he had killed lying where he was on the sand, lapped by the dark water and busily attended by the eels and fish, who nibbled at his kidneys and devoured his fat. Then he went after the Paeonians in their plumed helmets, who had been left beside the swirling river in a state of panic when they saw their leader fall in battle to the hands and sword of the son of Peleus. Thersilochus, Mydon and Astypylus; Mnesus, Thrasius, Aenius and Ophelestes – all these he killed. Indeed the swift Achilles would have slaughtered more Paeonians yet, had it not been for the eddying River, who in his resentment took human form to check him and caused his voice to issue from one of the deep pools. 'Achilles,' he said, 'you are more than man, both in your strength and your outrageous deeds. And the gods themselves are always at your side. But if the Son of Cronos really means you to kill all the Trojans, I implore you at least to drive them away from me and do your foul work on the plain. My lovely channels are full of dead men's bodies. I am so choked with corpses that I cannot pour my waters into the sacred sea – and you are wallowing still in slaughter. Have done with it, my lord! I am appalled.'

'Scamander, child of Zeus,' replied Achilles the great runner, 'your will shall be done. But I am not going to stop killing these arrogant Trojans till I have penned them in their town, tried conclusions with Hector, and found out which of us two is to be the conqueror and which the killed.'

With that he fell upon the Trojans once more like a fiend. But now Scamander of the Deep Eddies appealed to Phoebus Apollo. 'For shame,' he cried, 'god of the Silver Bow and Son of Zeus! Is this how you obey your Father? Did he not tell you many times that you were to stand by the Trojans and protect them till the evening dusk should throw its shadows over the fruitful fields?'

When he heard this, the great spearman Achilles leapt from the bank and plunged into the middle of the stream. Scamander rushed on him in spate. He filled all his channels with foaming cataracts, and roaring like a bull he flung up on dry land the innumerable bodies of Achilles' victims that had choked him, protecting the survivors by hiding them in the deep and ample pools that beautified his course. The angry waters rose and seethed around Achilles; they beat down on his shield and overwhelmed him. Unable to maintain his stance, he laid hold of a full-grown elm. But the tree came out by the roots, brought the whole bank away, and crashed into the middle of the river, which it bridged from side to side, clogging the stream with a tangle of branches. Achilles struggled out of the current and in his terror made a dash for the bank, where he hoped his speed would save him. But the great god had not done yet with Prince Achilles – he meant to put his exploits to an end and save the Trojans from destruction. He rose and menaced him with a black wall of water. The son of Peleus fled, gaining a spear-throw's start by swooping away with the speed of the black eagle, that great hunter who is both the strongest and the fastest thing on wings. The bronze rang grimly on his shoulders as he made his escape from the overhanging wave, and an angry roar came from Scamander rolling in pursuit.

Achilles was a great runner, but the gods are greater than men, and time and again he was caught up by the van of the flood, like a gardener who is irrigating his plot by making a channel in among the plants for the fresh water from a spring. Mattock in hand, he clears obstructions from the trench; the water starts flowing; it sweeps the pebbles out of its way; and in a moment it runs singing down the slope and has outstripped its guide.

Sometimes the swift and excellent Achilles tried to make a stand and find out whether every god of the broad sky was chasing him. But whenever he stopped, a mighty billow from the heaven-fed river came crashing down on his shoulders. Exasperated, he struggled to his feet. But the water still raced madly by, gripping him round the knees and sweeping the loose earth from under him. The son of Peleus groaned aloud, and looking up into the broad sky he cried: 'O Father Zeus, will no god have compassion and take it on himself to save me from the River? Then I should welcome any other fate than this. Not that I blame the other Heavenly Ones so much as my own Mother, whose false predictions fooled me. She said I should fall to Apollo and his flying darts under the walls of the embattled Trojans. Ah, why could Hector not have killed me? He is the finest man they have bred in Troy, and the killer would have been as noble as the killed. But now it seems that I was doomed to die a villainous death, caught in a great river, like a boy in charge of the pigs who is swept away by a mountain stream that he has tried to cross in spate.'

In quick response to his appeal, Poseidon and Athene came and stood beside him. Adopting human form, they took his hands in theirs and uttered reassuring words, Poseidon first. 'Courage,' he said, 'my lord Achilles! You have no reason for undue alarm when two such allies as myself and Pallas Athene come down to your help with the blessing of Zeus. Believe me, you are not destined to be overcome by any River. This one will soon subside, as you will see for yourself. And here is some good advice from us – you would do well to take it. Do not cease fighting, whatever the hazards may be, till you have every Trojan who escapes you penned up inside the famous walls of Ilium. And do not go back to your ships till you have taken Hector's life. We are vouchsafing you this victory.'

Their aim achieved, the two gods left him and rejoined the immortal company, while Achilles, much heartened by this encouragement from Heaven, went on across the fields. They were completely inundated, and afloat with the fine armour and the corpses of the butchered men. But stepping high, Achilles fought his way upstream, and Athene so enhanced his strength that the spreading deluge could not hold him back. Not that Scamander's rage had yet abated. Indeed, in a fresh access of fury with the son of Peleus, he flung up a mighty billow with a curling crest and called aloud to Simoïs: 'Dear Brother, let us unite to overpower this man, who will soon be sacking Priam's royal city, with not a Trojan to put up a fight. Come quickly to my help. Fill your channels with water from the springs, replenish all your mountain streams, raise a great surge and send it down, seething with logs and boulders, so that we may stop this savage who is carrying all before him. He thinks himself a match for the gods; but I am determined not to let his strength or beauty save him now. Nor shall that splendid armour. It shall lie deep in the slime beneath my flood; and as for him, I'll roll him in the sand and pile up shingle high above him. The Achaeans will not know where to find his bones, I'll bury him so deep in silt. His barrow will be ready-made for him, and there will be no need to build him another when they hold his funeral.'

As he finished, the heaven-fed River towered up and rushed upon Achilles with an angry surge, seething with foam and blood and corpses. A dark wave hung high above the son of Peleus and was threatening to engulf him, when Here in her terror for Achilles, whom she thought the swirling River was about to sweep away, gave a scream of alarm and turned sharply to her Son Hephaestus. 'To arms, my Child, god of the Crooked Foot!' she cried. 'It is you we have been

counting on to deal with Xanthus in this fight. Quick, to the
rescue, and deploy your flames, while I go and rouse the West
Wind and the bright South to blow in fiercely from the sea
and spread the conflagration till the bodies and armour of the
dead Trojans are consumed. You yourself must burn the trees
on Xanthus' banks, and set the very River on fire. He will eat
humble pie and beg you for mercy, but do not be deterred;
and do not mitigate your fury till you hear a shout from me.
Then you can let your raging fires die down.'

Hephaestus responded to his Mother's call with a terrific
conflagration, which started on the plain and consumed the
bodies of Achilles' many victims that were scattered there.
The shimmering flood was stemmed and the whole plain
was parched, like a freshly sprinkled threshing-floor that the
North Wind dries up in autumn to the farmer's delight.
When Hephaestus had thus dealt with the plain and consumed
the dead, he attacked the River with his dazzling flames.
Elms, willows, tamarisks caught fire; and the lotus, rushes and
galingale that grew in profusion by the lovely stream were
burnt. Down in the pools, even the eels and fish that had been
tumbling about in their beautiful home were tortured by the
hot breath of the Master Engineer. The River himself was
scalded. 'Hephaestus!' he cried. 'You are more than a match
for any god. I cannot cope with this white heat of yours. The
fight is off. Let the great Achilles go straight in and drive the
Trojans from their town. Why should I help in other people's
quarrels?'

The fire devoured him as he spoke. His limpid water was
already bubbling like the melted fat of a well-fed pig when the
whole cauldron seethes as the dry logs underneath blaze up
and bring it to the boil. Thus lovely Xanthus was consumed
by fire and saw his waters going up in steam. Conquered by
the blast of the great Artificer, he lost heart and ceased to flow.
In his distress he called to Here and besought her mercy.
'Here,' he cried, 'why has your Son picked out my stream for
persecution? Compared with all the others who are fighting
on the Trojan side, I have done little to deserve it. However,

if you bid me, I will stop – but so must Hephaestus. I will do more: I undertake on oath to make no attempt to save the Trojans from their doom, not even on the day when their whole city is consumed by the devastating fires that will be lit there by the warrior sons of Achaea.'

When the white-armed goddess Here heard this cry from Xanthus, she called out at once to her Son: 'Enough, my noble Child Hephaestus! We must not deal so harshly with a god merely to help a man.' Hephaestus, hearing this, put out the conflagration, and the stream began to flow again between its beautiful banks.

There was no more fighting between these two after the discomfiture of Xanthus. Here, though still resentful, saw to that. But now the feud between the other gods, driven as they were by their passions into opposing camps, came to a head in open violence, and they fell upon each other with a terrific roar, which made high heaven ring and the wide world groan again. Zeus, sitting on Olympus, heard the din. He laughed to himself in delight when he saw the immortals come to grips. For they did not waste a moment before closing. Ares, Breaker of Shields, began the fight by making for Athene, bronze spear in hand and shouting abuse as he came. He denounced her as the meddlesome vixen whose boundless impudence and high-handed interference had set the gods at each other's throats, and he reminded her of the time when she had incited Diomedes, Tydeus' son, to wound him. 'You made no secret of it,' he cried. 'You took his spear in your own hand; you drove it straight at me and cut my flesh. Now I am going to make you pay for what I suffered from you then.'

With that he struck Athene's tasselled aegis. So the magic cloak, which can withstand even the thunderbolt of Zeus, endured a blow from the long spear of the murderous War-god. Athene drew back and with her great hand picked up a block of stone that was lying on the ground, a big rough boulder which people of a bygone age had set up in the fields to mark a boundary. With this she cast and struck the rabid War-god on the neck, bringing him down. His armour rang out, and there he lay, covering nine roods, with his locks in the dust. Pallas Athene laughed and made him an insulting speech. 'You stupid fool!' she said. 'Did it never occur to you, before you matched yourself with me, to think of my superior strength? Now, you can regard yourself as working off your Mother Here's curses. She has wished you ill, ever since you angered her by deserting the Achaeans to fight for the insolent Trojans.'

Athene, having finished with him, turned her brilliant eyes away; and Aphrodite Daughter of Zeus took Ares by the arm and led him from the field – he had scarcely recovered his senses and was groaning all the while. But the white-armed goddess Here saw this move on Aphrodite's part and in her excitement called to Athene. 'Look,' she cried, 'unsleeping Child of aegis-bearing Zeus! There goes that hussy again, escorting the butcher Ares through the crowd and off the battlefield. After her, quick!'

Athene's heart leapt up. She sped after Aphrodite, closed with her, and struck her on the breast with her fist. Aphrodite, showing no fight at all, collapsed at once, and she and Ares lay there on the bountiful earth, with Athene crowing over them: 'May everyone who helps the Trojans in their fight against the Argive men-at-arms acquit himself like these and show as much daring and resolution as Aphrodite when she ran to Ares' side and braved me in my fury! Then we should soon have finished with the war and sacked the lovely town of Troy.'

The white-armed goddess Here smiled at this sally of Athene's. And now Poseidon the Earthshaker issued a challenge to Apollo. 'Phoebus,' he called to him, 'why are we two standing idle and apart? Is that a proper thing when others have begun? We ought to be ashamed to go back without a fight to Olympus and the Bronze Palace of Zeus. Take the first cast. You are my junior, and my greater age and experience make it unfair for me to start. But what a fool you are and what a short memory you have! You seem to have forgotten all the hardships you and I endured at Ilium when we were segregated from the gods and sent by Zeus to serve the haughty Laomedon for a year. He was to pay our wages and we were at his beck and call. My task was to build a wall for the Trojans round their town, a strong and splendid one to make the place impregnable; while you, Phoebus, looked after the shambling cattle with their crooked horns on the wooded spurs of Ida of the many ridges. We served our term, but when the happy hour for payment came, the unconscionable Laomedon refused outright to give us any wages, and packed us off, threatening to lash our feet and hands together and to send us for sale to some distant island. He even talked of lopping off our ears. So home we came discomfited, and very sore with Laomedon about the wages he had promised and withheld. That is the man whose people you are now so anxious to oblige, instead of joining us and seeing to it that these insolent Trojans shall be utterly wiped out, together with their children and their loving wives.'

'Lord of the Earthquake,' answered the Archer-King Apollo, 'you would credit me with very little sense if I fought you for the sake of men, those wretched creatures who, like the leaves, flourish for a little while on the bounty of the earth and flaunt their brilliance, but in a moment droop and fade away. No, let us call the battle off before it is too late, and leave these men to do their own fighting.'

With that Apollo turned and went. He thought it an improper thing to come to blows with his Uncle. But now he had to listen to the biting comments of his Sister Artemis, Mistress of Beasts and Lady of the Wilds, who did not mince her words to him. 'So the great Archer runs away,' she said, 'after handing Poseidon a victory, and a cheap one too! What is the sense, blockhead, of carrying a bow you never use? I have often heard you boast to the immortal gods in our Father's house that you would stand up to Poseidon. Never let me hear you talk like that again.'

The Archer-King Apollo had no retort for his Sister. But Here, Consort of Zeus, was infuriated with the Mistress of the Bow and gave her a piece of her mind. 'Impudent hussy!' she exclaimed. 'Are you proposing to stand up to me? I know your bow and arrows, and what a lioness you are to women, whom Zeus allows you to destroy at your discretion; but if you match yourself with me you will regret it. You would find it better sport to slaughter wild deer in the mountains than to fight your superiors. But since you dare me and would like to try conclusions, let this teach you how much stronger I am.'

Here broke off, and with her left hand seized Artemis by both her wrists, while with her right she swept the bow and arrows from her shoulders. Then she boxed her on the ears with her own weapons, smiling as her victim writhed and the arrows came tumbling out of the quiver. Artemis burst into tears and fled from her like a pigeon that flies before a hawk and has the luck to get away alive into a cleft or hollow in a rock. Thus the goddess fled in tears, leaving her bow and arrows on the ground. But her Mother Leto was reassured by Hermes the Guide and Giant-Killer, who called across to her and said: 'Do not be afraid, Leto, that I am going to fight you. People who come to blows with Consorts of the Cloud-compeller Zeus seem to have uphill work. No; you can boast to your heart's content and tell the gods that you got the better of me by brute strength.'

So Leto gathered up the crooked bow and the arrows that had tumbled here and there in the swirling dust, and retired with her Daughter's weapons in her arms. Meanwhile the Maid herself had reached Olympus and gone to the Bronze Palace of Zeus, where she sat down on her Father's lap and sobbed, with her divine robe quivering on her bosom. The Son of Cronos took his Daughter in his arms and asked her with a merry laugh: 'Which of the Heavenly Ones has so ill-used my darling Child?' To which the Huntress of the Lovely Crown replied: 'Father, it was your own Wife, the white-armed Here, who beat me. This quarrelling among the immortal gods is all her fault.'

While these two were talking to one another, Phoebus Apollo went into sacred Ilium. He had his doubts about the walls and was afraid that the Achaeans might forestall the day of Destiny and sack the splendid town forthwith. But the rest of the everlasting gods, some in dejection, others in great glee, returned to Olympus and sat down with the Father, the Lord of the Black Cloud.

Meanwhile Achilles continued to destroy. Men and their strong horses fell to him alike. He dealt out tribulation and disaster to the Trojans like the angry gods when the smoke goes up to the broad sky from a town they have set on fire, making all its people toil and many mourn.

Old King Priam climbed one of the bastions that Poseidon had built and saw the gigantic Achilles, and the panic-stricken Trojans driven before him in utter impotence. He gave a cry of alarm, and came down from the bastion to give fresh orders to the tried watchmen who were posted by the wall to look after the gates. 'Hold the gates open,' he said, 'till our routed forces reach the town. They have Achilles at their heels, and I fear a massacre. Directly they are sheltered by the walls and can breathe once more, close the wooden doors. I am appalled at the prospect of having that savage penned up in the city.'

The men unfastened the doors and thrust back the bars. With the gates swung open, there was some hope of saving the troops. Moreover, Apollo rushed out to meet them and avert a massacre. They were making straight for the city and the high wall, parched by thirst and covered with dust from their flight across the plain, while close at their heels came Achilles with his spear, intent on glory and still in the grip of the high fury that had seized him. Indeed Troy of the Lofty Gates would now have fallen to the sons of Achaea if Phoebus Apollo had not intervened and inspired Antenor's noble son Agenor, an excellent and mighty man of war. The god breathed daring into his heart, and leaning against an oak he stood by him in person, though hidden by a thick mist, to save him from the heavy hand of Death. In consequence, when Agenor saw Achilles sacker of towns approaching, he stood and awaited him, though with many dark misgivings in his noble heart, as he ruefully considered his position. He thought: 'If I fly before the great Achilles, joining in the general stampede, he will catch me none the less and slit a coward's throat. On the other hand I might leave the rabble to be chased by Peleus' son, and slip away from the walls on foot by that other way to the Ileian Plain. On reaching the foothills of Ida, I could hide in the woods, and after bathing in the river and washing the sweat off my body, I could make my way back to Ilium in the evening. But why do I contemplate such a course? Achilles is bound to see me sneaking away from the town into the open country; he'll come after me full tilt and catch me up. That will be certain death: he is far too good a man for me or for anyone else on earth. One thing remains – to go and meet him here in front of the town. He too is vulnerable, after all. He has only one life, and nobody believes that he is immortal, even if Zeus the Son of Cronos lets him carry all before him.'

This settled it. Agenor braced himself and waited for Achilles without a tremor, once he had made up his mind to stand up to him in single combat. Thus a leopardess steps out from her jungle lair to face the huntsman, and neither feels nor shows a sign of fear when she hears the baying of the hounds. Even if the man gets in first with a cast or lunge and she is pierced by a javelin, her courage does not fail her and she grapples with him or dies in the attempt. Thus the excellent Antenor's son, the admirable Agenor, refused to fly before trying conclusions with the son of Peleus. He held his circular shield in front of his body, and aiming his spear at Achilles challenged him boldly. 'My lord Achilles,' he shouted, 'no doubt you thought that you were going to sack the proud city of Troy this very day. That was a foolish error. Troy will survive to witness much hard fighting yet. While we are there, she has plenty of stalwart sons to fight her battles under the eyes of their parents and their wives and children. It is you that are rushing to your doom, redoubtable and all-daring as you are.'

With that, he launched the sharp spear from his heavy hand, and sure enough he struck Achilles on the shin below the knee, making the tin of his new shin-guard ring grimly on his leg. But the god's work stood up to the blow and the bronze point rebounded: it had hit but had not wounded him. The son of Peleus in his turn attacked the godlike Agenor. But Apollo did not let him win this fight. Hiding Agenor in a thick mist, he swept him off and dismissed him unmolested from the field. The Archer-King then practised a ruse on Peleus' son to steer him away from the rest of the Trojan army. Making himself look exactly like Agenor, he appeared in Achilles' path. Achilles started eagerly in pursuit and chased the god across the wheatfields, heading him off towards Scamander of the Deep Pools. Apollo kept a little way ahead, and all the time he fooled Achilles into thinking he could overtake him by running still harder. Meanwhile the rest of the Trojans reached the city in a mass, with grateful hearts, and filled it as they crowded in. They had not even enough spirit left to wait for each other outside the city-walls, in order to find out who might have got away or who had fallen in the battle, so hastily did they pour into the town, all, that is to say, whose legs had saved their lives.

XXII

THE DEATH OF HECTOR

SWEPT into their city like a herd of frightened deer, the Trojans dried the sweat off their bodies, and drank and quenched their thirst as they leant against the massive battlements, while the Achaeans advanced on the wall with their shields at the slope. But Fate for her own evil purposes kept Hector where he was, outside the town in front of the Scaean Gate.

Meanwhile Phoebus Apollo revealed himself to Achilles son of Peleus. 'My lord,' he said, 'why are you chasing me? You are a man and I am an immortal god, as you might have known if you had not been so much preoccupied. Are you not neglecting your business with the Trojans whom you put to flight? Do you not see that they have shut themselves up in the town while you have strayed out here? You will never kill *me*: I am immune from death.'

Achilles of the nimble feet was furious. He rounded on the Archer-King and called him the most mischievous of gods. 'You have made a fool of me,' he cried, 'by luring me here, away from the walls. To think of all the Trojans who might yet have bitten the dust and not reached Ilium! You have robbed me of a great victory by saving their lives, an easy task for you, who had no punishment to fear – much as I should like to pay you out, if I only had the power.'

With no more words, Achilles turned his thoughts to mighty deeds and dashed away towards the town, running with the speed and easy action of the winning horse in a chariot-race when he puts on a spurt and finishes the course. Old King Priam was the first to see him rushing towards them over the fields. As he ran, the bronze on his breast flashed out like the star that comes to us in autumn, outshining all its fellows in the evening sky – they call it Orion's

Dog, and though it is the brightest of all stars it bodes no good, bringing much fever, as it does, to us poor wretches. The old man gave a groan. He lifted up his hands and beat his head with them. In a voice full of terror he shouted entreaties to his beloved son, who had taken his stand in front of the gates in the fixed resolve to fight it out with Achilles.

'Hector!' the old man called, stretching out his arms to him in piteous appeal. 'I beg you, my dear son, not to stand up to that man alone and unsupported. You are courting defeat and death at his hands. He is far stronger than you, and he is savage. The dogs and vultures would soon be feeding on his corpse (and what a load would be lifted from my heart!) if the gods loved him as little as I do – the man who has robbed me of so many splendid sons, killed them or sold them off as slaves to the distant isles. Even to-day there are two of them I cannot find among the troops that have taken refuge in the town, Lycaon and Polydorus, children of mine by the Princess Laothoe. If the enemy have taken them alive, we will ransom them presently with bronze and gold, of which she has plenty, for Altes, the honourable old man, gave his daughter a fortune. But if they are dead by now and in the Halls of Hades, there will be one more sorrow for me and their mother who brought them into the world, even though the rest of Ilium will not mourn for them so long – unless you join them and also fall to Achilles. So come inside the walls, my child, to be the saviour of Troy and the Trojans; and do not throw away your own dear life to give a triumph to the son of Peleus. Have pity too on me, your poor father, who is still able to feel. Think of the hideous fate that Father Zeus has kept in store for my old age, the horrors I shall have to see before I die, the massacre of my sons, my daughters mauled, their bedrooms pillaged, their babies dashed on the ground by the brutal enemy, and my sons' wives hauled away by foul Achaean hands. Last of all my turn will come to fall to the sharp bronze, and when someone's javelin or sword has laid me dead, I shall be torn to pieces by ravening dogs at my own street door. The very dogs I have fed at table and trained to watch my gate will loll about in front of it, maddened by their master's blood. Ah, it looks well enough for a young man killed in battle to lie there with his wounds upon him: death can find nothing to expose in him that is not beautiful. But when an old man is killed and dogs defile his grey head, his grey beard and his privy parts, we plumb the depths of human degradation.'

As he came to an end, Priam plucked at his grey locks and tore the hair from his head; but he failed to shake Hector's resolution. And now his mother in her turn began to wail and weep. Thrusting her dress aside, she exposed one of her breasts in her other hand and implored him, with the tears running down her cheeks. 'Hector, my child,' she cried, 'have some regard for this, and pity me. How often have I given you this breast and soothed you with its milk! Bear in mind those days, dear child. Deal with your enemy from within the walls, and do not go out to meet that man in single combat. He is a savage; and you need not think that, if he kills you, I shall lay you on a bier and weep for you, my own, my darling boy; nor will your richly dowered wife; but far away from both of us, beside the Argive ships, you will be eaten by the nimble dogs.'

Thus they appealed in tears to their dear son. But all their entreaties were wasted on Hector, who stuck to his post and let the monstrous Achilles approach him. As a mountain snake, who is maddened by the poisonous herbs he has swallowed, allows a man to come up to the lair where he lies coiled, and watches him with a baleful glitter in his eye, Hector stood firm and unflinching, with his glittering shield supported by an outwork of the wall. But he was none the less appalled, and groaning at his plight he took counsel with his indomitable soul. He thought: 'If I retire behind the gate and wall, Polydamas will be the first to cast it in my teeth that, in this last night of disaster when the great Achilles came to life, I did not take his advice and order a withdrawal into the city, as I certainly ought to have done. As it is, having sacrificed the army to my own perversity, I could not face my countrymen and the Trojan ladies in their trailing gowns. I could not bear to hear some commoner say: "Hector trusted in his own right arm and lost an army." But it *will* be said, and then I shall know that it would have been a far better thing for me to stand up to Achilles, and either kill him and come home alive or myself die gloriously in front of Troy. I could of course put down my bossed shield and heavy helmet, prop my spear against the wall, and on my own authority make overtures to Prince Achilles. I could promise to deliver Helen and all her property to the Atreidae, everything in fact that Paris brought away with him to Troy in his hollow ships when he sowed the seeds of this Achaean war. I could undertake besides to share all the rest of our possessions with the enemy, and then induce my countrymen to swear in Council that they would hide nothing, but divide all the movable property in our lovely town into two equal parts. But why do I contemplate such a course, when I have every reason to fear that if I approach Achilles he will show no pity, nor any regard for my person, but will kill me out of hand like a woman, naked and unarmed as I should be? No; at this hour I cannot see Achilles and myself as a pair of trysting lovers, billing and cooing to each other like a lad and lass. Better to waste no time, and come to grips. Then we should know to which of us the Olympian intends to hand the victory.'

While Hector stood engrossed in this inward debate, Achilles drew near him, looking like the god of War in his flashing helmet, girt for battle. Over his right shoulder he brandished the formidable ashen spear of Pelion, and the bronze on his body glowed like a blazing fire or the rising sun. Hector looked up, saw him, and began to tremble. He no longer had the heart to stand his ground; he left the gate, and ran away in terror. But the son of Peleus, counting on his speed, was after him in a flash. Light as a mountain hawk, the fastest thing on wings, when he swoops in chase of a timid dove, and shrieking close behind his quarry, darts at her time and again in his eagerness to make his kill, Achilles started off in hot pursuit; and like the dove flying before her enemy, Hector fled before him under the walls of Troy, fast as his feet would go. Passing the lookout and the windswept fig-tree and keeping some way from the wall, they sped along the cart-track, and so came to the two lovely springs that are the sources of Scamander's eddying stream. In one of these the water comes up hot; steam rises from it and hangs about like smoke above a blazing fire. But the other, even in summer, gushes up as cold as hail or freezing snow or water that has turned to ice. Close beside them, wide and beautiful, stand the troughs of stone where the wives and lovely daughters of the Trojans used to wash their glossy clothes in the peaceful days before the Achaeans came. Here the chase went by, Hector in front and Achilles after him – a good man, but with one far better at his heels. And the pace was furious. This was no ordinary race, with a sacrificial beast or a leather shield as prize. They were competing for the life of horse-taming Hector; and the pair of them circled thrice round Priam's town with flying feet, like powerful race-horses sweeping round the turning-post, all out for the splendid prize of a tripod or a woman offered at a warrior's funeral games.

They were watched by all the gods – in silence, till the Father of men and gods turned to the others with a sigh and said: 'I have a warm place in my heart for this man who is being chased before my eyes round the walls of Troy. I grieve for Hector. He has burnt the thighs of many oxen in my honour, both on the rugged heights of Ida and in the lofty citadel of Troy. But now the great Achilles is pursuing him at full speed round the city of Priam. Consider, gods, and help me to decide whether we shall save his life or let a good man fall this very day to Achilles son of Peleus.'

'Father!' exclaimed Athene of the Flashing Eyes. 'What are you saying? Are you, the Lord of the Bright Lightning and the Black Cloud, proposing to reprieve a mortal man, whose doom has long been settled, from the pains of death? Do as you please; but do not expect the rest of us to applaud.'

'Be reassured, Lady of Trito and dear Child of mine,' said Zeus the Cloud-compeller. 'I did not really mean to spare him. You can count on my goodwill. Act as you see fit, and act at once.' With which encouragement from Zeus, Athene, who had been itching to play her part, sped down from the peaks of Olympus.

Meanwhile Achilles of the nimble feet continued his relentless chase of Hector. As a hound who has started a fawn from its mountain lair pursues it through the coombs and glades, and even when it takes cover in a thicket, runs on, picks up the scent and finds his quarry, the swift Achilles was not to be thrown off the scent by any trick of Hector's. More than once Hector made a dash for the Dardanian Gates, hoping as he slipped along under the high walls to be saved from his pursuer by the archery of those above; but Achilles, keeping always to the inner course, intercepted him every time and headed him off towards the open country. And yet he could not catch him up, just as Hector could not shake Achilles off. It was like a chase in a nightmare, when no one, pursuer or pursued, can move a limb.

You may ask, how could Hector have escaped when Death was so close at his heels? He did so only through the final intervention of Apollo, who came to him for the last time, renewed his strength and gave him speed of foot. Moreover, Achilles had been signalling to his men by movements of his head that they were not to shoot at the quarry, for fear that he might be forestalled and one of them might win renown by striking Hector with an arrow. However, when they reached the Springs for the fourth time, the Father held out his golden scales, and putting sentence of death in either pan, on one side for Achilles, on the other for horse-taming Hector, he raised the balance by the middle of the beam. The beam came down on Hector's side, spelling his doom. He was a dead man. Phoebus Apollo deserted him; and Athene, goddess of the Flashing Eyes, went up to Achilles and spoke momentous words. 'Illustrious Achilles, darling of Zeus,' she said, 'our chance has come to go back to the ships with a glorious victory for Achaean arms. Hector will fight to the bitter end, but you and I are going to kill him. There is no escape for him now, however much the Archer-King Apollo may exert himself and grovel at the feet of his Father, aegis-bearing Zeus. Stay still now and recover your breath, while I go to Hector and persuade him to fight you.'

Achilles was well pleased and did as she told him. He stood there leaning on his bronze-bladed spear, while Athene went across from him to Hector and accosted him, borrowing for her purpose the appearance and the tireless voice of Dei-phobus. 'My dear brother,' she said to Hector, 'the swift Achilles must have worn you out, chasing you at that speed round the city. Let us make a stand and face him here to-gether.'

'Deiphobus,' said the great Hector of the flashing helmet, 'I have always loved you far the best of all the brothers Hecabe and Priam gave me. But from now on I shall think even better of you, since you had the courage, when you saw my plight, to come outside the walls and help me, while all the rest stayed in the town.'

'Dear brother,' said Athene of the Flashing Eyes, 'I can assure you that our father and lady mother begged and implored me to stay where I was, one after the other. My men were there and did the same – they are all in such terror of Achilles. But I was tormented by anxiety on your behalf. Let us attack him boldly and not be niggardly with spears. We shall soon find out whether Achilles is to kill the pair of us and go off with our bloodstained armour to the hollow ships, or himself be conquered by your spear.' Athene's ruse succeeded and she led him forward. Hector and Achilles met.

Great Hector of the flashing helmet spoke first: 'My lord Achilles, I have been chased by you three times round the great city of Priam without daring to stop and let you come near. But now I am going to run away no longer. I have made up my mind to fight you man to man and kill you or be killed. But first let us make a bargain, you with your gods for witness, I with mine – no compact could have better guarantors. If Zeus allows me to endure, and I kill you, I undertake to do no outrage to your body that custom does not sanction. All I shall do, Achilles, is to strip you of your splendid armour. Then I will give up your corpse to the Achaeans. Will you do the same for me?'

Achilles of the nimble feet looked at him grimly and replied: 'Hector, you must be mad to talk to me about a pact. Lions do not come to terms with men, nor does the wolf see eye to eye with the lamb – they are enemies to the end. It is the same with you and me. Friendship between us is impossible, and there will be no truce of any kind till one of us has fallen and glutted the stubborn god of battles with his blood. So summon any courage you may have. This is the time to show your spearmanship and daring. Not that anything is going to save you now, when Pallas Athene is waiting to fell you with my spear. This moment you are going to pay the full price for all you made me suffer when your lance mowed down my friends.'

With this Achilles poised and hurled his long-shadowed spear. But illustrious Hector was looking out and managed to avoid it. He crouched, with his eye on the weapon; and it flew over his head and stuck in the ground. But Pallas Athene snatched it up and brought it back to Achilles.

Hector the great captain, who had not seen this move, called across to the peerless son of Peleus: 'A miss for the godlike Achilles! It seems that Zeus gave you the wrong date for my death! You were too cocksure. But then you're so glib, so clever with your tongue – trying to frighten me and drain me of my strength. Nevertheless, you will not make me run, or catch me in the back with your spear. Drive it through my breast as I charge – if you get the chance. But first you will have to dodge this one of mine. And Heaven grant that all its bronze may be buried in your flesh! This war would be an easier business for the Trojans, if you, their greatest scourge, were dead.'

With that he swung up his long-shadowed spear and cast. And sure enough he hit the centre of Achilles' shield, but his spear rebounded from it. Hector was angry at having made so fine a throw for nothing, and he stood there discomfited, for he had no second lance. He shouted aloud to Deiphobus of the white shield, asking him for a long spear. But Deiphobus was nowhere near him; and Hector, realizing what had happened, cried: 'Alas! So the gods did beckon me to my death! I thought the good Deiphobus was at my side; but he is in the town, and Athene has fooled me. Death is no longer far away; he is staring me in the face and there is no escaping him. Zeus and his Archer Son must long have been resolved on this, for all their goodwill and the help they gave me. So now I meet my doom. Let me at least sell my life dearly and have a not inglorious end, after some feat of arms that shall come to the ears of generations still unborn.'

Hanging down at his side, Hector had a sharp, long and weighty sword. He drew this now, braced himself, and swooped like a high-flying eagle that drops to earth through the black clouds to pounce on a tender lamb or a crouching hare. Thus Hector charged, brandishing his sharp sword. Achilles sprang to meet him, inflamed with savage passion. He kept his front covered with his decorated shield; his glittering helmet with its four plates swayed as he moved his head and made the splendid golden plumes that Hephaestus had lavished on the crest dance round the top; and bright as the loveliest jewel in the sky, the Evening Star when he comes out at nightfall with the rest, the sharp point scintillated on the spear he balanced in his right hand, intent on killing Hector, and searching him for the likeliest place to reach his flesh.

Achilles saw that Hector's body was completely covered by the fine bronze armour he had taken from the great Patroclus when he killed him, except for an opening at the gullet where the collar bones lead over from the shoulders to the neck, the easiest place to kill a man. As Hector charged him, Prince Achilles drove at this spot with his lance; and the point went right through the tender flesh of Hector's neck, though the heavy bronze head did not cut his windpipe, and left him able to address his conqueror. Hector came down in the dust and the great Achilles triumphed over him. 'Hector,' he said, 'no doubt you fancied as you stripped Patroclus that you would be safe. You never thought of me: I was too far away. You were a fool. Down by the hollow ships there was a man far better than Patroclus in reserve, the man who has brought you low. So now the dogs and birds of prey are going to maul and mangle you, while we Achaeans hold Patroclus' funeral.'

'I beseech you,' said Hector of the glittering helmet in a failing voice, 'by your knees, by your own life and by your parents, not to throw my body to the dogs at the Achaean ships, but to take a ransom for me. My father and my lady mother will pay you bronze and gold in plenty. Give up my body to be taken home, so that the Trojans and their wives may honour me in death with the ritual of fire.'

The swift Achilles scowled at him. 'You cur,' he said, 'don't talk to me of knees or name my parents in your prayers. I only wish that I could summon up the appetite to carve and eat you raw myself, for what you have done to me. But this at least is certain, that nobody is going to keep the dogs from you, not even if the Trojans bring here and weigh out a ransom ten or twenty times your worth, and promise more besides; not if Dardanian Priam tells them to pay your weight in gold – not even so shall your lady mother lay you on a bier to mourn the son she bore, but the dogs and birds of prey shall eat you up.'

Hector of the flashing helmet spoke to him once more at the point of death. 'How well I know you and can read your mind!' he said. 'Your heart is hard as iron – I have been wasting my breath. Nevertheless, pause before you act, in case the angry gods remember how you treated me, when your turn comes and you are brought down at the Scaean Gate in all your glory by Paris and Apollo.'

Death cut Hector short and his disembodied soul took wing for the House of Hades, bewailing its lot and the youth and manhood that it left. But Prince Achilles spoke to him again though he was gone. 'Die!' he said. 'As for my own death, let it come when Zeus and the other deathless gods decide.'

Then he withdrew his bronze spear from the corpse and laid it down. As he removed the bloodstained arms from Hector's shoulders, other Achaean warriors came running up and gathered round. They gazed in wonder at the size and marvellous good looks of Hector. And not a man of all who had collected there left him without a wound. As each went in and struck the corpse, he looked at his friends, and the jest went round: 'Hector is easier to handle now than when he set the ships on fire.'

After stripping Hector, the swift and excellent Achilles stood up and made a speech to the Achaeans. 'My friends,' he said, 'Captains and Counsellors of the Argives; now that the gods have let us get the better of this man, who did more damage than all the rest together, let us make an armed reconnaissance round the city and find out what the Trojans mean to do next, whether they will abandon their fortress now that their champion has fallen, or make up their minds to hold it without Hector's help. But what am I saying? How can I think of anything but the dead man who is lying by my ships unburied and unwept – Patroclus, whom I shall never forget as long as I am still among the living and can walk the earth, my own dear comrade, whom I shall remember even though the dead forget their dead, even in Hades' Halls? So come now, soldiers of Achaea, let us go back to the hollow ships carrying this corpse and singing a song of triumph: "We have won great glory. We have killed the noble Hector, who was treated like a god in Troy."'

The next thing that Achilles did was to subject the fallen prince to shameful outrage. He slit the tendons at the back of both his feet from heel to ankle, inserted leather straps, and made them fast to his chariot, leaving the head to drag. Then he lifted the famous armour into his car, got in himself, and with a touch of his whip started the horses, who flew off with a will. Dragged behind him, Hector raised a cloud of dust, his black locks streamed on either side, and dust fell thick upon his head, so comely once, which Zeus now let his enemies defile on his own native soil.

Thus Hector's head was tumbled in the dust. When his mother saw what they were doing to her son, she tore her hair, and plucking the bright veil from her head cast it away with a loud and bitter cry. His father groaned in anguish, the people round them took up the cry of grief, and the whole city gave itself up to despair. They could not have lamented louder if Ilium had been going up in flames, from its frowning citadel to its lowest street. In his horror the old king made for the Dardanian Gate, bent on going out, and when his people had with difficulty stopped him, he grovelled in the dung and implored them all, calling on each man by his name. 'Friends, let me be,' he said. 'You overdo your care for me. Let me go out of the town alone to the Achaean ships. I want to plead with this inhuman monster, who may perhaps be put to shame by Hector's youth and pity my old age. After all he too has a father of the same age as myself, Peleus, who gave him life and brought him up to be a curse to all the Trojans, though none of them has suffered at his hands so much as I, the father of so many sons butchered by him in the heyday of their youth. And yet, though I bewail them all, there is one for whom I mourn still more, with a bitter sorrow that will bring me to the grave; and that is Hector. Ah, if he could only have died in my arms! Then we could have wept and wailed for him to our hearts' content, I and the mother who brought him, to her sorrow, into the world.'

Thus Priam, through his tears. The citizens of Troy added their moans to his; and now Hecabe led the Trojan women in a poignant lament. 'My child!' she cried. 'Ah, misery me! Why should I live and suffer now that you are dead? Night and day in Troy you were my pride, and to every man and woman in the town a saviour whom they greeted as a god. Indeed you were their greatest glory while you lived. Now, Death and Destiny have taken you away.'

Thus Hecabe wailed and wept. But Hector's wife had not yet heard the news. No one in fact had even gone to tell her that her husband had remained outside the gates. She was at work, in a corner of her lofty house, on a purple web of double width, which she was decorating with a floral pattern. In her innocence, she had just called to the ladies-in-waiting in her house to put a big cauldron on the fire so that Hector could have a hot bath when he came home from the battle – never dreaming that far away from all baths he lay dead at the hands of Achilles and bright-eyed Athene. But now the keening and moaning at the battlements reached her ears. She trembled all over and dropped her shuttle on the floor. She called again to her ladies-in-waiting: 'Come with me, two of you: I must see what has happened. That was my husband's noble mother that I heard; and as for me, my heart is in my mouth and I cannot move my legs. Some dreadful thing is threatening the House of Priam. Heaven defend me from such news, but I am terribly afraid that the great Achilles has caught my gallant husband by himself outside the town and chased him into the open; indeed that he may have put an end already to the headstrong pride that was Hector's passion. For Hector would never hang back with the crowd; he always sallied out in front of all the rest and let no one be as daring as himself.'

As she finished, Andromache, with palpitating heart, rushed out of the house like a mad woman, and her maid-servants went with her. When they came to the wall, where the men had gathered in a crowd, she climbed up on the battlements, searched the plain, and saw them dragging her husband in front of the town – the powerful horses were hauling him along at an easy canter towards the Achaean ships. The world went black as night before Andromache's eyes. She lost her senses and fell backward to the ground, dropping the whole of her gay headdress from her head, the coronet, the cap, the plaited snood and the veil that golden Aphrodite gave her on the day when Hector of the flashing helmet, having paid a princely dowry for his bride, came to fetch her from Eëtion's house. As she lay there in a dead faint, her husband's sisters and his brothers' wives crowded around her and supported her between them. When at length she recovered and came to herself, she burst out sobbing and made her lament to the ladies of Troy.

'Alas, Hector; alas for me!' she cried. 'So you and I were born under the same unhappy star, you here in Priam's house and I in Thebe under wooded Placus in the house of Eëtion, who brought me up from babyhood, the unlucky father of a more unlucky child, who wishes now that she had never seen the light of day. For you are on your way to Hades and the unknown world below, leaving me behind in misery, a widow in your house. And your son is no more than a baby, the son we got between us, we unhappy parents. You, Hector, now that you are dead, will be no joy to him, nor he to you. Even if he escapes the horrors of the Achaean war, nothing lies ahead of him but hardship and trouble, with strangers eating into his estate. An orphaned child is cut off from his playmates. He goes about with downcast looks and tear-stained cheeks. In his necessity he looks in at some gathering of his father's friends and plucks a cloak here and a tunic there, till someone out of charity holds up a wine-cup to his mouth, but only for a moment, just enough to wet his lips and leave his palate dry. Then comes another boy, with both his parents living, who beats him with his fists and drives him from the feast and jeers at him. "Out you go!" he shouts. "You have no father dining here." So the child runs off in tears to his widowed mother – little Astyanax, who used to sit on his father's knees and eat nothing but marrow and mutton fat, and when he was sleepy and tired of play, slept in a bed, softly cradled in his nurse's arms, full of good cheer. But now, with his father gone, evils will crowd in on Astyanax, Protector of Troy, as the Trojans called him, seeing in you the one defence of their long walls and gates. And you, by the beaked ships, far from your parents, will be eaten by the wriggling worms when the dogs have had their fill, lying naked, for all the delicate and lovely clothing made by women's hands that you possess at home. All of which I am going to burn to ashes. It is of no use to you: you will never lie in it. But the men and women of Troy shall accord you that last mark of honour.'

Thus Andromache lamented through her tears, and the women joined in her lament.

XXIII

THE FUNERAL AND THE GAMES

WHILE the city of Troy gave itself up to lamentation, the Achaeans withdrew to the Hellespont, and when they reached the ships, dispersed to their several vessels. Only the battle-loving Myrmidons were not dismissed. Achilles kept his followers with him and addressed them. 'Myrmidons,' he said, 'lovers of the fast horse, my trusty band; we will not unyoke our horses from their chariots yet, but mounted as we are, will drive them past Patroclus and mourn for him as a dead man should be mourned. Then, when we have wept and found some solace in our tears, we will unharness them and all have supper here.'

The Myrmidons with one accord broke into lamentation. Achilles led the way, and the mourning company drove their long-maned horses three times round the dead, while Thetis stirred them all to weep without restraint. The sands were moistened and their warlike panoply was bedewed with tears, fit tribute to so great a panic-maker. And now the son of Peleus, laying his man-killing hands on his comrade's breast, led them in the melancholy dirge: 'Rejoice, Patroclus, even in the Halls of Hades. I am keeping all the promises I made you. I have dragged Hector's body here, for the dogs to eat it raw; and at your pyre I am going to cut the throats of a dozen of the highborn youths of Troy, to vent my anger at your death.'

Achilles, when he had finished, thought of one more indignity to which he could subject Prince Hector. He flung him down on his face in the dust by the bier of Menoetius' son. His soldiers then took off their burnished bronze equipment, unyoked their neighing horses, and sat down in their hundreds by the ship of the swift son of Peleus, who had provided for them a delicious funeral feast. Many a white ox fell with his last gasp to the iron knife, many a sheep and bleating goat was slaughtered, and many a fine fat hog was stretched across the flames to have his bristles singed. Cupfuls of blood were poured all round the corpse.

Meanwhile Prince Achilles, the swift son of Peleus, was taken by the Achaean kings to dine with the lord Agamemnon, though they had hard work to make him come, still grieving for his comrade as he was. When they reached Agamemnon's hut they told the clear-voiced heralds to put a big three-legged cauldron on the fire in the hope of inducing Achilles to wash the clotted gore from his body. But he would not hear of such a thing. He even took a vow and said: 'By Zeus, who is the best and greatest of the gods, it shall be sacrilege for any water to come near my head till I have burnt Patroclus, made him a mound and shorn my hair, for I shall never suffer again as I am suffering now, however long I live. But for the moment, though I hate the thought of food, we must yield to necessity and dine. And at dawn, perhaps your majesty King Agamemnon will order wood to be collected and everything to be provided that a dead man ought to have with him when he travels into the western gloom, so that Patroclus may be consumed by fire as soon as possible and the men return to their duties when he is gone.'

They readily agreed and set to with a will on the preparation of their supper, in which they all had equal shares. They ate with zest, and when they had satisfied their thirst and hunger they retired for the night to their several huts. But the son of Peleus groaning wearily lay down on the shore of the sounding sea, among his many Myrmidons, but in an open space, where the waves were splashing on the beach. His splendid limbs were exhausted by his chase of Hector to the very walls of windy Ilium; but he had no sooner fallen into a sleep that soothed and enfolded him, resolving all his cares, than he was visited by the ghost of poor Patroclus, looking and talking exactly like the man himself, with the same stature, the same lovely eyes, and the same clothes as those he used to wear.

It halted by his head and said to him: 'You are asleep: you have forgotten me, Achilles. You neglect me now that I am dead; you never did so when I was alive. Bury me instantly and let me pass the Gates of Hades. I am kept out by the disembodied spirits of the dead, who have not let me cross the River and join them, but have left me to pace up and down forlorn on this side of the Gaping Gates. And give me that hand, I beseech you; for once you have passed me through the flames I shall never come back again from Hades. Never again on earth will you and I sit down together, out of ear-shot of our men, to lay our plans. For I have been engulfed by the dreadful fate that must have been my lot at birth; and it is your destiny too, most worshipful Achilles, to perish under the walls of the rich town of Troy. And now, one more request. Do not let them bury my bones apart from yours, Achilles. Let them lie together, just as you and I grew up together in your house, after Menoetius brought me there from Opus as a child because I had had the misfortune to commit homicide and kill Amphidamas' boy by accident in a childish quarrel over a game of knuckle-bones. The knightly Peleus welcomed me to his palace and brought me up with loving care. And he appointed me your squire. So let one urn, the golden vase your lady Mother gave you, hold our bones.'

'Dear heart,' said the swift Achilles, 'what need was there for you to come and ask me to attend to all these things? Of course I will see to everything and do exactly as you wish. But now come nearer to me, so that we may hold each other in our arms, if only for a moment, and draw cold comfort from our tears.'

With that, Achilles held out his arms to clasp the spirit, but in vain. It vanished like a wisp of smoke and went gibbering underground. Achilles leapt up in amazement. He beat his hands together and in his desolation cried: 'Ah then, it is true that something of us does survive even in the Halls of Hades, but with no intellect at all, only the ghost and semblance of a man; for all night long the ghost of poor Patroclus (and it looked exactly like him) has been standing at my side, weeping and wailing, and telling me of all the things I ought to do.' Achilles' outcry woke the Myrmidons to further lamentation, and Dawn, when she stole up to them on crimson toes, found them wailing round the pitiable dead.

Meanwhile King Agamemnon sent mules and men from every part of the encampment to fetch wood. The officer in charge of the party was Meriones, the squire of the lovable Idomeneus. The men carried woodman's axes in their hands together with stout ropes, and the mules walked ahead of them. They went up dale and down by many a zigzag path, and came at last to the spurs of Ida of the many springs. There they set to work with a will felling the tall oaks with their long-bladed axes, and trees came crashing down. The Achaeans split the logs and then roped them to the mules, who cut up the ground with their feet in their efforts to haul them down to the plain through the tangled undergrowth. The woodcutters too all carried logs, by order of Meriones, squire to the amiable Idomeneus. When they reached the shore, they laid them neatly down at the spot where Achilles planned to build a great mound for Patroclus and himself.

Having stacked this huge supply of wood all round the site, they sat down and waited there in a body. Achilles then gave orders for his war-loving Myrmidons to put on their bronze and for every charioteer to yoke his horses. They hurried off and got into their armour, and the fighting men and drivers mounted their cars. The horse led off, and after them came a mass of infantry one could not count. In the middle of the procession Patroclus was carried by his own men, who had covered his body with the locks of hair they had cut off and cast upon it. Behind them Prince Achilles supported the head, as the chief mourner, who was despatching his highborn comrade to the Halls of Hades.

When they came to the place appointed for them by Achilles, they put Patroclus down and quickly built him a noble pile of wood. But now a fresh idea occurred to the swift and excellent Achilles. Stepping back from the pyre, he cut off from his head an auburn lock he had allowed to grow ever since its dedication to the River Spercheus. Then he looked out angrily across the wine-dark sea and said: 'Spercheus, is this your answer to my father Peleus' prayers? He promised you that at my home-coming from Troy I should cut off this lock for you and make you the rich offering of fifty rams, sacrificed beside your very waters, where you have a precinct and a fragrant altar. That was the old king's vow; but you have denied him what he prayed for. And now, since I shall never see my own country again, I propose to part with this lock and give it to my lord Patroclus.'

As he spoke, he put the lock in the hands of his beloved comrade. His gesture moved the whole gathering to further tears, and sunset would have found them still lamenting, if Achilles had not had a sudden thought. He went up to Agamemnon and said: 'My lord Atreides, you are the man to whom the troops will listen. Of course they can mourn as much as they wish; but for the moment I ask you to dismiss them from the pyre and tell them to prepare their midday meal. We that are the chief mourners will see to everything here, though I should like the Achaean commanders to remain.'

On hearing what Achilles wished, Agamemnon King of Men dismissed the troops to their trim ships; but the chief mourners stayed where they were and piled up wood. They made a pyre a hundred feet in length and breadth, and with sorrowful hearts laid the corpse on top. At the foot of the pyre they flayed and prepared many well-fed sheep and shambling cattle with crooked horns. The great-hearted Achilles, taking fat from all of them, covered the corpse with it from head to foot, and then piled the flayed carcasses round Patroclus. To these he added some two-handled jars of honey and oil, leaning them against the bier; and in his zeal he cast on the pyre four high-necked horses, groaning aloud as he did so. The dead lord had kept nine dogs as pets. Achilles slit the throats of two and threw them on the pyre. Then he went on to do an evil thing – he put a dozen brave men, the sons of noble Trojans, to the sword, and set the pyre alight so that the pitiless flames might feed on them. This done, he gave a groan and spoke once more to his beloved friend: 'All hail from me, Patroclus, in the very Halls of Hades! I am keeping all the promises I made you. Twelve gallant Trojans, sons of noblemen, will be consumed by the same fire as you. For Hector son of Priam I have other plans – I will not give him to the flames, I will throw him to the dogs to eat.'

But in spite of this threat from Achilles the dogs were not given access to the corpse of Hector. Day and night, Zeus' Daughter Aphrodite kept them off, and she anointed him with ambrosial oil of roses, so that Achilles should not lacerate him when he dragged him to and fro. Moreover, Phoebus Apollo caused a dark cloud to sink from the sky to the ground and settle on the corpse, covering the whole area in which it lay, so that the heat of the sun getting at this side and that should not wither the skin on his sinews and his limbs too soon.

There was some delay with the body of Patroclus also: the pyre refused to kindle. But a remedy suggested itself to the swift and excellent Achilles. Standing clear of the pyre, he prayed and offered splendid offerings to the two winds, Boreas of the North and Zephyr of the Western Gale. He made them rich libations from a golden cup and implored them to come so that the wood might kindle readily and the bodies quickly be cremated. Iris heard his prayers and sped off to convey his message to the Winds, who had all sat down together to a banquet in the draughty house of the Western Gale. Iris came running up, and when they saw her standing on the stone threshold, they all leapt to their feet and each invited her to come and sit beside him. But she excused herself, and went on to deliver her message. 'I have no time to sit down,' she said. 'I must get back to Ocean Stream and the Ethiopians' land, where they are entertaining the immortals at a sacrificial banquet I am anxious not to miss. But I have a message from Achilles for you, Boreas and the Western Gale. He is praying to you and promising you splendid offerings if

you will come and kindle the pyre under the body of Patro-
clus, for whom the whole Achaean army is mourning.'

Her message delivered, Iris went off, and the two Winds
rose uproariously, driving the clouds before them. In a
moment they were out at sea, blowing hard and raising billows
with their noisy breath. When they came to the deep-soiled
land of Troy, they fell upon the funeral pile and the fire
blazed up with a terrific roar. Howling round the pyre they
helped each other all night long to fan the flames; and all night
long the swift Achilles, using a two-handled cup which he
replenished from a golden mixing-bowl, poured out libations,
drenched the earth with wine, and called on the spirit of the
unhappy Patroclus. As a father weeps when he is burning the
bones of a son who has died on his wedding-day and left his
stricken parents in despair, Achilles wept as he burned his
comrade's bones, moving round the pyre on leaden feet with
many a deep groan.

At the time when the Morning Star comes up to herald a
new day on earth, and in his wake Dawn spreads her saffron
mantle over the sea, the fire sank low, the flames expired, and
the Winds set out for home across the Thracian Sea, where the
roaring waves ran high. Achilles was exhausted. Turning
from the pyre he sank to the ground and instantly fell fast
asleep. But the other chieftains, who had joined King Aga-
memnon, would not let him be, and the whole party now
approached him. Roused by their voices and footsteps, he
sat up and told them what he wanted done. 'My lord Atrei-
des,' he said, 'and you other leaders of the united Achaeans;
make it your first task to put out with sparkling wine what-
ever portions of the pyre the flames have reached. Then we
must collect my lord Patroclus' bones, being careful to dis-
tinguish them, though that will not be difficult, as he lay in
the centre of the pyre, separated from the rest, who were
burnt on the verge of it, horses and men together. We will
put the bones in a golden vase and seal it with a double layer
of fat, against the time when I myself shall have vanished in
the world below. As for his barrow, I do not ask you to con-

struct a very large one, something that is seemly but no more. Later you can build a big and high one, you Achaeans that are left in the well-found ships when I am gone.'

They went about the business as the swift son of Peleus had directed. First they put out with sparkling wine all parts of the funeral pyre in which the flames had done their work and the ash had fallen deep. Then, with tears on their cheeks, they collected the white bones of their gentle comrade in a golden vase, closed it with a double seal of fat, laid it in his hut and covered it with a soft linen shroud. Next they designed his barrow by laying down a ring of stone revetments round the pyre. Then they fetched earth and piled it up inside.

When the troops had built the monument, they made as if to go. But Achilles stopped them and told them all to sit down in a wide ring where the sports were to be held. For these he brought out prizes from the ships – cauldrons and tripods; horses, mules, and sturdy cattle; grey iron and women in their girdled gowns.

The first event was a chariot-race, for which he offered the following splendid prizes: for the winner, a woman skilled in the fine crafts, and a tripod with ear-shaped handles, holding two-and-twenty pints; for the runner-up, a mare six years old and broken in, with a little mule in her womb; for the third man, a fine kettle holding four pints, untarnished by the flames and still as bright as ever; for the fourth, two talents of gold; and for the fifth, a two-handled pan, as yet untouched by fire.

Achilles stood up to announce the contest to the Argives. 'My lord Atreides and Achaean men-at-arms, these are the prizes that await the winning charioteers. Of course, if we were holding sports in honour of some other man, it is I who would walk off to my hut with the first prize, for you don't need me to tell you that my horses are the best of all, being immortal and a present from Poseidon to my father Peleus, who passed them on to me. But I and my splendid pair will not compete: they are in mourning for their glorious driver. How kind Patroclus was to them, always washing them down with clean water and then pouring olive-oil on their manes!

No wonder they stand there and grieve for him. Their manes are trailing on the ground and in their sorrow they refuse to move. However, the event is open to anyone else in the whole army who believes in his horses and the build of his chariot. So take your places now.'

This announcement from Achilles brought out the ablest charioteers. The first to spring to his feet was Admetus' son Eumelus King of Men, who was an excellent horseman. Next, the mighty Diomedes son of Tydeus, who harnessed the horses of the breed of Tros that he had taken earlier from Aeneas on the occasion when Apollo saved their master's life. Then red-haired Menelaus son of Atreus, scion of Zeus, who yoked a fast pair, Aethe, a mare of Agamemnon's, and his own horse Podargus. Aethe had been presented to Agamemnon by Echepolus son of Anchises, on condition that he need not go with him to windy Ilium but could stay at home in comfort – he happened to be a very rich man, who lived in Sicyon of the broad lawns. This was the mare that Menelaus yoked – she was champing to be off. The fourth man to harness his long-maned horses was Antilochus. He was the noble son of the magnanimous King Nestor son of Neleus, and his chariot-horses were of Pylian breed. His father now went up to him and gave him some useful hints, though he knew his business well enough himself.

'Antilochus,' said Nestor, 'young as you are, you stand well with Zeus and Poseidon and they have taught you the whole art of driving horses. So there is no great need for me to put you right. But expert though you are at wheeling round the turning-post, your horses are very slow, and I am afraid you will find this a great handicap. Yet even if the other pairs are faster, their drivers do not know a single trick that is not known to you. So you must fall back, my friend, on all the skill that you can summon, if you do not wish to say good-bye to the prizes. It is skill, rather than brawn, that makes the best lumberman. Skill, again, enables a steersman to keep a straight course over the wine-dark sea when his good ship is yawing in the wind. And it is by his skill that one driver beats another. The average man, leaving too much to his chariot and pair, is careless at the turn and loses ground to one side or the other; his horses wander off the course and he does not correct them. But the cunning driver, though behind a slower pair, always has his eye on the post, and wheels close in; he is not caught napping when the time comes to use the oxhide reins and stretch his horses; he keeps them firmly in hand and watches the man who is leading.

'Now let me tell you something to look out for. It is obvious enough; you cannot miss it. There is a dead tree-stump, an oak or pine, standing about six feet high. It has not rotted in the rain, and it is flanked by two white stones. The road narrows at this point, but the going is good on both sides of the monument, which either marks an ancient burial or must have been put up as a turning-post by people of an earlier age. In any case it is the turning-post that my lord Achilles has chosen for this race. As you drive round it you must hug it close, and you in your light chariot must lean just a little to the left yourself. Call on your off-side horse, touch him with the whip and give him rein; but make the near horse hug the post so close that anyone might think you were scraping it with the nave of your wheel. And yet you must be careful not to touch the stone, or you may wreck your horses and smash up your car, which would delight the rest but not look well for you. So use your wits, my friend, and be on the lookout; for if you could overtake them at the turning-post, no one could catch you up or pass you with a spurt, not even if he came behind you with Adrestus' thoroughbred, the great Arion, who was sired in heaven, or the famous horses of Laomedon, the best that Troy has bred.'

Having thus expounded the whole art of horsemanship to his son, King Nestor went back to his seat. Meriones was the fifth man to get his horses ready. And now they all mounted their chariots and cast their lots into a helmet, which Achilles shook. The first lot to jump out was that of Antilochus son of Nestor; then came that of King Eumelus, followed by that of Atreus' son, the spearman Menelaus. Meriones drew the fourth starting-place, and the last fell to Diomedes, the best man of them all. They drew up side by side and Achilles showed them the turning-point, far away on level ground. He had posted the venerable Phoenix, his father's squire, as an umpire there, to keep an eye on the running and report what happened.

At one and the same moment they all gave their horses the whip, shook the reins on their backs and set them going with a sharp word of command. The horses started off across the plain without a hitch and quickly left the ships behind. The dust that rose from underneath their chests hung in the air like a storm-cloud or a fog, and their manes flew back in the wind. At one moment the chariots were in contact with the fruitful earth and at the next were bounding high in the air. The heart of each driver as he stood in his car and struggled to be first was beating hard. They yelled at their horses, who flew along in a cloud of dust.

But it was not till their galloping teams had rounded the mark and were heading back to the grey sea that each man showed his form and the horses stretched themselves. The fast mares of Eumelus now shot out of the ruck, and next came Diomedes' stallions of the breed of Tros, close behind, with very little in it. It looked as though at any moment they might leap into Eumelus' car. They were flying along with their heads just over him, warming his back and his broad shoulders with their breath. In fact Diomedes would have overhauled Eumelus then and there or made it a dead heat, if Phoebus Apollo, who was still angry with Tydeus' son, had not knocked the shining whip out of his hand. Diomedes, when he saw Eumelus' mares going better than ever and his own horses slowing down for lack of anything to spur them on, was so angry that the tears poured down his cheeks. But Athene had had her eye on Apollo when he fouled Diomedes. She sped after the great man, gave him back his whip and put fresh spirit in his horses. Moreover she was so enraged that she chased Eumelus too and used her powers as a goddess to break the yoke of his chariot, with the result that his mares ran off on their own and the shaft crumpled up on the ground, while Eumelus himself was flung out of the car and came down by the wheel. The skin was taken off his elbows, mouth and nose; his forehead was bruised; his eyes were filled with tears, and he was robbed of speech. Meanwhile Diomedes swept round the wreckage with his powerful horses, having left the others well behind. Athene filled his pair with strength and let their master triumph.

Next after Diomedes came red-haired Menelaus, Atreus' son; and next again Antilochus, who was shouting at his father's horses and urging them to spurt like Diomedes' pair. 'Show me your best paces now,' he cried. 'I am not asking you to race that pair ahead, the gallant Diomedes' horses, whom Athene has just speeded up so as to make her favourite win. But do catch up Atreides' pair and don't get left behind by them. Be quick about it too; or Aethe will be turning up her nose at you – and she a mare. Why are you hanging back, my friends? I tell you frankly what you can expect. No more attentions from King Nestor's hands for you! He will slit your throats without a moment's hesitation if you take it easy now and leave us with the smaller prize. So after them full tilt! Trust me to find a way of slipping past them where the track is narrow. I shall not miss my chance.'

His horses, taking their master's threat to heart, went faster for a little while, and very soon Antilochus, that veteran campaigner, saw a place where the sunken road grew narrow. It ran through a gulley: water piled up by the winter rains had carried part of it away and deepened the whole defile. Menelaus was in occupation of the track, making it difficult for anyone to come abreast of him. But Antilochus did not keep to it. He drove a little off it to one side, and pressed Menelaus hard. Menelaus was alarmed and shouted at him: 'You are driving madly, Antilochus; hold in your horses. The track is narrow here. It soon gets wider – you could pass me there. Be careful you don't hit my chariot and wreck us both.'

But Antilochus, pretending that he had not heard him, plied

his lash and drove more recklessly than ever. They both ran on for about the distance that a quoit will carry when a young man casts it with a swing of the arm to test his strength. Then Menelaus' pair gave way and fell behind. He eased the pace himself, on purpose, fearing that the powerful horses might collide in the road and upset the light chariots, in which case their masters, through their eagerness to win, would find themselves rolling in the dust. But red-haired Menelaus managed to give the other a piece of his mind. 'Antilochus,' he cried, 'you are the most appalling driver in the world. We were mistaken when we thought you had some sense. Well, have it your own way; but all the same, you shall not carry off the prize till you have answered on your oath for this affair.'

Then Menelaus turned to his horses. 'Don't stop,' he shouted at them. 'Don't stand and mope. That pair ahead of you will weaken in the leg far sooner than you. They are neither of them as young as they were.' His horses, frightened by their master's reprimand, sped on with a better will and soon were close behind the other pair.

Meanwhile from their seats in the ring the spectators were looking out for the horses, who were rapidly approaching in a cloud of dust. Idomeneus the Cretan King was the first to see them. He was sitting well above the rest on high ground outside the ring, and when he heard a driver shouting in the distance he knew the voice. He also recognized one of the leading horses, who showed up well, being chestnut all over but for a round white patch like the full moon which he had on his forehead. Idomeneus stood up and called to the other spectators: 'My friends, Captains and Counsellors of the Argives; am I the only one who can see the horses or do you see them too? It seems to me that a new pair are leading, and the driver also looks different. Eumelus' mares, who were ahead on the outward lap, must have come to grief out there, for I certainly saw them leading at the turning-post and now I cannot see them anywhere, though I have searched the whole Trojan plain. Perhaps Eumelus dropped his reins: he couldn't steer his horses round the mark and had an accident as he was

wheeling. Yes, that is where he must have been tossed out
and smashed his chariot, while his mares went wild and bolted.
But do get up and have a look yourselves. I cannot be quite
sure, but the leading man looks like an Aetolian to me, yes,
one of our Argive kings, the son of horse-taming Tydeus,
Diomedes himself.'

But Aias the Runner and son of Oïleus contradicted him
rudely. 'Idomeneus,' he said, 'why must you be for ever
showing off? Those high-stepping mares out there have a
long way yet to go; and you are not by any means the
youngest man among us, nor do you own the sharpest pair of
eyes. Yet you are always laying down the law. Here among
your betters you really must control your tongue. That pair
in front is the same that led before, Eumelus' mares. And
there's Eumelus, in the chariot, with the reins in his hands.'

The commander of the Cretans took offence at this. 'Aias,'
he retorted, 'you are a most cantankerous, ill-natured fellow,
and quite unlike an Argive in your lack of courtesy. But come
now, let us have a bet about the leading pair. We'll stake a
tripod or a cauldron, and have King Agamemnon as our
referee. You'll learn the truth when you pay up.'

Aias the Runner rose in fury to give Idomeneus an insolent
repartee; and the quarrel would have gone still further if
Achilles himself had not leapt to his feet and intervened. 'Aias
and Idomeneus,' he said, 'stop quarrelling. This interchange of
insults is a breach of good manners which you would be the
first to condemn in others. Why not sit down in the ring and
keep your eyes on the horses? They will soon be coming
along, all out for victory. Then each of you can recognize
them for himself and pick out the winners and the second pair.'

By now Diomedes was very close. He was driving with the
whip, swinging his arm right back for every lash, and making
his horses leap high in the air as they sped on to the finish.
Showers of dust fell on their driver all the time, and as the
fast pair flew over the ground the chariot overlaid with gold
and tin came spinning after them and scarcely left a tyre-
mark on the fine dust behind.

Diomedes drew up in the middle of the arena, with the sweat pouring to the ground from his horses' necks and chests. He leapt down from his glittering car and leant his whip against the yoke. Sthenelus, his gallant equerry, made short work of the prizes. He took possession promptly, giving the tripod with the ear-shaped handles to his exultant men and telling them to lead the woman off. Then he unyoked the horses.

Antilochus son of Nestor was the next man to drive up. He had beaten Menelaus not by any turn of speed but by a trick. Yet even so Menelaus and his fast horses came in close behind. There was no more in it than the space that separates a horse from the wheel of his master's car when he strains in the harness and pulls him along, trotting so close in front that the tip of his tail keeps brushing the tyre and there is hardly any gap, however far he runs. There was no more than that between Menelaus and the peerless Antilochus. It is true that at the time of the incident Menelaus had been left as much as a disk-throw in the rear. But he soon came up with him. Aethe's mettle had begun to tell – she was Agamemnon's lovely mare – and on a longer course Menelaus would have passed him. It would not even have ended in a dead heat.

Meriones, Idomeneus' worthy squire, came in a spear-throw behind the famous Menelaus. His long-maned horses were the slowest pair in the race, and he himself was the poorest racing-driver.

The last of them all to arrive was Admetus' son Eumelus. He was dragging his handsome chariot himself and driving his horses in front of him. When he saw this, the swift and excellent Achilles was sorry for the man. He stood up in the ring and made a suggestion: 'The best driver of the lot has come in last. Let us give him a prize, as is only fair. Make it the second, for of course Diomedes takes the first.'

Everyone welcomed this idea, and Achilles, encouraged by the men's applause, was about to give the mare to Eumelus, when Antilochus, King Nestor's son, jumped up and lodged a formal protest with the royal son of Peleus. 'My lord

Achilles,' he cried, 'I shall resent it keenly if you do as you suggest. You are proposing to rob me of my prize because Eumelus' chariot and horses came to grief – as did Eumelus, though he drives so well. The fact is that he ought to have prayed to the immortal gods; then he would never have come in last in the race. However, if you are sorry for the man and fond of him, there is plenty of gold in your hut, and copper and sheep, and you have women-servants too and splendid horses. Choose something later on from these and let him have an even better prize than mine. Or hand it to him now and hear the troops applaud you. But I will not give up this mare. Anyone who cares to try can come and fight me for her with his fists.'

This speech drew a smile from the swift and excellent Achilles. He had always liked Antilochus, his comrade-in-arms, and was delighted with him now. He gave him a gracious answer: 'Antilochus, if you really wish me to send for something extra from my hut and give it to Eumelus as a consolation prize, I will do even that for you. I will give him the cuirass I took from Asteropaeus. It is made of bronze and plated with bright tin all over. It is a gift that he will value.'

Thereupon Achilles told his squire Automedon to fetch the cuirass from his hut. Automedon went and brought it to him; and Achilles handed it to Eumelus, who was very pleased to have it.

But this was not all. Menelaus had by no means forgiven Antilochus and he now got up in a very ugly mood. A herald handed him the speaker's staff and called for silence. Then Menelaus spoke, looking the king he was. 'Antilochus,' he said, 'you used to be a very sensible fellow. Now see what you have done! By cutting in across me with your own far slower pair, you have made my driving look contemptible and robbed my horses of a win. My lords, Captains and Counsellors of the Argives, I appeal to you to judge between the two of us impartially, so that none of our men-at-arms will be able to say: "It was only by lying that Menelaus beat Antilochus and walked off with the mare. His horses really were much slower. It is his rank and power that bring him out on top." No, on second thoughts, I will hear the case myself. And I am not afraid that any Danaan will accuse me of injustice: it will be fairly tried. Antilochus, my lord, come forward here in the proper way; stand in front of your chariot and pair, holding the pliant whip you always drive with; touch your horses; and swear in the name of the Earthshaker and Girdler of the World that you did not hold up my chariot by a deliberate foul.'

'Enough,' said the wise Antilochus. 'I am a much younger man than you, King Menelaus, and you, my senior and my better, know well enough how a young man comes to break the rules. His mind is quicker, but his judgment not so sound. Forgive me then, and of my own accord I will let you have the mare I won. Moreover, should you ask for something more or better of my own, I would rather give it to you at once than fall for ever out of your majesty's favour and perjure myself before the gods.'

With that, great Nestor's son led the mare over and handed her to Menelaus, whose heart was warmed like the dew that hangs on ears of corn when the fields bristle with a ripening crop. Thus, Menelaus, was the heart within you warmed, and this was the answer that you gave:

'Antilochus, it is my turn to yield: I cannot be angry with you now. You have never been impulsive or unbalanced, though this was certainly a case where the high spirits of youth got the better of discretion. But another time be careful not to overreach your betters. No other Achaean would have found me so easy to placate. But you have suffered much and laboured hard in my behalf, and so have your noble father and your brother. I therefore accept your apology. And not only that, I will give you the mare though she is mine, to show our countrymen here that there is no pride or malice in me.'

With that, he handed over the mare to Noemon, one of Antilochus' men, and himself took the shining kettle. Meriones, who had come in fourth, took the fourth prize, two talents of gold. The fifth, the two-handled pan, remained un-claimed. Achilles gave this to Nestor. He carried it across the ring to him and said: Here, my venerable lord, is a keepsake for you also. Let it remind you of Patroclus' funeral, for you will not see the man himself among us any more. The prize I am giving you has no relation to the sports; for I know that you will not be boxing or wrestling, nor entering for the foot-race or the javelin-throwing. Your years sit too heavily on you for that.'

As he spoke, Achilles put the prize in Nestor's hands. Nestor was delighted and made him a speech. 'Yes, my dear boy, you are quite right in all you say: I am infirm of limb. My feet are not so steady now, my friend, and my arms no longer swing out lightly from the shoulder as they did. Ah, if only I were still as young and vigorous as I was when the Epeans buried my lord Amarynceus at Buprasion and his sons held funeral sports in honour of their royal father. There was not a man to match me there, either among the Epeans or the Pylians themselves or the mettlesome Aetolians. In the boxing I beat Clytomedes son of Enops. Ancaeus of Pleuron took me on at wrestling and I won. In the foot-race I defeated Iphiclus, who was a good man; and with the javelin I cast farther than Phyleus, and Polydorus too. It was only in the chariot-race that I was beaten, by the two Moliones, who grudged me this event and cut across me in the crowd, because a win for them meant that after all the chief prize stayed at home. Those two were twins. One of them used to drive from start to finish, while the other plied the whip.

'That is the kind of man I was. Now, I must leave this sort of thing to younger men and take the painful lessons of old age to heart. But at that time I stood in a class by myself. Well, you must get on with your own friend's funeral sports. Meanwhile I accept your gift with pleasure. I am delighted to think that you always realize how well disposed I am to you, and never let a chance go by of paying me the respect that our countrymen owe me. May the gods reward you graciously for what you have done.'

When he had heard all that Nestor had to say by way of thanks, Achilles made his way through the crowd of spectators and brought out the prizes for the boxing-match. For the victor in this painful sport, he fetched and tethered in the ring a sturdy mule, six years old and broken in – which is a hard job in the case of mules. For the loser there was a two-handled mug. Standing up, Achilles announced the contest to the Argives: 'My lord Atreides and Achaean men-at-arms, these are the prizes for which I want to see our two best men put up their fists and box to a finish. Apollo's favourite, the man who comes off best in everyone's opinion here, can take this sturdy mule to his own hut. The loser will receive this two-handled mug.'

There rose at once a huge fine-looking fellow called Epeius son of Panopeus, who was a champion boxer. He put his hand on the sturdy mule and said: 'Come on, the man who wants to carry off the mug. The mule is mine, and nobody is going to knock me out and take her, for I maintain that I am the best boxer here. True, I am not so good at fighting – no one can be a champion all round – but isn't that enough? At any rate, I'll tell you what I mean to do. I am going to tear the fellow's flesh to ribbons and smash his bones. I recommend him to have all his mourners standing by to take him off when I have done with him.'

This challenge was received in complete silence. The only man who dared to take it up was the heroic Euryalus, the son of King Mecisteus, Talaus' son, who, after Oedipus had fallen, went to Thebes for the funeral sports and there beat all the Cadmeians. Euryalus was got ready for the fight and was warmly encouraged by his famous cousin Diomedes, who wanted very much to see him win. He helped him on with his shorts, and bound on his hands the well-cut oxhide thongs. When the two men were dressed they stepped into the middle of the ring; they both put up their mighty hands, and they fell to. Fist met fist; there was a terrible grinding of jaws; and the sweat began to pour from all their limbs. Presently Euryalus took his eye off his man, and the excellent Epeius, leaping at the chance, gave him a punch on the jaw which knocked him out. His legs were cut from under him and he was lifted by the blow like a fish leaping up from the weed-covered sands and falling back into the dark water, when the North Wind sends ripples up the beach. His chivalrous opponent gave him a hand and set him on his legs. His followers gathered round and supported him across the ring on trailing feet, spitting clots of blood, with his head lolling on one side. He was still senseless when they put him down in his own corner. They had to go and fetch the mug themselves.

Losing no time, the son of Peleus brought out and displayed fresh prizes, for the third event, the all-in wrestling. For the winner there was a big three-legged cauldron to go on the fire – it was worth a dozen oxen by Achaean reckoning – and for the loser he brought forward a woman thoroughly trained in domestic work, who was valued at four oxen in the camp. Achilles stood up to announce the contest to the Argives, and called for a couple of entries for the new event. The great Telamonian Aias rose at once, and so did the resourceful Odysseus, who knew all the tricks. The two put on their shorts, stepped into the middle of the ring, and gripped each other in their powerful arms. They looked like a couple of those sloping rafters that a good builder locks together in the roof of a high house to resist the wind. Their backs creaked under the pressure of their mighty hands; the sweat streamed down; and many blood-red weals sprang up along their sides and shoulders. And still they tussled on, each thinking of the fine cauldron that was not yet won. But Odysseus was no more able to bring down his man, and pin him to the ground, than Aias, who was baffled by Odysseus' brawn. After some time, when they saw that they were boring the troops, the great Telamonian Aias said: 'Royal son of Laertes, Odysseus of the nimble wits; either you or I must let the other try a throw. What happens afterwards is Zeus's business.'

With that, he lifted Odysseus off the ground. But Odysseus' craft did not desert him. He caught Aias with a kick from be-

hind in the hollow of the knee, upset his stance, and flung him
on his back, himself falling on Aias' chest. The spectators were
duly impressed. But now the stalwart admirable Odysseus
had to try a throw. He shifted Aias just a little off the ground,
but he could not throw him. So he crooked a leg round Aias'
knee, and they both fell down, cheek by jowl, and were
smothered in dust. They jumped up and would have tried a
third round, if Achilles himself had not risen to his feet and
interposed. He told them they had struggled quite enough and
must not wear each other out. 'You have both won,' he said.
'Take equal prizes and withdraw. There are other events to
follow.' The two men readily accepted his decision, and after
wiping off the dust put on their tunics.

The son of Peleus went on at once to offer prizes for the
foot-race. The first was a mixing-bowl of chased silver, hold-
ing six pints. It was the loveliest thing in the world, a master-
piece of Sidonian craftsmanship, which had been shipped
across the misty seas by Phoenician traders and presented to
King Thoas when they put in at his port. Then Euneus son of
Jason had given it to the lord Patroclus in payment for Lycaon,
Priam's son; and now Achilles offered it as a prize in honour of
his dead friend to the runner who should come in first in the
foot-race. The runner-up was to have a large, well-fattened
ox; and the third and last man half a talent of gold. Achilles
stood up, announced the contest and invited competitors to
come forward. Aias the Runner and son of Oïleus jumped up
at once; so did Odysseus of the nimble wits; and they were
followed by Nestor's son Antilochus, who was the fastest of
the younger men. The three of them toed the line, and
Achilles pointed out the turning-post.

They went all out from scratch. Aias soon shot ahead; but
very close behind him came the good Odysseus, close as a
girdled woman brings the shuttle to her breast as she carefully
draws it along to get the bobbin past the warp. So little was
there in it. Odysseus' feet were falling in the tracks of Aias
before the dust had settled down again; and he kept up so
well that his breath fanned Aias' head. He was straining every

nerve to win, and all the Achaeans cheered him, shouting encouragement to a man who was doing all he could already. As they drew near the finish, Odysseus offered up a silent prayer to Athene of the Flashing Eyes: 'Hear me, goddess. I need your valuable aid. Come down and speed my feet.' Pallas Athene heard his prayer, and she lightened all his limbs.

They were just about to dash up to the prizes, when Aias slipped in full career. This was Athene's doing, and it happened where the ground was littered with dung from the lowing cattle that were slaughtered by the swift Achilles for Patroclus' funeral. So Aias had his mouth and nostrils filled with cattle-dung, while the much-enduring excellent Odysseus, having caught him up and finished, carried off the silver bowl. The illustrious Aias took possession of the farmyard ox. Then he stood there with his hands on one of the animal's horns, and as he spat out dung, remarked to the spectators: 'Damnation take it! I swear it was the goddess tripped me up – the one who always dances attendance, like a mother, on Odysseus.'

But they only laughed at him, delightedly. And now Antilochus came in. He took the last prize with a smile and made them a speech. 'Friends,' he said, 'I'll tell you something that you know already. The gods still favour the old crowd; for though Aias is only a little older than myself, Odysseus over there is the product of an earlier generation, a relic of the past. But his old age, as they say, is green; and it's a hard job to beat him in a race – for any of us but Achilles.'

This compliment to Achilles the great runner drew a reply from the prince himself. 'Antilochus,' he said, 'I cannot allow your tribute to go unrewarded. You have won a half-talent of gold: I will give you another.' And he handed the gold to Antilochus, who received it with delight.

The son of Peleus now brought out and put down in the ring a long-shadowed spear, a shield and a helmet, the arms that Patroclus had taken from Sarpedon. Then he stood up and told the Argives what was coming next. He said: 'I want our two best men to fight each other for these prizes before

the assembled troops. They must put on their armour and use
naked weapons. To the one who first gets through the other's
guard, pinks his man and draws blood, I will give this Thracian
sword, with its fine silver mounting, which I took from
Asteropaeus. The armour here will be shared between the
combatants and I will also give them a good dinner in my
hut.'

His challenge was taken up by the great Telamonian Aias
and by Tydeus' son, the powerful Diomedes. Each armed
himself on his own side of the ring, and the pair advanced
on each other in the centre, in fighting mood and looking so
fierce that all the spectators held their breath. They came
within range. They charged three times, and when they had
tried three lunges at each other, Aias succeeded in piercing
Diomedes' rounded shield. But the bronze failed to reach his
flesh: he was saved by the breast-plate underneath. It was now
Diomedes' turn. Thrusting repeatedly above the rim of
Aias' large shield he touched him on the neck with his glitter-
ing spear-point. The spectators were so terrified for Aias that
they called upon the combatants to stop and share the prizes.
However, the prince awarded Diomedes the big sword, which
he handed to him with its scabbard and its well-cut baldric.

The next prize offered by the son of Peleus was a lump of
pig iron which had already done service as a quoit in the
powerful hands of Eëtion, and had been carried off on board
ship with his other possessions by the swift and excellent
Achilles after he had killed him. Achilles stood up, announced
the contest and invited competitors to come forward. 'This
lump is big enough,' he pointed out, 'to keep the winner in
iron for five years or more, even if his farm is out in the wilds.
It will not be lack of iron that sends his shepherd or his plough-
man in to town. He will have plenty on the spot.'

In response to this, the dauntless Polypoetes rose to throw
the disk. So did the highborn and powerful Leonteus, and
Telamonian Aias and the noble Epeius. They stood in a row
and the good Epeius picked up the weight and hurled it with
a swing. But the spectators only laughed at his effort. Leonteus,

offshoot of Ares, was the next to throw. Then the great Telamonian Aias cast with his mighty hand and passed the marks of all the others. But when it came to the dauntless Polypoetes' turn, he overshot the whole field by the distance to which a herdsman can send his staff flying on its crooked course among a herd of cows. There was loud applause, and the mighty Polypoetes' men got up and carried off their king's prize to the hollow ships.

Archery came next, and for this Achilles offered prizes of violet-coloured iron in the form of ten double-headed and ten single-headed axes. He set up the mast of a blue-prowed ship a long way off on the sands; and for a target he had a fluttering pigeon tied to it by the foot with a light cord. 'The man who hits the pigeon,' said Achilles, 'can take the whole set of double-headed axes home with him. If anyone hits the string and not the bird, he won't have done so well, but he can have the single axes.'

The great Prince Teucer and Meriones, Idomeneus' worthy squire, rose to compete and shook lots in a bronze helmet. It fell to Teucer to shoot first, and he quickly let fly an arrow with tremendous force. But he had forgotten to promise the Archer-King a pleasing sacrifice of firstling lambs, and he failed to hit the bird – Apollo grudged him that success. Yet he did strike the cord by which the bird was tethered, near its foot. The sharp arrow severed the string and the pigeon shot up into the sky, leaving the string to dangle down. The Achaeans roared. But Meriones, who had been holding an arrow ready while Teucer aimed, snatched the bow hastily from Teucer's hands and promptly vowed a pleasing sacrifice of firstborn lambs to the Archer-King Apollo. He saw the pigeon fluttering high overhead beneath the clouds, and as she circled there he hit her from below, plumb in the wing. His arrow went clean through, came down at his feet and stuck in the earth, while the bird settled on the mast of the blue-prowed ship with drooping head and plumage all awry. In a moment she was dead and fell to the ground a long way from the man who had shot her. The spectators were lost in admiration. Meriones carried off the set of ten double axes, and Teucer took the single axes to the hollow ships.

Finally the son of Peleus brought into the ring a long-shadowed spear and an unused cauldron with a floral pattern, worth an ox. He put these down, and the javelin-throwers rose to compete. The two men that stood up were imperial Agamemnon, Atreus' son, and Meriones, Idomeneus' worthy squire. But the swift and admirable Achilles interposed, saying: 'My lord Atreides, we know by how much you excel the rest of us and that in throwing the spear no one can compete with your prowess. Accept this prize and take it with you to the hollow ships. But if you are agreeable, let us give the spear to my lord Meriones. That is what I at all events suggest.'

To this decision, Agamemnon King of Men made no demur. So Achilles gave the bronze spear to Meriones, and the King handed his own beautiful prize to his herald Talthybius.

XXIV

PRIAM AND ACHILLES

THE games were over. The soldiers left the ring and scattered to their several ships: they were thinking of their supper and a good night's rest. But Achilles went on grieving for his friend, whom he could not banish from his mind, and all-conquering sleep refused to visit him. He tossed to one side and the other, thinking always of his loss, of Patroclus' manliness and spirit, of all they had been through together and the hardships they had shared, of fights with the enemy and adventures on unfriendly seas. As memories crowded in on him, the warm tears poured down his cheeks. Sometimes he lay on his side, sometimes on his back, and then again on his face. At last he would get up and wander aimlessly along the salt sea beach.

Dawn after dawn as it lit up the sea and coastline found Achilles stirring. He used to harness his fast horses to his chariot, tie Hector loosely to the back of it, and when he had hauled him three times round Patroclus' barrow, go back and rest in his hut, leaving the body stretched face downward in the dust. But dead though Hector was, Apollo still felt pity for the man and saved his flesh from all pollution. Moreover, he wrapped him in his golden aegis, so that Achilles should not scrape his skin when he was dragging him along.

This was the shameful way in which Achilles in his wrath treated Prince Hector. The happy gods looked on and felt compassion for him. They even hinted to the sharp-eyed Hermes that he might do well to steal the corpse, an expedient that found favour with the rest, but not with Here, or Poseidon or the Lady of the Flashing Eyes. These hated sacred Ilium and Priam and his people just as much now as when the trouble first began and Paris fell into the fatal error of humiliating the two goddesses at their audience in his shepherd's hut

by his preference for the third, who offered him the pleasures
and the penalties of love.

Eleven days went by, and on the morning of the twelfth
Phoebus Apollo spoke his mind to the immortals: 'You are
hard-hearted folk, you gods – monsters of cruelty. Did Hector
never burn for you the thighs of oxen and of full-grown
goats? Yet now you will not even go so far as to save his
corpse for his wife and mother and his child to see, and for his
father Priam and his people, who would burn it instantly and
give him funeral honours. No, it is the brutal Achilles whom
you choose to support, Achilles, who has no decent feelings in
him and never listens to the voice of mercy, but goes through
life in his own savage way, like a lion who, when he wants his
supper, lets his own strength and daring run away with him
and pounces on the shepherds' flocks. Achilles like the lion
has killed pity. And he cares not a jot for public opinion, to
which most people bend the knee for better or for worse.
Many a man loses a dearer one than he has lost, a brother
borne by the same mother, or maybe a son. He weeps and
wails for him and then has done, since Providence has en-
dowed men with an enduring heart. But what does Achilles
do for *his* beloved friend? He kills Prince Hector first and then
he ties him to his chariot and drags him round the tomb. As
though that were an honourable thing, or were going to do
him any good! He had better beware of our wrath, great man
though he is. What is he doing in his fury but insulting sense-
less clay?'

White-armed Here bridled at this. She said: 'There would
be force in what you say, my Lord of the Silver Bow, if the
gods had it in mind to value Hector as they do Achilles. But
Hector is an ordinary man, who was suckled at a woman's
breast; whereas Achilles is the son of a goddess whom I
myself brought up and took under my wing and gave in
marriage to a man, to Peleus, the greatest favourite that we
had. Why, all you gods came to the wedding. And so did you,
Apollo, and sat down to the banquet lute in hand. You keep
worse company to-day! But you never were a loyal friend.'

Zeus the Cloud-compeller remonstrated with his Consort. 'Here,' he said, 'you must not lose your temper with the gods. There is no question of putting the two men on the same footing. But the fact remains that the gods loved Hector too; he was their favourite in Ilium. And he certainly was mine. He never failed to give me what I like. When banquets were afoot, my altar never went without its proper share of wine and fat, the offerings that are our privilege. But we must abandon this idea of stealing the gallant Hector's corpse. In any case it is not feasible without the knowledge of Achilles, whose Mother always stays beside him night and day. However, let one of the gods tell Thetis to come here to me. I have a wise solution to suggest to her. Achilles must accept a ransom from King Priam and give Hector up.'

Iris of the Whirlwind Feet started at once on this mission. Half-way between Samos and rugged Imbros she dived into the dark bosom of the sea with a resounding splash and sank to the bottom as quickly as the bit of lead that an angler attaches to his ox-horn lure with fatal consequences to the greedy fish. She found Thetis in her vaulted cavern, surrounded by a gathering of other salt-sea Nymphs, in whose midst she was bewailing the lot of her peerless son, destined as she knew to perish in the deep-soiled land of Troy far from his own country. Fleet-foot Iris went up to the goddess and said: 'Come, Thetis; Zeus in his unending wisdom calls you to his side.' To which Thetis of the Silver Feet replied: 'What does the great god want me for? I am so overwhelmed with sorrow that I shrink from mixing with the gods. However, I will come. No doubt he has some weighty matter to discuss with me.'

With that, the gracious goddess took a dark-blue shawl – there was nothing blacker she could wear – and set out on her journey, preceded by swift Iris of the Whirlwind Feet. The waters of the sea made way for them and they came out on the shore and darted up to heaven, where they found all-seeing Zeus with the happy everlasting gods in session round him. Thetis sat down by Father Zeus – Athene let her have her chair – and Here with a cheerful word of welcome passed her a lovely golden cup, which Thetis returned to her when she had drunk from it. The Father of men and gods then opened with these words:

'So, Lady Thetis, you have come to Olympus in spite of your troubles. You are distraught with grief – I know as well as you. Nevertheless I must tell you why I called you here. For nine days the gods have been quarrelling about Hector's body and Achilles sacker of cities. Hermes the Giant-Slayer has actually been urged to steal the corpse. But hear how I propose to settle the matter, with all honour to Achilles and in a way that will make sure of your future reverence and affection for myself. You must go quickly to the camp and convey my wishes to your son. Tell him that the gods are displeased with him, I most of all, because in his senseless fury he refused to part with Hector's body and has kept it by his beaked ships. I hope he may be overawed by me and give it up. Meanwhile I will send Iris to the noble-hearted Priam to suggest that he should ransom his son by going to the Achaean ships with gifts to melt Achilles' heart.'

Zeus was obeyed by Thetis, goddess of the Silver Feet, who at once sped down from the peak of Olympus to her son's hut. She found him moaning piteously while his comrades bustled round him in busy preparation of the morning meal, for which a large woolly sheep was being slaughtered in the hut. Achilles' lady Mother sat down close beside him, stroked him with her hand and spoke to him. 'My child,' she said, 'how much longer are you going to eat your heart out in lamentation and misery, forgetful even of your food and bed? Is there no comfort in a woman's arms – for you, who have so short a time to live and stand already in the shadow of Death and inexorable Destiny? Listen to me now and understand that I come to you from Zeus, who wishes you to know that the gods are displeased with you and that he himself is the angriest of them all, because in your senseless fury you refused to part with Hector's body and have kept it by your beaked ships. Come now, give it back and accept a ransom for the dead.'

'So be it,' said Achilles of the swift feet. 'If the Olympian is in earnest and himself commands me, let them bring the ransom and take away the corpse.'

While the two conversed down there among the ships – and Mother and son had much to say to one another – Zeus despatched Iris to sacred Ilium. 'Off with you, Iris, fast as you can,' he said. 'Leave your Olympian home and take a message to King Priam in Ilium. Tell him to ransom his son by going to the Achaean ships himself with gifts to melt Achilles' heart. He must go alone, without a single Trojan to escort him, except maybe one of the older heralds, who could drive the mule-cart and bring back to Troy the body of the man whom the great Achilles killed. Tell him not to think of death and to have no fears whatever. We will send him the best of escorts, Hermes the Giant-Slayer, who will remain in charge till he has brought him into Achilles' presence. Once inside the hut no one is going to kill him, neither Achilles himself nor anybody else. Achilles will see to that. He is no fool; he knows what he is doing, and he is not a godless man. On the contrary, he will spare his suppliant and show him every courtesy.'

Iris of the Whirlwind Feet flew off on her errand and came to Priam's palace, where sounds of lamentation met her. In the courtyard Priam's sons were sitting round their father, drenching their clothes with tears, and there in the middle sat the old man like a figure cut in stone, wrapped up in his cloak, with his head and neck defiled by the dung he had gathered in his hands as he grovelled on the ground. His daughters and his sons' wives were wailing through the house, thinking of the many splendid men who had lost their lives at Argive hands and now lay dead.

The Angel of Zeus went up to Priam and addressed him. She spoke in a gentle voice, but his limbs began at once to tremble. 'Courage, Dardanian Priam!' she said. 'Compose yourself and have no fears. I come here not as a herald of evil but on a friendly mission. And I am sent to you by Zeus, who, far off as he is, is much concerned on your behalf and pities you. The Olympian bids you ransom Prince Hector by taking presents to Achilles which will melt his heart. You must go alone, without a single Trojan to escort you, except maybe one of the older heralds, who could drive the mule-cart and bring back to Troy the body of your son whom the great Achilles killed. You are not to think of death, and to have no fears at all, since the best of escorts, Hermes the Giant-Slayer, will accompany you and remain in charge till he has brought you into Achilles' presence. Once inside the hut, no one is going to kill you, neither Achilles himself nor anybody else. Achilles will see to that. He is no fool; he knows what he is doing, and he is not a godless man. No, he will spare his suppliant and show you every courtesy.'

Her message delivered, Fleet-foot Iris disappeared. Priam told his sons at once to get ready a smooth-running mule-cart with a wicker body lashed on top. Then he went to his lofty bedroom, which was built of cedar-wood and was full of precious ornaments. He called to Hecabe, his wife. 'My dear,' he said to her, 'an Olympian Messenger has come to me from Zeus and told me to ransom Hector's body by going to the Achaean ships with gifts to melt Achilles' heart. Tell me, what do you make of that? I myself feel impelled to go down to the ships and pay this visit to the great Achaean camp.'

His wife cried out, 'Alas!' when she heard this. 'Where is the wisdom which people from abroad and your own subjects used to praise in you? How can you think of going by yourself to the Achaean ships, into the presence of a man who has killed so many gallant sons of yours? You must have a heart of iron. Once you are in his power, once he sets eyes on you, that beast of prey, that treacherous brute, will show you no mercy at all, nor have any respect for your person. No; all we can do now is to sit at home and bewail our son from here. *This* must be the end that inexorable Destiny spun for him with the first thread of life when I brought him into the world – to glut the nimble dogs, far from his parents, in the clutches of a monster whose very heart I would devour if I could get my teeth in it. That would requite him for what he has done to my son, who after all was not playing the coward when Achilles killed him, but fighting, without any thought of flight or cover, in defence of the sons and deep-bosomed daughters of Troy.'

'I mean to go,' said the venerable godlike Priam. 'Do not keep me back or go about the house yourself like a bird of ill-omen – you will not dissuade me. If any human being, an augur or a priest, had made me this suggestion, I should have doubted his good faith and held aloof. But I heard the goddess' voice myself; I saw her there in front of me. So I am going, and I will not act as though she had never spoken. If I am doomed to die by the ships of the bronze-clad Achaeans, then I choose death. Achilles can kill me out of hand, once I have clasped my son in my arms and wept my fill.'

Going to his coffers, Priam lifted their ornamented lids and took out twelve beautiful robes, twelve single cloaks, as many sheets, as many white mantles and as many tunics to go with them. He also weighed and took ten talents of gold; and he took two shining tripods, four cauldrons and a very lovely cup, which the Thracians had given him when he went to them on an embassy. It was a household treasure that the old man valued highly, but so great was his desire to recover his beloved son that he did not hesitate to part with it also.

There were a number of townsfolk in the portico. Priam gave these the rough side of his tongue and sent them all about their business. 'Away with you,' he cried, 'riffraff and wastrels! Have you no cause for tears in your own homes, that you must come and vex me here? Is it a trifling thing to you that Zeus the Son of Cronos has afflicted me with the loss of my finest son? If so, you will learn better. The Achaeans will find you easier game by far with Hector dead. And as for me, I only hope I may go down to Hades' Halls before I see the city plundered and laid waste.'

As he spoke he fell upon them with his staff, and they fled from the house before the violent old man. Next he fell foul of his sons. He shouted angrily at Helenus, Paris and the excellent Agathon; at Pammon and Antiphonus and warlike

Polites; Deiphobus, Hippothous and lordly Dius. He trounced all nine of them and then he told them once more what to do. 'Bestir yourselves,' he cried, 'my good-for-nothing and inglorious sons! I only wish you had all been killed beside the gallant ships instead of Hector. Ah, how calamity has dogged me! I had the best sons in the broad realm of Troy. Now all of them are gone, the godlike Mestor, Troilus that happy charioteer, and Hector, who walked among us like a god and looked more like a god's son than a man's. The war has taken them and left me these, a despicable crew – yes, rascals all of you, heroes of the dance, who win your laurels on the ballroom floor when you are not engaged in robbing your own people of their sheep and kids. Can't you get busy, sirs? I want the cart prepared at once and all these things put in it. I am waiting to be off.'

Priam's sons were terrified by his fulminations and quickly fetched a fine new mule-cart with strong wheels and lashed a wicker body on it. They took down from its peg a yoke of box-wood for the mules, with a knob in the middle and the proper guides for the reins; and with the yoke they brought out a yoke-band nine cubits long. They laid the yoke carefully on the polished shaft, in the notch at the end of it, slipped the ring over the pin, carried the yoke-band round the knob with three turns either way, then wound it closely round the shaft and tucked the loose end in. This done, they went to the bedroom, fetched the princely gifts that were to buy back Hector's corpse, and packed them in the wooden cart. Then they yoked the sturdy mules, who were trained to work in harness and had been presented to the King with the compliments of the Mysian people. Finally, to Priam's chariot they yoked the horses that the old man kept for his own use and fed at the polished manger.

As Priam and the herald stood lost in anxious thought while the vehicles were prepared for them under the high roof of the palace, they were approached by Hecabe in great distress, carrying a golden cup of mellow wine in her right hand for them to make a drink-offering before they left. She came up to the chariot and spoke to Priam himself. 'There,' she said. 'Make a libation to Father Zeus and pray for your safe return from the enemy's hands, since you are set on going to the ships. You go against my will, but if go you must, address your prayer to the Son of Cronos, the Lord of the Black Cloud, the god of Ida, who sees the whole of Troyland spread beneath him. Ask for a bird of omen, a swift ambassador from him. And let it be his favourite prophetic bird, the strongest thing on wings, flying on your right so that you can see it with your own eyes and put your trust in it as you go down to the ships of the horse-loving Danaans. But if all-seeing Zeus refuses to send you his messenger, I should advise you not to go down to the Argive ships, however much you may have set your heart on it.'

'My dear,' said the godlike Priam, 'I will surely do as you suggest. It is a good thing to lift up one's hands to Zeus and ask him for his blessing.' The old man then told his house-keeper to pour clean water on his hands. She brought a jug and basin and attended on him. When he had washed his hands he took the cup from his wife, went to the middle of the forecourt to pray, looked up into the sky as he poured out the wine, and made his petition aloud. 'Father Zeus, you that rule from Ida, most glorious and great; grant that Achilles may receive me with kindness and compassion; and send me a bird of omen, your swift ambassador, the one that you yourself like best, the strongest thing on wings. Let it fly on the right so that I can see it with my own eyes and put my trust in it as I go down to the ships of the horse-loving Danaans.'

Zeus the Thinker heard Priam's prayer and instantly sent out an eagle, the best of prophetic birds. He was one of those dusky hunters whose colour calls to mind the ripening grape, and when his wings were spread they would have stretched across the stout double doors of the lofty bedroom in a rich man's house. They spied him flying on their right across the town, and were overjoyed at the sight. He warmed the hearts of all.

The old man hastily mounted his chariot and drove out by the gateway and its echoing colonnade. He was preceded by the four-wheeled cart, drawn by the mules and driven by the wise Idaeus. Then came Priam's horses. The old man used his whip and drove them quickly through the town; yet even so a crowd of friends kept up with him, wailing incessantly as though he had been going to his death. But when they had made their way down through the streets and reached the open country, these people, his sons and sons-in-law, turned back into Ilium and went home.

Zeus, with his all-observant eye, saw the two men strike out across the plain. He felt sorry for the old king and turned at once to his Son Hermes. He said: 'Hermes, a task for you. Escorting men is your prerogative and pleasure; and you are amiable with those you like. So off you go now, and conduct King Priam to the Achaeans' hollow ships in such a way that not a single Danaan shall see and recognize him till he reaches Peleus' son.'

Zeus had spoken. The Guide and Giant-Killer at once obeyed him and bound under his feet the lovely sandals of untarnishable gold that carried him with the speed of the wind over the water or the boundless earth; and he picked up the wand which he can use at will to cast a spell on our eyes or wake us from the soundest sleep. With this wand in his hand the mighty Giant-Slayer made his flight and soon reached Troyland and the Hellespont. There he proceeded on foot, looking like a young prince at that most charming age when the beard first starts to grow.

Meanwhile the two men had driven past the great barrow of Ilus and stopped their mules and horses for a drink at the river. Everything was dark by now, and it was not till Hermes was quite close to them that the herald looked up and saw him. He at once turned round to Priam and said: 'Look, your majesty; we must beware. I see a man, and I am afraid we may be butchered. Let us make our escape in the chariot, or if not that, fall at his knees and implore his mercy.'

The old man was dumbfounded and filled with terror; the

hairs stood up on his supple limbs; he was rooted to the spot and could not say a word. But the Bringer of Luck did not wait to be accosted. He went straight up to Priam, took him by the hand and began to question him. 'Father,' he said, 'where are you driving to with those horses and mules through the solemn night when everyone else is asleep? Are you not afraid of the fiery Achaeans, those bitter enemies of yours, so close at hand? If one of them saw you coming through the black night with such a tempting load, what could you do? You are not young enough to cope with anyone that might assault you; and your companion is an old man too. However, I certainly do not mean you harm. In fact I am going to see that no one else molests you; for you remind me of my own father.'

'Our plight, dear son,' said the venerable old king, 'is very much as you describe it. But even so some god must have meant to protect me when he let me fall in with a wayfarer like you, who come as a godsend, if I may judge by your distinguished looks and bearing, as well as your good sense, which all betoken gentle birth.'

'Sir,' said the Guide and Slayer of Argus, 'you are very near the mark! But now I ask you to confide in me. Are you sending a hoard of treasure to some place of safety in a foreign land? Or has the time come when you are all deserting sacred Ilium in panic at the loss of your best man, your own son, who never failed to keep the enemy at bay?'

Priam the old king replied with a question: 'Who are you, noble sir, that speak to me so kindly of the fate of my unhappy son? Who are your parents?' To which Hermes replied: 'I suppose you are testing me, my venerable lord, and trying to discover what I know of Prince Hector. Well, I have seen him with my own eyes, and seen him often, in the field of honour. And what is more, I saw him hurl back the Argives on their ships and mow them down with his bronze, while we stood by and marvelled, since Achilles would not let us fight, having quarrelled with King Agamemnon. For I must tell you that I am a squire of Achilles, who came here in the same good ship as he. I am a Myrmidon and my father is Polyctor, a rich man and about as old as yourself. He has seven sons, of whom I am the youngest; and when we drew lots it fell to me to join the expedition here. To-night I left the ships and came onto the plain, because at daybreak the bright-eyed Achaeans are intending to assault the town. They are tired of sitting here, and so eager for a fight that the Achaean chieftains cannot hold them in.'

Priam replied: 'If you really are a squire of Prince Achilles, I implore you to tell me the whole truth. Is my son still by the ships, or has Achilles already thrown him piecemeal to his dogs?'

'So far, my lord, neither the dogs nor the birds of prey have eaten him,' said the Slayer of Argus. 'His body is intact and lies there in the hut beside Achilles' ship. And though he has been there for eleven days, his flesh has not decayed at all, nor has it been attacked by the worms that devour the bodies of men killed in battle. It is true that every day at peep of dawn Achilles drags him mercilessly round the barrow of his beloved comrade; but he does no harm to him by that. If you went into the hut yourself, you would be astonished to see him lying there as fresh as dew, the blood all washed away and not a stain upon him. Also, his wounds have closed, every wound he had; and there were many men who struck him with their bronze. Which shows what pains the blessed gods are taking in your son's behalf though he is nothing but a corpse, because they love him dearly.'

The old man rejoiced when he heard this and said: 'My child, what an excellent thing it is, whatever else one does, to give the gods their proper offerings! I am thinking of my son, who, as surely as he lived, never neglected the gods of Olympus in our home. It is for that that they are giving him credit at this moment, though he has met his fate and died. But now I beg you to accept this beautiful cup from me, and under the protecting hand of Heaven, yourself to see me safely to the ships and into my lord Achilles' hut.'

'Sir,' said the Guide and Giant-Killer, 'you are an old man

and I am young; yet you tempt me to take a bribe from you
behind Achilles' back. No! If I were to defraud my master I
should be thoroughly ashamed and terrified of the conse-
quences to myself. However, I am ready to serve you as
escort all the way to famous Argos and to be your faithful
henchman on board ship or on the land. No one would be
tempted to attack you through undervaluing your guard.'

With that, the Bringer of Luck leapt into the horse-chariot,
seized the whip and reins, and put fresh heart into the horses
and mules. When they came to the trench and the wall round
the ships, they found the sentries just beginning to prepare
their supper. But the Slayer of Argus put them all to sleep,
unfastened the gates, thrust back the bars, and ushered Priam
in with his cartload of precious gifts. And they went on, to the
lofty hut of Peleus' son.

The Myrmidons had built this hut for their prince with
planks of deal cut by themselves, and had roofed it with a
downy thatch of rushes gathered in the meadows. It stood in a
large enclosure surrounded by a close-set fence, and the gate
was fastened by a single pine-wood bar. It used to take three
men to drive home this mighty bolt and three to draw it;
three ordinary men of course – Achilles could work it by
himself. And now Hermes, Bringer of Luck, opened up for
the old king, drove in with the splendid presents destined for
the swift Achilles, and said to Priam as he dismounted from the
chariot: 'I would have you know, my venerable lord, that you
have been visited by an immortal god, for I am Hermes, and
my Father sent me to escort you. But I shall leave you now,
as I do not intend to go into Achilles' presence. It would be
unbecoming for a deathless god to accept a mortal's hos-
pitality. But go inside yourself, clasp Achilles' knees, and as
you pray to him invoke his father and his lady Mother and
his son, so as to touch his heart.'

With that, Hermes went off to high Olympus. Priam leapt
down from his chariot, and leaving Idaeus there to look after
the horses and mules, walked straight up to the hut where
Prince Achilles usually sat. He found him in. Most of his men

were sitting some way off, but two of them, the lord Auto-
medon and the gallant Alcimus, were waiting on him busily,
as he had just finished eating and drinking and his table had
not yet been moved. Big though Priam was, he came in un-
observed, went up to Achilles, grasped his knees and kissed his
hands, the terrible, man-killing hands that had slaughtered
many of his sons. Achilles was astounded when he saw King
Priam, and so were all his men. They looked at each other in
amazement, as people do in a rich noble's hall when a foreigner
who has murdered a man in his own country and is seeking
refuge abroad bursts in on them like one possessed.

But Priam was already praying to Achilles. 'Most worship-
ful Achilles,' he said, 'think of your own father, who is the
same age as I, and so has nothing but miserable old age ahead
of him. No doubt his neighbours are oppressing him and
there is nobody to save him from their depredations. Yet he at
least has one consolation. While he knows that you are still
alive, he can look forward day by day to seeing his beloved
son come back from Troy; whereas my fortunes are com-
pletely broken. I had the best sons in the whole of this broad
realm, and now not one, not one I say, is left. There were fifty
when the Achaean expedition came. Nineteen of them were
borne by one mother and the rest by other ladies in my
palace. Most of them have fallen in action, and Hector, the
only one I still could count on, the bulwark of Troy and the
Trojans, has now been killed by you, fighting for his native
land. It is to get him back from you that I have come to the
Achaean ships, bringing this princely ransom with me. Achill-
es, fear the gods, and be merciful to me, remembering your
own father, though I am even more entitled to compassion,
since I have brought myself to do a thing that no one else on
earth has done – I have raised to my lips the hand of the man
who killed my son.'

Priam had set Achilles thinking of his own father and
brought him to the verge of tears. Taking the old man's hand,
he gently put him from him; and overcome by their memories
they both broke down. Priam, crouching at Achilles' feet,

wept bitterly for man-slaying Hector, and Achilles wept for his father, and then again for Patroclus. The house was filled with the sounds of their lamentation. But presently, when he had had enough of tears and recovered his composure, the excellent Achilles leapt from his chair, and in compassion for the old man's grey head and grey beard, took him by the arm and raised him. Then he spoke to him from his heart: 'You are indeed a man of sorrows and have suffered much. How could you dare to come by yourself to the Achaean ships into the presence of a man who has killed so many of your gallant sons? You have a heart of iron. But pray be seated now, here on this chair, and let us leave our sorrows, bitter though they are, locked up in our own hearts, for weeping is cold comfort and does little good. We men are wretched things, and the gods, who have no cares themselves, have woven sorrow into the very pattern of our lives. You know that Zeus the Thunderer has two jars standing on the floor of his Palace, in which he keeps his gifts, the evils in one and the blessings in the other. People who receive from him a mixture of the two have varying fortunes, sometimes good and sometimes bad, though when Zeus serves a man from the jar of evil only, he makes him an outcast, who is chased by the gadfly of despair over the face of the earth and goes his way damned by gods and men alike. Look at my father, Peleus. From the moment he was born, Heaven showered its brightest gifts upon him, fortune and wealth unparalleled on earth, the kingship of the Myrmidons, and though he was a man, a goddess for his wife. Yet like the rest of us he knew misfortune too – no children in his palace to carry on the royal line, only a single son doomed to untimely death. And what is more, though he is growing old, he gets no care from me, because I am sitting here in your country, far from my own, making life miserable for you and your children. And you, my lord – I understand there was a time when fortune smiled upon you also. They say that there was no one to compare with you for wealth and splendid sons in all the lands that are contained by Lesbos in the sea, where Macar reigned, and

Upper Phrygia and the boundless Hellespont. But ever since the Heavenly Ones brought me here to be a thorn in your side, there has been nothing but battle and slaughter round your city. You must endure and not be broken-hearted. Lamenting for your son will do no good at all. You will be dead yourself before you bring him back to life.'

'Do not ask me to sit down, your highness,' said the venerable Priam, 'while Hector lies neglected in your huts, but give him back to me without delay and let me set my eyes on him. Accept the splendid ransom that I bring. I hope you will enjoy it and get safely home, because you spared me when I first appeared.'

'Old man, do not drive me too hard,' said the swift Achilles, frowning at Priam. 'I have made up my mind without your help to give Hector back to you. My own Mother, the Daughter of the Old Man of the Sea, has brought me word from Zeus. Moreover, I have seen through *you*, Priam. You cannot hide the fact that some god brought you to the Achaean ships. Nobody, not even a young man at his best, would venture by himself into our camp. For one thing he would never pass the sentries unchallenged; and if he did, he would find it hard to shift the bar we keep across our gate. So do not exasperate me now, sir, when I have enough already on my mind, or I may break the laws of Zeus and, suppliant though you are, show you as little consideration as I showed Hector in my huts.'

This frightened the old man, who took the reprimand to heart. Then, like a lion, the son of Peleus dashed out of doors, taking with him two of his squires, the lord Automedon and Alcimus, who were his favourites next to the dead Patroclus. They unyoked the horses and the mules, brought in the herald, old King Priam's crier, and gave him a stool to sit on. Then they took out of the polished waggon the princely ransom that had won back Hector's corpse. But they left a couple of white mantles and a fine tunic, in which Achilles could wrap up the body when he let Priam take it home. The prince then called some women-servants out and told them to wash and anoint the body, but in another part of the house, so that Priam should not see his son. (Achilles was afraid that Priam, if he saw him, might in the bitterness of grief be unable to restrain his wrath, and that he himself might fly into a rage and kill the old man, thereby sinning against Zeus.) When the maid-servants had washed and anointed the body with olive-oil, and had wrapped it in a fine mantle and tunic, Achilles lifted it with his own hands onto a bier, and his comrades helped him to put it in the polished waggon. Then he gave a groan and called to his beloved friend by name: 'Patroclus, do not be vexed with me if you learn, down in the Halls of Hades, that I let his father have Prince Hector back. The ransom he paid me was a worthy one, and I will see that you receive your proper share even of that.'

The excellent Achilles went back into the hut, sat down on the inlaid chair he had left – it was on the far side of the room – and said to Priam: 'Your wishes are fulfilled, my venerable lord: your son has been released. He is lying on a bier and at daybreak you will see him for yourself as you take him away. But meanwhile let us turn our thoughts to supper. Even the lady Niobe was not forgetful of her food, though she had seen a dozen children done to death in her own house, six daughters and six sons in their prime. While Artemis the Archeress killed the daughters, Apollo with his silver bow shot down the sons, in his fury with Niobe because she used to pride herself on having done as well as his own Mother, Leto of the Lovely Cheeks, and contrast the many children she had brought into the world with the two that Leto bore. Yet that pair, though they were only two, killed all of hers; and for nine days they lay in pools of blood, as there was no one to bury them, the Son of Cronos having turned the people into stone. But on the tenth day the gods of Heaven buried them, and Niobe exhausted by her tears made up her mind to take some food. And now she stands among the crags in the untrodden hills of Sipylus, where people say the Nymphs, when they have been dancing on the banks of Achelous, lay themselves down to sleep. There Niobe, in marble, broods on the desolation that the

gods dealt out to her. So now, my royal lord, let us two also
think of food. Later, you can weep once more for your son,
when you take him into Ilium. He will indeed be much
bewept.'

The swift Achilles now bestirred himself and slaughtered a
white sheep, which his men flayed and prepared in the usual
manner. They deftly chopped it up, spitted the pieces, roasted
them carefully and then withdrew them from the fire. Auto-
medon fetched some bread and set it out on the table in hand-
some baskets; Achilles divided the meat into portions; and
they helped themselves to the good things spread before them.

Their thirst and hunger satisfied, Dardanian Priam let his
eyes dwell on Achilles and saw with admiration how big and
beautiful he was, the very image of a god. And Achilles noted
with equal admiration the noble looks and utterance of Dar-
danian Priam. It gave them pleasure thus to look each other
over. But presently the old king Priam made a move. 'Your
highness,' he said, 'I beg leave now to retire for the night. It is
time that my companion and I went to bed and enjoyed the
boon of sleep. My eyelids have not closed upon my eyes since
the moment when my son lost his life at your hands. Ever
since then I have been lamenting and brooding over my
countless sorrows, grovelling in the dung in my stable-yard.
Now at last I have had some food and poured sparkling wine
down my throat; but before that I had tasted nothing.'

Thereupon Achilles instructed his men and maidservants to
put bedsteads in the portico and to furnish them with fine
purple rugs, spread sheets over these and add some thick
blankets on top for covering. Torch in hand, the women
went out of the living-room and busied themselves at this
task. Two beds were soon prepared; and now the great
runner Achilles spoke to Priam in a brusquer tone. 'You must
sleep out of doors, my friend,' he said, 'in case some Achaean
general pays me a visit. They often come here to discuss their
plans with me – it is our custom. If one of them were to see
you here at dead of night, he would at once tell Agamemnon
the Commander-in-Chief, and your recovery of the body

would be delayed. Another point. Will you tell me how many days you propose to devote to Prince Hector's funeral, so that I myself may refrain from fighting and keep the army idle for that space of time?'

To this the venerable king replied: 'If you really wish me to give Prince Hector a proper funeral, you will put me under an obligation, Achilles, by doing as you say. You know how we are cooped up in the city; it is a long journey to the mountains to fetch wood, and my people are afraid of making it. As for Hector's obsequies, we should be nine days mourning him in our homes. On the tenth we should bury him and hold the funeral feast, and on the eleventh build him a mound. On the twelfth, if need be, we will fight.'

'My venerable lord,' replied the swift and excellent Achilles, 'everything shall be as you wish. I will hold up the fighting for the time you require.'

With that, he gripped the old man by the wrist of his right hand, to banish all apprehension from his heart. So Priam and the herald settled down for the night there in the forecourt of the building, with much to occupy their busy minds, while Achilles slept in a corner of his well-made wooden hut with the beautiful Briseis at his side.

Everyone else, men under arms and gods, spent the whole night in the soft lap of sleep. But Hermes, god of Luck, kept wondering how he was to bring King Priam away from the ships unchallenged by the trusty watchmen at the gate; and he could not get to sleep. In the end he went to the head of Priam's couch and said to him: 'My lord, it seems that, since Achilles spared you, you have no misgivings left, to judge by the soundness of your slumbers in the enemy camp. Just now he let you have the body of your son – at a great price. Would not the sons that are left you have to pay three times as much for you alive, if King Agamemnon and the whole army came to know that you are here?'

The old man's fears were roused, and he woke up the herald. Hermes then yoked the mules and horses for them and drove them quickly through the camp himself. They passed unrecognized; and as Dawn drew her saffron cloak over the countryside, they reached the ford of eddying Xanthus, the noble River whose Father is immortal Zeus. There Hermes, taking leave of them, set out for high Olympus; and the two men, wailing and weeping, drove the horses on towards the town while the mules came along with the body.

Cassandra, beautiful as Golden Aphrodite, was the first among the men and girdled womenfolk of Troy to recognize them as they came. She had climbed to the top of Pergamus and from that point she saw her father standing in the chariot with the herald, his town-crier. She saw Hector too, lying on a bier in the mule-cart. She gave a scream and cried for all the town to hear: 'Trojans and women of Troy, you used to welcome Hector when he came home safe from battle. He was the darling of every soul in the town. Come out and see him now.'

Cassandra's cries plunged the whole town in grief, and soon there was not a man or woman left in Troy. They met the King with Hector's body at no great distance from the gates. His loving wife and lady mother fell upon the well-built waggon, to be the first to pluck their hair for him and touch his head. They were surrounded by a wailing throng. Indeed the townsfolk would have stayed there by the gates and wept for Hector all day long till sunset, if the old man, who was still in the chariot, had not commanded them to make way for the mules and told them they could mourn for Hector later to their hearts' content, when he had got him home. The people, thus admonished, fell back on either side and made a passage for the cart, leaving the family to bring Hector to the palace.

Once there, they laid him on a wooden bed and brought in musicians to lead in the laments and sing the melancholy dirges while the women wailed in chorus. White-armed Andromache, holding the head of Hector killer of men between her hands, gave them the first lament:

'Husband, you were too young to die and leave me widowed in our home. Your son, the boy that we unhappy parents brought into the world, is but a little baby. And I have no hope that he will grow into a man: Troy will come tumbling down before that can ever be. For you, her guardian, have perished, you that watched over her and kept her loyal wives and little babies safe. They will be carried off soon in the hollow ships, and I with them. And you, my child, will go with me to labour somewhere at a menial task under a heartless master's eye; or some Achaean will seize you by the arm and hurl you from the walls to a cruel death, venting his wrath on you because Hector killed a brother of his own, maybe, or else his father or a son. Yes, when he met Hector's hands, many an Achaean bit the dust of this wide world; for your father was by no means kindly in the heat of battle. And that is why the whole of Troy is wailing for him now. Ah, Hector, you have brought utter desolation to your parents. But who will mourn you as I shall? Mine is the bitterest regret of all, because you did not die in bed and stretching out your arms to me give me some tender word that I might have treasured in my tears by night and day.'

Such was Andromache's lament; and the women joined her. Next, Hecabe took up for them the impassioned dirge: 'Hector, dearest to me of all my sons, the gods loved you well while you were with me in the world; and now that Destiny has struck you down they have not forgotten you. Swift-foot Achilles took other sons of mine, and sent them over the barren seas for sale in Samos or in Imbros or in smoke-capped Lemnos. And he took your life with his long blade of bronze; but though he dragged you many times round the barrow of the friend you killed (not that he brought Patroclus back to life by that), you have come home to me fresh as the morning dew and are laid out in the palace like one whom Apollo of the Silver Bow has visited and put to death with gentle darts.'

Her words and sobs stirred all the women to unbridled grief. But Helen followed now and led them in a third lament: 'Hector, I loved you far the best of all my Trojan brothers. Prince Paris brought me here and married me (I wish I had perished first), but in all the nineteen years since I came away and left my own country, it is from you that I have never heard a single harsh or spiteful word. Others in the house insulted me – your brothers, your sisters, your brothers' wealthy wives, even your mother, though your father could not be more gentle with me if he were my own. But you protested every time and stopped them, out of the kindness of your heart, in your own courteous way. So these tears of sorrow that I shed are both for you and for my miserable self. No one else is left in the wide realm of Troy to treat me gently and befriend me. They shudder at me as I pass.' Thus Helen through her tears; and the countless multitude wailed with her.

And now the old king Priam told his people what to do. 'Trojans,' he said, 'bring firewood to the town, and do not be afraid that the Argives may catch you in an ambuscade. Achilles undertook, when he let me leave the black ships, that they should not attack us till the dawn of the twelfth day from then.'

At Priam's orders, they yoked mules and bullocks to their waggons and assembled speedily outside the town. It took them nine days to gather the huge quantity of wood required. But when the dawn of the tenth day brought light to the world, they carried out the gallant Hector with tears on their cheeks, laid his body on top of the pyre and set fire to the wood.

Dawn came once more, lighting the East with rosy hands, and saw the people flock together at illustrious Hector's pyre. When all had arrived and the gathering was complete, they began by quenching the fire with sparkling wine in all parts of the pyre that the flames had reached. Then Hector's brothers and comrades-in-arms collected his white bones, lamenting as they worked, with many a big tear running down their cheeks. They took the bones, wrapped them in soft purple cloths and put them in a golden chest. This chest they quickly lowered into a hollow grave, which they covered with a layer of large stones closely set together.

Then, hastily, they made the barrow, posting sentinels all round, in case the bronze-clad Achaeans should attack before the time agreed. When they had piled up the mound, they went back into Troy, foregathered again, and enjoyed a splendid banquet in the palace of King Priam, nursling of Zeus.

Such were the funeral rites of Hector, tamer of horses.

THE END

NOTE

WITH reference to the end of the *Iliad*, one of our manuscripts contains a remark by an annotator to the effect that certain authorities substituted for the last line the words: 'Such were the funeral rites of Hector. And now there came an Amazon . . . . . .'

This suggests that the line was used by poets following Homer as a link for the continuation of the story after the burning of Hector's body. We know that such continuations were made and that the next episode was the arrival at Troy of the Amazon Queen, Penthesilea, who comes to Priam's help, fights Achilles, and is killed by him. The story is told in detail by one Quintus of Smyrna, who lived in the 4th century after Christ and wrote a Greek epic in the Homeric manner under the title *Where Homer Ends*, which we possess.

GLOSSARY

THE Glossary is divided into three alphabetical lists and is confined to characters who are of some importance in the development of the story.

Information derived from writers later than Homer is given in square brackets.

Note that the word *Greek* was not used by Homer. The people he describes as fighting against Troy were known to him as *Achaeans*, though he calls them also *Argives* and *Danaans* with apparent impartiality. 'Troy' and 'Ilium' are used as synonyms for the Trojan capital.

I

ACHAEANS

ACHILLĒS. Son of Peleus and the Sea-Nymph Thetis; King, or rather, since his father is not dead, Prince of the Myrmidons of Phthia in Thessaly. Homer makes him the central figure of the *Iliad*, in which his death at the hands of Paris and Apollo is foretold. Odysseus meets his soul in Hades (*Od.* XI), and his funeral is described to him by Agamemnon's soul (*Od.* XXIV).

AGAMEMNON. Son of Atreus [and Aerope], often called Atreides; King of Mycenae and overlord of all Achaea. He is the [elder] brother of Menelaus (the pair are referred to together as the Atreidae), and Commander-in-Chief of the Achaean forces at Troy. He was murdered by his consort Clytaemnestra and her lover Aegisthus on his return to Greece (*Od.* I, IV, XI, XXIV).

AIANTES. Plural of Aias.

AIAS. Son of Oïleus; leader of the Locrians. He is distinguished from his greater namesake as the lesser Aias, or the Runner. There is also a marked difference of character. His insolence and self-conceit, which are brought out in the account of the games in XXIII, ended in his own destruction, as described by Proteus to Menelaus (*Od.* IV).

AIAS. Son of Telamon; King of Salamis. He is distinguished from his namesake, the son of Oïleus, as the great, or Telamonian Aias. He was defeated in the contest for the divine armour of the dead Achilles by Odysseus, who meets his still resentful soul in Hades (*Od.* XI). [Later poets tell us that this defeat caused Aias to go mad and kill himself.]

ANTILOCHUS. Son of Nestor; a young warrior who plays a more prominent part in the fighting, and also in the games, than his brother Thrasymedes. [He was killed by Memnon in the attempt to save his father.] His younger brother, Peisistratus, laments his death, during his visit to Menelaus (*Od.* IV).

ATREIDĒS. Son of Atreus. This patronymic is used by Homer both for Agamemnon and for Menelaus, who are often referred to as the two Atreidae.

AUTOMEDON. Son of Diores; a Myrmidon, and squire of Achilles, who serves as squire and driver to Patroclus when he fights without Achilles.

CALCHAS. Son of Thestor; the chief augur and prophet of the Achaean expedition.

DIOMĒDĒS. Son of Tydeus [and Deipyle]; King of Argos; one of the most attractive characters portrayed by Homer, who is very fond of his father too and makes such frequent and detailed references to his exploits that one is tempted to think that an account of them was one of his own earlier works. The character of Diomedes presents a striking contrast with that of Achilles. He returned safely to Argos (*Od.* III). [Later legends state that Aphrodite, in revenge for his attack on her in V, stirred up trouble for him at home and that he migrated to Italy.]

EURYPYLUS. Son of Euaemon, of Ormenion. This is the man who does some fighting in the *Iliad* and is wounded by Paris. Another man of the same name is mentioned in the 'Catalogue' (II); and another again in the *Odyssey* (XI).

HELEN. Daughter of Zeus [by Lede wife of Tyndareus]; sister of Castor and Polydeuces [and Clytaemnestra]. Married to Menelaus of Sparta, she ran away from him with Paris to Troy, where she spent nineteen years as the acknowledged wife of Paris (see her own statement near the end of XXIV). After the capture of Troy, she accompanied Menelaus to Egypt, and we meet her again (*Od.* IV) presiding over his palace in Lacedaemon.

[Homer, unlike later poets, does not seem to believe that Lede, her mother, was visited by Zeus in the form of a swan and that Helen issued from an egg. He even makes her in her exile regret 'her parents', forgetting for the moment that one of them was Zeus (III, p. 67).]

IDOMENEŪS. Son of Deucalion; King of Crete; one of the ablest and most amiable of Agamemnon's captains. In the *Odyssey*, Homer is careful to bring him safely back to Crete after the sack of Troy (*Od*. III).

MACHAŌN. Son of Asclepius, the famous physician. He and his brother Podaleirius are the chief surgeons serving with the Achaean forces.

MENELĀUS. Son of Atreus; King of Lacedaemon or Sparta, and [younger] brother of Agamemnon. His wife Helen was seduced and abducted to Troy by Paris. We meet him after the war, with the repentant Helen, in their palace in Lacedaemon (*Od*. IV), and his translation after death to the Elysian plain is foretold.

MENESTHEŪS. Son of Peteos; Prince of Athens and leader of the Athenian contingent.

MĒRIONĒS. Son of Molus; nephew and squire of King Idomeneus, and second-in-command of the Cretan forces.

NESTOR. Son of Neleus; King of Pylos. Though he was the oldest of the Achaean chieftains fighting at Troy, he survived the war and returned safely to Pylos, where Telemachus visits him nine years later during his wanderings in search of his father Odysseus (*Od*. III).

ODYSSEŪS. Son of Laertes and Anticleia; King of Ithaca; the hero of the *Odyssey*.

PATROCLUS. Son of Menoetius of Opus; the squire and close friend of Achilles.

PHOENIX. Son of Amyntor; King of the Dolopes; an old friend of Achilles, whom Peleus had made Achilles' tutor.

STHENELUS. Son of Capaneus; squire to Diomedes.

TALTHYBIUS. Chief herald to Agamemnon.

TEUCER. Son of Telamon and a mistress [Hesione, daughter of Laomedon]; half-brother of the greater Aias; the best bowman in the Achaean force. [After returning to Salamis he migrated to Cyprus.]

THERSĪTĒS. An unruly member of the Achaean rank and file. [He was

put to death by Achilles for jeering at him when he sentimental-
ized over the death of the Amazon Queen, Penthesilea, whom he,
Achilles, had just killed in battle.]

TLEPOLEMUS. Son of Heracles and Astyocheia; an Argive prince
who settled in the island of Rhodes.

TYDEIDES. See under *Diomedes* son of Tydeus.

II

TROJANS AND ALLIES OF TROY

ANDROMACHE. Daughter of Eëtion, King of Thebe-under-Placus;
wife of Hector and mother of Astyanax or Scamandrius. [She
was carried into captivity and married to Neoptolemus son of
Achilles.]

AENEAS. Son of the goddess Aphrodite and Anchises; a Trojan noble
who is second-in-command to Hector. He gives his pedigree to
Achilles in XX, showing that he is a third cousin of Hector's,
but belongs to the younger branch of the line of Dardanus.
Homer, in XX and in XIII, hints that he is disaffected towards
Priam and the reigning house. Poseidon (in XX) even suggests
that Aeneas may become King of Troy and establish the younger
branch. [It is probable that it is on this passage that later stories
of Aeneas, and in particular the Roman legends, were founded.
He survived the Sack, and migrated via Carthage to Italy, where
he sowed the seeds of Rome's greatness (see Virgil's *Aeneid*).]

ANTENOR. A Trojan noble, who advised his countrymen to give up
Helen. [Later stories make him a traitor, who was spared by the
Achaeans when they sacked Troy.]

BRISEIS. Daughter of Brises of Lyrnessus. When Achilles sacked the
town, he took Briseis captive. Agamemnon subsequently took
her from him to compensate himself for the loss of Chryseis (I).

CASSANDRA. Daughter of Priam [and Hecabe]. After the sack of
Troy, Agamemnon took her home with him, and she was mur-
dered by his wife Clytaemnestra (*Od.* XI). [She was a prophetess
who, because she rejected the advances of Apollo, was doomed
to see all her prophetic warnings ignored.]

CHRYSEIS. Daughter of Chryses, the priest of Apollo at Chryse near
Troy. Captured at Thebe by Achilles, she was allotted to Aga-

memnon, who was forced by Apollo to give her back to her father (I). She is not subsequently heard of [unless it is she who reappears, much altered, as Chaucer's Criseyde].

DEÏPHOBUS. Son of Priam and Hecabe; Prince of Troy. Accompanied Helen on her inspection of the Wooden Horse (*Od.* IV). [He married Helen after the death of Paris and was killed by Menelaus when Troy was sacked.]

DOLON. Son of Eumedes; a wealthy young Trojan who was very fond of horses.

GLAUCUS. Son of Hippolochus; a Lycian prince; second-in-command of the Lycian allies to Sarpedon, his first cousin.

HECABE. Daughter of Dymas the Phrygian, and consort of King Priam, to whom she bore many sons, including Hector, Helenus and Deiphobus. [After the sack of Troy she was carried off by the Achaeans.]

HECTOR. Son of Priam and Hecabe; Prince of Troy, and Commander-in-Chief of the Trojan and allied armies. Homer evidently intends us to regard Hector as Priam's eldest son and heir (see Hector's prayer for his own son in VI, and the laments in XXIV); but he does not commit himself, and everything else in the story points to Paris as the eldest son. It is Paris who is made judge of the three goddesses (XXIV), and sent on the mission to Sidon and Argos (VI) which ended in the abduction of Helen nineteen years before the *Iliad* opens (see Helen's lament in XXIV). If, as it is reasonable to suppose, he was at least twenty-one at the time of these exploits, he must be forty in the *Iliad*, whereas Hector is obviously a newly-married young man of at most twenty-five. It looks as though Homer had departed from older forms of the story in which Paris *was* the eldest son (but without properly adjusting the dates), and had 'invented' Hector as the heir apparent, because he needed a better foil for Achilles than was provided by the character of Paris.

HELENUS. Son of Priam and Hecabe; Prince of Troy. Like his sister Cassandra he was gifted with second sight. [He is taken by Neoptolemus son of Achilles to Epirus, marries Andromache after the death of Neoptolemus, and is visited by Aeneas in the course of his wanderings (Virgil, *Aeneid* III).]

IDAEUS. Chief herald to Priam.

PANDARUS. Son of Lycaon; a Lycian commander. He is a treacherous fool. [but there is no hint in Homer of the character that Chaucer and Shakespeare give him].

PARIS. Son of Priam [and Hecabe]; Prince of Troy; apparently junior to his brother Hector (but see under *Hector*). Homer refers throughout to his abduction of Helen as the cause of the war, making only one passing reference (in XXIV) to the famous Judgment by Paris of the three goddesses, Aphrodite, Here and Athene, when he was serving as a shepherd on Mount Ida. [Nor has Homer anything to tell us of Oenone, the first wife of Paris, or of Paris' death.] Homer also calls Paris 'Alexandros', but to avoid confusion I have ignored this name.

POLYDAMAS. Son of Panthous; one of the ablest of the Trojan leaders; apparently a commoner, or at any rate not a member of the royal house. He is a cautious, clear-headed strategist whom Homer uses as a foil for Hector.

PRIAM. Son of Laomedon, and descendant of Dardanus son of Zeus; King of Troy. [He was killed during the sack of Troy by Neoptolemus son of Achilles].

SARPĒDON. Son of Zeus and Laodameia the daughter of Bellerophon; King of Lycia and leader of the Lycian allies.

III

GODS

APHRODĪTĒ. Daughter of Zeus and Dione; the goddess of Love. She fights on the Trojan side, rescuing her admirer and protégé Paris, and her son Aeneas, and coming gallantly to the help of her lover, Ares the War-god. She is often called 'the Cyprian' (see *Od.* VIII).

APOLLO. Son of Zeus and Leto, also called Phoebus or Phoebus Apollo; the god of Prophecy, and of Poetry and Music. He is also the Archer-King and the patron of bowmen. The sudden deaths of men (not by violence but by disease) are attributed to his darts. He is also the protector of herds. He fights on the Trojan side, having a shrine in Pergamus, and is a bitter critic of Achilles (XXIV). [Later he was identified with the Sun.]

ARĒS. Son of Zeus and Here; the god of War. Though he has promised Here and Athene to aid the Achaeans, he fights on the

Trojan side, and in the battle of the gods is ignominiously disposed of by Athene. Aphrodite's gallant attempt to rescue him in XXI is no doubt to be explained by reference to the Lay of Demodocus (*Od.* VIII). The term 'offshoot of Ares' which Homer applies to several warriors is puzzling. 'Offshoot' does not appear to mean 'son', for in some cases the man's father is mentioned.

ARTEMIS. Daughter of Zeus and Leto, and Sister of Apollo; the goddess of the Chase, Mistress of the Bow, and Protectress of wild animals. It was one of her functions to kill women with her 'gentle darts'; i.e. she administered sudden death by disease. In the war she fights, not very effectively, on the Trojan side, no doubt following her Brother.

ATĒ. Daughter of Zeus; a personification of blind folly or infatuation, rather than a goddess.

ATHĒNĒ. Daughter of Zeus, also called Pallas Athene; the goddess of Wisdom and the Patroness of the arts and crafts. She is also the Protectress of cities and a fighting goddess (though not in the same sense as Enyo, the goddess of War), being on occasions entrusted with the magic arms of Zeus, whose thunder also she can wield. She plays a prominent part in the war on the Achaean side, although she has a shrine in Troy, no doubt because of her defeat in the Judgment of Paris (see XXIV). [Homer does not mention the legend which describes her as springing fully-armed from the head of Zeus; but he never gives her mother's name.]

CRONOS. Father of Zeus, Poseidon, Hades and Here; the ex-King of Heaven, who had been deposed by his Son Zeus.

DĒMĒTĒR. [Daughter of Cronos]; the goddess of Corn and fruitfulness. Homer has little to tell us about her. [Mother by Zeus of Persephone the Queen of Hades.]

DIŌNĒ. Mother of Aphrodite by Zeus.

DIONȲSUS. Son of Zeus and Semele. He is mentioned only twice in the *Iliad* (VI and XIV), and Homer does not state that he is the god of Wine but only that he was born to give 'pleasure to mankind'.

EILEITHYIA. Daughter of Here; goddess of Childbirth; often in the plural.

HADĒS. Son of Cronos and Rhea; the god of the Dead, who received the underworld as his portion when he and his brothers Zeus and

Poseidon divided the world between them. Homer several times mentions him in conjunction with Persephone, without stating the relations between them.

HĒBĒ. Daughter of Zeus and Here; a cupbearer and handmaiden of the gods. She was married to Heracles after his apotheosis (*Od.* XI).

HĒPHAESTUS. Son of Zeus and Here; the Master-smith and great Artificer and Architect of Olympus. In Homer he is apparently born a cripple and his lameness is not due to either of his two falls from Heaven (I and XVIII). In the war, he is on the Achaean side and, as the god of Fire, is called upon by Here to rescue Achilles from the River Xanthus. In the *Iliad* he is married to Charis (XVIII); in the *Odyssey* (not very happily) to Aphrodite (*Od.* VIII).

HĒRĒ. Daughter of Cronos and Rhea, and so a Sister of Zeus as well as his official Consort and Queen of Olympus. In the war she gives whole-hearted support to the Achaean arms. She is also the goddess of motherhood and in this capacity controls the Eileithyiae, the minor goddesses of childbirth (see XIX).

HERMĒS. Son of Zeus and Maia; the Ambassador of the gods (see XXIV and *Od.* V), though in the *Iliad* Iris is used more often than Hermes as go-between. He is also the Bringer of Luck and the Conductor of Souls (*Od.* XXIV). Homer constantly refers to him as the Slayer of the monster Argus. In the war he is on the side of the Achaeans, though he does little to help them.

IRIS. [The Rainbow]; a Messenger of the gods, especially in the *Iliad* where she seems often to usurp the functions of Hermes. Occasionally she obliges mortals of her own accord, e.g. Helen in III, and Achilles in XXIII.

LĒTO. [Daughter of Cronos and Phoebe]; Mother of Apollo and Artemis by Zeus. She is referred to by Hermes in XXI as a consort of Zeus, but she was not his official consort in the same sense as Here.

PALLAS ATHENE. See under *Athene*.

PERSEPHONĒ. Queen of the Dead. See under *Hades*.

PHOEBUS APOLLO. See under *Apollo*.

POSEIDON. Son of Cronos and Rhea, and a younger Brother of Zeus, who received the sea as his domain when the three brothers, Zeus, Poseidon and Hades divided the world by lot between them. He is also the god of Earthquakes. He supports the Achaeans in the war, having an old grudge against Troy (see XXI), but not always with such vehemence as his Sister Here.

STRIFE (Eris). Sister of Ares the War-god; a personification rather than a goddess in the ordinary sense.

THETIS. Daughter of the Old Man of the Sea [Nereus]; a Sea-Nymph who was married to a mortal, King Peleus, and became the Mother of Achilles. She is naturally a keen supporter of her son in his feud with Agamemnon, but is not otherwise concerned in the war.

XANTHUS. The god of one of the two chief rivers of the Trojan plain (Xanthus, alias Scamander, and Simoïs his brother). He is a Son of Zeus, who as god of the Sky is the Father of 'heaven-fed' rivers. Homer applies the same name to another river, in Lycia; to a horse of Hector's; and to one of Achilles' immortal horses. The word is nearly the same as that used for 'red-haired' Menelaus, and seems to indicate the colour of ripe corn.

ZEUS. Son of Cronos and Rhea; the supreme Olympian deity. As the minister of Destiny, he is neutral in the war. But he supports Achilles in his feud with Agamemnon; and he shows great sympathy for the Trojans, in particular for Hector and Priam.

FOR THE BEST IN PAPERBACKS, LOOK FOR THE

In every corner of the world, on every subject under the sun, Penguin represents quality and variety – the very best in publishing today.

For complete information about books available from Penguin – including Pelicans, Puffins, Peregrines and Penguin Classics – and how to order them, write to us at the appropriate address below. Please note that for copyright reasons the selection of books varies from country to country.

In the United Kingdom: Please write to *Dept E.P., Penguin Books Ltd, Harmondsworth, Middlesex, UB7 0DA*

If you have any difficulty in obtaining a title, please send your order with the correct money, plus ten per cent for postage and packaging, to *PO Box No 11, West Drayton, Middlesex*

In the United States: Please write to *Dept BA, Penguin, 299 Murray Hill Parkway, East Rutherford, New Jersey 07073*

In Canada: Please write to *Penguin Books Canada Ltd, 2801 John Street, Markham, Ontario L3R 1B4*

In Australia: Please write to the *Marketing Department, Penguin Books Australia Ltd, P.O. Box 257, Ringwood, Victoria 3134*

In New Zealand: Please write to the *Marketing Department, Penguin Books (NZ) Ltd, Private Bag, Takapuna, Auckland 9*

In India: Please write to *Penguin Overseas Ltd, 706 Eros Apartments, 56 Nehru Place, New Delhi, 110019*

In Holland: Please write to *Penguin Books Nederland B.V., Postbus 195, NL–1380AD Weesp, Netherlands*

In Germany: Please write to *Penguin Books Ltd, Friedrichstrasse 10–12, D–6000 Frankfurt Main 1, Federal Republic of Germany*

In Spain: Please write to *Longman Penguin España, Calle San Nicolas 15, E–28013 Madrid, Spain*

In France: Please write to *Penguin Books Ltd, 39 Rue de Montmorency, F-75003, Paris, France*

In Japan: Please write to *Longman Penguin Japan Co Ltd, Yamaguchi Building, 2–12–9 Kanda Jimbocho, Chiyoda-Ku, Tokyo 101, Japan*

PENGUIN CLASSICS

Aeschylus	**The Oresteia**
	(Agamemnon/Choephori/Eumenides)
	Prometheus Bound/The Suppliants/Seven
	Against Thebes/The Persians
Aesop	**Fables**
Apollonius of Rhodes	**The Voyage of Argo**
Apuleius	**The Golden Ass**
Aristophanes	**The Knights/Peace/The Birds/The Assembly**
	Women/Wealth
	Lysistrata/The Acharnians/The Clouds
	The Wasps/The Poet and the Women/The Frogs
Aristotle	**The Athenian Constitution**
	The Ethics
	The Politics
Aristotle/Horace/	
Longinus	**Classical Literary Criticism**
Arrian	**The Campaigns of Alexander**
Saint Augustine	**City of God**
	Confessions
Boethius	**The Consolation of Philosophy**
Caesar	**The Civil War**
	The Conquest of Gaul
Catullus	**Poems**
Cicero	**The Murder Trials**
	The Nature of the Gods
	On the Good Life
	Selected Letters
	Selected Political Speeches
	Selected Works
Euripides	**Alcestis/Iphigenia in Tauris/Hippolytus/The**
	Bacchae/Ion/The Women of Troy/Helen
	Medea/Hecabe/Electra/Heracles
	Orestes/The Children of Heracles/
	Andromache/The Suppliant Woman/
	The Phoenician Women/Iphigenia in Aulis

Hesiod/Theognis	**Theogony** and **Works and Days/Elegies**
'Hippocrates'	**Hippocratic Writings**
Homer	**The Iliad**
	The Odyssey
Horace	**Complete Odes and Epodes**
Horace/Persius	**Satires** and **Epistles**
Juvenal	**Sixteen Satires**
Livy	**The Early History of Rome**
	Rome and Italy
	Rome and the Mediterranean
	The War with Hannibal
Lucretius	**On the Nature of the Universe**
Marcus Aurelius	**Meditations**
Martial	**Epigrams**
Ovid	**The Erotic Poems**
	The Metamorphoses
Pausanias	**Guide to Greece** (in two volumes)
Petronius/Seneca	**The Satyricon/The Apocolocyntosis**
Pindar	**The Odes**
Plato	**Georgias**
	The Last Days of Socrates (Euthyphro/The Apology/Crito/Phaedo)
	The Laws
	Phaedrus and **Letters VII and VIII**
	Philebus
	Protagoras and **Meno**
	The Republic
	The Symposium
	Timaeus and **Critias**
Plautus	**The Pot of Gold/The Prisoners/The Brothers Menaechmus/The Swaggering Soldier/Pseudolus**
	The Rope/Amphitryo/The Ghost/A Three-Dollar Day

Pliny	The Letters of the Younger Pliny
Plutarch	The Age of Alexander (Nine Greek Lives)
	The Fall of the Roman Republic (Six Lives)
	The Makers of Rome (Nine Lives)
	The Rise and Fall of Athens (Nine Greek Lives)
Polybius	The Rise of the Roman Empire
Procopius	The Secret History
Propertius	The Poems
Quintus Curtius Rufus	The History of Alexander
Sallust	The Jugurthine War and The Conspiracy of Cataline
Seneca	Four Tragedies and Octavia
	Letters from a Stoic
Sophocles	Electra/Women of Trachis/Philoctetes/Ajax
	The Theban Plays (King Oedipus/Oedipus at Colonus/Antigone)
Suetonius	The Twelve Caesars
Tacitus	The Agricola and The Germania
	The Annals of Imperial Rome
	The Histories
Terence	The Comedies (The Girl from Andros/The Self-Tormentor/The Eunuch/Phormio/The Mother-in-Law/The Brothers)
Thucydides	The History of the Peloponnesian War
Tibullus	The Poems and The Tibullan Collection
Virgil	The Aeneid
	The Eclogues
	The Georgics
Xenophon	A History of My Times
	The Persian Expedition

PENGUIN CLASSICS

PENGUIN CLASSICS

Saint Anselm	**The Prayers and Meditations**
Saint Augustine	**The Confessions**
Bede	**A History of the English Church and People**
Chaucer	**The Canterbury Tales**
	Love Visions
	Troilus and Criseyde
Froissart	**The Chronicles**
Geoffrey of Monmouth	**The History of the Kings of Britain**
Gerald of Wales	**History and Topography of Ireland**
	The Journey through Wales and **The Description of Wales**
Gregory of Tours	**The History of the Franks**
Julian of Norwich	**Revelations of Divine Love**
William Langland	**Piers the Ploughman**
Sir John Mandeville	**The Travels of Sir John Mandeville**
Marguerite de Navarre	**The Heptameron**
Christine de Pisan	**The Treasure of the City of Ladies**
Marco Polo	**The Travels**
Richard Rolle	**The Fire of Love**
Thomas à Kempis	**The Imitation of Christ**

ANTHOLOGIES AND ANONYMOUS WORKS

The Age of Bede
Alfred the Great
Beowulf
A Celtic Miscellany
The Cloud of Unknowing and Other Works
The Death of King Arthur
The Earliest English Poems
Early Christian Writings
Early Irish Myths and Sagas
Egil's Saga
The Letters of Abelard and Heloise
Medieval English Verse
Njal's Saga
Seven Viking Romances
Sir Gawain and the Green Knight
The Song of Roland

PENGUIN CLASSICS